trials
death and the undead

written by
Kurtis Bissell

Trials: Death and the Undead

Second Print Edition:
Copyright © 2015 Kurtis Bissell
Artwork © 2015 H. Todd Liggett
Book Design © Kurtis Bissell and H. Todd Liggett

First printing, October 2013
Special Edition* printing, May 2014

    * Special Edition limited release: 50/50 hand-numbered copies;
      revised/expanded material & special cover art + event advertisement

All editions self-published by way of:
CreateSpace, a DBA of On-Demand Publishing, LLC

ISBN-13: 978-1508800910
ISBN-10: 150880091X

Dedicated to my parents.

I owe them everything.

Seriously. Everything. Even this book.

All my love – and all I can give.

And then some more.

Preface
The Story of a Story

†

This book is the result of many years of painstaking character development, plot and story alterations, false starts, premature endings, epiphanies, confusion, internal (and some external) debates, alcohol, weed and the eventual ultimatums given unto myself in the way of catalysts and creations that paved the way for the story that will follow this impromptu preface.

As far as characters go, those included in this story are close to my heart for many reasons. Though some may be despicable – and others downright nasty – I have formed a bond with each of them over the years. Many were birthed in my brain when I was still in middle school; many others just a few years ago. But even those that have been around for over half my life have much growth to undergo; their characters – in this story, at least – have much to learn and experience throughout the next two books.

As for the story itself, the characters within have had to deal with all my ludicrous changes to the world in which they live. In the beginning, a select few characters in this novel were to experience a different sort of apocalyptic scenario; instead of dealing with the undead, the characters had originally dealt with a *human*-induced apocalypse. By which I mean they had to deal with an entire world fighting itself. And the "hero" included in *Trials* had originally been a serial killer who was forced to fight against the anti-hero that was his nemesis since childhood. (I'm sure you can figure out just who that may have been from the context of this novel.)

And then one day (somewhere back in 2007) it struck me: *zombies.* I was big into zombies at the time and decided to write a novel about all these characters that included living in an undead world. But I began the story at the wrong point; I had started with the end of my "hero's" saga. Of course, at the time I had no idea of this; everything beforehand would have taken place in flashbacks. But as the backstory presented itself, I realized the true beginning of his journey.

So I shelved that story for another day and wrote the first lines of a story that you will not read. Sure, the general storyline is the same, but that intro (and much of the following first few chapters) was shoved into a deep, dark corner, never to be spoken of again…until now [insert cliché maniacal cackling]. That intro was too slow and off-putting; trust me, I was told so by a rather reliable source.

The story that follows is the real story…as best I can tell it, that is. But it's not the whole story. Our "hero" in this novel must learn and see and do and love and lose and hate and kill and grow much, much more than can possibly be written in one book. My hope is that my encapsulation of his – and all the other characters' – personas and aspirations and experiences draws you into this world enough to read the remaining tale.

~K.B.

Day Zero
Prelude to Mayhem

I

Reports were slow to hit the news of the mass hysteria striking in the southern Puget Sound region. Nobody could account for – or connect the dots between – all the belligerent and seemingly unconnected and unprovoked attacks sprouting up in various cities and towns along the I-5 corridor and Olympic Peninsula. These blips of random chaos failed to register on the radars of any major news networks in the area.

Although most of the attacks were sprouting up on or around college campuses, the very first attack struck in a sleepy town in the foothills of the Cascades. The man emerged, deranged and bloodthirsty, from the restroom of a local eatery and attacked a waitress and a cook before chasing his wife into the streets. This threat would quickly be quelled by the townsfolk (aided in part by a pair of tourists with a sketchy past) and therefore go unnoticed by the media. Stricken with grief, the man's wife would leave town before it was too late.

Most incidents like this would quickly be quelled – very few in major metropolises would receive nominal media coverage. Those who survived would be shaken and remain leery until the real threat struck in full force. This lingering fear would ultimately lead to many deaths in the first few days. For a select few, this fear would bolster their wherewithal and enable them to survive for months or years to come.

And as the chaos boiled over into hysteria in what would soon be considered "ground zero" in this new and deadly epidemic, one man sat alone in his hotel room, guzzling whiskey and popping painkillers. Distressed of his own accord and recent actions, this man roamed the past, swallowed up in grief and extreme intoxication (it's a wonder he didn't simply keel over). If he had seen the few reports scattered about the local news stations, he wouldn't have paid the situation a single thought.

But he hadn't even the slightest inclination to switch over to any broadcast that might inform him of anything beyond his own little world. He was content (relatively so) to wallow in his own misery and self-deprecation. The pills numbed his heartache and the whiskey twisted his thoughts until he had no cohesive string of reason left upstairs. His diminished attention flicked between the quiet cartoons playing on his television and the muted hustle and bustle of midday city life.

II

Smoking was definitely illegal indoors – especially in an establishment such as this. But he had paid the bellhop to ignore the stench of cigarettes that bled out the cracks of his door into the hallway. He also paid the bellhop to make special trips to the liquor store whenever he was in need of more whiskey and cigarettes. In the two weeks he had been staying in this hotel, he had paid the bellhop – the boy was barely of drinking age – more than three bills to keep him stocked.

From his eighth floor room (the top floor of this renovated – yet obviously rundown – hotel), the town looked squat and pretty. It was always squat, nobody could deny it; but it was prettiest in autumn, when the streets and buildings glistened eternal from the constant rains. Add to this the sheen of damp and decaying leaves that clogged nearly every crevice and corner – and blanketed nearly everything else in sight – and the city was nearly surreal in its glistening spectrum of colors, which were undoubtedly enhanced by the persistent film of moisture thus afforded by frequent precipitation. After all, the region was, is, and always shall be (until the end of times, barring any of a million calamities) famous for its persistent precipitation.

(The irony of autumn's beauty has always been a point of interest to many, including the man of this hotel room; the subject of this tale. The irony being this; though the colorful imagery of autumn is quite beautiful by most accounts, its beauty stems from decay. And decay is traditionally, despite its naturalness, conceived as an ugly ordeal. The reason, presumably, is mankind's mental conceptualization and connection to decay and how their own bodies shall, after death, *decay*; it is not viewed as a particularly *beautiful* event. But, as a species, mankind seems to *relish* in the decay of Mother Nature. This is the irony of autumn's beauty.)

The park across the street was a major source of entertainment for this man; transients and addicts of all sorts mingled about, trading drugs and booze for money and cigarettes and weed (and god knows what else). Their numbers weren't as strong as they would have been two months prior, but plenty remained to offer their antics to any who may watch (as this man now did from his hotel window). In fact, the only noticeable change in this man's dour demeanor happened when a police cruiser would roll by; these were the times he actually laughed aloud as everybody in the park would scatter.

But his good cheer would always dissipate too quickly and he would then traverse the mental plains back into a regretfully painful past.

III

He could remember all too well the look of death as it settled upon the eyes of the only man he ever killed. Blood vessels had popped, the eyelids and brow had relaxed, the pupils were dilated and staring away at nothing. He remembered the trickle of blood as it rolled down his cheek and onto the tile and the hot flow that continued to pool even after he withdrew the blade.

Kneeling in this growing pool, he stared for too long at the face he had once (long ago) considered friendly. His subconscious studied every detail of the scene in order to torment his dreams in the future while his conscious brain stared blankly at the dead eyes of this man. Up until this very moment in his life, he had thought of death as nothing more than another part of life. Never had he imagined killing, though the thought of such an act never irked him either. It wasn't until he actually took a man's life that he began to despise the act entirely.

He remained like that – kneeling by a familiar corpse in a pool of blood – for over an hour. He would look the body up and down, waiting for it to move or breathe – or maybe just waiting to die himself. Before leaving, tears started down his cheek and he wiped them away with bloody hands. (He barely remembered to wash up on his way out – as though it mattered since his jeans were soaked through.)

And then he was paid and caught a train and started drinking all the way home.

IV

A glass of whiskey in one hand, a little blue pill cradled in the other, and a lit cigarette dangling from his lips, he sat before the window, lost in images of dead eyes and blood. His own eyes were unfocused at the park, staring beyond the grass and transients at unchangeable events and actions of his recent past...

If he had been looking, he would have seen an interesting scene in which a police officer tackled a rather aggressive teenager. The officer was attempting to handcuff him when the boy whirled and ripped a chunk from his arm. The officer reeled and knocked the boy unconscious (or dead). Bleeding profusely, he finally slapped cuffs onto the boy and tossed his limp body into the back of his cruiser.

But, instead of watching this rather intriguing scene, this man's mind was elsewhere, so he failed to witness this blip of chaos.

Once the scene below was done, a rapping started on the door, startling him out of his dolor. He looked about the room, confused and delirious. When the rapping started again – more rhythmic this time – he shook the haze of his past from his vision and snuffed the cigarette in a plastic water cup. He swallowed the pill with a snort of whiskey and wobbled silently to the door. He peered through the peephole.

It was the young bellhop – a boy barely of drinking age.

He sighed and kicked the bedcover away (it had been stuffed along the bottom of the door in a feeble attempt to keep smoke in). He threw the latch and opened the door. "Come in, then," he said. "Quickly, though."

The bellhop bounced into the room and the door was shut. "Thank you, sir," he said. His eyes begged for the cash he was seeking, though he hadn't run any errands in two days. "I was just stopping in to see if you needed anything before I leave."

"A bit early, isn't it?" he replied, checking the clock – mid-afternoon still.

"Yeah, it is," said the bellhop. "It's my birthday, so I'm off early today. But I figured I'd see if you needed anything before I get this party started."

"Hmm." Looking around, he located the bottle of whiskey by the television. It was still half-full. "I could probably use one more," he said. He reached into his back pocket and came out with a Benjamin. "Here," he said without hesitation. "Get yourself something, too," he said. "Something to celebrate with."

Feigning reluctance at the overpayment, the boy took his money. "I can't take all this," he lied, holding the bill to his chest. "It's too much," he said.

"Just take it." He tired almost immediately of the boy's charade. "Have yourself a happy birthday. Get drunk and fuck bitches. Smoke weed and do blow, if you really want – it's your life. In fact..." He pulled a pillbox from his breast pocket and dumped a pill into his hand. "Here," he said. "Only take half, though."

The boy looked suspiciously at the little blue pill.

"Trust me," he said. "It'll make your night something...special."

"Umm...okay," replied the boy. He stowed the pill in the fifth pocket of his jeans. He would remember the pill later in the night and, ignoring this man's advice, take the whole thing at once. (Thirty milligrams of oxycodone were quite a bit at once for a seasoned pill-popper, let alone this mostly drug-free boy.) He would be higher than ever before and obliterated from the addition of copious amounts of alcohol. And somehow – *somehow* – this young man would manage to sweet-talk a pretty young lady into accompanying him to his little apartment down-town. The girl was actually younger (more than a few years younger) than her fake ID did claim, and very impressionable, as well. Unfortunately, she also carried a new disease that would change – and ultimately end – his life.

So it goes.

V

Just as his own pills began to settle in, this man received the bottle he requested. The boy thanked him again and again for the extra cash without actually offering to return any of the change. He left before annoying the man too terribly.

By nightfall, he was drunk; the rest of his previous bottle was gone and he was working hard on the next. Entertainment at the park below had ceased and the town was aglow with orange streetlights. He ordered a movie about a hitman that he barely watched (he scoffed when he did pay attention, despite the fact that he liked the movie).

At one point, he grabbed the ice bucket and some change and started for the door. Before he could leave, he fought with the bedcover, kicking and swearing at it until he opened the door. He staggered down the hall to the ice machine, filled his bucket and set it down to grab a couple sodas from the vending machine. After a ridiculous struggle with the quarter slot (his drunken aim was terrible), it finally dispensed some no-name cola (no joke; the can simply read *Cola*).

And then he staggered back to his room without the ice bucket.

Failing to realize his forgetfulness, he locked the door tight, tripped over the bedcover (without kicking it back into place), and shut the window. He plopped into the chair, cracked his can of cola and poured it over whiskey. It was at this point that he noticed the lack of ice. He briefly debated going back out for it, but decided instead that he couldn't move from this spot.

Moaning started up next door – and then the headboard started smacking the wall.

He groaned, turned up volume on the television, and lit a smoke. A vague memory of this hotel's stigma hit him and he wondered if the woman next door was a hooker. He shuddered at the thought of paying for disease-riddled sex and felt sorry for anyone who stooped so low.

When the movie was done, the moans next door were still not done. But he was drunk enough and high enough to ignore these sounds now. He killed the television, emptied his glass, snuffed his cigarette and stumbled over to the bed. He never remembered hitting the pillow.

But the dream that followed would haunt him for some time.

VI

Empty, omnipotent eyes hovered over the kingdom of one.

On his throne was the king of this land, hunched and brooding. Beside his gaudy, red-and-gold throne stood a faceless woman. Her pose and position suggested power and poise, yet she appeared submissive and reliant on this man – this *king*. This throne was atop a towering dais with steep steps leading down to a checkered courtyard. Near the top of these stairs were two headless bodies; blood flowed in rivers from their severed necks down, down, down, until it stained the courtyard red.

Incensed by this horror, the king drew his sword – large and lithe with a mysteriously bright sheen glowing from its dark blade – from its scabbard and howled in anger. He leapt into the sky, slashing and growling and cursing the eyes as they filled the sky with flame and fury and malice unparalleled.

And there, in the sky, a battle did rage – with no apparent victor.

trials

Day One

I

Weary eyes fluttered open.

A brief assessment of his faculties confirmed that the drugs, the alcohol were still swimming through his system. He also found himself still fully clothed in everything – boots, jeans, belt, flannel – everything except for his jacket. The bedsheets (minus comforter and standard issue hotel bedcover) were in a tangle around his knees, constricting him.

The glaring red clock read 8:13 a.m.

He groaned and rolled over, further tangling himself in the bedsheets.

For a time, he laid there, wondering how much sleep he got and wishing he could get more. But when his hazy mind wouldn't shut down – still caught up in a fit of guilt and self-pity – he rolled back over to check the clock again: 8:22 a.m.

With a huff, he rolled out of bed and staggered to the bathroom – he nearly tripped over the bedcover that was spread across the hall; the pain in his hip flared at the stutter-step he took to avoid it. He grumbled some more, withdrew a pillbox from his breast pocket and dry-swallowed a little blue pill.

He downed a short glass of tap water and stared at his reflection in the mirror. His ash brown hair was a mess; his curls were beginning to show and he thought of how he should probably get a haircut soon. His eyes (brown and hazel and speckled with greens and reds at closer inspection) were bloodshot and sporting bags. And – for the first time in his life – he began to notice the skin crinkling around the edges, forming his first wrinkles. His skin had drained most of its color in the past few weeks from lack of exposure (and a healthy mix of malnutrition and bingeing); he appeared older than his years and haggard.

Drinking and drugging aside, other, more avoidable factors, aged him further.

After another short glass of water, he brushed his grimy teeth, killed the light and staggered back into the main room, again stumbling over the bedcover. He grumbled and shot a delirious glare at it.

Head swimming, arms limp, eyes fuzzy, he stood between the bed and television without a clear thought as to what he should do. He wasn't looking at the empty bottles on the dresser or those scattered in and around the trash bin. He wasn't listening to the morning birdsongs or frantic, rushing traffic filtering in through the window. At times, his shallow, sleeplike breathing would catch and he wouldn't even inhale.

But when the racket next door began again, he took a deep breath and looked around, still hardly seeing a thing. He saw the clock, though; 8:31 a.m. – time was dragging. The banging on the wall (presumably the headboard) and the moaning (visceral, beastly moans and groans) caused him to shudder. *Don't they ever stop?* he thought. His notions from the night before regarding his neighbor hiring a hooker were challenged when he realized that ladies of the night probably don't stay until morning. And if they did…

Must cost a pretty penny for her, he thought.

Setting all thoughts of his insatiable neighbors aside, he ran his tongue over his teeth to verify he had brushed them. He eyed the single-serving coffee pot for just a moment before stepping over to the table to dig through his bag. He grabbed a few twenties and stuffed them into his back pocket. From the front pouch, he grabbed his last two packs of Camels, shoved one into each of the front pockets of his jeans. He snatched his old brown jacket and plain black baseball cap off the back of the room's only chair and headed for the door.

Once again, he was foiled by the bedcover.

II

The sky was a wash of clouds and smelled of rain, though none was falling. The air was brisk and mostly calm – his breath trailed like smoke as he walked along the boulevard. At the thought of smoke, he opened one of his packs and sparked a cigarette, huddling in an alcove to hide from the mild breeze that kicked up just in time to snuff his lighter's flame.

The streets were already alive with bustling businessmen, hipsters bundled up in awful, gaudy, outdated clothing and the grungy, over-encumbered (and often underdressed) transients that have become the staple of this town over the years.

Sirens blatted in the distance – people shouted in the park, the alleyways. Something raucous was going on in the apartments above a vacant corner store. Indifferent to the chaos and troubles of others, he carried on, secluding himself in a sorry world of his own creation.

Feeling grimy and groggy, he made his way down the boulevard, up an avenue and through an alley to arrive at a specific coffee shop (he passed at least four on this short trek). He pulled one last, fat drag off his cigarette and ditched the remainder into the street before entering the shop. The last tendrils of smoke drifting out his nostrils swirled at the threshold.

Within minutes, he was pushing back through the glass double doors with another cigarette poised between his lips and a latte warming his hands. For a moment, he stood just outside the doors, debating whether to sit at a table along the shop's façade or wander around the city. It felt like an eternity since he had been home, and he had yet to accomplish a thing besides sit in his hotel with whiskey and pills and self-loathing. Nobody – save for his drug dealer – was even aware of his return; and they would surely be curious to learn where he had been.

With the call of the city overriding his urge to observe the interesting – if not peculiar – local denizens, he decided to walk rather than sit. Leaving the cigarette poised, unlit, between his lips, he took off down the main avenue, heading east. He had no particular destination in mind and chose the direction based on a particular set of emotions associated with that side of town.

In the alcove of a theater the next block up sat a trio of beggars flying a sign that read SPARIJUANA FOR THE NUGLESS; drawn upon it was a crude picture of a weed leaf smoking a joint. The only one showing any bit of life was the boy holding the sign (really, it was just propped up against his knee) – his limp Mohawk was streaked with pink dye. The girl in the middle was slack-jawed with drooping eyes; the boy on the other end wore a ratty baseball cap adorned with metal lighter tops around the bill; it was pulled down so you couldn't see his face. None of them paid this passerby a single glance.

Amused with their sign, he dropped a handful of change into their basket. They didn't even shift at the clanging of coins.

Sipping his latte and lightly chewing on his cigarette, rather than smoking it, he ambled by bustling shops and empty bars. Passing by the fenced-off shell of a building that was yet to be built, he realized that he couldn't remember what used to be there, why it wasn't there anymore or how long it had been since anything actually occupied that space.

Along his path, many beggars held out their hands, held up their clever cardboard signs. Some hollered, some kept silent, some just moaned – all were dirty and disheveled. He ignored them all, his eyes locked firmly on the pavement.

Some blocks down, he spied the horrid glass edifice of city hall – a sight he never failed to notice as its modern styling clashed horribly with the rustic aesthetics of downtown. While debating making some obscene gesture at the building and all it stood for, he bumped into an older homeless man who appeared to be in his late sixties (at least). His arms were outstretched and he was unreservedly groping for something, all the while sputtering a series of phlegmy, vacillating sounds.

With a cursory glance – so brief he failed to notice the empty, red eyes – and a curt apology, he scurried across the road, taking a quick inventory of his pockets. When all was found to be in order, he glanced over his shoulder to find this extremely disheveled old man plodding after him through the crosswalk, arms still outstretched. Again, he failed to notice the empty, red eyes, though he did sense some sort of hunger or desire (he couldn't rightly figure which it was).

The old man groaned again; the sound seemingly permeated the air and (in his opiate- and hangover-induced haze) he could swear that the groans were coming from all around. But he put this out of mind and continued up the road.

The sights and sounds of the day – along with the strange old man on his trail – started nagging at the back of his mind. He couldn't remember so many sirens blaring both near and far – the city has always had its crime, its problems, but the persistence of this day's din was reminiscent to that of a larger city.

He felt out of place and distant, but attributed this to the months he spent away.

Still ambling along the main avenue, he noted how the cars dotted both sides of the street in an unusually sporadic fashion – some had a wheel on the curb, others were turned the wrong way – some were missing windows, others were smoking. These details did not escape him, but he pushed them out of mind and veered off onto an emptier residential side street. The houses on this road had an old, comfortable feel that helped him shake his sense of unease.

He kept his eyes on his feet or up in the trees, sipping his coffee and chewing on the butt of his cigarette, willfully ignorant to the disorder that swallowed up even this neighborhood. He failed to notice the broken windows, the wide-open front doors, or notice all the people staring at him – and subsequently ambling after him – with hungry eyes. Instead, he smiled contentedly and breathed in the tainted, yet crisp autumn air.

Sirens warbled in the distance – someone hollered – somewhere nearby a dog barked aggressively. He tried not to hear all this, but the sounds registered deep within and bounced around the back of his mind.

His smile faltered, but did not disappear. *You're being paranoid,* he thought. *Might wanna lay off the pills for a bit.* This last was rather superficial; if only subconsciously, he knew he wouldn't quit the pills – *couldn't* quit them – yet.

And despite the painkillers, his hip flared up and he stopped to rub the muscles beneath the scars. When he did so, he found himself standing at a grassy lot between two houses. Save for a few scattered trees, all that stood in this lot was a derelict trailer. It was an old, rusty, wooden thing with two flat wheels and sagging rails – it's anybody's guess the last time it was utilized. For just a moment, he wondered who owned this property and why, with all the recent developments in this town, nobody had built a house here.

A crow cawed from somewhere high behind him.

After a swill of his coffee, he started back up the road.

Towering trees reached down with their droopy limbs while daisies, dandelions and roses sang to him from gardens, yards and the grass-lined sidewalks that were now little more than stepping stones. The day was becoming more beautiful with every step – and by the next crossroad he had nearly forgotten about the incessant oddities of the day.

His brain felt as though it was wrapped in a warm blanket. He finally lit his cigarette and meandered through the neighborhood until he saw the park. A smile touched his face at this long lost sight and he strode across the open field.

The grass was slick from the morning dew. He ran his finger along the surface of a picnic table, drawing a line through the speckles of moisture still lingering there. For minutes, he wandered about the recently manicured field. He found himself by the tennis courts and ran his hand over the cold, damp chainlink that surrounded them. From there, he meandered over to the basketball court and stared blankly up at the backboard, thinking of games of his youth – games long gone.

At last, he found himself seated upon the jungle gym. He stared at the empty park, looking from tree to table, grass to fence – and finally his eyes moved up to the whitewashed sky. There was a crow up there, circling the park. Chasing it in concentric circles were two smaller birds. He took the last drag of his cigarette, held it, then exhaled slowly and watched the smoke melt into the sky.

Ditching the butt, he noticed movement across the park; no longer was he alone in this little haven.

Two things were immediately discernible about this newcomer: this person was male and walked with a limp. After closer inspection, one might notice that he was quite underdressed for the current weather, let alone the inclement weather. But he failed to look closer, thereby failing to register these details.

Instead, his attention returned skyward – to the clouds and the birds.

And, after a few beats, he let his eyes drift shut.

Trying further to distract himself from this peculiar day, he forced favorable memories to spring forth; his love, now gone and in the past, danced before his mind's eye. He relived select memories of her in an attempt to shut out the shady life he had since been living.

A tear stung his eye, but he did not let it loose.

III

It came with the rain.

A cool, refreshing sprinkle speckled his face – soft kisses descended from the sky which enhanced his fond revelry. A brisk wind whistled in the trees and played in his hair. Floating on this refreshing wind was an unfavorably rank odor and the muted chaos of the city – sensations this man tried his best to dismiss.

A large raindrop smacked him in the ear.

He felt the fierce grip, was rocked by the ferocious tug, heard the grunt of effort expelled – and his revelry came to a screeching halt (almost literally). With a quizzical, obscene exclamation, he jerked his arm free – thus acquiring a small tear on his jacket sleeve – and launched off his perch, leaving the last of his depleted latte behind. He landed on wobbly feet, but righted himself quickly, on the ready for his purported attacker.

Beyond the vertical bars where he had – moments before – been leaning, stood a scraggly young man whose gnarled and bloody arm – now through to the shoulder – whipped back and forth. This young man's hand – far worse than his arm with digits sticking out unnaturally in all angles and fingernails splintered or altogether missing – clenched spasmodically, groping at air. Around his mouth was a red froth and there was something amiss with the young man's eyes. He snarled – it was a horrid, inhuman sound.

This deranged and dirty transient (for what else could he be?) dropped to the ground. His arm popped as it was ripped from between the bars, falling with his weight. (It flopped unnaturally after that, and he wondered what could make someone break their own arm in such a fashion.) This transient then began crawling beneath the jungle gym. His face was contorted and he was still snarling and spewing that red, liquidy froth. The sight caused this dazed, drugged and hungover wanderer to clutch and reel; he barely found the strength to keep the meager contents of his belly stowed.

Whirling to run, he was confronted by a bloody businessman that was no less gnarly than the previous aggressor. And before any other thought could cross his mind, his right fist crossed this businessman's face, sending him sprawling to the dewy earth.

He took off across the field.

Nearing the road, he glanced over his shoulder; both men were up and staggering after him – but with no apparent haste in their steps (one hitched and bobbed as it lurched, which may have been a feeble attempt at some sort of haste). He vaguely noticed their complete lack of interest in one another and sheer determination to pursue him. He could also detect no sense of collusion, other than their apparent interest in *just him.*

Why me? This thought screamed and bounced about his skull with some force.

Panting from the brief sprint, he stopped and leaned against a tree, watching the pair of seething, groping lunatics and their shuffling gait. He noticed that neither man spoke; and still, neither exchanged a collusive glance – not even a single look between them at all. He shouted some questioning obscenities to an escalated retort of snarls and groans.

What do they want with me? This thought bounced about just as forcefully – and almost painfully – as the previous one had. And then he wondered if it was completely random; perhaps it wasn't just *he* that these – these – these *people* were after. Maybe it was larger than all this…

Through his confusion and panic drifted interconnected thoughts of disease and drugs and chemicals; he wondered the cause of this attack – the apparent *sickness* of this pair – thinking of every possible catalyst for such behavior. Was the city water poisoned? Was there a biological attack? Has the bath salt craze reached his home town?

Whatever the cause, he knew he couldn't linger.

His hand was throbbing and bloody from punching the businessman's face (he remembered the feel of cold skin and brittle bones crunching on impact). He wiped most of it off in the grass before leaving the park and stared – repulsed – at the remaining blood as he hurried down the street.

As the questions of who and how and why and what rattled around his muddled brain, he was struck dumb by a shambling crowd at the next block. Every single person in this crowd – this *horde* – was just as dirty, disheveled, and bloody as the pair back at the park. His jaw dropped and he almost tripped over his own feet; more frothy red mouths, empty eyes and upraised arms. But worse than all of that was the eerie chorus of groans that erupted as he passed before them.

The rain was now a steady drizzle and each footfall slapped audibly on the damp ground. Each was louder than the last – each was heavier, quicker. The rain smacked his face, covering it with cold, wet kisses (with mounting fear, the sensation was far less comforting than before). Checking over his shoulder at the crest of a small hill, he found his pursuers were still barely rounding the corner. Feeling a respite granted by this cushion, he slowed his pace – but his eyes remained sharp as he now watched every tree, every bush – every *rose*bush – and certainly around every corner for more of these deranged psychopaths.

Maybe it's just an overblown zombie walk, he thought. *Maybe, being unaware, they're now fucking with me on a rather grandiose – if not obscene – scale…?* But then he recalled the snapping of that young man's elbow – the *pop* as it was yanked back through the bars. Surely *that* couldn't have been faked…

A car whizzed through an intersection up ahead without slowing.

Sloughing his willful ignorance – to be sure, not without some inner turmoil – this wanderer, feeling more like a foxed rabbit now, finally began cataloguing his surroundings – *actually* paying attention. Every busted window and open door, every tire mark and bloodstain, was a glaring watermark of some profound, incomprehensible chaos.

Home! he thought – and immediately felt lost. The closest thing he had to a home anymore was his hotel room. And between him and this transitory home was a labyrinth of bedlam (he saw this now). He wasn't even sure how to proceed if he safely traversed the city streets; holing up in a ninth floor burrow would only prove to trap him further.

His room did hold a few useful treasures: a knife and his pistol (protection was paramount!), and his bag with all the money and extra clothes and –

My phone, he thought. *I can call someone, go somewhere…*

He hadn't touched his phone in months – hadn't spoken to anybody in nearly a year. But he knew his only chance at stability was contacting somebody that cared – somebody that wasn't afflicted by whatever was happening – somebody that hadn't written off his existence. He *must* get to his phone, if only to chase a pipe dream.

And then he saw her.

She was facedown and motionless – a young lady strewn across the front stoop of (presumably) her midcentury home. The rain was washing some of the pooled blood away – red rivers that disappeared into the lawn (perhaps a light stain was visible, but nothing more). He shook his head, horrified and stunned.

Before he could pull himself away, the woman – previously limp – twitched and craned her head. She pushed herself up, revealing a face drenched with dried blood and red froth. Her eyes were lifeless, hemorrhaged and blank. She reached for him, her face twisted in a snarl, and she howled.

Terrified into motion, he took off down the road – down the hill.

Visions of faceplanting on the slippery pavement flashed through his ragged, muddled mind as gravity turned his jog into a sprint. And any attempt to slow his increasing pace was foiled by the steep grade. After a minute (less, actually, though it felt much longer to someone so terrified of tumbling at this speed), this frightening descent finally leveled out. He silently thanked the tread of his new boots for holding true. Slowing to a fast walk, he stuck to the middle of the road with a shrewd eye on every house he passed – every tree, bush and rosebush, as well. And then he started down the next step of the hill, careful not to let gravity pull him quite so fast this time.

After this step, the descent into downtown would become mild, manageable.

The road came to an end at the next crossroad. Beyond the intersection were an expansive field and two schools. He remembered playing catch here before the elementary school was built; and later, after it was built, smoking pot and cigarettes with his pals in the parking lot.

Aways downfield was a group of schoolchildren – they were hunched over something he couldn't see. In truth, he didn't want to see their gruesome mastication (in all actuality, they were munching away on the school's band teacher). But even the distance between him and this gruesome scene couldn't block him from understanding what the kids were doing. What bothered him the most was that they were *children*; this sickness wasn't very discriminating. He found minor consolation in the fact that they didn't shift their focus to him. Presumably, they were "content" with their current meal...Soon enough, the school itself blocked his view of them – and he was quite thankful for this.

Maintaining a brisk pace now, he kept to the sidewalk; generally heavier traffic on this road kept him from walking down the middle, as he had previously. The steep residential roads (down which he'd nearly tumbled) were far less trafficked than this one. Though, at the moment, there were no passing cars.

He was lost in himself, failing to properly survey the land, when a bald man in a tattered suit smashed through the front doors of the school. He left bloody streaks across the glass on his departure. His white shirt was streaked in red; the tie, half undone, hung lopsided from his neck. The schoolteacher howled and grunted and lumbered after this wanderer and trailed more blood with every step.

The suddenness of it all made this wanderer run.

In its attempted haste to catch up, the schoolteacher tripped over a step and tumbled into the grass. Some time later, as it crawled along, this highly infectious schoolteacher would make a meal of a young lady as she carelessly ambled too near his position. Apparently she should have been watching her step.

So it goes.

The frightened wanderer (with his fantastic new boots) ran for blocks without stopping, without looking anywhere except at his own path. When crossing a major thoroughfare, he was nearly mowed down by a pickup that blindly careened across every lane before crashing through the bay windows of an office supply store.

And he ran some more, without a single thought toward helping these people – infected, or not.

A few more blocks down, as his pace was slowing (he had little stamina for such exertion any longer) a bicyclist zipped by and slammed a leather sap between his shoulders. He went sprawling and landed in a huff, the wind knocked from his lungs. The bicyclist flew around a corner and was gone, never to be seen by this man again.

Dazed and winded with minor lacerations on his hands, he pushed himself up and looked around, eyes blurry, unfocused. A group of hipsters were staggering after him from across the street. A homeless man, still overburdened with a hiking pack that slowed his already labored gait, staggered at him from up ahead.

CRACK! – the homeless man's head exploded.

The gunshot rang out from up above and echoed off every surface.

CRACK-whizz! – he heard the bullet in midflight, watched it chip a piece out of the sidewalk.

He rolled under an awning and thrust himself into an alcove beneath the shooter, panting and frantic (and still dazed). Moments later, the shooter fired off three more rounds – *CRACK-CRACK! CRACK!* – and two of the lumbering hipsters fell dead. The third one moaned and seethed and – *CRACK!* – crumpled in turn.

When the gunfire ceased, he took his chances and bolted down the street; no bullets chased him, though he could still hear the gunman at work behind him.

His heart leapt in his chest when a corner of the hotel was visible just two blocks away. He ramped up his pace, starting a beeline across an intersection. When he spotted a group of at least a dozen bloodied and shambling people in the park, he adjusted his speed and route accordingly. They groaned and moaned and lurched after him, but none got close enough to grab at him.

He pushed through the hotel's front door and boarded the elevator unmolested.

IV

Exiting the elevator on the ninth floor, he was passed by a frightened older couple. The man was pallid and holding a bloodied towel over his elbow; the woman was frazzled as she escorted him into the elevator. Before the doors closed on them, she called out some warning about the bellhop in a shrill voice.

Ignoring her warning, he scuttled along to his room.

Waiting for the keycard to register was painful – but he was inside the room in moments, throwing the bolt and latch on the door.

Stumbling over the bedcover, he threw himself onto the bed and snatched his pistol out from beneath the pillows. He chambered a round, tucked it into his waistband, snatched the eight-inch bowie knife from the nightstand drawer and stood to thread his belt through the knife's sheath.

When the ruckus began next door – the banging on the walls that he previously mistook for the headboard, the moaning he assumed had been a hooker – he finally understood what had transpired in there. Though, he still idly wondered if one of them was a hooker...

From the front pouch of his backpack, he withdrew two extra clips – both fully loaded – and stuffed them into his back pockets. From the same pouch, he withdrew his terribly outdated slider phone and turned it on. As it powered up, he zipped his bag and started pacing around the room. Before it turned on, he slipped another little blue pill into his mouth – to calm his nerves.

Names and places were flying through his head; whom to call, where to go – what in bloody *hell* he should do. He was torn trying to figure out who would answer a call from such a stranger. He thought about Tod – his mentor, advisor, friend, employer – but knew he'd be too far away to assist. He thought of his parents, no longer in town – no longer in state – and wished he could just run into their comforting arms.

His phone beeped and vibrated, showing that he had five new voicemails and eight new text messages. Scanning the inbox, he found the most recent to be from Louis – a close friend – a brother – and found a glimmer of hope in this predicament of his.

Without reading the messages – or listening to the voicemails – he called Louis.

The voice on the other end was loud, nearly frantic: "Vincent!" he cried. "How the fuck are you? *Where* the fuck are you?"

"I'm in town," he replied. "At the Governor. Need help. Shit's going down and I don't know what –"

"Dude, I know," said Louis. "I've seen it on the news, and now there are some *freaks* at my front door!"

"Can you get out of there?"

"Yeah. Truck's in the garage." He paused, keys rattled. "Where you at? The Governor?"

"Yeah."

"On my way."

"What are we gonna do?"

"I don't know. But we can't sit and watch." He paused again – a car door shut. "I'll be there soon – five minutes, tops. Just sit tight and don't let them bite you." He hung up before Vincent could inquire about such a peculiar warning.

Sliding the phone into his pocket, he winced at the stinging in his hands. At closer inspection, he found tiny pebbles lodged in the superficial lacerations on his palms. Again, he stumbled over the bedcover on his way to the bathroom. Cursing his luck, he washed his hands – the water in the basin was brown from dirt and blood.

For a moment, he inspected himself in the mirror. He wiped a dark smudge from his cheek with the back of his hand. His eyes were glassy and a little red, but alert, despite the cloud that lingered around his head. He noticed the tear on his jacket, the blood that streaked it – the grime from falling on the sidewalk. But, having nothing to replace it with, he figured his jacket would have to hold out a little while longer.

He retrieved his backpack (minding the bedcover at last) and checked the time: 10:10 a.m.

At the door, preparing to head downstairs, he heard a knock – just a single knock. He cocked his head, perplexed – and then he heard a scrape and a groan. He cursed and contorted his face, wondering how he would get out of the room safely. Through the peephole, he could see the gnarled jowls of the bellhop moving back and forth. He cursed again, formulating a plan.

Gun in hand, he threw the latch, undid the bolt. Cautiously – after one last look around – he hit the handle, letting the bellhop fall through the door. He jumped back over the bedcover and fired three deafening shots into his chest. But the bellhop didn't fall down – he just stumbled back a few steps before starting forward again.

Vincent backed away until he bumped into the table.

The bellhop's feet tangled in the bedcover, laying him out on the floor.

Leveling the pistol at his forehead – *at* its *forehead*, he thought, re-fusing to think of it as a person – Vincent finally took note of the hemorrhaged sclerae and pale pupils, the dark veins that streaked its ash-en skin. Looking at this, he almost faltered. But when he saw the bellhop's fingernails strain and crack as it groped at the carpet – attempting to pull itself along – he pulled the trigger.

BLAM! – the only sound remaining in his ears now was that of his heart.

For moments, he stood there, watching the coagulated blood ooze around the bellhop's head, forming a chunky puddle of sorts. Never had he seen anything like that blood – it was brownish and thick and nothing at all like blood. He hadn't seen brainmatter in person before, but he knew that wasn't it.

Before his stomach decided to revolt, he slipped into the hallway, his gun poised and ready to fire.

Something slammed into a door – he nearly squeezed off a round, but managed to hold off. This happened again and again, but he refused to jump at the sound again. When he reached the elevator, the entire floor was flooded with the racket – he briefly wondered how long the doors would hold up under such constant assault before ignoring the thought as inconsequential, if not stupid.

He hammered the elevator call button repeatedly, nervously glancing over his shoulder every few seconds. But after a minute of this, the floor indicator for this car still remained at the lower level. He gave up on the elevator and started for the stairs.

Bleak and utilitarian, the whitewashed stairwell echoed every sound he made; the door closing behind him rebounded back to his ears tenfold – his footfalls rang out above and below. He tried stepping lightly to diminish the noise, but the urgency of his situation resonated in his brain and he hastened his step by the first landing.

Three floors down, with no sign of danger, he hastened his steps even more, sometimes skipping three or four at a time. His quick and heavy footfalls and their riotous echoes covered the moans rising from below. He raced along, worrying about leaving Louis to wait outside while he dawdled in this barren stairwell –

He nearly crashed into the gnarled and blood-streaked housekeeper – a short and pudgy Hispanic woman with a gaping hole in her cheek. Narrowly missing her, he slammed into the concrete wall as she – *it* – lunged up the last step; she tripped and fell at his feet. Before he could react, the housekeeper latched onto his ankle, pulled it toward her seething jowls. He screamed and cursed and kicked, but she held tight, clamping her teeth around his foot – *oh, the pressure!* – he could feel her teeth through his leather boots. He fired blindly –

BLA-BLAM! – a quick double-shot and the weight of the deranged woman dropped from his foot. The bullets clanged off every surface, ricocheted dangerously close to this man's head, before finally burying themselves in randomly similar places on opposing walls.

His entire head was ringing from a deafening onslaught of echoes and his first thought was that he just lost his hearing. His second thought was that he shot off his foot, but he couldn't focus enough to open his eyes. He knew that the shock of the wound and the buzzing in his brain would be enough to block him from feeling the pain.

He groped at his foot and opened his eyes, not fully believing what he saw; his foot remained attached to his leg. The same could not be said for half the housekeeper's head; the stairs, the railing, the wall were all speckled with curdled blood and brainmatter (which, now that he thought about it, looked disgustingly similar to cottage cheese, if cottage cheese were crusty and reddish-brown or gray, as some of the bits of dead brainmatter were).

He two-stepped down the last three flights, his eyes alert and ears still ringing.

The scene beyond the lobby door was horrific: groups of gruesome people were hunched about the lobby, feasting in a scene of horrific mastication on various individuals, some of whom were still kicking and screaming – or trying to scream. The walls were sprayed red and the floor was a churning puddle as flopping limbs and gushing wounds stirred the growing red mess. A pair of infected teenagers ferociously gnawed on the corpses of the elderly couple at the elevator's threshold; the doors kept dinging and trying to close on them.

Vincent opened fire, blazing a path through the lobby. He slipped and stumbled over a dismembered leg which sent him sprawling in a puddle of untainted, fresh blood at the edge of the feast. Pushing himself up, he felt a tug at his ankle and instinctively twisted away – he leveled the pistol at a woman's head. Before squeezing the trigger, he had time enough to register the fear in her eyes, the trembling of her lips; a chunk of her hair had been torn out and blood spurted the walls from somewhere Vincent could not see.

"*Shoot!*" she whimpered. "*Please!*"

BLAM! – the bullet punched a dark red hole into the center of her pretty face.

He pushed himself up and bolted for the door.

V

Louis was not parked out front, nor was he in the drive or alleyway. Vincent saw no sign of his friend anywhere. But disheveled bodies lurched at him from everywhere, no doubt in response to his raucous gunfire. Their groans grated at him from every angle as he whirled this way and that, hoping to see his friend's arrival.

A deranged version of the hotel manager pushed through the front doors and started at him; he backed away, into the street.

Their numbers were steadily growing. They appeared from every corner of every street and alley and alcove, and swarmed on his position. With every step, he found he was farther from one and closer to another. Frantically whipping his gun from target to target, he was uncertain of where to focus his defenses.

Standing in the middle of the road, his breath catching and heart racing, he gave in to the inevitable meal he was to become. He lowered his weapon, looked himself over – *what a mess!* A wash of calm enveloped him as he conceded to defeat – he could nearly feel the stench of death as it crept up behind him.

He considered eating a bullet right then and there.

But they visibly hitched – each one of them did. They were listening to something – some were turning. Unable to hear a thing besides a steady ringing in his ears, Vincent whirled on the creeper behind him – *oh the stench!* – and slammed his pistol into its head. One hit, and he felt the skull crack and cave and watched the gnarled policeman weakly crumple to the cement. It was still clutching its baton.

He ran past other reaching arms, into the park. Only a few of them tried following, but their lumbering gait was no match for his sprint and he reached the gazebo untouched. Save for a few stragglers at the edge of the park, he was alone here. Some of them lurched in his direction, others turned away.

Peculiar, he thought, aware of how modest a descriptor this was.

Nothing lingered behind him; he glanced over each shoulder, and the nearest – what? *creeper? lurcher? stench? zombie?* (he refused to believe this last explication) – was thirty yards away. He dropped his pistol's clip, noted that it had one bullet remaining, and popped it back in. He started across the park –

The first sound he heard was a guttural churning. And then he heard the thump – the splat – and the high-revving engine became apparent. He gazed up the street, elated at the sight of Louis' pickup barreling through a shambling horde; chunks of graymatter and curdled blood were lodged in the grille. As it rumbled up to the hotel, Louis began tapping out a rhythm on the horn – even the nearest stench started toward the truck.

Vincent began hooting and hollering and jumping and waving his arms about in a ludicrous fashion. But Louis couldn't hear him over the ruckus of his own little world; his attention was on the hotel and his fist pounded the horn while the radio babbled about Judgment Day.

When the horde grew dense around the truck, Louis took off.

Vincent's heart sank.

He stood there, arms dangling, mouth agape. Questions and curses rattled around his brain – he couldn't figure why Louis hadn't waited just a moment longer – why he hadn't looked around and seen his flailing, wailing friend across the street. Worse, he couldn't figure what to do if left out here on his own, in the heart of a ravenous city. Best he actually could figure was that he should run – maybe back up to his room – to buy time and formulate a new plan.

His phone rang; it was a piercing, foreign sound (he hadn't heard it in months).

Every gruesome face contorted and turned in his direction.

Halfway through the second ring, Vincent answered it: "I'm in the park," he husked.

"What?" Louis called back.

A little louder now: "I'm in the park! Across from the hotel!"

"Two seconds!" replied Louis.

The roaring engine distracted the crowd again and the truck flew out from the alley, crushing a stunned-looking barista that stood in its way. The truck hopped the curb, slipped between two trees and ripped up wet grass before sliding to a stop in front of Vincent.

"Let's go!" hollered Louis.

Vincent raced around to the passenger side.

The radio was blatting something about Evangelicals and Judgment Day, but Vincent was far more concerned with the possible injuries he sustained in his escape. Ripping off his boot, he could feel Louis' eyes boring into him, no doubt enrapt by the blood-drenched enigma sitting beside him. But Vincent was focused on his foot, concerned with his friend's earlier warning of being bitten.

"What the...?" began Louis. "What happened to you?"

"Nothing," said Vincent – his foot proved to be unscathed (he silently thanked his boots for saving his skin once again). He sighed in relief. "Drive," he said. "This ain't no place to linger." Already, the lurchers were creeping on their position.

Louis floored the gas, throwing a rooster tail of mud behind them. "Did one of them get you?" he asked.

"Almost," replied Vincent. "Didn't even break the leather."

"Are you sure? These things are highly –"

"Dead sure," he said, vaguely aware of the irony. "What are these things?"

"Dunno," said Louis – the truck bounced off the curb and into the street. They mobbed around a corner, the truck listing hard to one side. "Haven't heard a definitive report yet. People are just rambling about

Armageddon and such. I'm thinkin' it's more likely some sort of biological attack on us from one of the many countries that hate western civilization."

"Seems more like something from a Romero flick to me," murmured Vincent.

There was a noticeable silence and Vincent realized they were heading deeper into town. "Where are we going?" he inquired.

"John called right after you," said Louis. "Didn't sound well – was mumbling something about his fiancée and offing himself. We're going to stop him – save him…save them both. I hope."

VI

They weren't too late – John was planted on the front porch, an untouched spray of blood streaking his face and a bloody bat at his side. He didn't even look up as the truck pulled across the front lawn – his shoes were far more interesting to stare at, apparently.

Vincent climbed out of the truck; Louis hopped out and raced around to John.

"Are you okay?" he asked, his voice brimming with concern. "Where's Lucy?"

John was silent, but his grave eyes rose to meet Louis'.

"Oh, buddy," he said. "I'm so sorry." He went in to offer a hug and John allowed it. "We're gonna get you outta here," he explained, releasing him. "We just gotta get outta town and we should be safe. We're gonna hit my parents' lakehouse and figure something out."

Standing back, silent, was Vincent. John's attention flicked over to him and, despite his grief, a glimmer of shock visibly registered on his face. "Where'd you come from?" he croaked – his words had a certain bite to them that stung at Vincent's heart.

"Long story," he said. "Come along and we'll talk." Vincent thought he saw a burning in John's eyes.

Looking back at Louis, John huffed and pushed himself up, being sure to grab the bat. He strode by both of them and flopped into the bed of the truck without a word.

Vincent shared a reproachful eye with Louis, sighed and climbed into the truck.

Once Louis settled himself behind the wheel, they were off.

VII

Almost immediately their journey was hindered by clogged streets. Cars and trucks and busses and vans all zipped carelessly around corners and through stop signs. Emergency vehicles warbled near and far – a trio of police cruisers were mobbing east when Louis maneuvered onto the main road. Vincent turned to watch them weave around obstacles at high speeds, their sirens blatting all the way.

Louis slammed his fist into the steering wheel. "I don't understand how everything could go from calm and quiet to sheer madness in such a short period of time!" he hollered.

"I couldn't tell you," said Vincent – he remained seated sideways on the pickup's bench seat. "I didn't even know of any of this until today." He regarded Louis suspiciously. "How long has this been going on?" he asked.

"First reports were out a couple days ago," replied Louis. "But it was being dubbed as another form of influenza – like the bird flu or the

swine flu. Standard precautions: stay away from sick people and such."
He scoffed. "Guess nobody heeds advice from the television anymore."

"And then...what?" pried Vincent. "It just spread like wildfire all of
a sudden?"

"Guess so," said Louis.

"Should we call anybody?" posed Vincent. "Maybe the police?"
Another cruiser whipped by them, this one headed toward the mall.
"What about your parents? Maybe they're already out at the lakehouse..."

"Nah," said Louis. "They're on vacation up at Whistler. Guess they
got a good early snow." He braked at the stop light; a school bus entered
the intersection, heedless of the light or cross-traffic and –

WHAM! – an armored truck slammed into its rear axle.

Both vehicles pirouetted through the intersection until the bus toppled and slid into a gas pump. People ran screaming in every direction,
fearful of the fireball that would surely follow. Some of these people
were tackled and devoured by infected individuals already lurking toward the scene.

"*Go! Go! Go!*" Vincent urged.

After a quick glance in either direction, Louis hit the gas and they
peeled rubber through the intersection. He muttered obscenities while
terrible scenarios rounded his brain. He skidded around a van that sat
dead across both lanes, its doors wide open. Vincent watched as John
was tossed from side to side in the bed at this sudden maneuver.

"Careful, yo," warned Vincent. "You're throwing John around like a
rag-doll back there."

The ground shook beneath their wheels...and then the concussion
hit them –

BOOM! – the gas pumps behind them exploded.

Vincent whirled, caught a glimpse of the massive fireball that rose skyward. John sat up at the sound, propped up on his elbows to watch the plume; Louis glanced the plume in his rearview. A cloud of red and black and orange twisted up, casting a hot shadow across the road – Vincent could feel it from inside the truck.

Louis watched this for too long; he looked back up barely in time to see an infected horde lurching across the road. He swerved to avoid them, tossing John against the wheel well again – but still clipped one with the front fender. The rest of its gruesome group groped at the doors and over the siderails, reaching for anything – reaching for John.

"*Shitshitshit*," he hissed, watching as John sat up, unscathed. After a quick glare at Louis in the mirror, he laid back down in the bed.

For a short time in their drive, the road was nearly deserted – only a few frantic drivers passed them in either direction. But the solace was quickly dissolved when they neared the freeway; panicky, terrified families raced from their homes toward hopeful havens in distant places along the peninsula or in the west.

One of the vehicles that broke away from the pack just after the southbound onramp carried an ill-fated crew of college students. The campus – less than a mile away – was overrun after the infection coursed throughout the classrooms. The majority of students attending figured an impromptu zombie walk had started without their knowledge (Vincent felt their pain on that misconception). By the time anybody realized the threat was real, most of the student body had turned.

The crew of students now heading south along rural roads would soon fall prey to infection as well. Only one of these four Greeners would survive the subsequent wreck and forge some semblance of a life in this new, twisted world.

But none of these men – not Louis or John or Vincent – would know this man as their paths were never destined to collide. And they drove on with barely a thought toward the rickety van save for their immediate stereotyping of the occupants as hippies and Greeners.

Just before merging onto the freeway, they passed a familiar bar. Vincent puzzled over the haphazardly packed vehicles along the side of the building and those parked in a neat row out front – he couldn't fathom the need to hit the local watering hole in such a crisis.

Despite this mass exodus from the city, the highway was fairly calm. A few cars were abandoned along the shoulder, but not so many as in the city. The line of vehicles in which they had been driving divided at the interchange for 101 up the peninsula. The few remaining vehicles heading west all sped out of sight before Louis turned off the highway. And then they were all alone, bopping up and around and down and along the windy two-lane road that brought them to the lakehouse.

The neighborhood was quiet – nobody was out, not healthy or otherwise. Most of the houses appeared to be unoccupied, their tenants most likely trapped in town or gone away – some lucky few may have even skedaddled in time to avoid the immediate catastrophe altogether (though Vincent wasn't very optimistic about the latter).

Upon arrival, it was apparent that the lakehouse was empty; shades were drawn with no shining lights either inside or out. The driveway, the lawn were blanketed with leaves and pine needles in such a way that the property screamed *VACANT!* at anybody who should care to look. Vincent noticed this as Louis backed the truck through the side yard and around to the back (he didn't bother to ask why they were parked around back on soft earth instead of out front on pavement; he trusted Louis' judgment).

John was drenched from riding in the truckbed (at least the rain had washed away most of the blood from his face). He was sitting up and vaguely scanning the property when Vincent climbed out of the truck. But his gaze was distant; he was lost in the nightmarish, surreal moments when he took what remained of his fiancée's life.

Sensing this, Vincent stood aside, knowing his help would not be appreciated.

Louis popped the tailgate. "C'mon, buddy," he said to John. "Let's get outta the rain, have a drink, get some food." His voice was soft and soothing, but John just glared. And, after a few beats, when John didn't move, Louis said, "It's safer in there anyhow; nobody to bite us – nobody to kill."

John dropped his eyes. A moment later, he stood and stepped off the tailgate, extending his hand to Louis. "You're a terrible driver," he said. And as Louis chuckled at this gibe, he said, "Thanks," his voice barely above a whisper.

Taking John's massive hand in one of his own, Louis said, "Anything for you, brother." He smiled. "The worst is behind us now."

John pursed his lips, still gripping Louis' hand. He glanced at Vincent; their gaze met for a moment before Vincent looked down and away. "Hey," said John – and Vincent looked back up. "I'm glad to see you're still alive."

"Same to you," Vincent replied with a wan smile.

VIII

Once the house was secured, they sat around the dining room table, each locked in a distressful spell. Silence engulfed them – entranced them – a silence that seemed to drape them with a deeper, darker gloom. They were chainsmoking, using a small saucer for an ashtray, and sipping on whiskey (John mostly swirled his drink, mesmerized by the amber whirlpool). Faint light sputtered across the table from a lone candle set in the middle; layers of smoke lingered, lazily drifting around their heads.

Time was gauged not by the clocks but by the growing pile of cigarette butts in the saucer between them and the thickening cloud in the air. At one point, Louis stood up to open the kitchen window; still, nobody spoke. Vincent wondered what they were thinking – he tried to read their faces; John was apparently too stricken to be thinking of much; Louis appeared to be chewing through miles of information and trying to formulate a plan. Of his own thoughts, Vincent had very few; he wished to detach from the world – at least for a little while; he felt restless at their inaction, though he was thankful for the reprieve.

The only immediate solution he saw fit for these internal struggles lay in drinking more whiskey and taking more pills – at least he could detach emotionally, if not physically.

Without a word, he stood up – his chair squalled on the linoleum – and made his way to the restroom. Unloading the first two glasses of whiskey from his bladder, Vincent slipped another pill into his mouth, swallowed it dry.

He looked at himself in the mirror: his hat was now speckled with dried blood; his jacket was a complete wash of muck and gore; a red smear stretched up his neck and cheek and dappled his ear. Looking down at himself, he found his jeans and boots in a similar state; it was all soaked through.

His head swam suddenly and he had to grab hold of the counter to steady himself. He looked back into the mirror, barely able to focus on the fuzzy reflection that stared back, awkward and wobbly.

Moments later, after his head cleared, Vincent backed out of the bathroom.

John sat alone at the table while Louis crouched before the refrigerator in the adjoining kitchen. In the dim room, bathed in white light from the refrigerator, Louis appeared to glow. It was at this moment that Vincent noticed just how clean and unspoiled he was – especially in comparison to his own bloodstained self. He felt almost as though he were in the presence of something ethereal – this feeling was amplified by the fact that Louis had gone out of his way to rescue him after such a long silence between the two of them.

It wasn't until Louis stood to open the freezer that the magic melted away.

Vincent found his voice: "Yo, Lou," he said. "Know if I can get a change of clothes? Maybe a shower, too?"

Turning toward Vincent, Louis was visibly appalled – again – at his appearance. "Yeah, dude," he said, tossing both the freezer and fridge doors shut at once and marching out of the kitchen. "Follow me." He led Vincent down the hall – the bathroom light was still shining – and into the master bedroom. "I'm sure you can borrow some of my dad's clothes." He opened a drawer containing shirts. "Doubt he'd mind right now."

"Thank you," replied Vincent, opening another drawer – this one was full of jeans.

"Towels are under the sink in the bathroom," Louis explained. "I'm gonna make some food. Got any preferences?"

"Anything will do," said Vincent. "I haven't eaten all day."

IX

Vincent showered, changed into a fresh set of clothes that fit him surprisingly well. The pants were a touch loose and the longsleeve was a bit billowy, but the jacket he found fit him perfectly and was heavier and warmer than his ruined one. After shoving another longsleeve into his pack, he rejoined his friends.

The house smelled of pizza; Vincent's stomach lurched at the aroma.

John was lounging on a chair in the living room, staring at the ceiling. The television was on and muted with closed captioning. It was tuned into a news channel that was showing a grainy video of a residential street scene. The subject of the video was a horde of lurchers staggering aimlessly through the middle of the street. A moment later the horde stopped at once and turned. And then an old white box truck careened through the heart of the horde.

The video cut back to a flustered young anchorman. A moment after his lips started moving, the captions caught up:

NOBODY IS CERTAIN AT THE CAUSE FOR THESE MASS HOMICIDES, BUT EARLY SPECULATION FROM SCIENTISTS SUGGEST A BIOLOGICAL OR CHEMICAL AGENT. NO WORD FROM THE PENTAGON YET AS TO THE VALIDITY OF A POSSIBLE TERROR ATTACK, THOUGH THE QUESTION HAS BEEN POSED.

AGAIN – I WILL REPEAT FOR THOSE OF YOU JUST TUNING IN. LOCALIZED INCIDENTS OF MASS HOMICIDE HAVE BEEN REPORTED IN THE SOUTH PUGET SOUND REGION. THE AT-

TACKERS IN EVERY REPORTED CASE HAVE BEEN SLOW AND
SHAMBLING AND EXTREMELY AGGRESSIVE. THE ATTACK-
ERS DO NOT RESPOND TO REASON, NOR DO THEY SEEM TO
BE IN COLLUSION.

THE GENERAL PUBLIC IS ADVISED TO REMAIN INDOORS
AND AVOID ALL CONTACT WITH ANYBODY WHO IS SICK OR
UNRESPONSIVE. ANY CONTACT WITH THESE ASSAILANTS
COULD LEAD TO INFECTION.

STAY TUNED ALL DAY AND NIGHT FOR CONTINUING
COVERAGE AND SAFETY TIPS.

"Food's almost done," said Louis, poking his head around the corner. "Just took it out of the oven. Should be ready in five minutes." He
glanced at the television. "Any good news?"

"They still don't know what it is," replied Vincent – he had taken a
seat in a plush wingback by the front window and was now smoking a
cigarette. "Might be some terrorist attack is what they're saying, but
they're not sure who or what or why."

"A terrorist attack? Here?" he said in disbelief. "Highly doubtful."

"My thoughts exactly." Though his thoughts were also muddled by
a poor mixture of oxycodone and horrific events (the booze would soon
play a part in this tragedy as well), he truly doubted the legitimacy of the
newscaster's report.

"How bad is it out there?" asked Louis.

"Still a local phenomenon," said Vincent.

John pushed himself up and off the couch. "I'ma hit the shower," he
said and trudged down the hall.

When the bathroom door was shut, Louis said, "I feel so bad for him."

"Me too," said Vincent. "I can't imagine what he's feeling." Through the haze, he was hit by smiling images of Isabella – his one true love. The thought of her had a debilitating effect – moreso when the images morphed into her crying, screaming, contorted face. He was suddenly interested in the cigarette smoldering between his fingers.

Moments later, Louis was shoving a plate in front of his face – half of a small freezer pizza was on it. He took the plate, but continued smoking. Louis sat on the couch across from him.

"Should I ask you what happened," said Louis, "or are you going to tell me?"

Vincent looked up at him, perplexed. He raised an eyebrow at his friend.

"I know her side of it all," Louis explained, "but I'd like to know just what the hell you were thinking. And – *and!* – I'd like to know where you've been for the past year."

Vincent flushed, shook his head and pulled hard on the cigarette.

"I'd rather not involve John just yet," said Louis. "Not in his current state."

"I don't think this is a good time –" began Vincent.

"When would be a better time?" Louis interjected.

Vincent was silent, staring at his pizza.

"Listen," began Louis – he set his plate aside and leaned forward. "I know about the job."

Vincent glared, suspicious. "What job?" he asked.

"I know you left to pursue greener pastures," replied Louis, equally suspicious now. "Only I was under the impression that you had taken a lucrative position with Tod overseas." He studied Vincent's physical response. "But that's not the case, is it?"

"Oh no," said Vincent. "It was very lucrative. And you could say there was lots of travelling involved."

"Working with Tod?"

"Yes."

"Doing what?"

"I'd rather not discuss this right now."

Louis chuckled sardonically – almost maniacally. "I can't believe you, Vin. You left an amazing woman – a woman who would have given the world for you – probably would have taken a bullet for you! And you left her – *why?* – to work with that psycho sonofabitch!"

Vincent's face slacked. He gazed thoughtfully into his friend's eyes. And then he reached over the arm of his chair, snatched his back-pack and tossed it over to Louis. "Open it up," he said. "And while you're in there, remember that I never ended anything with her. I told her I'd be gone for a while and she flipped – she said she never wanted to see me again."

Louis unzipped the bag; his eyes widened and jaw dropped.

"There's just under thirty thousand in there," said Vincent. "I did it for her. I did it for the benefit of our society. I did it…because I needed to."

"You really took the job," breathed Louis. "You really fucking did it."

Again, Vincent grew suspicious. "What do you know?"

Holding a stack of hundreds in one hand and the bag in the other, Louis said, "I know he approached me first. I have no idea why; he should have known I'd reject the offer."

"Must have known you wouldn't do a thing about it."

"He promised me August," said Louis, and his lips quivered. "He said he could have her released."

"Oh, Jesus!" husked Vincent. "Why didn't you tell me? I'm sure I could talk to him –"

"No!" Louis shouted. "I don't want any favors from that asshole. I'll get her out myself."

"But how?"

Louis looked at the stack in his hand, at the bag, and back up at his friend.

"You honestly think money can get her out of there?" inquired Vincent.

"It could help."

"I doubt it. And that's not nearly enough to begin to bribe someone. Not these days."

Louis dropped his head, resigned to Vincent's logic. He ruminated on their situations a moment longer and said, "You really thought she'd wait for you? What about when you returned with this money and your story – do you think she would have stayed with a killer?" He brought his eyes up to meet Vincent's.

And Vincent dropped his in turn. "I don't know. Maybe she would have respected my intentions."

"You really think that?"

Vincent pulled the last hefty drag off his smoke, pitched it into the fireplace and shook his head. "No," he said. "Maybe. I don't know."

"I doubt it," said Louis.

"You gonna tell John?"

"No," replied Louis. "Not yet. I'll let him broach the subject. When he's ready." He shoved the stack of cash back into the bag, zipped it up and tossed it at Vincent's feet. "You know I love you, brother. That's why I care so much."

Vincent sighed and picked up a piece of pizza.

X

Vincent's pistol was dismantled and spread out across the dining room table. Blackened cotton swabs were in a heap beside a box of fresh swabs. He was pulling a brush through the barrel when Louis announced he was going to gather some supplies. Focused – and mostly indifferent to seeking out supposed "essentials" – Vincent continued unabashedly at his meticulous scrubbing.

He was setting the brush down when John sat beside him.

"Got something I can help with?" he asked.

"Sure," said Vincent. "I already got the slide. But you can hit the frame."

After dabbing the end of one swab with the cleaning solution, John started scrubbing away. At first, Vincent was worried his friend would start off on the same line of questioning that Louis had. But after a few minutes of cleaning, he was certain John would remain silent and brooding.

Just when Vincent began melting back into the process, John said, "Welcome home."

Astounded – and after a few beats – Vincent said, "Good to be home."

"How was your trip?"

He thought a moment. "Interesting. Enlightening."

John grunted, dabbed more solution onto a fresh swab and went back to work. A minute later, he asked, "Was it worth it?"

Vincent thought about this for a while – John granted him the time. At last, he said, "No. I don't think it really was."

"You miss her?" he asked.

"More than you know. But," he let the word hang for a moment. And then: "There are worse things in life than having loved and lost."

Again, John grunted.

Vincent shuddered, realizing how harsh the words may have sounded. "Sorry," he said. "That came out the wrong way."

"It's all good," replied John. "I get your meaning."

Silence flourished between them again; only the rain outside and the wind blowing in through the open window could be heard. Time was allowed to slip by at its own pace and Vincent was finally given a moment to detach completely from this world. His head was warm and fuzzy, wrapped up in a mingling haze of pills and alcohol (a familiar comfort these past few weeks). Despite this haze, his nimble fingers worked a swab into every crevice, collected every speck of gunpowder from in and around the barrel. Occasionally, he would glance over at John to be sure the frame was receiving as meticulous a cleaning. These practiced fingers then applied oil to every moving part and contact surface.

He was reassembling his gun when Louis marched back into the dining room, proudly presenting his haul. He laid out a series of weapons – a wooden baseball bat, a hatchet, a bolt-action .22-caliber rifle – and set down two boxes of ammunition and a banged-up, faded blue first aid kit (it looked ancient and was, in fact, older than any of them).

"Well," said Vincent, "two guns should be better than one." He started reloading his empty clip.

"Check this out," said Louis – and he popped open the first aid kit. Aside from the standard bandages and alcohol wipes, this kit was also equipped with basic survival supplies: from iodine drops and windproof matches to collapsible cups and Mylar blankets. "It's my dad's old one-stop-camping-shop; got everything you need to survive in nature except sustenance itself."

Vincent thought Louis was a little too upbeat for their current predicament. He managed to hold his tongue on the matter. "Should be handy," he said, "if we find ourselves in the forest." Finished reloading, he slapped the clip onto the heel of his hand three times and popped it back into the pistol.

John reached for the rifle. He looked it over for two seconds before breaking it down. He handed Vincent the bolt and action and started on the long barrel. They plunged right back into the calming routine of cleaning and oiling.

Louis poured three whiskeys, kept one and sat opposite them, smoking.

XI

Outside was pitch black and dumping buckets of rain.

Inside was dim – lit by a single candle – and quiet. Louis was spread out on the couch, watching the candlelight dance about the textured ceiling. John sat stolid in the straightback, unpadded, wooden chair at the foot of the dining room table, brooding over unthinkable – and unchangeable – events. Vincent sat, drunk and stoned, smoking in the wingback by the front window, occasionally peeking through a thin gap around the edge of the curtains.

Once, Louis had suggested checking the news again. But he was quickly denied by both Vincent and John.

"They ain't got shit else to tell us," said John.

And Louis didn't press the subject; he figured this postulation to be correct. He let his hunger for knowledge – the common mortal hunger for knowledge – fade with an understanding that the media was as ignorant to the situation as they were, if not moreso as they were most assuredly locked away in some fortified building with no personal experiences from which they could draw.

As it were, the very station they had been tuned into was now overrun with infection from an executive that turned after the doors had been locked tight. Only one little room was left unaffected. And while this frantic news crew fought to stay on the air, this trio of silent survivors drifted in and out of consciousness until being rudely awoken in the early hours of dawn.

Day Two
Hide & Seek

I

Yellow and pink tendrils of dawn filtered through thinning rain-clouds offering a minor reprieve from the sheer darkness of this lakeside drive. The rain had diminished from its earlier assault into a mild sprinkle, but the road was still a cascade of rushing water and slick leaves. Despite some mild slips and slides – and the occasional hydroplane – Maurice Enderby managed to captain his Comanche effortlessly down this familiar road. And even the gushing, gaping wound on his wrist did little to detract from his practiced piloting.

All day, Maurice had been working his route delivering baked goods to shops and marts in remote locales from the city to the coast. Not once in his route had he been exposed to any effects of this horrifying epidemic – not even a glimpse of a news report or clip of a radio broadcast. Until his unfortunate – and ultimately deadly – encounter at the warehouse, Maurice had been living a normal, uneventful day.

And in a flash it all changed.

Some people will complain about their boss. Some will even talk idly about killing them, though very few actually follow through with such empty threats. But on this formerly regular day, Maurice Enderby found reason enough to bludgeon his boss – his *friend* – a person with whom he had never become angry even once in their years of friendship – he bludgeoned him to death.

Then again, he had never once been terrified of his boss – his friend – not until those last snarling, gnashing, bloody moments of his life.

The wound that Julius left him was no longer painful – *Shock,* he assured himself; it was numb and clotted, but still spurted some when his arm would inadvertently shake and seize at a crest or corner.

His vision blurred and eyes fluttered – *So much rain!* cried his brain – over a crest, over a bump. Checking the mirror, he saw a hazy brown lump – *Tree…*he thought with uncertainty. *Whatever.* He drove on, continually justifying his recent predicament.

A small dip, a broad corner, a crest and a straightaway – and his vision blurred again – *Damn rain!* Something worse than rain – worse than his condition – obscured his vision – *What the…?* He swerved, fishtailed, dodged a shambling bluehair – and then he lost consciousness.

II

In his chair, glass in hand, smoldering cigarette between his lips, Vincent opened his eyes to a dreary scene beyond the curtains. In his semiconscious delirium, he was reminded of late nights with Isabella, sipping cocoa or hot buttered rum, watching the dark rain drip through barren trees.

And again he drifted away.

Angels' kisses smacked him here and there; a cool blast caressed his ear and heated up to a burning, passionate suckling. She slowly dragged her warm, moist tongue seductively down his belly. Endearing emptiness escaped his quivering lips.

Staring into her lustful, keening eyes, he could sense the boiling of her blood – it was pungent, it was palpable.

She was kissing his neckline – her lips were hot.

She was licking his belly – her tongue grew cold.

She was – somehow – in both places at once.

And he continued to proclaim his love for her.

Drawing her chilly tongue below his beltline, he thought his pecker might freeze.

Again, he met her lustful, keening eyes.

To his surprise, she glowered, snarled – shrieked and pounced, shattering into a million pieces –

He awoke with a start – his neck was hot, his stomach cold – his crotch was frozen.

Upon inspection, he found a half-lit cigarette on his shoulder and his glass was tilted over his belly. He grimaced at the burn on his neck and wiped absently at the spilt whiskey down his frontside. And then he remembered the sound that awoke him to begin with –

"What the hell was that crash?" called Louis from the couch.

"It shook the whole house!" cried John.

Vincent threw open the curtains to find an overturned white hulk resting against the home's brickwork façade. In its tumble, the truck had bowled over a barren sapling and left the street-side fenceline in shambles.

"Oh," said Louis, wide-eyed. "Shit."

For a time they stood in awe, too shocked to react.

And then John spoke up: "Should we help?" he asked. "I don't see any movement."

Nobody responded immediately – they were all still too stunned.

"Well," said Louis. And, after a pause, "It's hard to believe none of them heard that," he said, gesturing to the fire station across the road.

Vincent looked nervously at the small stretch of dim road he could see. "I think we should see if they're alright," he said at last.

"And what if they're dead?" asked John. "What then?"

"Then there's not much we can do," replied Vincent. "But we have to see."

"I don't know about you," said Louis, addressing John, "but my conscience won't let me sit idly by while somebody could be dying before my eyes." The morning felt darker with the dim morning glow casting deep shadows across the deluged yard; Louis could not see much as he scanned this dreary scene, but he could not see any imminent threat. "And," he said, turning to face John, "we should probably check before any...any..."

"Lurchers," said Vincent. "That's what I see when I look at them."

"Yeah, sure," said Louis. "*Lurchers*. We should check before *they* show up."

Cold rain, amplified by the blustering wind, smacked Vincent in the face upon opening the door – it nearly ripped the door out of his grip. Scowling at the sensation, he stepped from the comfortable darkness into the dim, piercing morning drizzle.

Scuttling through the soggy lawn, soaking their shoes, their socks, their pants – just as the falling rain was soaking their heads, their jackets, their shirts – each felt the tug of dismay. And when he dropped to his knees, Vincent was certain of the fate this truck's sole occupant had suffered; a motionless, bloody body dangled awkwardly from the seatbelt. After checking the pulse – he felt a faint thumping from the man's carotid – he noticed the gaping wound on the man's wrist.

"He's alive," said Vincent, staring at the wound. "But he's been bitten. He doesn't have long."

Audible over the patter of rain falling on the truck's skyward undercarriage was a chorus of inarticulate groans.

"C'mon, Vin," said John. "We should get going now."

For a moment, Vincent remained on his knees beside the fated Maurice Enderby – a man he had never known – a man he would never know – a man he would never forget. The deluge laid his hair flat – water dripped from his nose, his chin, and coursed down his face. It soaked through his thin jacket. He was drenched from toe to top, hot with rage and dismay.

He rose to his feet slowly, smoothly. He nodded at John. And with one last glimpse of the man he never knew, Vincent followed his friends back inside. Quickly, they gathered the weapons Louis had collected the night before, a couple grocery sacks of canned food and supplies. Vincent grabbed his backpack, which now carried a half gallon of cheap whiskey. Within a minute, they were running down the back steps and climbing into the truck.

With Louis behind the wheel of his truck and John jammed illogically in the middle of the small cab, they ripped around the house, throwing mud and grass and sliding out as a result of the disproportionate weight ratio and soggy conditions. A scattered horde staggered after the truck from around the capsized Comanche. More of them marched intentionally in their path, heedless of any consequences. The impact jarred them not just physically, but mentally as well. The gory splatter across the windshield jarred them further.

III

Twice before reaching the highway, they were passed by reckless drivers risking it all to zip down this storm-soaked, winding road. "Idiots," Louis said after the second reckless car – a dirty station wagon – slipped and skidded along in the wrong lane. "All wheel drive doesn't mean you can't lose control," he scoffed.

Five minutes later they rolled to a stop at the intersecting highway.

Hardly surprising to any of them, emergency vehicles – a pair of WSDOT (Washington State Department of Transportation) Incident Response Team vehicles, along with an ambulance – were flanking a stalled minivan. They watched as a trio of paramedics frantically worked to revive an unconscious elderly man lying on the wet pavement.

Someone flew by, nearly clipping the ambulance. They hardly noticed.

"Well," said Louis. "We have a decision to make now."

A member of the Incident Response Team looked curiously over at them.

"I'm in no hurry to head back to town," said Vincent.

"If we're not heading back to town," Louis said, "then where do we go?"

"Forward," said John, staring at the entrance to a familiar forest road.

They considered this in silence for a moment.

"Not a bad idea," said Vincent. He glanced over at the frantic paramedics and spotted a man with a hardhat and khaki vest swiftly crossing the road. "What's this guy want?" he asked. The man started waving his arms at them.

"I'm not particularly inclined to find out," said Louis. "I'd rather –"

An empty car was careening down the road at a frightening clip. It listed over the road's bevel from the fast lane, as though a ghost driver was piloting it directly at the man in the road. Incidentally, the driver had already dived from the car moments prior when dementia began to settle into his infected brain.

And, just as Louis was trying to say what he'd rather do, the man, trying to jump onto the shoulder, was mowed over by the ghost driver. The car wrapped around a light pole with the man trapped beneath its wheels – the sound of which was horrendous. His hardhat – which proved quite worthless in this situation – was thrown halfway across the highway, and wobbled to and fro before coming to rest on its top. It was speckled with blood that would soon wash away with the rain.

"Holy shit!" cried John, clapping a hand over his mouth.

Vincent gaped and climbed out of the truck – rather mechanically.

"Where are you going?" shrieked Louis.

But Vincent ignored him; he moved swiftly toward the wrecked sedan.

The rest of the response team, ignoring the minivan and surrounding scene, raced across the highway. The paramedics all stood and, after a brief exchange, two of them took off toward the wreck. The remaining paramedic knelt down beside the elderly man whose eyes had just opened. A brief smile faded quicker than its onset when this paramedic noticed the strange discoloration of the man's eyes.

While John and Louis raced from the truck to assist Vincent in his efforts to help the crew with the wreck, this lone paramedic watched a dark, frothy goo bubble and ooze from his patient's mouth. Gurgling and groaning, the patient – *former* patient – snatched his arm with a ferocity uncommon to men of his age.

The paramedic screamed – blood sprayed and squirted from his arm, keeping perfect time with his heartbeat. But soon enough, the flow would fade, the wound would clot. (It would, in fact, clot far sooner than it ever should with a healthy human body…)

As the car was being rolled off of the flattened (and rather unfortunate) member of the WSDOT Incident Response Team, the paramedic started bashing the old man's skull with his bare hands. And when the broken, pulpy mess of this man was uncovered, the paramedic was rocking the old man's head off the pavement. He continued until the old man's skull cracked and spilled a grossly discolored substance (curdled blood which may have contained fragments of bone and brainmatter) spilled out onto the pavement.

Panting, and holding one hand over the gaping hole in his arm, this lone paramedic stood on wobbly legs and started around the ambulance. He was crossing the road when the paramedics across the way were confirming the mangled body to indeed be dead (as though it weren't blatantly obvious already). Shaking his head, one of these paramedics gently closed the man's eyes.

The other looked up in time to see their other colleague wobbling his way across the highway. "Pat!" he cried – and he was up and aiding Pat without a moment's hesitation. The other paramedic followed on his heels. Together, they helped their injured colleague into the ambulance to assess his condition. Neither noticed the bloody mess of a man they had been assisting before the wreck; his corpse was less than four feet away.

Abhorrent to the woes of this freshly infected paramedic, the remaining Incident Response Team members crouched beside the mangled remains of their fallen friend and colleague. One of them had his head bowed and was mouthing a silent prayer; he repeatedly kissed the crucifix hanging from his neck.

Nobody seemed to notice the audience of horrified, perplexed young men despite their recent efforts to assist in the tragically futile rescue attempt.

Louis grabbed at Vincent's arm, insisted that he get back in the truck, told him they should leave before things escalated. But he pulled away, captivated by the mangled corpse; he noticed the deluge was already washing much of the blood away.

At last, Louis jolted him from this morbid reverie. When Vincent met his stern gaze, Louis said, "Let's go."

For a few beats, he just stared blankly back at Louis. Once his mind cycled back into gear, Vincent nodded solemnly. With one last glance at the conglomeration of bereaved and traumatized (and apparently underpaid) men, he followed Louis back to the truck. He was numb – shock and horror overwhelmed him.

He watched the scene drift by as the truck rolled across the highway. He absently noticed one of the men turn to watch them leave. He was entirely unaware that their quick exit would leave a lasting impression on this man regarding current affairs of the region.

In fact, a direct link could be formed between their flight and his; after another brush with death, this man would recall their truck rolling apathetically along, and he would flee to the coast in a futile attempt at saving his own life. It was there that he quickly discovered the true scope of this epidemic. Unfortunately, this lesson also made him a party to the epidemic.

So it goes.

IV

"What the fuck was that?" cried Louis.

But Vincent wasn't listening; he just continued staring out the window at the fading highway scene. He was wondering about the paramedics, now; he'd seen the body by the ambulance and watched as two of them were working hurriedly over the convulsing body of the third.

A brief pause through the median to check for traffic and they were on gravel.

"I said –" began Louis.

"I heard you," said Vincent. "I was trying to help."

"Doesn't look like you helped much!" He was irate. "If anything, you put us in danger!"

"Fuck you, Lou," said Vincent. He was surprisingly calm and his voice held no malice, though his callous words and glowering eyes would suggest otherwise. "Trying to help another human is worth the risk, don't you think?"

"Not if you want to live!" He was still irate.

"If I want to live with a healthy conscience, I will help whenever I can." His conscience was already overladen with grief and self-loathing. He wondered briefly if Louis, having so recently learned of his darkest secret, could understand the inner turmoil he felt at every passing moment.

Louis huffed, but said nothing.

The persistent churning and crunching of gravel filled the truck and rattled their bones while the numerous potholes fiercely jounced them this way and that. Vincent even bumped his head on the ceiling once, just hard enough to shock his spine and disrupt his thought process. After the road smoothed out a bit, Vincent asked, "Can't we cross over to Rochester or something from here?"

"Already on it," said John. "I'm a little hazy on the route, but I'm sure I can figure it out."

"I'm sure you can, too," muttered Vincent. He was staring at the sharp cliff to their left, recalling a very unpleasant memory from his youth. His body suddenly felt weightless at the thought – just as it had on that drug-induced, reckless night. As if to strike this terrible memory home, the truck hit a deep, jagged pothole that threw Vincent's knee into the dash – just as it had that long ago night (only this time, they did not end up on a cliffside wrapped around a tree). He lightly groaned and rubbed his knee, shifting his attention out his own window at the passing hillside. Inwardly, he grumbled at being a passenger on this road; he never drove off a cliff while in control of a vehicle, only as a passenger. Granted, John hadn't either. But Vincent remained uncomfortable, regardless.

Within minutes, the deluge broke down to a light drizzle.

"Gotta love the weather up here," commented John.

And then the drizzle let up altogether.

John grunted. "It'll probably start up again in five minutes." He spoke low, more to himself.

Miles later, near what might be considered the peak of this particular hill, they came to a gentle stop behind a trailer half-filled with fresh lumber.

"What's all this, now?" grumbled John.

"It would appear to be," said Louis, "an inconvenient obstacle."

"Agreed," sighed Vincent. "Extremely inconvenient."

"Can we clear it?" inquired Louis.

"How?" said John. "Pull it into the next turnaround?"

"I don't know," replied Louis. "Something…anything."

"We could drive it off the cliff," mused Vincent. "That would get it out of our way."

"Great idea," said Louis, not short on sarcasm. "Nobody would miss *that* rig."

"They just might not," said Vincent. "Looks like it's been abandoned already, anyhow."

"What about an alternate route?" posed Louis. "Gotta be multiple ways through the forest."

"None that I know of," replied John. "But I'm not all *that* familiar with these roads. And I'm not supposing you guys are, either."

"Nope," said Vincent.

"Yeah, not quite," said Louis.

"Let's check it out, at least," said John. "Maybe we will be able to move it…somehow…somewhere…" He killed the engine. "I hope…"

They filed out of the truck. Vincent drew his pistol; Louis shouldered the rifle; John gripped the wooden bat in one hand. They moved cautiously forward, spanning the road, with John at point, flanked on either side by Louis and Vincent. At the rig, Vincent kept between the trailer and hillside while John led Louis around the narrow path along the cliffside. The sweet, musty mixture of fresh cut timber, diesel and hot metal lent an air of power to the scene that amplified its intrinsic eeriness.

All three stopped just short of the cab. From here, they detected an underlying coppery stench of death and the must of pestilence.

Locking eyes with Vincent, John gestured toward the cab. Vincent nodded and strafed around front, pistol ready, eyes locked on the wind-shield. He strafed around until he was covering the door John was about to open. Louis pulled the rifle into his shoulder and readied his finger on the trigger guard (the barrel waggled under his nerves).

Time stopped for a moment – that's how Vincent remembered it, anyhow.

John was staring at Louis, resting the bat on his shoulder. Louis was staring back at him with a frozen expression of anxious trepidation. Vincent's breath was locked tight in his chest, his face was hot. His mind escaped him, careening wildly through a plethora of wild imaginings at boggling speeds. He thought his heart might stop or explode – or maybe he'd just drop from an embolism or the like.

Such a moment as this proved unwarranted by any means; John threw open the door to no assault from within. Vincent released a shuddering sigh and drew a similarly shuddering breath – noting, quite nostalgically, the crispness of the fresh autumn air. It took him a moment to detect the odor of rot that emanated from the cab.

John started to speak: "See guys –"

But he was cut off by a yelp from Louis followed closely by the POP of his rifle. The bullet went wild, ricocheted off the trailer and buzzed by Louis' ear. It buried into a tree somewhere; its final resting place was unseen and inconsequential (except maybe to the injured tree, but nobody cared to question its feelings on the matter). Louis was pulled to the ground by an infected lumberjack that had stealthily climbed up the hillside behind him. He kicked at the groping hands, the gnashing teeth, the deathly, lacerated face with its vibrant spiderweb of blue veins.

While Vincent stood afar, unable to react for lack of a clear shot,

John lunged at the lumberjack, arching the bat down onto its brittle skull (the sound of which was unforgettable, no matter how hard one might actively try to forget). Again, he sighed relief.

The cab rocked – a muffled groan floated out the door. A bloody, disemboweled lurcher scrambled out of the cab and landed with a dull plop on the gravel. Before it could crawl an inch, Vincent splattered its brains with a practiced aim.

John whirled, bat upraised. When he spotted the dead lurcher, he relaxed. "Thanks," he said.

Louis sat up to catch his breath. At his feet, still hanging half off the cliff, was the lumberjack whose head John had so courteously crushed. Still panting, he grimaced and kicked the body back over the ledge. From the sound of it, the body rolled a fair way down. "Well then," he breathed.

"Well then, indeed," said Vincent. He stepped over to Louis and offered his hand.

Waving him off and pushing to his feet, Louis said, "Think there'll be more?"

"I'm sure we'll know soon enough," replied Vincent. He turned to the cab.

John was already peeking inside. He stepped up and climbed in, rummaged here and there.

Vincent waited impatiently for two minutes before dragging his smokes out and sparking one. He puffed a few times and asked, "Anything?"

"You'd know if I found anything," John grumbled. He sat up in the passenger seat and looked at his hands. "Gross," he said. "I think I touched someone's intestines." He lurched and nearly reeled before quickly composing himself. He snatched a rag off the dash and thorough-ly wiped his hands. "And still no keys." He slid out of the cab.

"Now what?" said Vincent, deflated.

"Can we just pop it into neutral and roll it?" posed Louis.

"You gonna push it, Hercules?" John mocked.

"It's definitely too heavy to push," said Vincent. "Shit." He drew hard on his smoke. Through the resulting cloud, he said, "Guess we gotta turn back."

"Maybe we find another road," said Louis. "Try to feel our way through."

"Nah, fuck that," replied John. "It seems safer to me to stick to what we know rather than getting ourselves lost in the forest and trapping our-selves in worse scenarios than this."

"So…what should we do?" asked Louis – he was desperately lost in fear.

"I don't know," replied John.

"Why don't we find a pull off," Vincent suggested. "We'll get away from this unpleasantness for a minute, maybe formulate a plan of action and a place to go."

"Maybe we should just get to the police or something," said Louis. "Somebody's got to have a handle on all this – somebody's got to know what to do."

"I'm not terribly opposed to that idea," said John.

"Me neither," said Vincent. "Why don't we give it until tomorrow, though?" He pulled the last drag off his cigarette and ditched the butt to the wayside. "We got enough supplies to last the night. And then we can venture into town tomorrow to check in with the local authorities."

"Are you being sarcastic?" Louis asked.

"Only slightly," said Vincent. "How about we keep an ear on the situation via radio and decide what to do in the morning? Say the shit hits the fan; we can seek help elsewhere – somewhere farther away. If it's better, we head into town. Can we agree on that?"

"I can," said John without hesitation.

Louis was slower to respond, but not from reluctance to agree; he was just that scared and lost. "Yeah," he said at last.

"Cool," said Vincent. He clapped a hand on Louis' shoulder. "It'll be alright, buddy. We'll get through this, the three of us. We can do it."

Louis feigned a smile. "I sure hope so," he sighed.

V

A few miles back down the hill, they discovered a fair-sized cove of trees in which they could settle for a while. John backed them in beside a firepit littered with crushed cans, melted bottles, spent fireworks, bullet casings, shotgun shells and countless cigarette butts (to which this group would add their own expansive collection before moving on).

Another decent drizzle had started up again and none were quick to feel the chilly rain. Each of them sat, staring at nothing with blank eyes and raging minds. It was at this time that Vincent could feel the lingering effects of the copious amounts of booze and pills he had consumed throughout the night. He figured another pill should level him out just right.

"So yeah," said John. "What do we do now?"

Silence – it was well understood that this question was rhetorical.

"Let me see the whiskey," said Louis.

Without a word or any hesitation, Vincent produced the large bottle and promptly handed it over. He watched Louis take two large pulls then offered a cigarette that was initially denied, but ultimately accepted.

"Sorry I flipped on you earlier," said Louis. He took another large pull and handed the bottle to John.

"No need to apologize," said Vincent. "I don't even know where my brain was at that point." He popped a cigarette in his mouth and opened the door. He snortled at himself and said, "I don't even know where my brain is *now*." He stepped out into the rain.

His hair was quickly laid flat across his head – the curls along his brow straightened out with the added water weight. Before lighting his cigarette, Vincent turned his face toward the sky and let the rain wash over his face. It was cold – and so was the mild breeze – but he did not mind. Perhaps his recent bingeing was clouding his nervous system – perhaps events of the last twenty-four hours detached something important in his brain. More likely, the combination was working in tandem.

"You alright there?" asked Louis.

Face still upturned and mind still drifting in the clouds; "Mm," he grunted. "Sure."

The spark of Lou's lighter brought Vincent back down. "Here," he said, offering his lighter. "Though you might want a new smoke."

Pulling the cigarette from his mouth, Vincent found it was drenched through. "Hmm." He drew a new one from his pack, took Louis' lighter and, shielding his smoke and flame from the rain, sparked it.

"Thanks," he said.

"No problem," said Louis. He wandered away and found a wild fern he decided needed a good watering (though the rain would have been more than sufficient). He groaned his delight at unleashing his bladder.

John stepped outside and leaned over the truck's bed. "This is kinda odd," he said. "Normally I'm in the forest to have fun." He paused. "What sort of fun can we have now?"

"Well," said Louis as he finished watering the fern, "I don't think we'll be having much fun and I don't have a clue as to what we should do." He smoked and strolled back to the truck. "I sure as shit know I don't want to stay up here in this miserable weather all day, but what else can we do?"

Vincent watched globs of rain pummel the smoke he exhaled.

"We have plenty of provisions to last us a good while," continued Louis. "Food and water and booze and clothing. But I'm not looking forward to living in the forest in the middle of fall." He smoked, his eyes flicking between his two silent friends. He hung his head.

John opened his mouth to say something, had a vision of his girl-friend with her bared teeth and hungry eyes, and decided against speaking. He took a drag of his cigarette instead. In the interim, more images of gnarled, nasty faces, soulless, hungry eyes and bloodied base-ball bats flashed through his head.

Slamming one massive fist on the side of the cab, John shouted at nobody – shouted at his god – shouted at his devil – shouted at all the entities that wouldn't answer him: "What the *fuck* is going on out here?" His outburst was the sum of all their thoughts.

Speaking slowly, giving each word its own space, Vincent said, "No fucking clue." He squeezed his eyes shut, but found no relief there. He looked up to the sky again and still found nothing. When he tried looking at one friend or the other, he found something worse than noth-ing: he found a reflection of his own confusion and horror, a discovery that left him feeling substantially more dismayed than before.

After a pause, Vincent drew the last puff of his smoke, flicked it and started poking around in the cab of the truck. Moments later he came back out with a bottle of water. He downed over half while his friends blankly stared. He smacked his lips. "Still cold," he said.

"Well, that's something," said Louis.

"Yup," agreed Vincent.

"Wanna toss me one of those?" asked Louis.

"Me too," grumbled John.

A moment later, Vincent tossed a bottle to each.

After filling their bellies with water, the three of them exchanged a look.

"So now what are we doing with the rest of the day?" asked Louis sardonically.

"If this rain would quit, we could start a fire," said John.

"Well," said Louis, tapping the rifle. "We could go hunting for dinner."

"We have dinner," said Vincent. "Plenty of cans in the truck."

Louis cast a sprightly glare at him. "Seriously, dude?" He raised an eyebrow and shook his head. "If we hunt we'll eat up time, not to mention something possibly tasty. And besides, it might distract us."

"Would you rather stand here in the rain and stare at each other?" asked John. Not a moment later, he turned to Louis and said, "I saw a trail down the road aways. We could check it out."

Louis nodded. "I'm down." He looked expectantly at Vincent.

"Well yeah," said Vincent, responding to Louis' expressive gaze. "You know I'm down."

Nobody was quick to move. Nobody spoke, coughed, sighed or

otherwise made a sound for better than five minutes. Nobody noticed the crow that lit upon an evergreen or the rustling of a critter in the bushes. Each was in his own brain, wondering what happened to the world in which they had spent so many frightless years.

With a stub of a cigarette dangling from his lips, John pushed back from the truck. He pulled one last drag from his smoke and flicked it into the firepit – he watched it bounce off a broken bottle and out of sight under a rogue piece of blackened wood. Louis followed suit; he similarly shoved off from the truck and ditched his butt in the pit. Vincent didn't move until Louis walked by, tapping the rifle.

"Shall we?" inquired John.

"Guess I'm ready," replied Vincent.

"I know I am," said Louis, tapping the rifle again.

Vincent checked his pistol and grabbed the hatchet; John snatched the baseball bat and they were off.

VI

Each was nervous as they left their small cove – each was on guard and scanning the road, the bushes, the steep dropoff. And as the rain continued to taper, its dampening of ambient noise (including the crunching of gravel underfoot) began to decrease. The bone-chilling breeze decided to die down as well. Somewhere up above, the sun broke briefly through a gap in the clouds. This trio did not notice any of these seemingly insignificant events.

The trail John had noticed on their drive was blazed for (and by) dirt bikes; they had to enter the trail by stepping around the tall dirt hump that blocked the trail from larger vehicles (or inexperienced riders). Vincent took the lead with John holding the rear; each man was spaced with room enough to wield his own weapon. Their steps were careful and each did his best to avoid snapping any twigs or getting slapped by low-hanging branches. Occasionally they would stop for the chirping of birds or rustling of nearby bushes. They only saw two of these birds and could not get a clear shot on either of them before something startled them away.

The day's deluge managed to elicit every ounce of vitality and beauty from the very lush and vibrant forest floor. Deep, resounding colors that are somehow subdued even in the brightest of sunlit days were brought to light. Every leaf of every color on every tree or bush or along the path and underfoot assailed the senses to the point that you could taste the greens, hear the reds and smell the yellows just by setting your eyes upon them – and there was no single place you could set your eyes without spying a leaf of some color. The trees themselves appeared to have been carved from crimson clay and softened with dark felt.

Something snapped behind them; Louis whirled and his friends ducked.

With the rifle butted up to his shoulder and eyes peeled, Louis scanned either side of the path; his friends did the same with weapons brandished, ready for action. The moment passed without a sound – each man heard only his own heavy heart; not one of them could even take a breath. Their eyes searched the screaming reds and palpable greens, watching for fluttering wings or shuddering shrubs.

And then they saw it: a bird in the trees nearly ten feet up and thirty feet away. Louis swept the rifle in its direction. In the brief moment it took him to train the muzzle on that hopeful meal (as meager as it may have been), that little bird chirruped, fluffed its tail feathers and took flight. His attempted tracking of the bird was immediately foiled by dense foliage.

He lowered the rifle, scanned the trees.

"Damn," he breathed.

"That sucks," said Vincent.

They continued down the path.

Somewhere up above, just out of sight, was a crow. It made no noise and did not follow until their attention was focused elsewhere. They were totally unaware of their stealthy stalker – dark as the night and nearly as silent. Only once would it make its presence known.

There was no way for these men to see the clearing through the thick forest, but they sensed an intangible change in the surrounding wood. The clearing they could not see was occupied by a group of hunters and self-proclaimed revolutionaries with enough ammunition and ordnance to supply a small militia. These men had been in the forest for three days now and had no clue that the world was crumbling around them (if they had known, they would have been on the front lines blasting anything that moved into oblivion).

In addition to their ordnance, this group had with them enough provisions to last a week or more and planned on using up everything before heading back for supplies. They kept two guard dogs – one Rottweiler and one pitbull. The former was patrolling the trail's end and becoming agitated as it picked up the scent of three strangers.

It was in this very moment when the Rottweiler – his nametag read Maximus – began to grumble its displeasure that the crow made its presence known by belting a very loud caw, knocking a pinecone loose and taking flight. The men whirled, scanned the trees above. The crow lit upon a nearby tree, knocked another pinecone loose, and took to the skies again. And as Louis tried to locate the source of these sounds, a doe was startled out of hiding – they watched it streak by not twenty yards away. He was once again foiled by foliage and a total lack of experience. They chased it back down the trail but lost sight as their speed and agility were no match for that of the little whitetail.

From the commotion of this chase came the scuttling feet of rabbits, squirrels and the fluttering of some birds in the trees above. Each man looked in a different direction, pointing at all sorts of critters that had just been scared out of hiding; Louis couldn't lock onto any of them. After a moment there was nothing to be heard but their labored breathing.

"Shit!" exclaimed John. "Now what?"

"Keep on truckin'," said Louis. "Obviously plenty to hunt."

"I say we hunt from the truck," proclaimed Vincent.

"Probably just as fruitful as this," said Louis. "We're obviously not hunters."

"Speak for yourself, city boy," said John.

"Oh yeah?" said Louis. "When was the last time you went hunting, John?"

"It's been a few years," he replied. "But at least I have experience tracking *and* hitting moving targets."

"If you think you can do better..." He thrust the rifle at John.

And they traded; Louis shouldered the baseball bat and fell in behind the others.

A chilly wind kicked up, whistling through the trees, rustling the leaves and shaking shrubs; a screaming red leaf drifted before Vincent's face and landed on his shoulder. He brushed at it, shifting his focus from the path; something was watching him from a distance, shrouded by foliage – this was more of a sensation than an observation. Further surveillance of the surrounding revealed a doe in the distance; it was standing still, staring as though it were caught in headlights.

"*Yo!*" he hissed.

And John whirled at once.

By the time his eyes shifted to the spot the deer was, it had already vanished.

Another breeze kicked up, knocked some raindrops free and loosed more leaves.

With the path's end in view, they heard a rustling in a low bush; John whirled, swinging the muzzle toward the sound. Not a moment passed before the varmint darted across the path. And before it could dip beneath another bush, John squeezed the trigger, plugging the poor rabbit in the rump.

A nearby bird took flight.

A crow cawed up above.

And a few hundred yards up the trail came the distant cacophony of barking dogs.

The bird, quick as it was, fell to John's deadeye – just as the rabbit had.

The crow took off; the dogs were disciplined by drunken revolutionaries.

After retrieving the critters John had effortlessly bagged, they heard the crunch of gravel followed by the roar of a diesel. They exchanged an apprehensive gaze and listened. The vehicle – each of them figured it was a large truck (their assumption was correct) – was close, but moved slowly. They crept down the path, gripping their weapons with one eye watching for the glint of painted steel through the foliage.

Upon sighting the pickup, they ducked behind trees and shrubs;

each was universally wary of the newcomers. It was a massive green, four-door dually with a slanted canopy – a large Seahawks emblem was emblazoned on the back window. As far as any of them could tell, the truck carried two people – a man and a woman.

"You think they're okay?" asked Louis.

"I don't know," replied Louis.

The truck passed, they stepped out of hiding and slunk along to the trailhead.

The truck stopped just outside their camp.

"Ah shit," whispered John. "What're you doing?"

"You think we should see what they want?" asked Louis.

"I don't think I care about what they want," replied Vincent.

"I'd rather keep our numbers low for now," said John. "I *know* I can trust you two."

A crow cawed in the distance; a dog barked its response.

Brake lights gave way to tail lights and the truck trundled away.

With one last look of trepidation, they pushed up and off the trail's hump and stepped onto the gravel road. With bewilderment and reasonable uncertainty wracking each of them equally, this trio started toward their cove.

The rain had diminished to a bearable mist and the breeze was inconsistent, mild.

VII

Using tree sap and moss – with whatever dried twigs and leaves they could find – this trio finally managed to create a meager flame in the litter-strewn firepit. When the flames would dwindle, they would shove in scraps of paper and shave more sap off chunks of bark. And once the fire was a steady blaze that required minimal tending, John beheaded and hung his kills to drain.

Feeling mildly useless, Louis flipped on the truck's radio.

"– the righteous shall ascend to Heaven while the wicked will be left at the mercy of Satan's army." The volume was up and all three stopped to listen.

A deep, raspy voice broke in over the man's sermon: "But what of the confirmed reports of biological attacks on several –" the radio crackled and fizzed into silence. A moment later, the raspy voice resumed: "I would also like to point out that if this is the rapture, why haven't we noticed anybody ascending to Heaven, like you said they would?"

"They have not ascended yet," began the sermonizer, "because this is just the beginning – this is just the First Horseman –"

"There is nothing to back your –"

"If you please!"

"I do!" hollered the raspy voice. "I see no proof of this *rapture*. I see disease that stems *directly* from –"

"From *what*? The supposed biological attacks? Even if that *is* true – since no word has been officially sent down –"

"I have the report right here!"

"And who wrote that report? I see no official insignia –"

"It shows right here; CDC. That's enough for me."

"And who runs the CDC?"

"Not the Pope, that's for sure," grumbled the raspy man.

"He might offer them some enlightenment."

"You're too far off base. The Pope –"

Louis turned the dial. "Holy shit," he said. "I can't handle all that right now."

"No shit," mumbled Vincent. He began collecting meatier chunks of wood; fallen limbs and heavy logs – some were mildly rotted, but he figured he could work with them somehow.

A mechanized voice scratched its way through the radio: "– local FEMA shelters. Local law enforcement and military personnel have been activated to escort all citizens who are unable to safely travel on their own. The 911 call center is down due to the volume of calls, so please just remain in your home until an escort arrives. For the safety of yourself and law enforcement, do not make any attempts to leave your homes or confront anyone infected.

"Again: an outbreak of an unknown biological agent has been reported in your area. Citizens have been instructed to report to their local FEMA shelters. Local law enforce –"

"Well that's not much information," muttered Louis. He twisted the dial again.

"– BACK!" cried the radio. "LOCK IT UP! NOW!" The man started panting into the microphone. "*Shit*," he said. Someone spoke beyond the microphone's range. "Fuck the FCC," said the radio personality. "They can fine me all they want. I was just fucking attacked by a shit-eaten nigger-fuck." The person beyond the mic spoke inaudibly once again. "Oh, give me a break. And get me a bandage, would ya?" The man breathed heavily.

"What the fuck was that?" said Vincent. He was staring with wide eyes at Louis.

"I'm not quite sure..." replied Louis. "But we all know what it sounded like."

The radio spoke up again: "Sorry about all that. But I hope you'll pardon my French in this instance. And let me explain it briefly before turning you back over to the tunes you love so much. Moments ago, as I'm sure you all heard, our producer crashed into the booth here and laid into me – but not with his words. No, he laid into me with his teeth. I'm not sure exactly what that means for me, but from what I've seen so far, it can't be good." He puffed audibly on a cigarette. "I think we killed him," he said. "I think – oh, thanks, man. Much appreciated."

Now within the mic's reach, a resonate baritone said, "You're welcome."

The DJ seethed for a moment. "Ouch," he said. "Just bandaged my wound. Shit hurts like the dickens. Anyhow. Enough of my problems. If you wanted drama, you'd listen to the news stations that are all banding on about terrorists and Satan. But if you're here, listening to me, then all you'll want to hear is this –

The unmistakable bass riff of Tool's 'Sober' took over the airwaves.

Louis went to twist the dial.

"Leave it," said Vincent. "You never kill Tool." He dropped an armload of sticks beside the fire. "Now get over here and help me with some logs I found."

As they scavenged wood from the surrounding forest, John began splitting logs and setting them out to dry by the flames – the constant mist was a frustrating impediment to this effort. After an hour of splitting and gathering, they paused for lunch; a can of ravioli apiece that they had acquired from the lakehouse. They washed the ravioli down with water and whiskey. The sun was somewhere in the west, behind a veil of clouds, and dinner had yet to be gutted and skinned, but their bellies were full and their thoughts were miles from their predicament.

"Anybody got a bowl?" Vincent asked as he chucked a damp log to one side of the fire.

Louis snorted. "I wish." He looked hopefully at John.

"I hardly smoke anymore," said John.

"I can't even remember the last time I smoked pot," said Vincent. "But damn does it sound good right now."

"No shit," said Louis woefully. He stoked the fire with a skinny stick.

They shared in a cigarette before returning to work: John continued splitting wood; Vincent continued tending the fire; and Louis began fashioning a jury-rigged canopy from a tattered tarp that nearly extended the length of the truck and covered half the firepit. He used two fallen tree limbs for supports and secured them to the tarp with bright orange tie-downs.

Just before dusk, the clouds moved east, revealing a surreal cobalt sky with a single star shining bright straight above their heads. The moon was in the east, already risen, like God's thumbnail hanging on a string unseen. A sight so lovely would have normally sparked a sense of relaxation, comfort – nostalgia and inspiration – if Vincent's mind had not already been so thoroughly ravaged by current events and relatively recent misdeeds.

Current – and recent – events aside, this moon, this time of year, kindled unpleasant memories of greater losses and hardships from his childhood. He remembered staring up at this same moon in this same month on multiple occasions and praying. It was under this moon that he denounced religion in all its forms as his prayers – however specific and urgent they may have been – always went unanswered...

He was roused from this dolor by John plopping down beside him with the bird and rabbit in one hand and a large buck knife in the other. Vincent noticed that the carcasses were headless; the bird was already plucked.

"So," began John – he wore a demented smile. "You wanna learn how to clean a meal?"

"Uh," said Vincent, poking the fire. "Sure."

"Great," said John. He set the rabbit aside and held the grouse firmly in his left hand. "We'll start here." He suddenly snapped both legs back. "When you do this, you want to make sure you pull the tendon all the way out." He grunted, tugged and removed a leg, tendon and all. "You wanna try the other?"

Tentatively, Vincent reached for the bird's leg.

"No," said John. "You've gotta hold it tight." He thrust the bird into Vincent's open hand.

All that Vincent could think of was the bacteria this grouse must carry in its feathers. He held it gingerly at first and thumbed the broken leg. His first tug did nothing. He bore down harder and ripped the leg free.

"There's a start," commented John. "Now pull that tendon out."

It was slimy to the touch; his fingers slipped right off when he tried again.

John snortled. "Really yank it," he said. "You should be well practiced at that by now."

Vincent glared at him for the untimely jab. But then he pinched the tendon and ripped it free.

"That's right!" said John. "Now take this knife and slit the bird from here to here," he ran the blade from sternum to anus, showing Vincent where to cut.

His lip curled at the thought, but he took the knife and buried the blade into the soft flesh. Blood poured out of the incision, coating his hand. It felt cool and oily; it smelled ripe and coppery. A wave of nausea passed over him.

"Good," said John. "Now reach on in and pull it all out."

"How 'bout you show me how best to do this," said Vincent. Truthfully, he thought he might puke if he had to shove his hand into a bird's body cavity.

John chuckled. "Greenhorn." He snatched the grouse from Vincent. "You do it just..." he slid two fingers into the cavity, "...like..." and slid them down, "...this." A stream of fleshy, bloody guts slid from the carcass into a pile in the dirt. "And now," he said, holding up the plucked and gutted bird, "we just gotta take care of the wings."

Vincent handed over the knife, handle first.

Using his thumb and forefinger to spread the wing, John slipped the blade gently into the joint, careful to heed the placement of his fingers. And when he was satisfied, John sliced effortlessly through the joint, removing the wing in one swift motion.

"Don't worry," said John, "I got this." He sliced off the other wing a moment later.

Though removal of the wings did not bother Vincent, he allowed this without protest.

"*Voila!*" said John, presenting the headless, legless, wingless bird.

Using a grocery sack for a table, John proceeded to show Vincent the process of skinning and cleaning the rabbit. He began by removing the legs at the elbow. After that, he showed Vincent the finer points of removing the pelt; one cut and he removed it like a wet sweater – Vincent's stomach churned at the sight, but he kept his composure, knowing that this information would someday be important and wondering how he had not already learned such things.

And then he wondered, briefly, how he could kill a person without even a hint of nausea.

Some color had drained from his face. He wasn't aware of this, but John noticed his pallor and decided against having him clean the rabbit – *Some other time,* he thought. A practiced incision, a flick of the wrist and a pile of entrails slid out into the grocery bag. He went back in for a second look, pulled out something puffy and pink and set the clean carcass beside the grouse.

"How's that?" asked John. "Not so bad, yeah?"

The meat before him had Vincent feeling warmer already – he was suddenly able to ignore the gory aspect of the matter. He grunted an affirmation.

VIII

The moon was up, the sun was down – the stars were shining bright. The hot fire was a welcome contrast from the deepening cold and the scent of roasting meat on the rudimentary spit was enough to cause instant salivation. If not for the constant crackle of distant gunfire, one might actually forget their problems and enjoy the atmosphere.

The gunfire they heard was that of a military compound that had been constructed at a bottleneck on the highway. The operation was set up all around the area considered to be "ground zero" for the epidemic in a desperate attempt at staving off the spread of infection. But even with this checkpoint and its strategic positioning, the infection was spreading beyond anybody's control.

But without any of this gunfire sounding in the surrounding woods, they were able to relax some, though a somber aura permeated every facet of their doings. Occasionally, John or Louis would stoke the fire and turn the rotisserie – occasionally they would smoke and drink. At one point, Louis cracked a large can of chicken and dumpling soup and set it in the coals.

Vincent mostly drank and stared into the fire. If the flames grew too warm or the images he saw within the flames grew too vivid, he would turn his attention to the trees, the stars – the bright thumbnail in the sky. But when he was tired of craning his neck, he would turn right back to the flames as they danced up and around the cooking grouse. The pill he had taken an hour ago was starting to work its magic – though that did nothing to ease the dull ache in his back and pelvis from sitting on the hard ground.

His crossed legs began to tingle. "I'ma hit the head," he said, rising slowly to his feet.

"Don't go too far," said Louis.

"Don't worry," said Vincent as he started across the alcove. "I'm just pissin' in the corner is all." He puffed on his cigarette and ran a hand through his hair.

Vincent was urinating when John – lounging against the truck tire – began whistling a tune of his own design. He paused once for a snort of whiskey and began again with the same tune. The whistling was diminished – like background music – and neither Louis nor Vincent recognized exactly when he transitioned into the Star Spangled Banner.

When he did notice – halfway back to the campfire – Vincent hummed along.

Somewhere after the second verse, Louis began singing a solemn parody:

"No refuge could save the walking dead slave

from the terror of flight, or the gloom of the grave."

The whistling then faltered – as did the singing, the humming – and all was silent again, save for the crackling of the fire, the wind in the trees; his tasteless parody rendered them speechless, distraught.

A few minutes later, John moved the grouse from the spit to a smooth cross-section of an old fir and began carving. While he was occupied with that, Louis skewered the rabbit and set it over the fire. Vincent watched it all with abject curiosity while another cigarette dangled from his lips.

"You know, Vin," began Louis, "you've been chainsmoking all day."

"Yes," said Vincent. "I have been chainsmoking all day. I've been chainsmoking all week. Kinda happens that way sometimes."

"Still down?"

Vincent puffed on his smoke to cover his hesitation. "Yeah," he said through a cloud.

"Can't stop thinking about her, can you?"

Nodding, lost in the dancing flames, he breathed, "Yeah."

"I know how you feel, buddy." Louis pulled hard from the bottle. He, too, was lost in the dancing flames, dreaming of his someone – a lovely young lady who was wrongfully locked away in a rather scandalous turn of events. He would never discover the truth behind her disappearance.

Vincent regarded his friend with sorrow in his eyes. "I can't imagine –" he began, unable to finish the sentence.

"No need, bud," said Louis. He was holding back a well of tears.

John slammed his knife into the chopping block, clenching it with white knuckles. So recent was his love taken that hearing this must be torture.

After a beat – after cooling his head a touch – John said to Vincent, "Who knows, maybe you'll find her again. Maybe in all this madness, you and her will reconnect and fall right back in love. At least the possibility is there." Sorrow manifested as rage in John, and he felt it boiling toward the surface again.

And the subject was dropped.

They ate grouse and soup and passed around the bottle while the rabbit slowly roasted.

Staring out into the bejeweled night sky, Vincent fell into a warm cloud of intoxication. Hardly a thought passed through his head once the cloud fully descended. He found familiar constellations and built new ones from the brighter stars. He did this until the next round of meat was served.

The rabbit was meatier and fed them well and each of them began to feel the pull of sleep tugging at their eyelids.

"We gotta keep watch," said Louis groggily. "And I call *Not It*."

"*Not It*," blurted John.

"We should probably stay in the truck," said Vincent. "Out of reach to any passersby. Just throw the tarp over the back and we'll be good."

"Sure," said Louis, yawning. "Whatever you say." But he didn't move – he was lost in the fire somewhere between wakefulness and sleep, already dreaming of dancing beauties (though his dreams later this night would be wrought with shambling ghouls).

The tarp was laid across the truckbed with a gap by the cab large enough for them to shimmy in and out of quickly. And before they bedded down (or prepared to keep watch, as in Vincent's case), each of them smoked one last cigarette and shared a few swills from the large bottle of whiskey.

John and Louis crawled under the tarp and shared a thin blanket Louis kept in his truck for emergencies (this was its first use). Vincent donned a bright yellow poncho and climbed atop the roof of the cab with the rifle across his lap and pistol in his waistband.

Despite the full bellies, weary minds and exhausted bodies, neither John nor Louis was able to fall asleep for some time. They laid there, tossing, turning – bumping shoulders, bumping knees. But even distressed minds must run out of gas at some point, and John's went kaput around midnight. Louis followed him into slumberland thirty minutes later.

Vincent heard all of this from his perch. He had no trouble staying awake, despite the exhaustion that had taken hold of him as well. He was posted up for hours in silence with his eyes trained mostly on the moon – sometimes he would glance at the campsite's entryway, but only when he thought he heard something.

After a time, the rifle sat beside him, untouched, as he found no reason to utilize it.

Twice in the night he left his post; both times he stood and urinated off the hood of the truck only to sit right back down and gaze around. He smoked, he drank – and every few hours he would pop another pill. And somehow – after the terror and trauma and drugs and booze – he managed to stay awake until the dawn and beyond.

Day Three
Lost & Found

I

After hours of bearing the frigid night air with but only a few winks and blinks toward sleep, Vincent was at last granted the sight of this morning's thick fog enveloping and radiating the colors of the rising sun; his world turned orange. The dew dappled trees were given that same orange glow, and in some places the light was refracted in such a way that these trees appeared to be adorned with candles.

The birds were out, singing their morning hymns nearby and far away. A goldfinch landed on an evergreen, sending a spray of orange water to the ground below. It chirruped, fluffed its tail feathers and took to the sky again as a phoenix from a fire; a string of fiery droplets trailed behind this golden streak.

Though he noted this beautiful sight – aptly attributing some of the optical trickery to sleep deprivation and drugs – Vincent hardly catalogued it; in minutes he would forget (just as he had already forgotten about the sounds of panic and pain he'd heard in the midst of the star-speckled, frigid night).

A light breeze combed the trees, knocking free some loose leaves and feathering his face with chilly fingers; he pulled the poncho up to his nose, blinked his glossy eyes. Even with sleep deprivation muddling his vision, Vincent could see the individual water particles within the fog dance and swirl (or maybe that, too, was optical trickery). An aspen leaf, still green, joined the soiree, overshadowing these entrancing particulates with its comparatively colossal size. And for minutes, he was captivated by this low-hung fire-dance of stagnant precipitation.

And then this mesmerizing revelry was over; the leaf twirled, flipped, juked and jived around his head to land atop the truckbed tarp. The fog then swirled and churned until it was nothing but another dense conglomeration of sluggish water particles that appeared to be avoiding one another rather than comingling, as before.

With the breeze came a soft whirling sound. And as the breeze died down, the whirling did as well. What replaced it was something far less comforting – even before recognizing the sound, he found it disquieting. Over the dying breeze came a low moaning and the crunching of gravel beneath uneven footfalls. The sounds were muffled by the forest; Vincent found it difficult to pinpoint the distance, but he figured it was close.

He snatched the rifle off the cab.

For minutes he sat, hugging the bolt-action .22 with one finger stretched across the trigger-guard. His eyes were sharp, searching the fiery mist for anything unusual. The only entrance to the campsite was no wider than two car lengths; the campsite itself was surrounded by dense forest with even denser underbrush. Despite these facts, Vincent scanned his surroundings with a restrained, calculated cool – each rock, each shrub, each shadow was inspected until he felt certain that there was no immediate danger to himself or his friends.

He returned his attention to the road.

A brief moment elapsed with this man's pair of eyes scanning a bright morning haze for some sign of life – some silhouette – some shadow – to move across his vision. During that moment there was peace in the world – a peace that he had previously allowed to go unacknowledged. What set this moment apart was that not one thing of importance happened anywhere around the globe. Nearby, in the city from which they came, the soldiers, mercenaries and militias all ceased fire for reasons they would never know. In truth, so little happened in that moment that nobody even noticed the complete lack of anything. Some people found they had an extreme sense of eerie déjà vu, others felt nauseous.

Curiously enough, one man in a London supermarket dropped dead of an aneurism the very moment this anti-occurrence was over. The current epidemic had not yet traveled to Europe, but this man's sudden death would spark fear in many. Ironically, the very same morgue in which this man's body would be stored would also be the very same one from which Europe's first reanimated corpse would come.

Vincent would never learn of this.

Instead, Vincent would learn many skills in the way of survival. And the first rule of survival is *Kill or Be Killed* (or was it the second rule?) – a rule with which he was still struggling to cope. So when that silhouette shambled around the wall of trees, he paused. At first he could see nothing but a dark shape moving through a golden haze. The shape was strangely human; it had upraised arms that bobbed with every uneven step, stiff legs that caused these uneven steps, a head that lolled every whichway. It even had a foot askew that worsened its shambling gait.

As if it could smell him – for he made no noise to alert the thing – this shambling humanoid shape turned on a heel and moaned, hastening its meager pace.

Vincent's anxious eyes locked on this hungry aggressor.

As it got closer he could see the clotted gouge on its neck and the blue veins that spiderwebbed from this gory epicenter. It wore a blood-streaked, torn tee-shirt and grungy pants with one shredded leg. Its eyes were empty and red, its jowls foamy and caked with dried blood.

It moaned again and he fired instinctively, stopping the thing in midstride – his friends jumped at the shot, startled out of disturbing dreams to the sound of gunfire. But it moaned again and took another step. Vincent fired again and the thing snarled, but kept moving – his friends were scrambling out from under the tarp.

He took aim at the thing's head – a process that he felt took far too long – and fired true, his heart hammering as it fell to the ground. As with the bellhop at his hotel, Vincent marveled at the thing's persistence after receiving two shots to the chest.

After a beat, he turned to see Louis' gaping awe. Another beat and his heart calmed some. "Good morning," he said shakily, turning back for another peek at the ghoul, ensuring that it was still on the ground, still dead.

With a curious eye, Vincent said, "He's not really bleeding." And he was right – the spilt blood couldn't even fill a shoeprint. "Does it," he started. "Does it look…?" he searched for the right word. "Is it…is the blood…is it…*curdled?*" he asked at last.

"Oh God," blurted Louis – he threw himself over the side of the truck and retched.

Vincent grabbed at his belly as it lurched.

John covered his mouth, swallowed hard. "What the *fuck,* man?" he bellowed. "What the *fuck* is going on?" He was irate, screaming questions to nobody in particular. His friends did not try to stop his bawling tirade, not even when he leapt from the truckbed or started screaming his questions at the sky or down at the corpse. And not even when he dented the tailgate with one mammoth fist. By this time, Louis was huddled uncomfortably against the cab; Vincent remained seated throughout.

After a few minutes, he calmed a bit. Though still visibly heated and baffled over this rather sudden (and exceptionally massive) change in their lives – in the world – he was able to cool himself enough to think rationally enough to ask, "Where should we go from here?" The question's validity was solidified with his next statement: "We can't exactly go home if these, these…these *things* – these *people* – are *out here*, too!"

"What can we do?" asked Louis.

"We can try the radio," said Vincent. "Maybe they got some news for us."

With a nod John stepped to the cab, flung the door open and turned the key. The truck rumbled to life. A moment later the cab was filled with a mildly frantic, yet well-controlled man explaining the proper procedure for evacuation of the city. Having come into the middle of these instructions, they first learned that they should not panic (to which Vincent abruptly rolled his eyes – but he listened intently nonetheless). They were instructed to cooperate with all law enforcement and military personnel (there was no mention of any lawless behavior taken by evacuees).

"Sounds like nothing much has changed," said Louis.

According to the broadcast, refugees unable to leave the city by their own means were to report to their local FEMA shelter followed immediately by a lengthy listing of several shelters from Seattle to Portland and up the peninsula – a couple listings on the outskirts of Aberdeen and Bremerton.

"It's spreading," said Vincent – his focus was faraway, contemplative.

They learned that the shelter nearest these men was at the armory and that safe transportation outside the quarantined areas was guaranteed (to which John snorted his cynicism).

"And again," said the voice on the radio, "I must remind everybody out there the extreme danger of coming into contact with the infected. It seems that the infection is only contagious from direct contact with infected individuals. In most cases, these individuals bite their victims."

Vincent noted the man's cautious avoidance of certain gruesome details.

"I'm being advised now that if contact with the infected is unavoidable," continued the voice on the radio, "one must fatally damage the attacker's brain." He paused, audibly gulping at a frog in his throat. His voice was shaky upon resuming: "Reports are in that attempts to bring down the attackers by any other means..." he trailed off. And when he resumed this time, his voice was noticeably weaker: "Attempts to bring down the attackers by any other means will not work."

"I do believe we figured that one out," sneered Vincent.

John hit a random preset button on the radio and the cab was filled with a heated theological debate between a religious radical and a scientist. John hit another preset; another listing of shelters. He twisted the volume knob, killing the voices.

"That was helpful," commented John, careful not to leave out a heavy layer of sarcasm.

"So now what?" asked Louis. "Where the hell do we go?"

Silence – each pondered the question seriously.

And then Vincent said, "East." He looked over at his friends who were now looking back at him, clearly thinking this through. "We'll head east until we're clear of the quarantine."

"How far east does it stretch?" asked John.

"Who knows," replied Louis.

"And who knows how fast this is spreading," said Vincent. "Could be that we're screwed anywhere we go. But there's a lot of open country between here and the Cascades."

"Lower populations," said Louis, catching Vincent's reasoning.

"Why not the ocean?" proposed John.

"I'm pretty sure everything from Aberdeen to Astoria is quarantined," said Louis. "Same with the peninsula. And God knows we're not heading toward Seattle."

"Fuck no," said Vincent.

"Another option," said Louis, "is to head south. There are plenty of options once we're out of this area."

"That's true," replied Vincent.

"You got maps on your phone, John?" Louis asked suddenly.

To which he replied, "Uh, yeah, I think so," and promptly pulled it from his pocket.

"Maybe find a route that takes us southeast," Louis instructed. "One that gives us the option to head one way or the other –" the frustration on John's face made him falter. "What's wrong?"

"My service is all fucked up," John complained.

"Hasn't it been all fucked up for a while now?" asked Vincent.

"True," replied John.

"You still got maps?" asked Louis.

"Yeah, I think so," he said. "But it's not letting me use the GPS function." He fiddled a moment longer. "*And* I have no reception! Great!" He scowled and continued fiddling with the phone.

With a stiff look of consternation, Vincent said, "The question still remains: Where the hell do we go? The direction is fantastic and all, but the destination is far more important. At least a tentative or temporary destination – a waypoint, if you will."

"How 'bout the mountains?" suggested Louis. "Fairly remote, low populations."

"Cold," John interjected.

"Especially this time of year," replied Louis. "And even colder in the coming months – but I wouldn't suggest staying the winter."

"Cold," he said again, fiddling with the maps on his phone.

"Yes," said Louis. "Thank you. Everybody down?" His eyes shifted from Vincent to John and back again.

Vincent was nodding.

After a moment, John shrugged. "Which one?" he asked.

"Whichever one provides the least path of resistance," said Vincent.

And they all nodded.

II

He heard them through a haze – "Think there'll be more?" and "Not many" and "I like this route" – without actually listening to the words. His severely sleep deprived and opiate-riddled brain couldn't process the words any longer; his eyes could only look through the fire. The occasional spark or sizzle would bring his focus back and he might see a lick of flame or notice the cans of chili were about to boil over – but only momentarily.

He sat that way for quite some time. Only the pressure of his blad-der roused him; he stood at once and walked around the truck. His hip was bothering him now from sitting so long on the cold, hard ground. Just before he lit a cigarette, Vincent dry-swallowed another little blue pill.

With his bladder empty and pecker away, he started back to the fire.

Behind a cloud of smoke, he plopped back down beside the fire.

"We can always figure something else out," said John. "But those are our current options – the shortest route is highlighted in red."

Louis held John's phone close, tracing the routes with his eyes. "Check it," he said, leaning over so Vincent could see the screen. "He's mapped out a variety of routes for us to take."

Vincent looked upon the map with uncomprehending eyes; he saw a vague haze of green and blue and yellow and red and orange spiderweb-bing from the center of a topographical map – that much he recognized. After a few moments he placed the map, traced the lines. And finally he recognized what he was seeing. "Great," he said. "I like this one for starters," he said, indicating the first leg of the green line.

"Me too," agreed Louis. "Low trafficked areas."

"Which one?" inquired John.

"The green one," replied Louis. "For starters, at least."

"It leads toward endless possibilities," said Vincent. A little conver-sation was all he needed to jumpstart his brain on this chilly and tired morning. "It also intersects the freeway down south. Maybe we could skip down to Highway 12 right quick and be done with all this."

John was nodding. "I was thinking that as well," he said.

"Let's see how viable an option that is," said Louis.

"Until then," said John, "let's eat! I don't know 'bout y'all, but my stomach be a-grumblin'." With a large gloved hand, he grabbed out the cans of chili one-by-one and passed them over to his friends.

The food was hot and they gobbled it quickly.

By the time they finished, the sun was nearly to the treetops and the fog was lifting. The mystical orange glow of dawn that previously captivated Vincent's imagination was rapidly fading. And overhead the clouds were reforming – soon they would blot out the sun. By mid-afternoon it would be raining, though none of these men would see – or care – about such things.

III

After snuffing the fire and tearing down their makeshift shelter, Vincent felt the warmth of his pills as they began to assuage the pins in his hip and head-off the approaching headache. It was this familiar warmth that caused him to set in the truckbed rather than the cab – "I'll watch our back," he had said to the guys. Though trepidatious, they allowed this with little protest.

And they started down the narrow logging road with Louis at the helm.

Their return trek through the hills was relatively smooth; though the road was rough and rugged, they did not encounter a single body, whether live or lurching (nor did they see another vehicle). It wasn't until they were driving under an avenue of power lines near the highway that they ran across another group.

In the large parking lot at the entrance to this section of forest was a tight square of trucks parked bumper-to-bumper and mirror-to-mirror. The man standing guard beside this cluster raised a shotgun to his shoulder and scowled – his compatriots did nothing more than glance in their direction.

Upon closer inspection, one would find a pair of wounded individuals crowded in a corner of a truckbed. The pair were a bright, beautiful couple before the lurcher found them canoodling on a dock when their convoy had stopped for gas. Much to their surprise, the thing came from the lake, first grabbing the girl's ankle and tearing into it with jagged teeth. And when the boy attempted shoving the thing away, it ripped into his arm. The outbreak being a fairly new development, this attack from below was one of the first recorded underwater attacks – a fact that actually caused its occurrence to go mostly unnoticed as only a handful of living people witnessed it (most of these witnesses would die shortly thereafter from ignorance in handling the recently deceased – a skill most would not properly develop for some time).

"I wonder what that was about," said Louis absently.

"Not our problem," said John. "And I don't think they wanted it to be our problem."

Along the final stretch of this gravel road they encountered their second lurcher of the day. And with their lingering trepidation regarding outright murder, Louis steered the truck around this hungry wanderer as it staggered toward them with outstretched arms. His speed was low enough that Vincent could see the gnarled teeth gnashing at nothing. And through this phantom chomping he could see that this woman (for it had been a woman at one point in time) was missing her tongue. But this was not the focus of his attention as he was far more intrigued by the bloodshot, vacant eyes with electric blue pupils and the pasty, grungy skin laced with an intricate weave of blue veins that radiated from a gaping wound on her shoulder.

He scooted closer to the edge of the truckbed – her hand came within a foot of his face. Locking eyes with this very sick and disoriented woman – a terrible snarl plastered to her pasty face – he felt sorrow, he felt anger; he felt a range of emotions that were indescribable and bewildering. He found that after they had left this woman in the dust (quite literally), that he had absolutely no words to describe her features – his feelings – his mindset. Watching her single-mindedly shamble after them through the cloud of dust – still reaching, still gnashing (and still groaning) – Vincent found himself in a haze not unlike the trailing cloud.

His brain remained in this cloud on the highway, as they drove through the grassy median to pass one vehicle or another. Even when they stopped for gas and he stood, he was thinking about those eyes, that face, that weave of blue veins – the unrelenting need to catch up to them.

He was in this haze until roused by a bullhorn and gunshot.

Cursing their luck, Louis brought the truck to a stop.

IV

At the time of their arrival, three cars and an ambulance were parked helter-skelter before a cordon of barbed wire and jersey barriers. They were parked behind a red Honda. Beyond the barriers were a series of stark-white tents surrounded by canvas-backed flatbeds that were no doubt mobile barracks for the patrolling soldiers.

At this scene's foreground was a .50-caliber equipped armored Hummer flanked on either side by a row of locked and loaded M16s. Someone bellowed through a bullhorn at them from the Hummer's cab: "STEP OUT OF THE VEHICLE."

Astonished and slack-jawed, the trio sat stupefied.

"I REPEAT," bellowed the bullhorn-man, "STEP OUT OF THE VEHICLE."

They were astonished at the garb these soldiers wore: combat fatigues appeared to now include full respirators and goggles along with drawstring hoods and elbow-high gloves and thigh-high galoshes.

"THIS IS YOUR LAST WARNING –" began the bullhorn.

Vincent hopped from the truckbed.

"– STEP OUT OF THE VEHICLE," continued the bullhorn.

Louis and John scrambled out their respective door – nearly simultaneously.

"DISCARD ANY WEAPONS," advised the man.

Vincent placed his pistol on the pavement.

"ARE THERE ANY INJURED?' he asked.

They shook their heads – John said, "No."

"STAY WHERE YOU ARE," he instructed and lowered the bullhorn.

A pair of hazmat suits, accompanied by an entourage of armed soldiers, walked through a maze of barbed wire – there was no haste in their step. They were ever-mindful of the barbed wire and the threat it posed to their suits.

A breeze drifted in, chilling them to the bone – with it came the coppery scent of decay mixed with gunpowder and smoke and some unidentifiably repulsive odor, the source of which they dared not imagine. The bursts of gunfire in the background did not ease their concerns.

And then the hazmat crew began its work, visually surveying them head to toe, patting them down, pulling up their sleeves and pant legs, removing their headwear and checking their scalps. Their eyes and mouths were given special attention. And when each of them passed these preliminary exams, they began trifling the trio with questions: *what's your name who do you pick for the big game how old are you what's your favorite show where are you from* and, just for good measure, the all-important *have you been bitten.* Regardless of the absurdity of certain questions, the trio answered each in turn, though their bewilderment occasionally radiated uncontrollably.

In less than two minutes the hazmat crew was ushering them through the maze and beyond the cordons and immediately into the first tent. One-by-one they were taken through a series of tents and tests; extensive examinations of their bodies, delousing, needles, new clothes – hospital gowns on their first run and plain white longsleeve shirts with matching pants and slippers on their second run through the same process. The redundancy of these examinations irritated each of them in turn, but what irked them worse was that none of the doctors (most wore hazmat suits) would speak to them.

John was the first to crack; he screamed at one of them that wanted to give him a shot. And when he got irate, a soldier walked in with a stun gun and dropped him to the hard floor. When the seizures stopped, the doctor shot him full of something followed by another shot of something (one of the two – or the combination – made him dizzy and happy at the same time and he was calm).

Louis was the second to crack, but his retaliation was to keep quiet and stolid. When he wouldn't budge from the delousing room on his second visit there, they shot him up with something equally as euphoric as John's cocktail and hauled his naked body into the next tent and laid him out on a stretcher.

Vincent did not crack – he was too high already and figured compliance was the best card he could play. Even with his severe distaste for needles, he managed to not cringe or cry when they stuck him repeatedly. He gave up quickly on his attempts to communicate with the doctors and soldiers and waited for them to begin their questioning.

By the end of the tests, each was trimmed and swabbed and cleaned – and still they felt dirty and violated. And throughout it all, none of them were in the same place at the same time. Being the most compliant, Vincent was the first to be finished with the process. He was left alone in a bright tent with three stretchers; he picked out one and sat placidly for some time.

Within minutes he was dozing.

V

Somebody was chasing him down a glowing corridor lined with barbed wire. He was naked and frightened – and when he looked over his shoulder he saw a ginormous white figure, faceless yet fierce, wielding an outrageously large hypodermic in one hand. Its other hand was a disfigured red mass dripping scarlet rivulets onto lumpy, white earth. A nauseating ripple spread from under its feet with every step.

The corridor zigged and zagged, taking him this way and that, always lined with barbed wire. Each time he glanced over his shoulder the figure grew larger and more grotesque. At one point the hypodermic had a swordlike appearance.

His hip flared with pain and he tumbled into the barbed wire.

The figure roared with pleasure and when he saw it again it was lumbering after him, groaning audibly and dragging behind it...

VI

…an office chair with plastic casters that clattered over a floor that was little more than white tarpaulin over concrete. But the doctor wasn't wearing a hazmat suit. Nor was he wearing fatigues – just the respirator and plain white scrubs. He was carrying a clipboard.

Though the nightmare faded quickly, he couldn't shake the distress that lingered.

Without a clock for reference, Vincent hadn't a clue how long he'd been out.

Dutifully, he sat up.

"It's okay," said the doctor – his voice was almost machinelike speaking through the respirator. "You can lie back down. There are no more tests. I just have some simple questions for you to answer and you can go back to sleep."

He remained seated and demanded to know where his friends were.

"They should be done shortly," said the doctor. "We had to sedate them, so the tests went longer than we expected."

Vincent snortled, amused at his friends' resistance.

The doctor glanced at the clipboard. "Turns out you were self-medicating – which might explain your acquiescence." He watched Vincent blush a tad at having been called out on his drug usage. "But don't worry; drugs are the least of our concern here. Though I am a bit surprised that you survived being as doped-up as you are."

"It's hard to run from the walking dead when you can't move your hip," replied Vincent.

The doctor nodded, jotted something down. "And what's wrong with your hip?" he asked.

"Pain," said Vincent. "All the way down to my ankle sometimes."

The doctor nodded some more, jotted something else down. "I'm just going to need some basic information from you," he said. "Simple stuff; your name, birth date, address – stuff like that."

"Vincent Anton Andrews," he replied.

And the doctor jotted this down.

"I was born February 12th, 1985 in Edmonds. Currently, I'm living at the Governor Hotel in downtown Olympia. My social security number is five-three –"

"I'm not worried about that part," said the doctor, cutting him off. "Any family?"

"Yes. My parents live in Arizona –"

"What part?"

"Peoria," he said, mildly peeved at having been cut off once again. "My brother lives in California, just outside of L.A. I have no clue where my sister's at – we don't talk much these days…haven't in years."

"Well, they are lucky to be away from this madness," said the doctor.

Vincent grunted.

"What is your relation with the two men you came here with?"

"They are my friends," he said. "Like brothers."

"How long have you known them?"

"Over ten years each."

The doctor was writing all of this down. "And what are their names?"

"Louis Friend and Johnathan Miller." As an afterthought: "John's the big'un."

The doctor was nodding again, still writing. He reviewed his notes and said to Vincent, "Alright then. I think I have all I need for now. You can lie back down and we'll be back for you in a little while when your friends have been processed."

"Do you have anything for my hip?" Vincent asked. "It's starting to act up."

The doctor smiled behind his respirator. "We sure do." He stood up. "I'll send somebody for you." He walked back out the canvas door, raucously dragging the chair behind him. Vincent would never see this man again.

And nobody came to give him drugs.

VII

He awoke without realizing he had ever fallen asleep, greeted by Louis, who wore an uncharacteristically slack face. He was telling Vincent to wake up and shaking his shoulder. "Wake up!" he called when Vincent was roused.

"I'm awake! I'm awake!" proclaimed Vincent. "Jesus Christ, I'm awake!"

"Thank God!" said Louis. "I was afraid they'd knocked you out cold."

"Nope," said Vincent. "Didn't even know I was sleeping."

"Like a rock."

"Where's John?"

"Don't know," replied Louis. "I was hoping you could answer that question."

"Wish I could. Last I heard, you two were being stubborn."

"How'd you hear that?" asked Louis.

"Some doctor came in asking all sorts of questions," he explained.

"Oh," said Louis, genuinely shocked. "I can't believe you got one to talk to you."

"He came in specifically to talk to me," said Vincent. "Said I was done with the tests and had some questions. When I asked about you he said they had to sedate you." He chuckled. "Not surprised, really – especially with John's bull-headedness."

A nearby shriek startled them – *BLAM!* – and it was cut off by a shot that startled them worse. They locked troubled eyes, concurrent chills running up their spines.

Vincent swallowed hard. "Didn't sound like John." He wasn't entirely convinced.

They sat in silence for a few minutes, paranoid thoughts torturing their overstressed brains.

And then Louis asked, "Did they tell you anything?"

"I didn't ask," said Vincent. "They probably wouldn't have said shit anyhow."

"No," agreed Louis. "I guess they wouldn't, would they."

"Do you know how long we've been here?" inquired Vincent. "An hour? Two?"

"More like four or five," replied Louis. "Their damn repetitive exams exhausted most of the day. But I was out of it for a long time – maybe we've been here longer." He shot to his feet and started pacing. "I wish I had a fucking cigarette right now. The stress is killing me."

"Agreed," said Vincent. "But at least we're safe."

Louis whirled on him. "I don't know how safe we are after hearing that scream."

"I bet you we're safe as long as we're not infected with whatever they're looking for – whatever is causing the mayhem out there."

"I'm not counting on anything anymore," said Louis. "I wish they would leave us to our own devices – let us go away and hide from the world for a while."

"I'm anxious too, Lou," said Vincent. "But I don't see the harm in letting the government take care of us for now."

"You're too trusting, Vin."

"I'm just rolling with the flow."

VIII

Within twenty minutes of being reunited, they were moved to a sprawling tent filled with cots. The room was still as white as the rest of the tents, but the cots were a drab olive color with matching pillows and blankets. Three people shared the space with them: a man (*why is he so familiar?* Vincent asked himself) was in the far corner, hanging his head between slumped shoulders; and a woman sat beside her sleeping child opposite from the man. All three shared in the plain white garb.

Vincent sat on the first cot he came across; Louis sat on the next one over.

"Isn't that the paramedic from yesterday?" Louis asked, pointing with his chin at the man in the corner.

"That must be where I recognized him from," replied Vincent, looking over at the man who remained slumped.

They watched as the man slowly raised his clasped hands up to his brow, mouthed something. He crossed himself and looked up at the woman and child. His attention was on that silent pair for a moment before turning his dazed attention on them. He nodded and looked back at his feet, all the while expressionless.

"He looks more fucked up than I am," commented Louis.

Just then, Vincent's hip screamed and he cursed the doctor that never brought him drugs. He looked around at the door through which they had entered, hoping to spot someone of authority who might be able to help his pain if only he could –

John was pushed through the canvas door.

"John!" cried Vincent.

The woman turned, the man looked up.

"Holy shit!" cried Louis when he saw John.

But John staggered to a cot and fell onto it without a word, throwing an arm over his eyes to shade the harsh white light.

His friends raced over and knelt beside him.

"Are you okay, buddy?" asked Louis.

"What happened?" asked Vincent.

"Thought they mighta snuffed you," said Louis.

"It's all good," mumbled John. "Just kinda toasted."

"I'll say," said Vincent. "Heard you gave 'em hell."

"Uh-huh," breathed John.

"Let him sleep," said Vincent. "Shit, let *me* sleep, too."

But when he laid down, Vincent didn't fade very fast. He laid there for quite some time while his friends snored on either side of him – while the man in the corner mouthed his silent prayers – while the woman watched over her snoozing child – while the gunshots rang out both near and far. More than once these shots were preceded by the shriek of a man or woman. One time he thought the cry was from a little girl.

Just before sleep took him, someone else was shoved into the tent.

Day Four
Humanity

I

Around six in the morning – though he had no concept of time without a clock for reference – Vincent awoke in pain. Bolts of lightning were shooting down his right arm, which was tingly from fingertip to shoulderblade. Grimacing, he rolled onto his other side, well aware of the cot's tight discomfort.

Around seven, he awoke with both arms tingling up and down. He rolled onto his belly and waited until the tingling went away before drifting back into slumberland.

But his rest was disrupted twenty minutes later when the woman began shrieking.

II

Two hazmat suites entered the holding tent, escorted by four armed soldiers. Two of the soldiers flanked the door and regarded the detainees shrewdly. The remaining pair flanked the suits as they marched stolidly toward the sleeping child.

The girl's mother was still sleeping when they entered.

And when the girl yelped her surprise at being hoisted out of bed, the mother leapt to her feet. The soldiers held her back as she reached for her child, hollering and shrieking for them to give her baby back. The girl was hauled away, but she made hardly a sound. The mother was blatting away until her daughter was gone.

One of the soldiers plunged a needle into her arm and laid her back down on her cot. They left cautiously, glowering behind their respirators.

III

With a headache ripping through his brain – and still no doctor to help his pain! – and the horrific scene with the girl and her mother, Vincent found sleep hard to regain. After all the tests he had endured, he found it hard to imagine that such a little girl could have slipped through their screenings. And if the girl wasn't taken because she was infected, then why would they take her? If she could be infected, without a visible wound, then couldn't he be infected as well? Was there some way he could have contracted this affliction?

He didn't think so.

But he did believe the girl had to be taken for some previously unseen symptom.

IV

He awoke some fifteen minutes later, heaving.

A pile of vomit – *chili*, he thought, with a shudder – was massed around his face and dripping to the white floor. He coughed hard and retched again, reeling as his stomach cramped and churned.

A pair of hazmat suits, accompanied by another four soldiers, came in and escorted him out of the holding tent. They walked him down a bright corridor and into a small examination room, then strapped him to a stretcher and started poking him, probing him. When he retched again, this time a thin stream of bile and mucus, they collected a sample to add to their already copious array.

He grimaced and flinched when they checked his eyes; the light they used bored into his retinas and stabbed his brain. The doctors wrote something down and checked his vitals – his blood pressure was a little elevated, but that's to be expected.

His exhausted brain gave in and he passed out.

V

He was jostled awake from a bump to his head and a racquet in his ears. The bright lights flashing above him added to the raucous din that assailed his senses. He coughed and flailed and found he was no longer strapped down and that his stretcher was being rolled through the corridor.

A moment later, the stretcher stopped and he was helped to his feet by a pair of hazmat suits. They lifted him gingerly and guided his wobbly body back into the holding tent where his friends were still sleeping.

The man in the corner – the paramedic from the other day – watched them set him down upon his cot. They left at once.

Delirious, Vincent unfolded onto the cot and fell asleep.

VI

When he awoke again, the woman was gone.

Somebody was curled up on a cot on the far side of the room.

The paramedic was still seated where Vincent remembered he had always been.

His friends were still asleep.

He was awake because somebody had just injected something into his arm and was pulling the needle back out. Before he could turn or speak, his back seized and he was captivated by a wave of cool warmth that spread throughout his body. By the time the hazmat suit had left the room, he was back on that cozy river, floating toward the land of nod.

At last, the doctors had brought him the fix for his menagerie of problems.

VII

Nothing woke him except for some subconscious understanding that he was alone.

At least, that's what he figured it was when he awoke suddenly and saw that he was in fact alone in this vast room of drab cots. He looked at the places his friends had been, thinking that they'd be back any moment. He thought maybe they were using the toilet.

The steady sound of gunfire from outside unnerved him.

A thought occurred to Vincent, and he realized that they couldn't be in the bathroom, because the bathroom here was little more than a hole in the far corner, by where the paramedic had been seated for so long. And nobody was at the toilet, because nobody was in the room.

Still wobbly – but still riding the river – Vincent staggered to the canvas door.

He pushed through and found he was still alone.

One tentative step after another brought him to another small canvas door – white, of course. He peeked through the door's small window – a murky piece of clear plastic – and saw a stretcher and table, but no chair. And, more importantly, no people.

He was almost to the next canvas door when he was confronted by a doctor in scrubs, wearing a respirator, but no hazmat suit. The doctor grinned at him – the look of which was almost sinister behind the respirator.

"Mr. Andrews," the doctor said, his voice sounded mechanized from the respirator. "Glad to see you're up and about. How are you feeling now?" He read the perplexity on Vincent's face. "Why don't you lie back down, Mr. Andrews?"

"Where are my friends?" croaked Vincent.

"They are fine," replied the doctor. His seemingly sinister smile, his mechanized voice did nothing to soothe Vincent's bewilderment. "You'll be briefed when you're properly rested. Now let's get you back –"

"No!" cried Vincent – he staggered back a step. "I want to find them. I want to know what's going on!"

"Don't you worry, Vincent," assured the doctor. "You're no good to anybody in your current condition. I want you to get some more rest. Doctor's orders." His smile persisted, creepy as ever.

"Fuck your orders!" cried Vincent.

Something pinched his shoulder and he crumpled to the floor.

VIII

Voices were babbling somewhere nearby, too low to hear, especially under the ever-present gunfire from the blockade outside.

He mumbled and croaked, but they continued babbling.

And then they got closer.

He moved to ward them off, but found his arm wouldn't move. He could move his head without restraint, but quickly discovered that every other appendage was locked tight to a most uncomfortable plastic board – a stretcher, he figured, like the one from before. His eyes popped open and confirmed the fear.

Two people were approaching, both wearing respirators. One was wearing plain white scrubs and looked vaguely familiar. The other was wearing olive fatigues with all sorts of insignias – he was older with a short-cropped white horseshoe of hair and shrewd, soul-piercing blue eyes.

"How you feeling there, kid?" asked the latter – his name was M. Johnson, according to his fatigues.

Vincent groaned. After a brief assessment, he discovered that he was still riding the river. He dropped his head back and mumbled, "I could be better."

"Well don't you worry, son," said M. Johnson, "these guys will fix you up real good. Fix you up so you don't need the drugs anymore. Just sit tight." He turned to leave.

"Wait," said Vincent.

M. Johnson turned back. "Yes?"

"Where are my friends?"

"They're fine," said Johnson. "They're out of quarantine now. You would be, too, if it weren't for your sickness."

"I'm not…" he began.

M. Johnson laughed. "No. You're not infected. Well, not with *the disease*, that is. No, you're infected with something called *addiction,* and these docs here got the cure. Give it some time, Vincent, and you'll be on your feet again. But for now, let these guys do their work."

Vincent turned red.

"It's okay, son," said M. Johnson. "Everybody's got their vices. It's just that some're worse'n others." M. Johnson turned to leave.

"One more thing," said Vincent.

M. Johnson stopped, cocked his head. "Yes?"

"When can we get our things back?" he asked. "I got some ...valuables in my bag I couldn't stand to live without."

Slowly, M. Johnson spun on his heel, brimming with delight and chuckling lightly. "You must be referring to the enormous – if not *illegal* – sum of cash you were toting around so carelessly." He paused a moment to watch Vincent's eyes flare with alarm. "I imagine you took a few hefty withdrawals when all this started going down. You must have been overwhelmed with paranoid delusions of a crumbling society on the horizon to empty such a sizeable bank account." He cackled, amused with himself at creating such a string of plausible postulations.

When Vincent didn't reply – he just sat on the exam table, slack-jawed and stunned – M. Johnson tried to ease the tension he no doubt felt (though his persistent, sinister smile behind the respirator countered his meager efforts); "Don't you worry. I won't report you. And when this is all over, you'll get it back, free and clear, to do with it as you will."

Still unsure of how to respond, Vincent slowly nodded.

M. Johnson cackled again. "You feel better," he said. And he left the room without another word. With a cursory smile of his own, the doctor followed.

Vincent looked around – stoned, uncomfortable and troubled.

And, once again, all alone in a stark-white, alien room, listening to the gunfire outside.

But at least his hip didn't hurt.

IX

He didn't remember drifting to sleep. But he did remember waking up to a nurse undoing the straps around his wrist. With his arm free, he immediately went to work scratching the end of his nose. He sighed, relieved.

"That's been itching for *hours*," he told the nurse.

The nurse chuckled lightly and undid his other arm.

"Thank you, man," said Vincent, genuinely appreciative.

The nurse nodded, his smile completely gone now – all business.

"Mr. Andrews," came a voice from somewhere behind the nurse – Vincent saw quickly that it was the same doctor from before. "There's only so much I can do for you today, seeing as you were as stoned as a drug mule whose bag popped. But, in time, I think we can wean you off the drugs for good."

Vincent was silenced – stunned – from the doctor's bluntness.

"I will ask you to inform myself," continued the doctor, "or any of the medical staff, if you feel nauseous at any point – especially after eating." He glanced at his ever-present clipboard. "We have not informed your friends of the condition you're in, so it will be up to you whether to disclose such information to them – I have no care for what you do in that regard." He glanced again at his clipboard. "If you notice anything out of the ordinary with any of the refugees – particularly, loss of appetite, increased hostility, delusional or demented dialogue – please inform the nearest guard, nurse, doctor – whathaveyou – and avoid contact at all costs." He repeated this: "At *all* costs."

He let this settle on Vincent's mind – and it did, heavily. With his straps undone and the nurse gone, Vincent sat up, rubbing his wrists.

"Those are the ground rules," explained the doctor. "Any questions?"

Considering the situation for a moment, Vincent asked, "Do we get those fancy respirators, too?"

The doctor cackled – the sound, the look, were both sinister in appearance. "No," he said, still cackling. "No. Refugees don't get respirators."

"Then what's the point of saving us if you don't protect us?" argued Vincent.

"We are fairly certain *the disease* isn't airborne," said the doctor with a lingering smile.

"Then why wear them?" asked Vincent, fairly certain of the question's futility.

The doctor said, "Standard operating procedure."

Just the sort of answer Vincent predicted. "Right," he breathed.

No sound but the steady *POP-POP-POP* of gunfire outside filled the air.

The nurse came back into the room with a small paper cup and an unopened bottle of water. He handed these to Vincent. "Take these," he said, "and be sure to drink the entire bottle of water afterward." He twisted the cap off the bottle while Vincent held it firm.

Vincent looked into the cup; two large white pills were inside. He washed them down with half the bottle. "What were they?" he asked.

"They're what the doctor ordered," replied the nurse as he left the room.

The doctor smiled when Vincent looked at him. "Let's get you some food," he said.

X

The cafeteria was almost claustrophobic – four folding tables and a long banquet table crammed into a space smaller than the holding tent. Two hotplates – one of something resembling macaroni and cheese, the other some thin-sliced, marinated beef – sat in the middle of the banquet table, flanked on either side by toast, hardboiled eggs, green salad and bananas. Two large air-pots stood tall on the far left side of the banquet table; one contained coffee, the other, hot water. You had to ask the only person tending this cafeteria what the hot water was for, and he would only respond by saying, "Hot drinks."

At a table by the coffee pot – it was in arm's reach – sat Louis, John and Vincent. Each was haggard; each wore bags under his dopey eyes. Each was too engrossed in mastication to speak much, despite their recent separation. The coffee was weak and lukewarm, which made it easy to drink. Before they were finished eating, each of them was wired from several cups – not to mention a lingering (or on-setting, in Vincent's case) haze from the drugs.

Vincent was enjoying the cross-fade of caffeine and methadone, despite the circumstances.

"Oh fuck yeah," said John, pushing back from an empty plate. "I don't know how or why, but that was a fucking awesome meal."

Vincent was picking at his food, eating bits here and there.

"If you say so," said Louis, lazily stabbing a piece of beef.

"It's got all the substance you need," said John, patting his belly.

"And whatever that sauce is for the beef, it's delicious."

The chef snorted inaudibly and stole a glance at their table.

Louis bit into the beef, nodding. "Yeah," he agreed. "It's not bad."

Vincent continued prodding his macaroni, poking his beef. He picked up a slice of toast and bit a corner off. The pills he was given were taking effect and he was beginning to slip away from the conversation entirely. He spied the chef picking his nose in the corner, then watched as he flicked the booger and returned to the banquet table to slice some more meat.

He inspected his plate, shrugged, and bit off another piece of toast.

The paramedic sauntered into the room, shoulders slightly hunched, and grabbed a banana and a cup of hot water. "Could I get a packet of apple cider?" he asked the chef.

The chef handed him a packet of powdered apple cider.

"Thank you," said the paramedic. He dumped the powder into his water, glanced at Vincent, his friends, and sat across the small room, facing the white canvas wall.

"Hey," said John, addressing the chef. "Who do we talk to about what's happening around here? Do you know?" This last came out as one word: *dyaknow.*

The chef shrugged, grunted. "I just work here," he said, laying a cover over the beef. "They don't tell me shit." His eyes flicked to the canvas door and his pale face became as red as his eyebrows.

Two soldiers – respirators, gloves, galoshes – entered the cafeteria and strode over to their table; one of the soldiers eyed the chef for a moment. He shifted his attention to the table and, looking only at Vincent, said, "Come with us."

When they didn't move, the soldier insisted: "Now."

Vincent downed his coffee and stood.

His friends followed suit.

And the soldiers led them out of the cafeteria; one led the troupe, the other followed.

The paramedic watched as they were escorted out.

XI

The room smelled of coffee and tobacco and copper and gunpowder. It was bright and white like the rest of this place and hazy from the smoke of M. Johnson's cigar. It was also the first tent they had seen with either a window or a ceiling vent. The window was a murky and translucent view of a double chainlink fence (complete with razor wire) – beyond this were two canvas-backed personnel vehicles and a tree-lined hillside. The vent was simply a hole in the ceiling with a view of the unappealing gray sky. Beneath the vent was a large swatch of wet canvas.

M. Johnson was seated behind a makeshift desk littered with papers that surrounded a lone laptop. A trio of plastic folding chairs sat before the desk. "Have a seat," he said to the men entering his field office. He stood up and walked to the only other table in the room – a small table with a coffee pot, a bottle of whiskey and four mugs. "Would anybody like a drink?" he asked. "Coffee? Whiskey? Both?"

"Coffee, please," replied Vincent. "Black."

"I could use some whiskey," replied John. "Straight."

"Coffee will do," said Louis. "Black, as well…please."

M. Johnson delivered their drinks appropriately and mixed an Irish coffee for himself before taking his seat behind the desk. His gaze pierced them each in turn – the silence of his gaze was deafening. Their own silence only added to the discomfort.

"I suppose," began M. Johnson, "that I should begin by introducing myself." His smile was broad – a full smile, not sinister in the least as he wasn't wearing a respirator. He puffed once, twice, thrice on his cigar, swiveled on his chair and rested his elbows on the desk. Removing the cigar from between his lips, he said, "Colonel Marten Johnson, United States Army National Guard." He saluted them.

Dutifully – patriotically – they returned the salute.

"Now," he said, "before we begin, I must know: would any of you like a smoke?"

"Yes please!" they said in unison.

Colonel Johnson chuckled and swirled a mahogany humidor around, flipping open the lid. Inside the spacious humidor, split by a strip of wood – more mahogany – was a row of fine cigars on one side and a pile of filtered cigarettes on the other. Neither the cigars nor the cigarettes were branded with a distinguishing label or emblem.

"They're Cuban," he explained. "All of them." He smirked. "But don't tell."

Each of them grabbed a cigarette and sparked it with the matches offered by Johnson.

Colonel Johnson sat opposite them, puffing on his cigar and studying their faces. He said nothing – and neither did they; the colonel was content to watch them squirm with impatience and curiosity. The growing silence in the room was punctuated by the steady gunfire sounding outside.

Vincent became irked with the colonel's flippancy and opened his mouth to speak –

"I bet you're all wondering," began the colonel, layering his voice over anything Vincent might offer, "what is going on out there." He was nearly as content watching them hush and shift to listen as he was when he watched them squirm. "Well," he continued, "I've been wondering the same damn thing: *What on God's Green Earth is going on out there?*" He removed the cigar from between his teeth and slammed a fist onto his desk – his coffee sloshed and spilled. "I can't figure it out," he said, a faint cloud of smoke lingering around his head. "What I can tell you is that we are doing everything in our power to maintain our national security and head off this threat."

Nobody commented on the pun, though it crossed each of their minds.

"Have you even made any progress?" inquired Louis. "The infection just seems to be spreading."

Vincent was inwardly abashed that his overly stoned brain was too slow to ask such an obvious question. "Yeah," he squawked. "It's spread to the coast now."

Colonel Johnson raised an eyebrow at him. "And where did you learn that?" he asked.

"It's all over the news," replied Louis. "Last I checked, most of western Washington is under quarantine. And who knows how far it's spread since we've been locked up in here, *incommunicado* from the outside world."

Raising another eyebrow, plugging the cigar between his teeth, Colonel Johnson leaned back and said, "Some of what you say is true; we *have* quarantined many regions after receiving reports of possible outbreaks. But as of yet, there are no confirmed incidents outside of the southern Puget Sound region. Any remaining quarantines outside of this region are purely precautionary at this point."

His lies were almost believable.

"So you're saying that you're winning," said Vincent, not without an underlying cynicism. "You're saying that the worst is over and we'll all get to go home soon."

"I'm not saying one way or the other," replied Johnson. "Even if we eradicate the infection, there will be months of follow-up and observation –"

"Wait," snapped Louis. "We'll still be under lock and key *after* the 'threat' –" he used rather sardonic quotation fingers, "– has passed?"

Colonel Johnson regarded him with shrewd eyes, drawing hard from his Cuban. "I'm saying that the threat may now be everpresent, regardless of physical eradication."

"What does that mean?" snapped Louis.

On the heel of that question, Vincent said, "You think the disease is in us already."

That statement caught the colonel off-guard.

"You think that once the immediate threat is quelled," he continued, "that we might still be carrying the infection in some form or another." His level stare caught the colonel's astonished eyes. "You think the infection can't be stopped."

His friends were staring at him now.

Colonel Johnson composed himself quickly. "I think you're jumping to conclusions now," he said. "Observation after quarantine is standard operating procedure. We wouldn't want this infection sprouting back up after we think we've defeated it."

Vincent was not convinced. "There's something you're not telling us," he said. "You know something about this infection. You know if it really was a terrorist attack or just some government fuck-up and you're just not –"

"I will not stand for this abuse," thundered Johnson. "Nor will I argue the terms of this quarantine with a civilian. You wanted information,
and I'm delivering." His face was red and furious now.

A soldier appeared by the canvas door.

"For now," began the colonel, "you'll stay in the civilian quarter
with the other refugees." He sneered at Vincent. "If I desire your *coun-
cil*," he said spitefully, "I will call for you." He motioned for the soldier.
"PFC Webb will escort you."

XII

Night had fallen, but still the lights were burning bright – both inside and out.

"You sure know how to get under peoples' skin," mused Louis.
"Under the circumstances, I'm not sure whether that'll be good for us, or
bad." He was smoking on one of the colonel's Cuban cigarettes in the
civilian quarter's designated smoking area. A small section had been
walled-off with translucent tarpaulin in one corner of this tent and was
even equipped with a tall propane heater, two plastic chairs and an ashtray. A makeshift overhead vent allowed the smoke to escape.

With him in the tent was Vincent – John had ventured over to the
cafeteria for more coffee and a snack.

"Yeah," agreed Vincent. "You're not the only person to tell me
that."

"I think it's fucking awesome," said Louis, smiling. He took a drag
from the rather robust cigarette, savoring the rich flavor. "If these guys
wanna play hardball when all we want is some simple answers, then I

say give 'em hell."

"I'm not really sure how simple those answers actually are," said Vincent. "Especially when that old fuck doesn't know a damn thing."

"I think he knows more than he'd like us to think," countered Louis.

"I'm sure you're right," said Vincent. "But he doesn't know how it's spread, other than the obvious. His anger was proof of that."

"Are you a psychologist now?"

"Not a psychologist. Just observant."

"Speculative," said Louis. "And speculation won't get us very far."

"I don't think we're going very far anyhow." Vincent drew the last puff of his smoke and snuffed it in the pedestal ashtray that sat in one corner, against the outside wall. "They got us locked up tighter'n a nun's vagina."

Louis grunted, patted the canvas wall. "Could be a *little* tighter."

"'Cause we'd get so far," replied Vincent, standing.

Louis shrugged, snuffed his cigarette and followed Vincent into the common area.

They found John had returned and was seated at a table in the far corner, conversing and playing cards with the paramedic. Rather than intrude on their game, Vincent sat upon a nearby cot he had previously picked out of the lot. Louis seated himself on the next cot over.

They were silent for minutes.

After a time, Vincent stretched out, but did not fall asleep.

And then Louis stretched out – he was asleep in minutes.

Vincent just stared at the glaring white canvas ceiling. He was worried about his family – he was worried about Isabella – he was worried for himself and his companions. He even found himself wishing for Tod's good fortune in all this madness.

And then he found – despite all his self-loathing and depression – that he was no longer overwhelmed with the atrocities he had committed. As far as he could tell, the murder of a confirmed terrorist was noble. Couple that with all the murders he had committed (or felt he committed) since the start of this outbreak, he felt as though he could move on. Perhaps he could even stop hating himself so much. Naturally, though, a lingering resentment of his actions would haunt him – if only marginally – for some time to come.

But the void in his life that was once filled with unconditional love would cause far more grief than any of his self-loathing.

Day Five

Deliverance

I

Vincent didn't recall having drifted away.

The inside lights had been dimmed, but the place was glowing from the exterior stadium lights. Despite the glow, darkness was dancing in every corner. His internal clock told him the sun should be up within the hour.

His gut was churning – the stroganoff they served him for dinner was trying to make its escape. His hip was aching, sending flares down to his knee, his ankle, his toes. His right arm was tingling, so he rolled onto his back – this caused his stomach to lurch again.

When his head began to swim, he sat up and held his gut, moaning.

Within minutes, a nurse was striding toward him – he was a silhouette against the dim yellow backdrop. He knelt before Vincent and handed him a Dixie cup of pink stuff (which Vincent downed instantly), followed by a water bottle and another Dixie cup – this one contained two pills. The nurse took the empty paper cups and left Vincent with the bottle. The exchange was utterly silent.

He waited some time after the queasiness subsided before laying back down.

II

And he awoke once more, but this time of his own accord.

His friends were at the card table, drinking coffee with the paramedic. After a stretch – he noted how fine his body felt this morning with some curiosity – he stood and sauntered over toward the table.

"Morning," he croaked.

They turned, offering salutations of their own.

"Vincent," said John, "meet Mark."

Vincent shook Mark's hand. "Nice to meet you," he said. He couldn't help but glance at the pendant of the Madonna that Mark wore from his neck.

"You as well," replied Mark.

Louis began saying, "Mark was telling us –"

"Hold that thought," said Vincent. "There are some pressing matters at hand." After a weary – and awkward – pause, Vincent strode away, leaving his friends – and Mark – in bewildered silence. But when he stepped behind the curtain for the john, they understood at once. They resumed conversing amongst themselves while Vincent relieved himself.

Urination was not his only goal; after the toilet, Vincent headed directly for the cafeteria. He loaded up a plate of toast and ham and eggs and one banana – along with the requisite cup of coffee – before heading back into the civilian quarters. He could feel the buzz of the drugs he had taken in the night running around his sleepy brain. Diving into his breakfast, he was thankful that his stomach wasn't churning any longer.

Listening to the ongoing conversation, Vincent gleaned the general theme and decided to chime in; "All religion aside, what else can we do but try to survive? I hate to bring up a Darwinian theory while setting aside religion, but that is our general purpose, is it not?"

"Survival is fine," said Mark. "But while the gates of Hell overflow from the sinful times we live in, this curse shall not be lifted. And Hell will continue to overflow as long as there are people committing the atrocities of murder and suicide in such proportions."

"I am sorry, Mark," said Vincent, "but murder is defined by rage rather than resistance. And suicide that results in one less *lurcher* – one less tortured soul to terrorize humanity – should be forgiven by any rational god. What are we to do but protect our species, no matter the cost?"

"These tortured souls you speak of are the collective army of Hell," seethed Mark.

"And we are the collective army of life," said Vincent. "We are far more badass – and far more clever – than anything the underworld can conceive." He sipped his coffee. "I don't intend on giving in. I have faith in us."

"I have faith in Our Lord Jesus Christ," replied Mark. "I have faith in the righteous that will thus be delivered in this time of trials."

Vincent scoffed at this, but said nothing to further incense this God-fearing man.

After an uncomfortable silence, filled only with the sounds of rapid gunfire – it was louder this morning – and Vincent's smacking lips as he finished his meal, Mark said, "I will pray for your eternal soul."

"Thank you," said Vincent, pushing back from the table. "But you'll have to pray really hard to save my damned soul." He stood up and walked to the smoking area, leaving his mess for somebody else to clean up. Before pushing through the tarpaulin door, he could hear John apologizing for Vincent's agnosticism.

Not one minute later, Louis was seated beside him in the small, translucent room.

"I wonder…" began Louis, speaking slow and deliberate. "I wonder if we can't have some of our things back. A change of clothes would be fantastic right about now." He plucked at the stark-white cotton pants he wore.

Vincent shrugged, nodded, grunted, but did not respond, despite his own feelings on the matter. He was listening to the gunfire outside, pondering the increased frenzy.

A muffled voice from beyond the canvas wall: *"Get him! He's right there!"*

Somebody cried out, the sound muted from distance and barriers.

The gunshot that followed was loud, startling the wide-eyed smokers to their feet.

A group of shadows raced across the outer wall.

The gunfire grew louder, more frantic. The shouting was panicked.

And then they heard the moaning – their jaws dropped. A helmet-clad, bulky shadow appeared on the canvas. But it was shambling, not walking. And as it shambled closer to the light source, its shadow grew to the size of a giant.

And then it stopped, its arms slumped and it fell – its shadow disappeared.

The bullet that tore through this lurcher's head also tore through the tent. Vincent was relieved that the bullet did not strike a foot to the right, or he would not be standing.

He turned and saw that there was a hole through the tarpaulin as well. He wondered where the bullet stopped – he wondered who got shot. What he would never know is that it miraculously took out another lurcher that was making its way through the northern gate of this temporary military compound.

Colonel Johnson raced into the room, accompanied by a familiar doctor and three soldiers – one of whom Vincent recognized as PFC Webb, the soldier from the previous day. They came bearing too many weapons to fairly utilize and started handing them out. When Vincent and Louis left the smoking area – still stunned, still smoking – Colonel Johnson slapped a rifle in each of their hands. The doctor handed him his extra and the colonel was armed again.

"You've just been drafted," he said. He started hastily away and called back at them: "We're abandoning the post. It's time to evacuate!"

The doctor followed on his heel.

Before they could follow as well, PFC Webb addressed them: "Stay with us."

The other two soldiers led the way, clearing the hall before waving for the rest to follow. The group moved in single file with two soldiers in the lead and Webb bringing up the rear. They stopped at every intersection before turning one way or another. Vincent was amazed at the size of this maze of tents. After an impossible number of twists and turns, they emerged into the sunlight. Now in the midst of it all, his heart was hammering in his chest – the pulse in his ears was deafening – as were the flurries of gunshots.

And all he could think was: *adrenaline is a beastly drug*.

III

Outside, the gunfire had already diminished greatly. The group hunkered down between the tent and double chainlink. Another soldier –

his nametag read D. Sanchez – addressed them as a whole: "Our goal is a truck just beyond the barricade. Once on board, we will make our way south to the rendezvous point." He regarded the civilians for a moment. "You got two choices," he said to them. "You can either stay alive or stay behind. But I ain't gonna babysit you, so watch your own ass and keep up."

Keeping low, D. Sanchez moved to the first gate and pulled it open. In the same fashion, Webb moved past him to open the second. And the other soldier – H. Lee, read his nametag – was first beyond the double chainlink with Sanchez in tow. The four civilians followed close behind this pair with watchful, wary eyes and shaky trigger fingers – it's a wonder they didn't shoot themselves. Webb took up the rear again.

Sanchez and Lee led them around APCs and Hummers and stacks of supplies unmolested. They paused beside the latrine (even outside its walls it stank of shit and bleach) to explain the maze of cordons and razor wire. Everybody nodded as they had been escorted through a similar maze not two days prior.

H. Lee stayed back with the civilians while D. Sanchez and C. Webb moved swiftly forward to clear the first leg of their path. Webb fired one round at a mangled lurcher – a fallen soldier – that was entangled in a coil of razor wire. He waved the group on and marched down the tight path.

Keeping low, Vincent scuttled to the barricade with Louis and John hot on his trail.

Mark crossed himself – one would hope this gesture saved him from damnation. *Time is precious* – a phrase Mark should have thought of before being so devout and frightened. As he did not think of this phrase, the time it took to sign the cross cost Mark his life; had he followed on John's heels, the lurcher that crawled out of the latrine would have snatched H. Lee's ankle instead. But since he had taken the time to sign the cross, the lurcher snatched Mark's leg and tore into his calf. The previously stark-white pant leg he wore turned red at once.

He crumpled to the cement.

His shrieks halted the group and brought unwanted attention to their exodus by living and lurching alike. People hollered and cursed from a distance; lurchers groaned near and far, save for the satisfied ghoul munching on Mark's leg. Gunfire erupted at the northern fenceline as soldiers – one of which was Colonel Johnson – blasted infected brothers in arms in a feeble attempt at traversing the sprawling grounds to intercept this group of deserters.

Seeing as Vincent didn't realize he was being escorted by deserters, this sudden eruption of gunfire and obscenities did not even register as out of the ordinary (not after the events of the last few days). Instead, he was focused – as were his friends – on Mark as he wailed and writhed and pleaded for help.

"*Keep going!*" cried Sanchez. He took off down the cordon maze.

Webb hesitated, his attention flicking between Mark and Colonel Johnson. Fear of penalties or punishment overwhelmed him and he took off after Sanchez.

Before Vincent could move to help, H. Lee had kicked the ghoul away from Mark and crushed its skull with his heavy boots. Vincent watched the skull concave and crack and squirt brownish graymatter across the pavement – he reeled, sickened at the sight. But he couldn't manage to hold it in this time; he whirled and retched. John steadied him before he could fall into the razor wire. And when he recovered, H. Lee was running by with Mark (still wailing) slung over one shoulder.

Vincent caught sight of Colonel Johnson at the northern gates; he was watching them, a rifle propped on one shoulder and a bag slung over the other. Doctors and soldiers raced by him, through the cordons, toward a series of waiting trucks. Vincent wondered briefly why they were heading north when Sanchez said the rendezvous was to the south – but then he was overcome with the desire to have his bag and money and clothes and –

John tugged his shirtsleeve. "Let's go," he said, his voice raised over the ruckus.

Hesitant to abandon his money and numerous possessions, Vincent glared across the grounds at Colonel Johnson. He wondered if he had his bag and what would happen to it if he never saw the colonel again – and he was certain he would never see him again. He cursed the world and followed John down the cordon maze.

H. Lee was surprisingly swift, carrying another man, and they had to push all the harder to follow (it didn't help that Vincent's head was still spinning and his joints all hurt from stress; the lingering drugs did nothing to assuage his pain). Louis raced ahead to offer assistance while John kept pace with Vincent, fearful that he might take a spill.

Distracted by Louis, Lee missed the crawler that reached out from the razor coils. It snatched his boot, throwing him off balance. With the added burden of Mark and his persistent writhing, they tumbled to the ground; Louis managed to hop and skip to avoid tumbling with them.

"*What are you doing, you fool?*" cried Sanchez as he looked back – he was nearly to a canvas-backed personnel carrier. "*Leave that guy! He's infected now!*"

John stomped on the crawler's outstretched hand and shot it in the face.

Louis helped H. Lee to his feet.

Vincent raced past them.

With one last look at Mark as he pleaded and groped at his bloodied leg, John jogged toward the truck. Louis was only a few steps behind him.

But H. Lee stopped, his compassion besting him, and went back for the man. And as he was leaning over to haul Mark back onto his feet, a gangly and gruesome girl lunged at him from behind a Jeep, tackling him into the razor wire. H. Lee – Harland was his name, Private Harland Lee – kicked and squirmed, but to no avail; her teeth ripped through his fatigues and sank into his flesh. He screamed and flailed and wildly swung at her face.

A boy of similar age and appearance to the girl lurched from behind the same Jeep.

Harland's thrashing attracted the attention of his comrades.

"*You fucks!*" cried Sanchez as he unloaded into the advancing lurchers. "*Motherfucker!*" he screamed. "*Cocksmoker! Piece of shit!*" And more of the like – more senseless denigrations of mindless, primal ghouls – but nobody could hear him over his thundering rifle.

Vincent raised his rifle, leveled it at H. Lee's head – a difficult task as it was whipping from side to side. D. Sanchez was still irate – still shooting – when Vincent pulled the trigger –

BLAM! – one in many shots currently ringing out in the area, but this one had a definite finality; H. Lee no longer wailed or thrashed.

The entangled lurcher continued feasting – *BLAM!* – until Vincent plugged its brain with a bullet. And with one more shot – *BLAM!* – he answered the pleas of Mark, though this form of help was not what Mark had in mind. At least his pains were at an end and life – or the inevitable infection that would have ended his life – wouldn't be troubling him any longer.

"C'mon, man," said Webb, coaxing Sanchez to cease firing and head to the truck.

He was reluctant, but when he saw that Lee was dead on the ground – motionless in the jaws of a monster – he stopped firing at the lurcher he hadn't managed to subdue (though it was now full of holes). He glared at Vincent with true malice in his eyes. But he said nothing and marched toward the truck.

Webb motioned the civilians into the back and started around front.

IV

"That little fucker blew our cover!" bawled Sanchez.

"Then Harland deserved his fate," replied the driver – his nametag read P. Cooper. Before hijacking this truck, he was Master Sergeant, but he highly doubted he would retain that rank if this whole mess blew over.

"I think we'll be fine," said Webb. "We're free and clear and *no-body's* gonna chase us down."

Cooper snorted at this. "Nobody left to chase us down."

"The colonel's left," said Sanchez.

"He ain't tryin' to roll *this* way," said Webb. "We're not worth his time."

"Whole damn system's gonna fall apart anyway," said Cooper. He maneuvered around an abandoned station wagon and onto the first offramp he found. "So what's with the meatballs in the back of my truck?"

"Colonel had us rescue them," replied Sanchez. "Kinda had to go along with it."

"Okay," said Cooper. "But how'd *you* end up with them? Why didn't *he* take them?"

"He was already gone," replied Webb. "We couldn't very well send them off on their own. That woulda been inhumane."

"Fuck humane. I don't need these pissants ruining my leave."

"Way I figure it," began Webb, "is we drop them somewhere safe where they can hole up or grab a car or something. They've done us no harm so far." He offered a cigarette to his fellow deserters before lighting one of his own.

"We'll drop them when I feel like it," said Cooper. "Or when they become a burden." He lit the cigarette his (former) subordinate had offered and, keeping to the backroads, Master Sergeant Patrick Cooper maneuvered along a familiar path away from town.

V

Benches ran the length of the truckbed on either side; Vincent and John sat opposite Louis on one. There was no window into the cab and this trio couldn't see or hear the occupants therein. The only view afforded them was out the back of the canopied bed. They watched the chaotic world trundle away.

Soon they turned south – Vincent knew the road very well, even from this limited perspective. It almost made him laugh aloud when he realized that they were headed along the same route – the very same country road – that he and his friends had previously planned on taking. But instead of commenting on this, he said, "I wonder where they're taking us."

"The one guy said something about a rendezvous point down south," said Louis. "Probably part of some fallback plan if shit should hit the fan. And sure enough, shit hit the goddamn fan."

"I'm just thankful," began John, "that they decided to rescue us in the process." He was staring at his feet with his fingers steepled beneath his chin. "It's a shame that Mark met his fate so cruelly, so suddenly." He looked across at Louis. "It makes you think of the times we live in – it makes you think of how quickly it can all be snatched away." His face contorted. "And to think, his vessel will now be a tool of the devil."

Vincent gazed sideways at his friend. But he kept silent, not wishing to debate theology with a man he would always consider family. Moreover, he was well aware that John had his beliefs and respected those of his friends – chastening him over religion would be rude.

"I say we figure out what we're gonna do," proclaimed Vincent, steering the conversation back to more pressing matters. "I am not a fan of how the military is handling this situation thusfar." His head swam suddenly – he listed momentarily to the left before sitting straight and continuing as though nothing happened; his friends took no notice. "We have to break away somehow."

"What are we gonna do?" asked Louis. "Jump out the back around a corner?"

"And risk breaking a leg?" replied John. "I don't think so."

As if on cue, a bolt shot through Vincent's leg, making him wince.

"Why don't we just ask them to let us make our own way?" posed Louis.

"I highly doubt they'd let us go and risk breaking the quarantine," replied Vincent. "They seem pretty serious about locking this thing down tight."

They heard a cry and a roar – the truck jolted and jounced. Two bodies unfurled behind them as the truck rumbled along, unabated. One of the bodies started chewing on the other, which remained motionless.

And then some exuberant hollering erupted from the cab.

"Fuckin' animals," muttered Vincent.

"Vin's right," said John. "They won't let us leave until they get things under control."

Louis sighed. "Guess we're fucked for now."

Time slowed to a crawl and they rode in silence.

With a cigarette poised between his lips, Vincent sat at the rear hatch watching the world drift away. Interspersed scenes of chaos dotted the road and surrounding landscapes. They passed more than a few cars that had managed to wrap themselves around trees, each in its own intriguing fashion. Sometimes they slowed to crawl around one wreck or another; a van that T-boned a hatchback; a Jeep that rolled into a Cadillac; a dump truck that crushed a Bug. The disturbingly requisite number of half-chewed bodies and dried pools of blood surrounded each of these scenes.

Only once did they spot another moving car, but it zipped by at such a rate in the opposite direction that they could hardly discern what make it was.

And then Louis, desperate for warmth, dug into a trunk at the nose of their canvas-topped – and uncomfortably close – quarters. Above the trunk were masks like those the soldiers and doctors had been wearing. Inside were heavy green overcoats, boots, galoshes and gloves.

Vincent was still watching the world slip away. They passed under the dense canopies that interspersed the farms and fields and homes; they passed under a whitewashed sky that threatened rain. Every house appeared empty and every field just a touch macabre. But in one particular pasture, he spied two figures racing from the forest. He guessed them to be a woman and a child. They were frantic – *possibly injured or bitten*, he thought – their path was unnecessarily windy. And before they were lost behind another veil of trees, he spied a dozen or more lurchers stumbling after them.

"*Shit!*" he hissed.

Just as he was cursing his inability to help this pair, Louis howled with delight; "Ah fuck yeah!" He snatched out a few jackets and tossed them over his shoulder. "Motherfuckin' *jackets*, y'all!" He pulled one on and zipped it up to his nose.

With one look, John could see that Louis had tossed him a jacket three sizes too small. "Uh, dude," he said with one eyebrow raised. "I don't think this'll work."

So Louis rifled through the trunk some more and came out with one that might work.

He was pleased when it did.

VI

Perched in a roadside tree, napping like a panther, was a young man – a college student. The boy's clothes were dirty, charred, and torn; his beard was twisted and growing thicker by the day; his long, dirty blonde hair was greasy and matted, and would soon clump into irregular dreadlocks. He was thin, but this was only in part due to malnourishment. Before the outbreak, he had already been athletic, and his mostly – *mostly* – raw veggie diet did little to pad his belly. (He was a self-proclaimed purist who occasionally claimed to be vegan in a vain attempt to avoid GMOs and MSG – or anything else that wasn't "free-range" or from a local farm; this was a dietary lifestyle common to the area at the time…)

Never have trees offered the luxury of tossing and turning – nor have they ever offered proper neck support. If your leg were to dangle uncomfortably, it may turn to pins before you ever noticed. But lurchers – even to this day – have proven that they cannot climb anything greater than a slight-to-moderate incline. So, while this young man dozed (nestled in the tentative embrace of this grand Aspen), a pair of lurchers milled about below. This pair was howling and groaning in response to his shifts and coughs – and his snores set them off in greater fits.

When the rumble of an oncoming engine reached their ears, the pair of lurchers started off toward the road. And while the boy was snoring away, lost in another brief – if not tumultuous – slumber, the rumbling truck pulled up to a stop not fifty feet away. It sat there for some time while the soldiers within bickered about which way to turn.

Upon sighting the approaching lurchers, the driver decided to turn left.

The boy awoke with a start and hopped to the ground, ready for a fight and content when he didn't find one. Without any immediate resistance, he sprinted toward the road, chasing the taillights of a military-type Kaiser personnel carrier.

Spotting the lurchers that were nearly to the road by now, this boy unsheathed a three-foot bamboo staff from his back. He tripped one, brained the other and continued to the road without missing a step.

The truck was pulling away quicker than he could run.

Forty yards down the road, he stopped to breathe, leaning over his bamboo staff.

In the back of the Kaiser sat a man this boy would never know – Vincent Anton Andrews. Vincent saw this young man at a distance, leaning over his staff, and figured him to be yet another lurcher hounding for a meal it couldn't have.

After a quick survey of his surroundings, this young man decided to continue down this road, wondering if he might indeed find rescue from another passing vehicle – military or otherwise.

Instead of such salvation, he would find a bicycle in a driveway. Other than a little blood splatter along the frame and tires, it was in fair condition. He would ride this sturdy mountain bike until the sun went down and he found another perch, many miles east of this location.

VII

"What the hell do you think you're gonna find there?" contended Sanchez. "Your moms gonna be waitin' up for ya? Gonna be keepin' dinner warm in the oven and rifles loaded and ready to pop? Keep dreamin', kid."

Ignoring the gibe, Webb said, "I need to grab a few things." And, as an afterthought: "Since we're in the area."

"And what's worth risking our lives for?" asked Sanchez. "Gotta grab your sister's titties one more time?"

"No sir," replied Webb, trying to hide his growing resentment of Diego – and naïvely trying to respect the now unofficial (yet lingering) chain of command. "I would like to pillage my father's cache of ammunition and ordnance. I think that's worth the risk."

Sanchez was silent.

The truck remained at a stop.

In the back, the civilians were debating jumping ship.

When Cooper saw the lurchers stumbling through the foliage, he hit the gas, turned left. "How do I get there?" he asked.

VIII

"I doubt we'd get very far," argued Vincent. "These guys would probably see us bail and come after us. And with their training, I bet it wouldn't be hard for them to take us down."

"And I doubt they'll care enough to chase after us," countered Louis. "What are we to them besides a burden? The military has far more pressing matters than some runaway civilians left to their wits in *B-F-E*." Meaning: *Bum-Fuck-Egypt*, as the saying went.

The truck started rolling.

"I guess we'll have to wait a little while longer," piped John. "But I'm sorry, Lou: I agree with Vincent on this one. There *will* be a better opportunity to bail."

Looking out the back, Vincent saw a hunched-over lurcher, apparently too feeble to chase after them any longer. *Or maybe*, he thought, *it found some easier prey.* Little did he know, it was a young man leaning over a bamboo staff...

"And besides," said Vincent. "I've seen *dozens* of those things out there. Some of 'em were running in packs." He thought about that comment for a moment. "Well, they weren't exactly running..."

This road came to a T at another rural thoroughfare – the intersection was a heaping mess of mangled cars and similarly mangled bodies. They felt the intentional impact when the driver pushed through the mess – the jolt was light, but it rattled them nonetheless.

Something moaned and groped at the canvas – Louis jumped and leveled his rifle at the sound. But the truck rolled on and away, leaving this hapless, shambling body in a cloud of black exhaust. Vincent watched it stagger after them – *Him*, insisted his mind, *it's a* him, *not an* it! (He was also sure to note his change in perspective regarding what they were since his first encounter.)

"Proof," said Vincent. "Those things are *everywhere*. We need to find suitable and easy-to-access transport before we can bail."

They turned onto another arterial road.

Minutes later, they were cruising down a long, shady gravel driveway. The vibrations of the uneven road were chattering Vincent's teeth, displacing his spine, his hip. Wincing at the mounting pain, he extended his leg and massaged his lower back. The driveway was just over a quarter mile, but Vincent thought it might as well have been two.

He was grateful when they stopped, leaping straight to his feet to stretch. His friends, having known him for many years, didn't even think to look at him sideways when he began his little dance of twisting this way and that, leaning forward and back, wincing and moaning when something creaked or cracked or otherwise ached – it was a dance they had seen far too many times to count.

They left him there, twisting and turning, and hopped to the ground. John extended his arms to loosen his back muscles; Louis leaned over, touching his toes for a moment before straightening himself – but neither came close to Vincent's elaborate routine. Once these brief stretches were complete, they looked about, admiring the scenery while scoping the area for danger.

Webb crossed the lawn toward the front door. Sanchez was a few steps behind him. He called over to them: "Stay put." They were in the house a moment later.

The driver – P. Cooper – came around the other side. His eyes caught John's. Though his face remained stern and calculating – sizing up the big man – he extended a gloved hand. "Cooper," he said. "Patrick Cooper." After shaking John's hand, he shook Louis'.

They introduced themselves in turn. "And that's Vincent up there," said Louis.

Breaking from another twist, Vincent waved.

Cooper returned the wave with a wan smile. Perplexity crossed his face and he turned back to Louis. "What's wrong with him?"

"Nothing," replied Louis. "He's just a bit broken." He rolled his eyes. "You'd think he was ninety at times the way he complains about his back and knees."

"Never even busted anything," murmured John, shaking his head.

Vincent thought of how wrong John's statement was – but he couldn't say anything without revealing his secrets to those who need not know.

"Well then," breathed Cooper, raising his eyebrows. He glanced up into the truck once more before turning his attention to the surrounding countryside. "Beautiful property," he said. "Always wanted a place like this."

Wind swept through the trees, rustling the few remaining leaves; the grass rippled. A pair of squirrels chased each other up a skyscraping fir tree; a crow lit upon the clothesline. And just to ruin the serenity of this quiet scene, the wind brought with it the muddled stench of decay and scorched earth.

Vincent eased himself to the ground, landing mostly on his right leg. "Where are we?" he asked.

"Webb's house," replied Cooper, turning his back to the wind.

"I'm guessing this isn't the rendezvous point your boys spoke of earlier," said Vincent.

Cooper shot him a suspicious eye. "No," he said. "Just a stop along the way." He turned toward the house, hoping nobody saw the look for what it was. But despite facing the house, he watched the civilians with his periphery while wondering which soldier had told them such a worthless lie.

Such a lie could get them into deeper, darker water.

Such a liar must be reprimanded.

Nobody saw his suspicious eye – nobody cared to look for it. Idle conversation was Vincent's tactic for distracting this man while he scanned the property for a vehicle worth commandeering. His friends were capitalizing on this tactic as well with the very same prize on their minds.

"You mind if I ask," began Vincent, keeping up with his concerned charade, "where that rendezvous point might be?"

"I do mind," replied Cooper, "because you do not need to know."

"Fair enough," said Vincent, giving up the search – there were no vehicles in sight, not even a bicycle or scooter or otherwise futile contraption. "Will we be safe there?" he asked, expecting another stock response.

"Would you rather stay here?" Cooper turned back to Vincent. "You think you'd be safe? Limited rations. Limited defenses. Nobody to back you up. No cordons to keep the walkers at a distance. And God knows about communications out here – cell phones probably don't even work."

Definitely not the response Vincent was expecting – he was stunned into silence.

"I'll tell you one thing," continued Cooper, "as long as you're chummin' with the United States military, you got the biggest, baddest backup and safest, most well-guarded installations on the motherfuckin' planet." And now he was lying – they wouldn't be chummin' with any country's military now that this group had deserted – but he would never feel the need to reprimand himself. "So if you wanna live, you might want to think about stickin' around a little while." More lies from the former Master Sergeant.

Vincent felt as though Cooper had seen right through his previous guise and somehow surmised their plan to break away. He had no idea that Cooper was flying by the seat of his pants. He was almost swayed by Cooper's obsequious arguments for the military before recalling the swift meltdown of their former outpost – not to mention the near tor- turous poking and prodding of their doctors.

After a beat, Vincent said, "I would never speak ill of the United States Army." Cooper's outburst had shocked him – had shocked them all – but he was able to retain his calm and self-assured demeanor. "It was a simple question. *Sir*."

Cooper looked him over coolly with a furrowed brow, trying to find something out of place on Vincent's face. He glanced at the others, but not for long. When he looked back at Vincent, his brow unfurrowed and he smiled. "Sorry about that," he said, clapping a hand on Vincent's shoulder. "It's been a rough few days, as you well know. And to top it all off, I lost one of my best men in our escape."

"It's all good," he said, absently noting that Cooper was more con- cerned for the one soldier than the rest of the soldiers that died this day. And then he wondered why a group of four – depleted now to three –

would be the only ones to flee the installation in such a large personnel carrier. Surely it wasn't just to rescue a few civilians. And surely it wasn't because that many soldiers had turned or died – not with such a fight still raging during their departure.

He wondered idly what happened to the colonel.

While Vincent was aptly theorizing, Webb and Sanchez emerged from the house, armed to the teeth with rifles, revolvers, bandoliers and swords.

"Look what's cookin' here!" howled Cooper. "These guys are seriously strapped." He noticed a new medal pinned to Webb's uniform – one he hadn't quite earned. "What's this?" he sneered, tapping the Purple Heart. "Another medal you'll never receive?"

"It's my father's," replied Webb, pushing past Cooper. He set a rifle and sabre in the back of the truck. "I'm sure he'd want me to honor him." His dour eyes told the story his lips could not manage.

"You'd honor him more by burying him with it," said Cooper.

Webb whirled on him with a solid right hook, knocking him to the dirt.

Sanchez pounced on Webb, hammering his ribs with lightning jabs, one after the other, until Webb was beside Cooper on the dirt.

In the moment it took John to step over and lift him off, Webb's face was bloody and busted. He lifted the wiry Latino with little effort and tossed him to one side – he earned a few fists to the gut for this, but he hardly noticed.

When he bent over to help Webb up, Sanchez scrambled to his feet and charged, only to meet Vincent's outstretched arm and fall, choking, to the dirt beside his commander. As he writhed, gasping for air, Cooper pushed up onto his haunches.

"You shouldn't speak ill of the dead," John told Cooper.

Checking his lip for blood, Cooper's gaze shifted between the men now standing over and around him – his eyes were calculating, menacing. He shot a quick glance at Sanchez (still gasping for air in the dirt) before returning his menacing gaze to the men around him.

When he saw the bloodied mess that was Webb's face, his lips cracked into a smile and he started cackling. He slapped his knee, shook his head and held his chest – all while cackling. After a moment of this, he stopped to look upon Webb's broken face once more; the sight of it sent him into a fresh bout of mad cackling that genuinely baffled the men around him.

"What the fuck is wrong with you?" bawled John, grasping at Cooper's collar.

"That's what you get, *fucker*!" Cooper croaked between guffaws.

John slowly stood up and took the former Master Sergeant with him. Once his feet were off the ground, the massive paw gripping his neck was choking out the laughter – but somehow the smile remained.

Cooper – mad with pain and revenge – waved sweetly at John, grinning ear to ear.

And then he flung his foot directly into John's crotch, immediately dropping him to his knees and thus releasing his grip.

But before he could celebrate this minor victory, Vincent clubbed him with his rifle. "You don't hurt my family," he told Cooper (though Cooper was now unconscious from the heavy blow to the head). Turning the business end of his rifle on Sanchez – who was finally able to breathe again – he asked, "You gonna try something?" His eyes were sharp, his hands were steady – the barrel didn't waver.

"Don't shoot him," said Webb – his face still busted and bloody.

"He was just protecting his commander."

"He went apeshit," said Vincent. "So did your commander. I can't trust either of them."

"You don't have to kill them!" called Webb.

"I'm not gonna kill them," said Vincent. "But I'm not gonna rescue them, either."

John was standing now – huffing and puffing, holding his crotch. "Agreed," he said.

"But we rescued *you*," said Sanchez.

"And I thank you for that," replied Vincent. "But your motives weren't genuine – you were acting under the guise of duty. I can't blame you for that. Now I can see through your façade and no longer wish to accompany you on this one-wheeled rollercoaster to Hell." Rifle leveled at the former corporal's face – his eyes similarly fixed on this target – Vincent instructed anybody to disarm the man.

"You can't do this!" cried Sanchez when John approached him.

"Apparently I can," replied Vincent, thankful that Webb hadn't moved to stop him.

And when John was stripping his loads of ordnance – two rifles crisscrossed over his shoulders, two revolvers in his waistband, a pistol in his holster – Vincent said, "Just put his guns a safe distance away."

John placed the guns to one side of the driveway beyond the nose of the truck.

As an aside to this, Louis stripped Sanchez of two sabres he had acquired and the dagger strapped to his ankle.

"Now go," Vincent instructed. "Get inside the house until we're gone."

"You can't do this!" Sanchez cried again as John hauled him to his feet.

"If I ever see you again," said Vincent, "I won't be so kind." He lowered his rifle, popped a cigarette in his mouth and sparked it.

"This is fucked up, man!" He was being shoved along a dirt path toward the front porch. "You can't strand me like this! You can't steal my truck! This is *inhumane!*" He was still squalling as such after John shoved him in the house.

When he raced back out the front door, Vincent fired a round at his feet, the bullet narrowly missed. He stopped dead in his tracks. "Don't make me use rope," he said. "Then you'd really be fucked."

Sanchez backed away, but didn't go back inside. He stood atop the porch with his hands upraised.

Without turning – still wary of letting Sanchez out of his line of sight – Vincent said, "So I'm guessing by your lack of resistance that you aren't trying to stay here with these psychopaths."

"Oh hell no," replied Webb. "I wasn't trying to hang around them for long anyhow."

"Good," said Vincent. "Let's go."

IX

From the cab, Vincent noticed more of the devastation than he'd seen riding in the back. Cars and trucks of every size and variety were ditched on either side of the road. A tractor was smoking in a field, its driver beside it, facedown in the mud. A pack of lurchers – a half-dozen blood-streaked, shambling, humaniform creatures – laboriously trudged through the soggy field, their progress even slower than usual.

"It feels kinda wrong," Webb told him while maneuvering the rig around a truck that was blocking an entire lane. "Those guys were my friends. Hell, they were my *superiors*. And I just ditched them in the sticks."

"They were loose cannons," replied Vincent. "And I'm pretty sure they had plans for us."

"I don't think they would have killed you."

"We left them with weapons," said Vincent. "That's better than they would have done for us."

"I'm sure they would have left weapons," said Webb, blushing. He turned south.

Vincent watched the gruesome scenery float by outside with vague interest. "There never was a rendezvous," he said. "You deserted."

Webb glowered at him. "We did what we could. And when word came that the outbreak was spreading beyond our control, that's when it started spreading throughout our unit. We had to save ourselves."

"Don't be so defensive," said Vincent. "I wasn't attacking you. If anything, I was commending you for all the reasons you just listed."

Ahead, in the middle of the road, was a gory throng of slithering mastication as over a dozen lurchers were piled atop a heap of half-eaten corpses, stuffing their gnarled faces with bits of intestine and shoulder and rib and thigh – one of them was gnawing on an entire foot, sans leg.

The scene caught the attention of these men.

"Oh, that's just not right," groaned Webb. He mashed the accelerator.

Still held tight in the dead hand of a victim of this horde was a fourteen-inch spike, which was picked up by the front passenger side tire of the Kaiser. The spike and tire survived the first rotation; the second rotation slammed the spike into the concrete at such an angle as to rip a golfball size hole in the tire.

Webb fought to correct the flailing vehicle in a panic. With white knuckles and wide eyes, this inexperienced kid from BFE, Washington, found that he could not stop this oversized truck in the allotted distance. Once the tire had shredded completely and they were riding on metal, they struck an old pickup that stalled half in, half out of a gravel driveway.

The force of this impact sent the Kaiser skidding sideways.

It dipped into the drainage ditch and flipped onto its side, throwing the occupants about – Vincent banged his knee and bumped his head. Dazed, he watched Webb tumble out the window – a rifle landed on his head, a knife in his belly – but Vincent didn't see this through his boggled vision.

The rear passengers were tossed out as the canopy ripped away.

X

Sounds of this wreck were heard for over a mile around – by infected and uninfected alike. Though he was not so fortunate with his eventual fate, one man was given a brief respite when a group of lurchers turned toward the twisted exclamation of certain devastation; he was given the extra two seconds required to climb atop a rickety shed. A young woman running through a nearby field – avoiding a litter of burning bodies – skirted an aggressing horde as their attention shifted.

A boy riding east on his bicycle heard the sound, but paid it little mind.

A pair of soldiers – armed to the teeth with rifles and sabres and bandoliers – marching down a long and winding gravel driveway heard the twisting metal and smiled, wishing the worst for the occupants.

XI

Two things registered before John landed: Louis' arm bending the wrong way on a canopy crossbar; and the rifle flying barrel-first at his face. And then the air was zapped from his lungs upon impact while the rifle speared his forehead, leaving a red crescent imprinted there.

John's head lolled from side to side. His eyes fluttered.

After a minute, he shook off the pain and focused his eyes.

He sat up fast, smacking his forehead into a sapling that stood between his legs – he winced and rubbed at the dueling pains.

Straight ahead was a grove ripe with damp underbrush. To his right, at a distance, was a pair of shambling bikers. To his left, only two yards away, was Louis, his head resting against a tree. He twisted around to see what was behind him, but a bolt of pain shot down his spine and he turned back around, grimacing and holding his neck.

Glancing over at the pair of lurchers again, something clicked; John hopped to his feet, ignoring the flares that shot up and down his spine, and ran over to Louis. He started spitting his name, trying to keep quiet, tapping his cheeks lightly.

The lurchers were still a good twenty yards away, but John's impatience was mounting. He started husking Louis' name even louder and slapping his face even harder, but the man remained unconscious through it all.

"Hey!" he belted, only inches from Louis' face. "Wake up!" he called, pinching his arm.

Louis sat bolt upright and tried moving his busted arm to soothe the pinched skin and screamed as his bones crunched. He reeled at the agony and lost his breakfast in a spray that coated John's pants.

Something moaned and groped at his shoulder – John jumped and punched a gnarled postman in the face. He scrambled for the rifle while the seething postman clutched at Louis' boots. It was gnawing on the left one when John brought the rifle down on its head – three blows with the stock and it was done.

Louis sat against the tree, heedless of the incident. His boots were virtually unscathed.

John whirled, leveling the rifle at a leather-bound oaf.

BLAM! – the lurcher fell with one shot to the brain. And –

BLAM! – so did the other.

He caught a glimpse of another lurcher's head bobbing and listing in the drainage ditch, moving toward the overturned truck – John had thusfar been ignorant to the state of this truck and its occupants.

He trained the rifle on the bobbing target, timing the sway of its head.

He exhaled.

BLAM! – this round did not find its target.

BLAM! – neither did this one.

He sighted his target again, exhaled again…

BLAM! – he watched its dead brains splatter the grassy embankment of the drainage ditch – some pieces even sprayed the pavement beyond.

"C'mon," he said to Louis; he hooked under his good arm and hoisted him to his feet. "Let's go check on Vincent." Together, they limped and stumbled through the foliage and into the ditch beside the highway.

At once, John could see the state of things; Webb's unconscious, bloody body lying just below the truck with a rifle draping his face. And, through the spiderwebbed windshield, he could see Vincent was suspended in air, still strapped in by the seatbelt. He laid Louis in the culvert – mindful of his busted arm – and dragged Webb's body into the open before crawling under the cab. He stood up through the open window, unlatched Vincent's seatbelt, and gently lowered him down and out of the truck.

With two of his friends dazed – one in nauseating pain, the other mildly concussed – and an unconscious soldier, John now had a line of three hapless bodies in a rural culvert. He already had a headcount of three dead lurchers and no way to know how many more might arrive at any given moment after having heard such commotion.

John poked his head back up into the cab. Moments later, he came back out with a blue steel box emblazoned with a large red cross. He popped it open – two large gauze pads and a heap of small bandages scattered instantly. Ignoring the mess, he went straight to the hypos, reading the labels on each until he found a pair that he liked; a local anesthetic and a cocktail of sedatives, painkillers and anti-nausea medication.

He jammed the anesthetic beside the knife that protruded from Webb's belly and injected its contents. Following this, he found a good vein on Webb's arm and injected the cocktail. The boy didn't move a muscle throughout this.

He packed a handful of gauze around the blade and gripped the handle.

*One...*he started counting. *Two...*he breathed deep, exhaled slowly. *Three!*

Blood sprayed him up and down – some went up his nose – as the knife was pulled free.

Webb screeched, arched his back, thumped the ground with his fists and kicked the air – John fought to keep the gauze on the wound, but too much blood was escaping. He was relieved when Vincent threw himself over the heaving body, locking his hammering arms and leveling his arched back.

With one hand keeping pressure on the wound, John rifled through the medical box with the other. He found a sterile package containing a curved needle, held this between his teeth and went back in to find the thread.

Webb passed out beneath Vincent, thus alleviating his duties to restrain him.

"You know what you're doing?" asked Vincent, huffing and pushing himself up.

"Sure," replied John, coming out with a package of thread. "Just like sewing up my sweater, but with more blood."

"Shit," breathed Vincent.

"Yeah, pretty much." He began stitching the wound while it was still gushing. "I just hope there isn't any serious internal damage." His stitching was sloppy and most definitely improper, but the wound would heal if Webb didn't die from internal bleeding. Since neither of these men were doctors, they would not be able to diagnose any such condition. They could only hope and pray for his well being. He taped a gauze pad over the wound.

"Let's get this show on the road," said Vincent, standing.

Something groaned nearby – something else joined in from farther away – something else snarled and seethed. And a chorus, like a wave,

rolled at them from everywhere; a driving sound that attacked their senses, disrupted all thought.

"Agreed," said John, tapping Webb's cheeks. "C'mon, man. Wake
up. We gotta go."

Vincent helped a wobbly Louis to his feet and guided him onto the
street.

"Ah fuck it!" hissed John – he lifted Webb up into a fireman's carry
and followed.

Only a few lurchers were visible as of this moment, but from the
chorus, they knew more would be shambling after them shortly.

They started down the road, their pace a notch above that of their
pursuers.

XII

Now equipped with a pistol in his good hand, Louis was hobbling
alongside Vincent, free of his aid. Together, they were firing off rounds
at many targets – some would land them kills, others would buy them
time. But with every shot they broadcast their location.

They were everywhere, it seemed. From behind every bush, every
car – every culvert and every driveway – another one would emerge. Selective gunfire became necessary; they would aim only for the nearest
targets.

And then Vincent found himself face to face with a gnarled farmer
– they went down in a tangle. Vincent thrust the rifle between his face
and the lurcher's gnashing teeth and kicked hard at its groin. But the
thing kept gnashing and groaning and pawing.

Another one – a scraggly woman with patchy, matted hair – caught

John's leg before he could kick at Vincent's assailant – he dropped Webb in a blackish puddle and stumbled forward, tripping over the tangled legs of Vincent and his assailant. He went down hard on his shoulder.

BLAM! – Louis painted the road with the scraggly woman's brains.

Vincent was now atop his attacker, one knee pressing hard into its chest – it continued pawing at him, seething and snarling. He repeatedly jammed his riflestock into its face – it flailed and pawed – and eventually it ceased all movement.

BLAMBLAM! – Louis put two rounds into the chest of a tall, bald – and bloody – lurcher, momentarily halting its progress toward John.

BLAM! – and it fell when he put a round in its head.

Webb groaned, his head lolled.

BLAMBLAM!

BLAM!

All three able bodies were now up and firing in every direction.

Webb rolled onto his back and looked about with weary eyes. And something within – some innate instinct to survive – told him to rise up and face this challenge. He had the skill, he had the will – he had the training – to survive. With one hand on his father's Purple Heart, he rose to his feet. Three imminent dangers were dropped in the first three seconds. Four more in the next six. His eyes were predatory – his aim was deadly.

I got it! he thought. I got the –

His abdomen exploded with pain – he doubled over, all thought cut off at once. His hand groped at the pain – he found the bloodied bandage and felt another surge as colored spots flashed before his eyes. He almost fainted – but the pain diminished and his vision cleared.

The gunfire hadn't ceased.

John threw an arm under his for support – he was almost mistaken for a lurcher and shot (thank goodness for Webb's slow reaction time in his state of near blinding pain). And then they ran, moving as swiftly as the tandem gait of John and Webb would allow.

Clear of the mass, they shouted their discontent at one another – they blurted obscenities and queries and ran at their stifled gait. Being able-bodied and without the burden of another man over his shoulder, Vincent raced ahead at times to clear their path of random lurchers. Louis attempted to assist, but mostly wasted ammunition in his untrained attempts at firing his pistol with only one hand (his left one, at that).

After a mile, they found a white box truck with the ghost of a logo lingering on the side – it stood alone in the middle of the road without a single ghoulish being to be seen. The rollup door at the back was shut, but they could see that the driver's door was ajar.

From somewhere far behind them came a brief thunder of gunfire.

"C'mon," husked Vincent. He unlatched the rear door with one hand, but it was sticky on the runners and he had to involve his other hand to open it; with a heave, he pushed it up.

Amidst a clutter of cardboard and industrial plastic wrap scattered about the back, there was an ancient floral print sofa and a stained twin mattress – but no lurking lurchers. "Get in there," he said, motioning for Louis to hop up. "And get him in there, too," he said, referring to Webb – he noticed the soldier was covered in blood and oil. He pondered this while racing to the driver's door, rifle on the ready.

But the cab was empty.

BANG! – the truck shook and Vincent whirled at the clatter.

Following this startlement, he heard the familiar clank and clack of the rear latch and realized the source of the clatter; John had slammed the rollup door. With a huff and a sigh, he climbed behind the wheel, pulled the door shut and set his rifle between the seats. He was fortunate to find the key still in the ignition rather than seek it out or fiddle with trying to hotwire the engine (a skill he did not possess).

John climbed into the passenger seat.

Vincent turned the key and silently thanked the heavens when the engine turned over.

"We gotta hit the gas station," said Vincent as they started down the road. "This thing's on fumes."

"Hey look," said John, holding up a credit card he found in the cup holder. "Free gas." He turned it over in his hand. "Corporate card, it looks like."

"Good," replied Vincent. "Should make this a quick stop."

XIII

Many times in their history, each of this truck's passengers had stopped at this gas station for last-minute camping essentials – beer, buns, smokes, snacks, gas. On this occasion, their needs were similar, but the circumstances of their visit were much less pleasant.

A bloody body was splayed out before a dingy blue minivan – it was an older model with rust stains on the hood and roof. Vincent pulled the box truck up to the pump opposite this van with a watchful eye – it appeared to be abandoned, but he remained leery all the same.

Once the truck was in park, John hopped out and went around back to open the rollup. Vincent was out a moment later. He swiped the card and – after the long authorization process in which he miraculously picked the proper zip code – plugged the nozzle into the tank. With the handle locked in place, he joined his friends at the rear of the truck.

"How you doin', Lou?" he asked.

With a hand on his busted elbow, Louis grimaced. "Not so hot," he said.

"I can imagine," replied Vincent. "Think you could keep watch real quick? John and I are gonna grab some supplies."

"Oh, sure," he said, drawing out his pistol. "Could someone check this for me? I think it's about empty."

John took the pistol, cleared the chamber, locked the slide and switched out clips. "Here ya go, buddy," he said, releasing the slide. "Locked and cocked and ready to rock." He held it out, grip first.

Taking the gun, Louis said, "Thanks." He eased himself to the ground.

Pointing his chin at Webb, Vincent asked, "How's he doin'?"

"He's out," replied Louis.

"He was barely conscious anyhow," said John. He turned to Vincent. "Let's do this."

They started off toward the store.

The place was bright and orderly – nothing was amiss on the floor, besides the absence of employees. And with this absence, Vincent took the liberty of snatching a sheaf of plastic bags from behind the counter. He handed a few to John and they set about grabbing items from every aisle; canned or boxed foods, bottled water and coffee drinks, beer and cigarettes, flashlights and motor oil, mapbooks and pocket knives...

Every bag they filled was set beside the front door.

Vincent bagged an ill-equipped first aid kit, wishing they had not left behind the extensive kit John had found in the Kaiser. He set this bag beside the others and spied a door behind the counter.

"Hey, yo," he called out to John. "I'ma check back here – see what I can find."

John grunted as he examined a cooler of dairy products and pre-made sandwiches.

Vincent popped open the door behind the counter; he started at the scene within.

On a chair in the middle of this claustrophobic room was a man without a face. In his lap, his limp hands loosely cradled a short-barrel shotgun. Above his chair was a smattering of blood and brains. And as Vincent looked on with horror, a scarlet drop fell directly onto the chrome of the shotgun.

With no time to turn or find a corner, his belly emptied at the dead man's feet in a spray. He reeled some, glanced once more at the faceless man in the chair, switched off the light and left the room. He pulled the door shut with a loud clap.

"You okay there, buddy?" asked John, genuinely concerned. "I heard ya yakkin'."

Vincent nodded absently, obviously distressed. "Don't go in there," he puffed.

Arching his brow, John said, "Okay." He studied Vincent's face with concern. "You sure you'll be okay, Vinnie?"

"I'll be fine," he replied. "But don't fucking call me that." Behind his revulsion was a faint twinkle.

John tittered and walked away.

After recovering from the gruesome backroom scene, Vincent joined his friend in gathering the collection of bags clustered about the front door. With a grip of bags dangling from both hands each, they left the store. Never again would they enter the doors of this nostalgic site.

They set their cache of supplies in the back of the truck.

And then something most peculiar happened: a white minivan pulled up to the stop sign directly in front of the store. The driver – an elderly woman with poufy white hair – looked over at the trio gassing the large, white truck and waved. She wore massive bifocals and had a large grin plastered upon her face. This woman was somehow ignorant to the wider world's current state. She would find out soon enough just how horrid it was.

They watched as she cautiously rolled forward and drove out of sight.

Each jumped when the gas pump snapped off.

They looked between one another, perplexed, intrigued.

"Did that just happen?" asked Louis.

"Did *what* just happen?" asked John.

"That did just happen," said Vincent.

"A woman," began Louis, speaking slowly, pausing every other word, "just drove…and waved…and smiled." He paused. After a beat, he said, "She *smiled*." He was staring after the white minivan, now long gone.

Perplexity spread throughout these three. Webb missed this strange occurrence as he was still out cold on the mattress.

"Awfully peculiar," said Vincent.

"How 'bout we go now?" proposed John, replacing the gas nozzle in its cradle.

"Yar," agreed Vincent. "It's definitely time to get going."

"Shut me in with Lou," said John. "I'ma splint that arm of his." He tapped a pair of long ice scrapers before pulling himself up into the truck.

Just the thought of it made Louis' busted elbow throb – it was purple and red and hanging awkwardly at his side. The movement caused by climbing into the box exacerbated the throbbing and his face was sketched with a grimace.

Vincent shut them in the back and climbed behind the wheel – he opened the door between the seats that led to the back and switched on the dome light so John wouldn't have to play doctor in the dark. Louis groaned plenty, yelped a handful of times, but otherwise made a good patient, despite the lack of painkillers or anesthetics.

But when Vincent heard the grinding of bones, he switched on the radio – partly to cover the stomach-churning sound (along with the seething groans), and partly in hopes of finding actual advice or information – news, hopefully. Something was said about the occult, something was said about Hell on Earth, something was said about "rage-infected monkeys" – each theory was ridiculous, and no story contained true news about the infection. There was nothing real to be said about its cause, treatment or possible cure – and Vincent doubted there would be any such news at the rate this infection was spreading.

More of the same, he thought.

One station referred to the infection as a "nationwide epidemic" and reminded its listeners to stay in their homes at all costs and avoid contact with anybody outside their homes. They were reminded often that Martial Law was still in effect and would remain so until the epidemic could be contained. All American borders and ports were on lockdown, all flights – personal and professional alike – were grounded. Nothing was said of infection outside the States.

Overwhelmed, he turned the volume down.

Now finished playing doctor, John squeezed through the small doorway into the cab and plopped into the passenger seat. He lit two cigarettes; when Louis was seated in the threshold to the cab, John handed him one.

Vincent opened a small package of miniature powdered donuts and popped one in his mouth.

After an uncomfortable silence, Louis piped up with some comment about the batty old lady that had smiled and waved without a care in the world. And they started dreaming up stories about her. Maybe she had been holed up for the past week with her collection of cats, which would explain her ignorance to the prevailing ailment quickly spreading across the nation. Maybe she was freshly infected and waved to wish them well as she departed on her last great venture. Or maybe – and Vincent particularly liked this theory – this old woman had grown to detest this society and was honestly enjoying the dire circumstances that had befallen it.

These distractions faltered the moment they approached the freeway onramp; a sea of cars – most of which were smashed together or otherwise crunched and crushed – sat before a deserted blockade that included a tank in its array of abandoned vehicles. And in the midst of this wreckage were a fair amount of bodies, both dead and undead alike. Some of the latter were busy feasting on the former, but plenty began to stagger through the mess in a futile attempt at catching this new feast on wheels.

"Well then," breathed John. "We're not going that way."

"Apparently not," said Vincent. "I guess we're moving right along to Plan B, then."

"And what was Plan B?" inquired Louis.

"Plan B is anything but this," replied Vincent.

John shrugged. "Guess we should just continue heading east then

...or something to that effect." He snatched a mapbook from the center console. "Let's find an interesting route," he said, thumbing through the pages.

Safely beyond the freeway scene, Vincent dared to throttle it a touch more.

Louis switched the radio back on and scanned the channels until he found an oddity among the news broadcasts: a station playing music. The song was nearly over and quite familiar to each of these men, though the band was rather obscure and none had ever heard their music played over the radio. A soothing baritone broke in over the outro: "And that last one was 'Shot Down' by The Beautiful Girls."

The song transitioned into some soft and smooth background music.

"Amazing band," praised the disc jockey. "I wish I could expect another album from them, but alas..." he intentionally left this hanging.

He let the jazzy background music fill an otherwise soundless void.

"My listeners," said this cool baritone after a few soothing measures. "My faithful listeners. I have something I must tell you." They were easily enrapt by this man's pleasing voice and the near-plodding pace at which he spoke – an attribute that kept him on the air for so long and acquired so many truly faithful listeners.

"With all this madness going on," he continued, "people eating people, people shooting people – we must ask ourselves: *When will my time come?* Well, my friends," he paused, audibly pulling a drag from a cigarette. "My time is growing shorter with every passing breath."

And he paused again, allowing for the proper amount of suspense, drama.

He started suddenly, coolly: "During the last set of music, Yours Truly was accosted by one of these mean green people eaters." He smoked again, letting this information settle into his listeners' heads. He resumed: "That mean green people eater was a longtime colleague of mine. And to tell you the truth, my friends, I held reservations about harming this fellow. I held these reservations until his jagged jowls tore away a piece of my arm – and then I did what we all find ourselves doing these days: I killed a man."

During another dramatic pause, a bubbling sound accompanied the jazz. He coughed and hacked and wheezed.

"I killed a friend," he coughed. "I killed a colleague. I killed a *human being.*"

He sighed, smoked, hacked, wheezed, coughed, sighed.

"It has been my pleasure to broadcast for you these many years," he said upon resuming. "My only hope is that all of you still listening – if anyone is still listening – that all of you have enjoyed the time we've spent together as much as I have. So now, before I bid you the fondest of fond farewells, I beg you: please don't let your heart hinder your survival in these especially tough times as I have let mine hinder my own…"

Another interval passed, filled with that soft jazz and his soft suckling of smoke.

The trio remained silent throughout this monologue.

In the back, Webb silently stirred; a finger twitched, his eyes fluttered.

"There's an endless array of music in this studio," continued this strangely serene voice, "and I'm about to hit play on infinite repeat. And you need not fret, my friends – my faithful listeners – as there will be no more pesky commercials trying to sell you useless products or costly services you will no longer need."

Soulless red eyes popped open on the mattress behind Louis.

"My listeners," said the DJ, "you are about to hear the widest range of uninterrupted music ever to hit the airwaves."

Webb craned his neck and pushed himself up.

"So here it is, my friends, my last toke, my last swill, my last drag, and even I am wondering what words to leave you with."

Webb stood up – the mattress creaked.

Louis turned. "Webb?" he said.

Wild hacking erupted from the speakers.

"But," continued the DJ, "all I can think to say..." he trailed off, leaving another dramatic gap in his monologue.

"Oh shit," breathed Louis.

"...is good luck," finished the soothing baritone.

Louis drew his pistol before his friends could even turn.

A moment before pressing play and killing the mic (and, subsequently, himself), this strangely calm, amazingly soothing disc jockey spoke one last word: "Adieu."

BLAM! – Webb's infected body fell back into a pile of plastic.

XIV

Ears ringing, heart slamming, adrenaline pumping – Vincent slammed on the brakes, leaving twin sets of tire marks stretching out behind the truck. Louis tumbled into the cab, slammed into the center console and whacked his busted arm against the hard plastic – he cried out at the pain; he grimaced and reeled, holding his elbow.

"*Holy shit!*" belted Vincent – his hands were crushing the steering wheel.

"*Motherfucker!*" cried John.

Louis continued rocking and reeling.

"What the hell was that?" yelled John.

"He turned," spat Louis.

"What?" yelled John, clearly in disbelief, his ears still ringing – all of their ears still ringing – from the deafening gunshot.

"Webb turned!" Louis hollered.

The box was dark when the pair whirled to verify this. Vincent fumbled around the dash until he found the correct dial and flipped on the dome light. A spattering of blood streaked the back door and a pair of legs stuck out of the plastic wrap at odd angles. Webb was otherwise buried in the midst of the semi-translucent wrap.

Vincent remembered the blood and oil that covered Webb's chest – *It wasn't all his*, he thought with a chill.

"We should bury him," suggested John – his eyes were focused on a field and farmhouse at the end of this road, beyond the intersection.

"That's one helluva risk," said Vincent, not entirely opposed to the idea.

"He's an American soldier," argued John. "He's an honorable young man. We owe him that much."

"'Don't let your heart hinder your survival,'" Louis said, quoting the fated DJ.

"This isn't my heart," John contested. "This is honor. This is right. That man – that *boy* – fought for our country. He saved our lives. It's the least we could do for him."

When nobody replied to this, he said, "There's a field straight ahead."

"I guess it's worth a look," said Vincent.

Louis did not argue.

John said, "We can bail if there's any sign of trouble." He looked over at his friends, each in turn. "I do understand the danger here. And maybe we don't bury him. But if nothing else, we should say a few words for him. And I don't know about you, but I'd rather not ride around with a corpse."

"I understand, John," replied Louis – he was still holding his busted elbow.

A low mist blanketed this fenced-in field that might have been farmland, though there wasn't a sign of crops or livestock. Beyond the gate – a service entrance, no doubt – was a grassy tract that ran between the fence and a line of trees. Set back aways, near dead-center of the property, was a tall white house.

Vincent piloted the box truck through the open gate, trundled through damp grass.

XV

In the day's fading light, a pair of luminous green eyes – belonging to a striking young redhead – watched this truck wade through the mist with trepidatious curiosity. This girl was not a resident of the attic she occupied; this house was simply a haven she had stumbled into while fleeing a shambling horde of demons. She found the place abandoned and had yet to find a chance to relocate.

The horde that chased her here had finally dispersed the night before.

Using a pair of binoculars she found in a random box, this girl watched a husky fellow – a tall, heavyset fellow with a thick growth of unkempt beard settling upon his face – step from the passenger door. He wore a heavy camouflage jacket over white cotton garb, all of which was spattered with blood and mud and something else (*vomit maybe?* she thought). Though interesting, she did not ponder this strange garb too much until the driver stepped into view wearing the same mismatched attire (also specked with mud and gore).

They exchanged some words and threw open the rollup door.

Inside was a smattering of curdled blood and brainmatter surrounding a dead soldier – this one wore full fatigues. This was not her first glimpse of death, but she was by no means accustomed to the sight of gore. She recoiled, dropped the binoculars to her side and squeezed her eyes tight. Gripping a golden locket that dangled from her neck, she mouthed a calming mantra her father had taught her if ever she should be upset. In the past four days, she had recited it countless times.

Her first glimpse of death was closely linked to one of the first known infected humans; while Vincent – a man she had never met – was reflecting on certain life choices in a smoky hotel room (aided, of course, by alcohol and pills), she was making dinner for her father (chicken with asparagus and a mixed green salad – a healthy meal to combat his standard fast food diet).

While watching Letterman, her father told her of the sickly woman who had accosted him in a downtown parking garage. As though this incident was a barometer for modern society, he went on to gripe about a nation that could cause frail old ladies to become outlaws. Not wishing to instill any fear in his daughter, he did not tell her of the horrid stench surrounding this lady or the wicked scratch she left on his arm.

If he knew the implications of the scratch he had sustained, he may not have omitted it from his telling. If he had known, he may not have gone home that night. If he had known, he may have sent her away and eaten a bullet.

But he hadn't known, and so his omission caused her great suffering.

Having never known about her father's ignorance to the situation, she could only ever speculate on how he got infected. And despite all her attempts at remembering his smiling face and ludicrously cynical demeanor, she couldn't help but focus on the way she saw him last: the snarling, snapping jowls and empty, bloodshot eyes.

Pushing these unpleasant thoughts aside, she relinquished the grip on her locket and refocused her eyes on the scene below.

The soldiers – she couldn't help but think of them as such – had wrapped the body of their fallen comrade (or enemy, for all she knew) in a large sheet of clear plastic, creating a grotesquely translucent cocoon. Her stomach churned but she refused to look away, even when they rolled the cocoon off the back – it was mercifully swallowed by the mist.

Another man – cropped blonde hair with a matching fuzz covering his face – dressed in the same interesting combination of soiled camo and cotton, hopped from the box. The three of them exchanged tremulous sorrow. In perfect synchronicity, they bowed their heads.

She watched their dismal memorial with mounting grief.

Binoculars still in hand, she snatched her backpack and bolted – down the attic ladder, around the banister, down the stairs, through the hall and out the back door. She bounded off the stoop, through the slick lawn.

The truck's rear door was shut – the big man was climbing back into the passenger seat.

"*Oi!*" she squawked – her foot slipped into a pothole and she faceplanted into the mist – the impact forced a grunt and cleared the air from her lungs. She was vaguely aware of her proximity to the dead soldier's cocooned body.

XVI

The eulogy was brief – they did not know enough to make it any substantial length. In his honor, they vowed to never forget Webb's bravery in rescuing them and his continued protection from the dead and undead alike. In closing, this trio vowed to carry on this legacy of protecting one another until the end.

"And you must promise," began Vincent, addressing Louis and John, "to kill me the very moment I turn into one of them, if not sooner."

"I'll promise you that," said John, "if you promise me the same."

"Likewise," said Louis.

"Agreed," said Vincent.

"Agreed," said John.

"Then we have an accord," said Louis, grimly nodding.

They offered the soldier – Private First Class Christopher T. Webb – another moment of silence in his memory.

When this moment passed, Vincent sparked a cigarette and ambled toward the driver's door hanging his head.

After helping Louis into the back, John shut him in and started toward the cab. Climbing through the door, he heard a shriek and a grunt – he whirled and caught a glimpse of a falling figure. He whistled at Vincent through the cab, motioned with his chin and stepped back to the damp earth. He thumbed the safety of his rifle to the off position.

They started simultaneously around either side of the truck.

"Hello?" offered John, keeping his voice low. "Anybody there?"

The figure groaned, stirred.

He stopped in a shooter's stance with the rifle trained on the veiled figure.

Vincent stepped around the other side, similarly leveling his rifle.

"Show yourself," commanded John, his tight grip on the trigger.

The figure groaned again and rose out of the fog, onto all fours.

"Hello?" he offered again. "You best respond before I plug ya."

The figure – clearly a young girl, though not so clearly uninfected – coughed and hacked and wheezed and coughed. "Wait," she gasped, holding up a hand. "Don't shoot," she pleaded. "Please don't shoot."

"Well, shit," said Vincent, lowering his rifle – John lowered his as well. "It's just a girl."

"Yes," she said, looking up at them – her face, though dirty and red from the fall, was soft and pretty. "Just a girl."

Louis came up swiftly behind John, pistol poised. He stopped when he saw the girl.

"Have you been bitten?" asked Vincent.

She found the question to be queer. "What?" she asked, falling back onto her haunches.

"Have you been bitten?" he asked again. "Have you been scratched?"

"What?" she asked again. "Why would I be bitten?" She was now wide-eyed and panicked from all the guns and ruing her decision to seek their aid. "I don't understand your questions," she said, wanting to run but fearful they would shoot her. *Shoot me dead like the other one!* she thought, disregarding the anguish she had seen during their vigil. She raised her hands in surrender.

They studied her curiously for a few beats.

And then Vincent posed, "I take it you haven't been in contact with the lurchers."

"*Lurchers?*" she said, tasting the unfamiliar word.

"Lower your hands," said Vincent, tiring of her drama. "You look silly."

She wouldn't – her unsubstantiated fear wouldn't allow her to.

"You've nothing to worry," he said. "We won't harm you unless you're infected."

"*Infected?*" she said, still in bewilderment. "Infected with *what?*"

The trio exchanged puzzlement. And then Vincent asked, "You don't know about the infection?"

"It's a fucking epidemic," added Louis.

"Well," she said, "I know that *something* is going on." Her mind's eye focused on the image of her father's hungry eyes, his snarling face. She recalled, in perfect clarity, the growls and snarls as he chased her through the house and into the street. She could still hear the crunch and pop of his skull beneath the car's tire. "I just didn't know…" she trailed off – a tear rolled down her cheek.

"Do you live here?" asked Louis.

Another tear rolled down her cheek. "No," she said, beginning to sob. "I live down th-th-the r-r-road." Her breathing hitched repeatedly, causing her to stammer. "My f-father," she began – but the sobs were too frequent and she couldn't form the words.

"It's okay," said Vincent, stepping forward, wrapping her up in his arms. She accepted this stranger's comfort, clutching his jacket with her small hands and burying her face in his chest. Her eyes were bursting with tears. "You don't need to explain it right now," he said, rubbing her back.

John asked, "So you're sure you haven't been infected?"

"No!" she bawled into Vincent's chest. "I've told you already!"

"C'mon, man," Vincent murmured with a disapproving head-shake.

While he held Vincent's gaze, John mouthed, *What the fuck?*

Vincent read each word, but paid it little mind. "Is it safe here?" he asked the girl while glowering at his friend. "I mean, would it be safe for all of us if we needed a place to rest?" He held the glower.

John threw up his arms and mouthed those words again.

She nodded. And then she shook her head. Her sobbing had subsided, but the tears continued rolling down her wet face. She pushed away from Vincent, wiped her nose with her sleeve. "I can't stay here anymore," she proclaimed. "Can I go with you?" Her gleaming eyes and rosy, tear-streaked face – her slumped shoulders, clasped hands, crossed legs and heaving, hitching chest – begged for them to rescue her.

"Well…" began Vincent – he turned to his friends.

Before they could discuss or ponder this, she said, "You can't just leave me here! I'd be much safer with your protection." And, as an aside: "I'm just a girl." She lowered her chin and gazed up helplessly at each of them in turn – her shoulders remained slumped; her hands clasped; her legs crossed – and she added a childish swaying of her hips.

Louis said, "I couldn't very well abandon a young girl in Hell."

"Well, shit," sighed John. "I don't think I could either." Despite his reluctance, John truly felt for her plight. "Sorry to be so crass," he said to her, pursing his lips bashfully. "It's just been a rough few days.

"I think we can all understand that," said Vincent, nodding – he would have taken her along regardless. With a faint smile, he faced her again. "We'll take good care of you," he said, planting a firm hand on her shoulder.

XVII

Using a crumpled polo shirt found behind the passenger seat, Vincent cleaned the mess left behind from Webb's scattered brainmatter. Chainsmoking with a beer always in arm's reach, he was recanting the last few days for the attentive girl – Kathryn was her name, but she had asked that they call her Ryn (a self-chosen nickname that her father had refused to recognize).

When his story was complete – along with a mediocre mop-up that left the door and laminate flooring still streaked with blood – he tossed the spent shirt aside and took a seat next to her on the couch. "By the way," he said, "I'm Vincent." He offered her his hand, and she shook it. "And those two assholes up front are John and Louis. They're my brothers. Sort of."

"Are you, like, blood brothers or something?"

After chortling at her naïveté, Vincent said, "No, we've just known each other forever. We're good enough friends to consider one another brothers. Don't you have any sisters you're not related to?"

"No," she said, blushing and shying away. "I don't really have many friends. The ones I do have are more of acquaintances than actual friends. And they're probably all dead now anyway with what's going on out there." Looking back up at him, her blush fading, she said, "My father was my only real friend."

"Oh," replied Vincent, aware of the shaky ground he was traversing. "Don't worry," he said, silently pledging to protect this girl. "You've got us." He smiled at her and threw an arm over her shoulders.

Her face lit up. "You mean it?" she asked, giddy. "For realzies? You don't mind?"

Her discourse made him smile. "I don't mind at all," he said.

After a moment, he said, "So tell me: how'd you end up at that house?"

When she looked down, unresponsive, he said, "You don't have to tell me if it's too painful a subject."

"No," she said. "It's okay. If you can bare the painful truth, then so can I." Her eyes fixed on his cigarette. "But could I…" she pointed at it timidly. "Could I have one of those? It would really help me…focus…"

His eyebrows rose. "Are you sure?" he asked. "Have you smoked before?"

"I have," she lied. "Once."

And though he read her fib, Vincent surrendered one of his cigarettes. "I bet you're not even old enough to smoke," he guessed, handing her a lighter. And when she shied away, he said, "How old are you anyway?"

"I'm eighteen," she lied, sparking the smoke.

"Bullshit," said Vincent, correctly assessing her fib once again. "You're not a day over sixteen."

She blushed. "Fifteen," she disclosed, taking her first pull off a cigarette – she failed to inhale, but the smoke turned her face a light shade of green.

Vincent chuckled. "No shit?" he asked. "So young!"

She took another faux drag off the cigarette and coughed lightly. "How old are you?"

"I'm twenty-nine," he replied.

"Just a baby," added Louis – he had spun around to join their conversation.

"So sad," John murmured – only Louis could hear him. He did not elaborate on this.

"It's cool," said Vincent, watching her attempt to smoke. "I started smoking when I was eleven. I won't judge you. But if you're gonna smoke, you might want to inhale."

She looked at him quizzically, smoke drifting from her mouth. "What do you mean?"

Chuckling again, he held his cigarette before his lips. "You don't puff on it like so," he said, drawing the smoke into his mouth and pushing it right out. "You have to actually *inhale* it," he explained, drawing the smoke into his lungs and exhaling a moment later. "Just like that."

She looked at him curiously. And when she drew the smoke into her own lungs, she coughed it right back out, gagging and hacking – her face turned three more shades of green and she held the cigarette out for Vincent to take.

Tittering, he took it and snuffed the cherry on the sole of his boot.

When her episode was over, she looked contemptuously at his cigarette.

Amusement lingered at the corners of his upturned lips. He said, "Still think this will help you focus?" He waved the cigarette in front of her twisted green face.

She snatched his smoke, inhaled, held it, exhaled – and coughed only once. "I do," she said, powering through the discomfort. After a few tentative drags, her face grew sad once more. "So," she said – her mind awhirl with overwhelming memories.

Vincent sparked the cigarette he had snuffed.

She began slowly, telling of her last meal with her father. "I was in bed when he started just banging on the door, howling and clawing. I didn't know it was him – not at first. I was scared. I called for my papa –

I called for him over and over and over, but he never responded. I only heard the howling, the scratching.

"And then he opened the door and I could see it was my papa and he was sick. Very sick." She hitched, holding back the tears, the sobs. Her hand went to the locket. "I saw it was him that was howling. Even in the dark I could see that his eyes and face were discolored.

"He came right at me but tripped over my hope chest. I remember screaming and running as he chased me. I remember stumbling and falling and still he was chasing me, not concerned that I might have hurt myself – my father was always concerned if I fell.

"He was sick. Very sick." She hitched some more – a tear rolled down her cheek. She drew on the cigarette – a long, deep puff that filled her lungs – and did not cough or sputter. She exhaled and continued her story.

"I remember running out into the street, screaming and crying. He was stumbling – I think the sickness made him slow." She thought for a moment and looked at Vincent with gleaming red eyes. "That's why you call them lurchers, isn't it?"

He nodded solemnly, lips pursed, brow furrowed.

"Makes sense now," she breathed, bowing her head, smoking – she was beginning to enjoy the toxic smoke that was polluting her lungs. "He was unresponsive," she said. "I kept screaming at him to stop, it wasn't funny, it was scary, and he should just stop." Her youthful discourse was no longer amusing. "But he didn't stop. He kept coming after me, howling and staggering and swiping. I stopped in the middle of the road, screaming at him. I was screaming and screaming, and he was howling away, staggering after me.

"And then a car flew around the corner and smashed into him. It screeched to a stop and he was thrown about ten feet. The driver hit the gas when he was trying to stand up again and crushed him." She winced at the recollection – the popping of his skull sounded in her brain.

After a moment, she looked back up at Vincent with large, watery eyes.

He pulled her into his chest and she let loose with moist bouts of strident sobs.

XVIII

The daylight withered away, leaving a darkness that enveloped the world. Kathryn had cried herself to sleep in Vincent's arms and he now sat introspectively with a beer in one hand and a cigarette in the other. Her story had depressed him – had depressed each of them. And he now sat, exhausted and in pain – his hip was on fire and sending flashes down his leg and up his spine. He was wishing for more drugs when John hit the brakes.

"What's up?" called Vincent, his voice low – he didn't want to wake Kathryn.

"There's a wolf," said John, perplexed.

"Weird," whispered Louis – Vincent could not hear this.

"Excuse me?" replied Vincent, craning his neck.

Sure enough, a large, white wolf stood in the middle of the road, perhaps ten yards from the truck. It had stopped directly over the double yellow lines on a now-defunct railway and was staring at them. It was smiling – tongue out, tail up and wagging.

They watched it with mounting curiosity.

And after a few moments – John could swear it was staring directly at him – its head whipped around, no longer smiling or wagging. With one more glance in their direction, the wolf took off down the railroad tracks, into the forest.

Before he could release the brake pedal, a large gray-white streak – another massive wolf – zipped along the tracks after it. It didn't bother stopping to inspect the truck.

Breathless, Louis said, "You think they might be…?"

"Infected?" said Vincent. "I don't think so…"

"I hope not," said John.

Slowly, they started down the road.

Another awkward scene behind them, Vincent reclined once more. With true sorrow in his eyes, he gazed upon the girl as she slept silently with her head in his lap. And as he started drifting away, Vincent heard John explaining to Louis the route he had devised before the incident with Webb. He couldn't make out all of what John was saying, but he heard enough to know the plan was sound.

They were parked shortly thereafter, doors locked and backed into a mass of brambles that wouldn't allow a thing to open the rear rollup door. After locking up, John climbed onto the mattress while Louis stretched out on the linoleum. They chatted quietly about immediate plans and postulations regarding the world. Vincent tuned them out and fell asleep relatively fast.

An hour later, the truck was full of snores.

Day Six

Conjecture & Confidence

I

A cool summer breeze wafted in, tussling his hair – a current rippled through the sea of green that spread out before him. In the distance, amidst a lush forest, stood an ancient ziggurat, ripe with vines that cascaded down the massive feat of masonry. Something round and glimmering sprouted from its peak and he was drawn to it at an incredible speed.

Beneath his hovering feet, the field moved swiftly by – he could almost feel the blades of grass tickling his toes. The forest parted for him – it was enchanted, this forest, with all the fancies of youth – and he remembered, vaguely, pondering over the abundance of fallen leaves in summertime. But the forest quickly gave way to a flagstone path – this was when the gliding came to an end.

He was awed by the structure at the end of the path – how massive it was! The vines enwrapping the edifice were an intertwining of olive and grape – but he couldn't reach them, no matter how close he got. And when he leaned closer, he fell into a moat he had previously not seen.

The freefall was not so scary – he watched the water below quickly approach, but did not fear its imminent impact. Spread out and calm, he fell through the air, wishing only that he had been able to taste the fruits that adorned the mystical ziggurat above.

And when he hit the water, there was no splash, only a –

II

THWAP! – Vincent grunted and grabbed at his face.

"Ow." He groaned, rolling through plastic, onto his back.

Kathryn was snickering.

"Don't laugh," he groaned, sitting up. He looked around, a twisted grimace still plastered to his face. Gauging his current position to that of the awful floral couch, Vincent pieced together the events that led to his rude awakening.

And then he glared at Kathryn – the look was devoid of any true malice. Despite covering her mouth now, Vincent could see that she was still snickering. He stuck his tongue out at her playfully – and she returned the gesture, adding to it a grin.

A brief assessment of his faculties told Vincent of the pain, not only in his face, but in his hips, his knee, his arm, and the ache that had settled in the middle of his back. He shrugged and rolled his shoulders, stretched his legs and popped his neck – he shook his elbow, twisted his back and popped his hip. His brain was clouded with endorphins just long enough to make him believe the pain might go away.

He stood up and stretched toward the roof.

The truck was already in motion – John was driving again with Louis sitting copilot. Kathryn (or Ryn, as she so adamantly explained the night before) was seated in the doorway between them.

The cloud of endorphins started to recede, leaving in its place a deep, dull ache at the base of his skull.

He plopped down hard on the couch with a grunt and a grimace.

"Oh? And what's that about?" asked Ryn.

"You'll know when you get older," replied Vincent, knowing very well that his aches had more to do with a lack of drugs than his relatively young age. He also knew that she would buy this line, being that he was nearly twice her age and therefore must be ancient.

"But you're not even thirty," she said, proving his theory to be – in fact – incorrect.

"Trust me," he said, continuing his aged charade. "It's been a hard knock life." This, at least, was not false – though it wouldn't explain the deep pains now assailing his drug-deprived body. "Just be sure to treat your body better than I have mine," he warned inauspiciously.

She raised an eyebrow at him – and then her face lit up and she was distracted by a grocery bag at her feet. After moments of rustling, she tossed him a canned espresso drink and an entire bag of bagels. "Breakfast," she said with a smile.

Vincent couldn't fathom her happiness – the world was still chaotic and to top that off, he was in terrible pain constantly. But then he remembered that she was holed up in an attic by herself for days. He attempted a return smile, but it was weak and appeared insincere. "Thanks," he said, shaking the can, shoving the bagels to one side.

"Headache?" she asked, still chipper – more chipper than he could handle.

He nodded. "Mm-hmm." Cracking the can of espresso, he said, "It'll pass." He downed half the can, relishing the silky flavor of the coffee-milk mixture. When the aftertaste started to fade, he downed the other half. He crushed the empty can, tossed it into a corner by the rollup.

The truck slowed to a crawl – "*Holy Jesus!*" husked John.

Ryn gasped; Vincent knelt beside her.

Every house along this backwoods residential development was streaked with blood – most had bodies strewn about the front yard. Cars were smashed and overturned – and one was on fire, burning from the inside. If any dangers lingered, they were out of sight.

A gut-wrenching smoke drifted in through Louis' cracked window, choking each of them. He rolled it up, but much too late; they could smell burning flesh and hair and gas and oil and wood and clothing…

Somewhere nearby, a dog barked.

Somewhere far off, a crow cawed.

"This is just awful!" Ryn gasped – her eyes were welling up.

Vincent patted her shoulder, knowing the action could not soothe such a sight.

John maneuvered the truck through a blood-streaked lawn to avoid a large SUV that was lying on its side in the middle of this narrow road. He mowed over a series of bushes and crushed a row of perennials while uprooting a rosebush that got caught in the undercarriage – not like the homeowners would mind.

A minute later – beyond the housing development – they were stopped before a wreck they couldn't skirt.

"Shit," breathed John – he checked the mirrors, scanned the road, inspected the surrounding trees.

"Looks like a monster truck rally gone wrong," murmured Louis, staring at the lifted pickup that had apparently driven partway over a hatchback before landing on its side.

"We gotta move one of 'em," said Vincent.

John sighed. "Yup," he agreed. "Excuse me, doll," he said to Ryn, reaching under her legs for the rifle that rested there.

"Let me out," said Vincent, tapping her shoulder.

Ryn rolled into the back, allowing Vincent to climb through to the cab.

"You two stay here," he said to Louis. "Keep an eye out."

Before Louis – or Ryn – could respond, Vincent followed John out the driver's door with a rifle of his own in hand.

Sweeping their surroundings – eyes peeled, ears alert – the pair stepped cautiously toward the hatchback.

A light wind whistled through the cracked and twisted metal of the wrecked vehicles and rustled the bushes and combed the trees, knocking free some dead leaves of screaming yellows and pungent oranges. It tousled Vincent's greasy hair.

Something moved inside the hatchback –

BLAM! – Vincent fired instinctively before the thing could make a sound.

Glass shattered; a wiry figure slumped in the passenger seat.

Louis popped his head out the driver's door, pistol ready.

The figure in the car was small – a child – with pasty cheeks and red eyes. It was missing an ear and wearing – even in death – a perpetual snarl. It was covered now with a blanket of broken glass, but Vincent was focused more on the black, bloodless hole above the child's right eye and the blue spiderweb that radiated across its face. He couldn't help but think of the youth that was stolen so viciously from this child.

A well of rage sprang up inside, but he refused to lose his composure just yet.

"It's okay, buddy," said John, patting his friend on the back. "He was infected. Nothing you could do." But John, too, was fighting the urge to cry out. He started away before his weakness could show, distracting himself by scanning for danger that may have been drawn to the sound of gunfire.

They were able to pop the hatchback's standard transmission into neutral and push it into the shallow culvert on the northern side of the road, thus creating enough open space for the box truck to bypass the devastating wreck. Emotions would soon abate, but the memories would linger – for far too long, of course – adding to the already overwhelming cache. In time, these memories would boil over into blind apathy.

III

The Beatles' "Girl" was playing on the airwaves of infinite shuffle and repeat; the absence of this station's late disc jockey and his cool baritone was noticeable, but the music he left broadcasting throughout the region would fill the void quite well for some time.

But Louis had not turned on the radio to listen to music; he flipped through station after station, pausing on those that were still airing long enough to catch the general subject of each. Plenty had already gone off-air, and the news stations still broadcasting were no longer listing appropriate FEMA shelters – nor were they explaining how to kill the infected attackers. Nothing was said of the Quarantine Zones or the Army National Guard – everything they heard was one ostentatious theory or another.

Judgment Day! shrieked one station. *Armageddon! Repent!*

Unofficial reports are claiming terrorist activity, claimed another.

Another said something about some government facility in the

Northwest…

And one particularly hackneyed station claimed that North Korea, being the First Horseman of the Apocalypse, had breached a military compound in the Northwest and…

"Holy crap!" cried Louis, switching off the radio. "Fucking fanatics!"

On the couch, out of sight to those in the cab, Vincent shook his head, eyes wide.

John spoke slowly, contemplatively: "Do you think there's truth to any of those stories?"

"Which part?" Vincent posed sardonically. "The part about Satan's Army rising from Hell? Or the part about North Korean terrorists and government conspiracy?"

"Well," he thought about it. "Both, I guess. But mostly I wonder about the government conspiracy aspect."

Vincent scoffed at this. "I think it's crap," he said. "They're just playing the blame game right now, and North Korea's an easy target. Not to mention the obligatory religious response – but we'll save that for later." He lit up a cigarette. "But, hell," he said, through a cloud of smoke, "I guess this gives us a reason to nuke 'em now." The devious smirk that momentarily appeared was quickly replaced by a brooding frown. "I bet you we will, too," he said. "We'll nuke 'em just for the hell of it. Why not, right? Fuck the Geneva Convention when our countrymen are dropping like flies and becoming cannibalistic freaks." He took a long drag of his smoke and let it burn his lungs for just a moment before exhaling.

John snorted. "That's fucked," he said. "It's fucked because of how likely it is."

Louis chimed in: "We couldn't risk a backlash in such a weakened state."

"I don't know why you're all so worried about the government," said Ryn. "Or terrorists, for that matter. Look around you; we have far more pressing matters to worry about what with the world coming to a screaming halt and all."

Whirling in his seat, Louis said, "You watch too many movies, my dear. The world won't end just because of an epidemic – we've lived through some tough times, I doubt a little cannibalism will defeat us."

She retorted: "But law and order is gone. Just look at us; we're out-laws now." Her eyes flickered and her lips curled upward just a smidge.

Spying this devious glimmer, Louis said, "I'm sure you'll find the reality of being an outlaw is a far cry from the romance of novels and the silver screen. Hollywood has greatly embellished the glory of such a life."

After a beat and, seemingly off-topic, she inquired, "Do you think you killed people out there?" And when nobody immediately responded, she added: "I mean *healthy* people....Do you think you killed *healthy* people out there? *Living* people?"

After a beat, Vincent responded: "I'm certain of it." He swallowed hard his emotion. "I'm sure we all did."

Louis met his gaze and they silently bathed in the troubling secret that Vincent had yet to share with John – or Ryn, now that she was a part of them indefinitely.

"You know," she said, "you'd all likely be dead if you'd stayed."

"Yes," replied Vincent in a whisper.

"Wouldn't that be justice though?" said John.

"Would it?" she replied. "Would it really be justice?" Her eyes burned on the side of his head – the only part of him she could see from the couch. "Would I deserve to be alone in that house until I died of malnutrition or straight attrition? Because that's what would have happened had you never showed up." She was seething, but John couldn't see this.

"Our inaction probably wouldn't have killed you," he said. "But it may have saved innocent lives."

Vincent held up a hand to silence her rebuttal – he shook his head when she turned to him; *there's no need*, this look told her – *leave it alone*. Recent events had apparently affected John in ways none of them fully understood; inner turmoil was ravaging him.

Against his better judgment, Vincent said, "We cannot be entirely certain our actions helped or hindered anybody's life."

In his tumultuous silence, John wrung the steering wheel.

And all were silent for a while.

Speaking only to Vincent, keeping her voice low – all they could hear from the cab was an incomprehensible murmur between John and Louis (not that it mattered) – Ryn asked timidly for one of his cigarettes. Her lower lip was pushed ever-so-slightly out; her head was tilted a touch forward so she had to look up. She batted her eyes twice – a nearly comical (and fairly juvenile) accompaniment to her existing intimation.

Vincent chuckled at her faux pout. "I'd hate to get such a pathetically adorable young girl addicted to such a bad habit," he teased, relinquishing a cigarette.

"Hey now!" she gasped, theatrically taken aback. "Don't laugh at me," she whined. And she snatched the cigarette from him.

"I can't help it," he said; a lingering smile played at the corners of his mouth. "You just looked so ridiculous." He sparked his lighter before her poised cigarette – and she drew the flame to cherry the tip.

"Like a pro," he commented. "But hey," he said suddenly, his face washed of any humor. "Don't you be tellin' no cops where you got that smoke." He was completely deadpan, staring at her with wide eyes and straight lips.

She raised a quizzical eyebrow.

And he winked with a smirk.

From the cab came John's voice. He was saying something about Armageddon.

IV

In an attempt to diminish his various aches and pains, Vincent started drinking.

He was alone on the couch now, feet kicked up over one arm; Ryn had taken a seat in the doorway to the cab – she was studying mapbooks and idly conversing with John and Louis. And though he liked the girl (despite being nearly half their age, she seemed to fit with this trio as though she were their missing link), he was glad to be rid of her long enough to collect his thoughts. He was also rather fond of stretching out for a time.

Only recently had Vincent returned to his hometown from the grand adventures that taught him the art of killing a man without leaving himself suspect. And only once had he put this training to use. The man he killed was a dangerous political target that threatened national security, but he had known the man from his past – had, at one point, been close friends with the target.

His emotions on the murder varied from anger to remorse to pity to fear – and always back to remorse. But as the days went on in this new, hellish world, Vincent found it increasingly easier to stow these uncomfortable emotions in order to focus on the present, which was markedly more disturbing than the past.

A troubling image of the woman at the hotel flashed through his mind – *Shoot!* she had whimpered. *Please!* He shuddered, remembering how he shot her without a moment's hesitation and ran without a second look...The infection was still fresh – he wasn't yet aware of the true implications of the events unfolding – and yet he shot a living, breathing – *speaking* – human being. (At the time, he had no way of knowing her wounds were irreversibly fatal.)

And then he thought of all the others that had perished so recently: the man in the toppled Comanche at the lakehouse; H. Lee and Mark at the military outpost; Sanchez and Cooper just outside of Littlerock (though he couldn't be certain this pair had perished, he still thought of them as deceased); and Webb, even though Louis had pulled the trigger on that one. Each of these deaths weighed heavily on his shoulders. (He failed to realize that most of these deaths, including that of the young woman whom he shot in the hotel lobby, were not his responsibility.) Add to this all the lurchers he'd killed in the last few days – most recently, the child in the hatchback – and the burden was overwhelming. By his flawed tally, he counted only one life – albeit a fragile, youthful life – that he had managed to save. But this did nothing to assuage his feelings of grief and guilt. He thought, then, that keeping her safe would be the only penance that might possibly, in time, assuage his overwhelming feelings of inadequacy...he somehow failed to factor in all he'd done to keep his closest friends – his *brothers* – safe in the last few days.

As if to further compound this hopelessly futile self-deprecation of his, Vincent found his thoughts listing toward memories of Isabella. He pushed his mind toward happier memories of their trips; all the impressive views of rolling hills and vast tracts of farmlands and the endless coastline of the Pacific. He recalled, with fondness, their jovial banter regarding livestock and wheat fields. He could still see – with painful clarity – the expanse of her slight lips whenever her luminous smile would light upon her face; her cute and scrunchy nose; her radiant eyes. He could even hear – still, with painful clarity – the melodic chortle that so complimented her lovely mirth in times of such joy.

But now there was a hole in his life in the place where she had been. And it was his doing – or *un*doing, as it were – that ended them. All the brightness of his previous memories shattered at this. He guzzled some more beer.

The universe tends to unfold as it should, he thought with a silent scoff. And, as usual, this phrase did nothing to ease his depression. Nor could it stop the wells from filling behind his eyes. Sometimes he would try similar aphorisms: *you did what you had to*; or: *there are other fish in the sea*; or: *it's not the end of the world* (this one sent a morbid tickle down his spine on this occasion); or: *there will be water if God wills it*; or: *if it's meant to be...*all of which were frustrating and none did anything to ease his troubled mind. In the end, he reminded himself of this: *You did it to yourself, jackass.*

He sighed and shook his head.

In a futile attempt at distracting himself, he guzzled more beer and lit a cigarette. At least the nicotine would calm his nerves some. Though, he longed for something harder (of course); namely the pills, which had done the trick quite nicely, right up until the military confiscated them (right along with his last remaining personal effects). Even just some weed would have been handy right then – just a little bowl would set him right...But, aside from his addiction, the pills (or any opiate-based drug) would truly have helped with the sickness he felt; without the proper de-tox regimen, he was feeling quite a bit *off* this particular morning. His stomach was churning, and he felt a chorus of tiny aches and pains pep-pering his body – some old (from his reckless youth or unfortunate scenarios of the last few years), and some new (from sleeping so awk-wardly and infrequently as of late). But, with *far more pressing matters at hand* (to loosely quote Ryn), he was determined not to show this dis-comfort to any of the others.

He went for another drink only to find his beer was empty.

Apparently, he had been so lost in himself that Vincent also lost all track of time. So when the truck eventually slowed before a scene of gruesome and perplexing violence, he was shocked to discover how far they had actually traveled.

Mustering what little energy he had, Vincent swung his creaky legs over to sit up; his muscles protested all the way. He crushed his empty beer can, tossed it aside, and moved lazily toward the cab. One short step and he was there, kneeling beside Ryn and gazing solemnly out the dirty windshield. He marveled at the mass of Kevlar-clad bodies and bullet-riddled vehicles; small town militants, from the look of it all.

At one point, these vehicles had formed a tight, circular roadblock that stretched from shoulder to shoulder. The only gap in this roadblock (before someone had smashed their way through the middle of it) was a small path into a driveway on the north side of the road. Tall hedgerows flanked this driveway and completed the blockade. The *what* and *why* of this roadblock were quite the mystery. But it would seem that their ef-forts at blockading this road were trounced by a troupe with far better firepower or training...the military, perhaps. Or maybe they were trounced by the pure and simple willpower of survivalists; brave civilians who refused to fade into the ether without having put up a fight.

By whichever means they were trounced, it was evident that their ranks weren't compromised by lurchers. Too many bullet holes and blood; none of the bodies about this ringed blockade appeared to have been infected.

"So sad," sighed Ryn. "Why would anybody be so mean to other human beings?"

Louis replied, "The constant struggle for supremacy." He plugged a cigarette between his lips and sparked it. He spun the window's crank a half turn to roll it down just a notch. "Nobody's content with what they have."

"Who knows," said Vincent, "maybe they were infected." He knew this was not so; he just wanted to ease their minds (if possible).

"Whatever they were," said John, "at least we don't have to deal with them."

Maneuvering through a hole in the blockade, he crushed the helmet – and skull – of a militiaman (quite unintentionally, of course, as he had no other route). He winced (and almost reeled) as an image of the head popping like a grape flashed through his mind.

From the opposite wall of the blockade sprang a half-dozen men, all of whom were aggressively exercising their second amendment rights. (Not that the Constitution held much water in those days – if it ever would again.) Vincent was fairly certain that most of their weaponry had been lifted off of (presumably) dead soldiers. And he was curious whether the rest of their extravagant rifles and machine guns were ever legal at all for civilian use.

Despite the urge to plow desperately through, John recognized their vulnerability. Being in an unarmored vehicle with naught but factory safety glass between their faces and such large-caliber weaponry, John wisely hit the brakes. The truck's occupants swayed in time with this sudden stop.

Movement in his peripherals caught his attention; he whipped his head in that direction. Vincent, Ryn, and Louis all turned their heads a moment later, to see what had caught John's eye.

A pair of men now stood in the driveway (the house beyond was a dingy, gray split-level with blacked-out windows). The pair had emerged from either side of the driveway's flanking hedgerows. One was around Vincent's age, the other was a generation older – Vincent figured him to be father to the other.

The older *gentleman* (to use the term loosely) sported a paunch, but was otherwise thin in the extremities. He had long, stringy white hair surrounding a blotchy, bald dome. His upper lip curled back into his mouth, hugging the toothless upper gum line within. His lower lip – it was a craggy, cracked, and thin thing – did not curl in, proving that he wasn't completely toothless.

The younger one was thin; his hair was considerably shorter and darker – but equally unkempt. Just like his presumed father, his face was painted with three-day stubble. And though his lips were just as thin and craggy, they did not curl in from lack of teeth.

Both men wore stained white tanks under unbuttoned, olive jackets with blue jeans and hiking boots. A shotgun rested on the young one's shoulder; the presumed father – the paunchy fellow – held at his side a very large revolver. The latter – the older one, with the white hair and paunch – motioned for John to roll down his window.

John obliged.

One of the men outside the blockade gestured to the pair at the driveway. To Ryn, this gesture looked like some sort of baseball signal; *steal third*, it said; or *swing away*. Though, it was contextually obvious that this gesture meant something entirely different indeed – something unpleasant, if not downright sinister.

The paunchy fellow turned to the thin one and nodded; the thin one returned this nod.

Regarding John now, the paunchy fellow croaked, "Put 'er in park."

On the heels of this, the thin one squawked, "Shut 'er down."

John thrust the truck into park. But he did not *shut 'er down*.

The thin one drew a deep bellyful of air, thrust his head back, and screeched, "*Shut 'er down!*" He grasped the shotgun with both hands and fired into the air. Ryn nearly jumped out of her seat; the other three were rattled and taken aback, but none reacted quite the same. Based on the volume and recoil of this blast, John guessed that the 12-gauge was loaded with something other than the typical birdshot. It was probably loaded with lead slugs. *Or maybe worse*, he thought, wondering if it might be some sort of homemade shrapnel-based round (which would undoubtedly include a heavy lead ball at its center; such things were not unheard of in this region).

The paunchy fellow chuckled (John still hadn't *shut 'er down*, as the saying apparently went.) "Now," he croaked in his froggy, phlegmy voice – a voice which carried with it notes of a low-register alto who had obviously drank and smoked most of his life away. But the paunchy fellow – the *white skullet fellow* who was almost certainly a tweaker, from the looks of him – did not immediately continue. Instead, he paused to scratch his cheek with the barrel of his very large revolver. Nobody spoke during this moment and Vincent thought that maybe he could hear the prickling of steel on stubble. Though, this could have just been his imagination.

(He also thought of how ironically satisfying it would be to watch that revolver erupt in the paunchy fellow's hand while so close to his supposedly inbred brain. The thought was fleeting. And the revolver did not erupt, much to Vincent's dismay.)

"Y'all're gonna do what m'boy says," continued the paunchy fellow. "It's in yer best int'rests to do so."

Vincent marveled at this man's stereotypical hillbilly accent; an accent which was uncommon to the region — no matter how deep in the backwoods one might venture. He wasn't sure, but thought that maybe it was Southern. He also wondered if it was a genuine accent, or if it was affected, and whether the paunchy fellow's missing teeth played into this accent.

With these inconsequential questions rolling through his head, Vincent glanced out the windshield. The half-dozen men out front were now filing in through the gap in the blockade. He was discomfited in their vigilance; not a single rifle barrel wavered from the cab of this truck.

The paunchy fellow's voice dropped a touch, but his volume was still ample; "Don't look to them for assistance, *boy*," he said, speaking directly to Vincent. "They'll kill you dead in three seconds if your friend don't kill that engine."

Vincent smacked John's shoulder.

But John was already reaching for the key.

After the engine was shut off, the paunchy fellow croaked, "There's a good boy." His voice was a tad more jovial then.

From the corner of his mouth, Vincent said to Ryn: "Stay down." He was timorous of what this bunch was after. "They'll leave us alone if we just play along right now."

Once inside the barricade, the six other militants split around either side of the truck; three around the passenger side, three around the driver side. One man from either trio continued around back and out of sight while the remaining pairs stopped just short of the cab's doors. Moments later, the rear latch was thrown and the rollup door opened. Vincent whirled at the sound.

"Nobody else back here," said one; he was a slightly shorter near replica of the thin one in the driveway. But his voice wasn't nearly as squawky, and he was slightly heavier around the waist – not much, though, as he still had the scrawny build of a tweaker. He even wore similar garb; the only difference was the Pantera shirt he wore beneath his olive jacket.

The other one – same olive jacket, but of no immediately discernible relation to the rest – said nothing. He held a cold and menacing gaze and kept his rifle trained firmly on Vincent.

Great, thought Vincent, *we're gonna get cooked and filleted by an inbred family of tweakers.* He wondered where their wives and sisters – or cousin-daughters and sister-mothers, or whatever other complicated and depraved female relations they might have – were at. He loathed the answer to this, should he ever find out. (He hoped he would never find out.)

The paunchy fellow spoke again in that froggy voice of his: "I'ma need y'all to get of the truck now." And when they didn't immediately obey, he said, "Now don't make me tell you twice."

The men outside the driver's side approached. One of them – a scruffy fellow with a long, dark goatee and longer curls that spilled out from beneath a green-and-white trucker's cap – opened the door. The other one – a scrawny kid of maybe 20 years with a shaved head and sores like mishappen pepperoni covering his face – remained a few steps back. The barrel of his .22 waggled; his eyes were wide and wild, and Vincent noticed the extreme dilation of his pupils. He was high as a kite – had probably done a line of some shitty, homemade meth right before this encounter – and looked as though he might inadvertently squeeze off a round at any moment. Vincent only prayed that, with his faltering aim, the bullet would go astray.

"Why don't we just shoot 'em right now?" said the scruffy fellow.

"Don't go gettin' all trigger happy on me, now," said the paunchy one. "We ain't tryin' to kill nobody here. Just collectin' our dues for them passin' through our land is all." His thin, craggy lips cracked into a broad – and obscenely false – smile. But his cheap words – and cheaper grin – fooled nobody; they were obvious sociopaths, made all the worse by the drugs. Without some luck, they wouldn't be leaving this property alive – if they left it at all.

Someone appeared around the driver's side, from behind the truck; Vincent recognized him as the man who was of no immediately discernible relation to the rest. From a sheath on his hip, he produced a large bowie knife. "I want to feed their faces to the *herd*," he said. His was the first voice that wasn't overly laden with the permuted and pervasive hillbilly bumpkin accent. But his vicious words betrayed any shred of affluence that may have been conveyed on this seemingly educated accent.

"You'll get yer chance," replied the paunchy fellow. "Now," he said, elevating his voice to address the occupants of the truck, "I want y'all to disembark in an orderly fashion."

"What do you want with us?" John demanded. "Why don't you just let us go about our business? We're all just trying to survive out here."

The paunchy fellow allowed him the space to speak – surprisingly so with how obtrusive he'd been thusfar. And when John was finished, he said, "The way I see it, without the tyranny of our socialist government oppressing their ways upon us anymore, this here plot of land has since been liberated by the Brothers of the Prairie – which is us – and is now under our control. By rule of the land, then, it is at our discretion to charge a toll for anybody crossing said land. But with the American dollar now worthless, we ask to be paid in blood. If we don't receive our requisite payment, then we'll kill you. 'Tis the *law of the land*." His craggy lips parted again to reveal his near-toothless grin. The teeth that did remain were yellowed and ringed with black rot. They looked as though they might fall from his face without notice.

Vincent wanted to laugh in the man's face – would have, had the situation not been so dire – for his attempted eloquence. Everything the paunchy fellow had just uttered sharply contrasted everything he exuded – from his demeanor and dress to his feinted hillbilly bumpkin accent, which was accompanied by the mushy lisp of a near-toothless man. Despite wanting to laugh at all of this, Vincent recognized the perilous predicament in which they now rested. "Do as he says," Vincent whispered – his voice was lost in fear; a shaky husk of its normal amplitude. "Don't worry," he said. "We'll figure this out."

"Y'all ain't figurin' shit out," snarled the scruffy one. "Now get the fuck out the truck." He reached in at John –

But John smacked his hand away with a glare.

(Vincent was sure the wily kid would shoot him then.)

When nobody shot him, John slid off the vinyl seat. The men (or man and boy, for the kid, after all, was no more than 20 years) gave him way with a step back. But from his blindside – from the frontside of the truck – came an older, portly fellow with long, blonde hair and a beard that rivaled this in length. He held his machine gun high, butt-first above his head. He brought the stock down – hard – on the side of John's head. The blow sent him sprawling at the boy's feet, but he did not lose consciousness.

"What the fuck was that?" cried Ryn, and she was out the door in a flash. Before Vincent could react or climb out after her, the portly fellow snatched her by the hair and shoved her to her knees. She wailed and thrashed and clawed at his arm, all of which seemed to excite him further. He yanked her head back and stared down at her with hungry eyes. His low, keening moans – or growls, perhaps – were enveloped by her seething cries and groans.

And then he said something vile to her, but his words were drowned out by Vincent's voluminous shouts: *"Get your fucking hands off of her, you sick fuck!"* He wasn't quite out the door – his head was barely outside – when the riflestock connected with the side of his head. (He should have known this would happen – he *did* know it would happen – but chivalrous bravado took hold of him when the portly fellow snatched Ryn by the hair.) He fell onto John, who was still a writhing heap at the feet of the sore-faced kid.

Louis was extracted from the passenger side by a gruff hand. This one was fit; he was broad at the shoulders and trim at the waist (but not tweaker-thin like the others). And though Louis was broken and put up no resistance, he, too, received a riflestock to the head.

V

Through his concussed haze, Vincent was vaguely aware of being dragged across pavement and gravel, and eventually through damp, cold grass and mud. He tried to make use of his legs to ease the drag – especially across the coarse gravel – but found the task too difficult to manage; neurons were obviously cross-firing. He was thankful, then, when the convoy came to a rest. Though, he wasn't so thankful of being released so violently or the sickly sensation of his throbbing noggin bouncing off the earth, no matter how soft and soggy it was at the moment.

Of his companions, he was by far the most coherent.

What he could tell of his immediate surroundings upon coming to rest in this yard: John was to his right, moaning quietly through semi-consciousness; Louis was to his left, lacking any consciousness at all; two men were hovering over him, a treeline at their backs; three more men were somewhere beyond his feet, a gray split-level with blacked-out windows at their backs. And though he noticed all this through blurry, bleary eyes, he had trouble making sense of it all. After a few brain-rending moments in which Vincent could scarcely recall who or where – or what – he was, a crow cawed above and he remembered it all at once. (Strange, yes, but that's exactly how it happened.) Stranger yet, his brain somersaulted around an obscure sort of situational-association (the cause of which mystified even him) and he croaked one word: "*Ryn*." His voice was cracked and raspy.

"No," said one of the men (through his haze, Vincent couldn't tell who had spoke). "That there's a *crow*." He spoke as if addressing a small child. And then one of the men (presumably the man who had been speaking) raised his rifle – *CRACK!* A muted, wet thump of something hitting soft earth a short distance away followed the gunshot. "And now it's a *dead* crow," said the man.

Vincent found himself smiling grimly up at whoever might see him. "That there's bad luck," he croaked. He added a feeble chuckle that quickly deteriorated into a bout of choked coughs and spurs.

"Shut up!" barked one of them – a steel-toed boot connected with his ribs, knocking the air from his lungs. Gasping to replenish his newly depleted air supply – his chest rattled uncomfortably – he wondered if any of his ribs had broken from the impact.

A distant shout (the unmistakable mushy croak of the paunchy fellow): "I told you not to kill them yet!"

"I didn't!" was the hollered response from one of the men. "I just shot a damn crow!"

"Well don't do that!" shouted the paunchy fellow. "I got business in here, and your damn ruckus ain't helpin' me get it done!"

"Sorry, Uncle Pete! Won't happen again!"

The paunchy fellow – *Uncle Pete* – mumbled something inaudible at this distance and ducked back out of sight. Vincent heard a door shut – a slider, from the sound of it. But just before it snapped shut, he heard the shrill cry of a girl in pain. And the only girl around was Ryn...

Business? thought Vincent with scorn – and he knew at once where to find Ryn. He rolled around, clutching his belly, but really he was taking stock of his captors and friends. John was coming to; his eyes were open and gazing blankly at Vincent. He blinked intermittently, trying to regain focus. As for the captors, none were really paying much heed to their prisoners. The only one watching them was the man with the bowie knife. Vincent could feel this man's eyes crawling over every curve and line of his face, plotting the course for his knife's future incisions. Two of the others were jabbering about the crow; and the remaining pair was arguing over something while gesturing toward the house.

Vincent clenched his eyes, clutched his belly, and lightly groaned, feigning more pain than he actually felt. His mind was awhirl with fleeting escape plans and combative countermeasures. But even with John's aid (which he wasn't certain he would have any time soon), two unarmed men against five gun-toting, knife-wielding militants was a bit lopsided – and not in their favor. And since it was almost certain to be just him combating these captors – while concussed, at that – then he was ready to resign himself to defeat.

If it weren't for his overblown survival instincts which screeched at him to fight through this, then he may very well have done just that: resigned. As it was, his mind wouldn't cease maneuvering about options for survival, no matter how farfetched they may have been. He was trying to quiet these maneuverings when one of the men started briskly away from the rest – toward the house.

The man nearest him – the portly fellow – snatched at his jacket, but he pulled away with ease. The others, with the sole exception of the quiet one and his large knife, started after him, as well. "Where you goin'?" the portly fellow barked at the scruffy one.

"To get mine!" replied the scruffy fellow, sharply. "I ain't waitin' around like some jackal while they get the good parts. Y'all would be wise to be rid of *them* and join me."

"But we're not supposed to kill them outright," said the kid with the sore-splotched face as he stepped over John. He raised a finger to one of his sores and started picking at it, quite unconsciously.

"Then don't," said the scruffy fellow, still marching away. "I'ma get mine before it's too late."

That phrase entered Vincent's head with ferocity. *Before it's too late*, he thought with a start. He sat up at once, and was met by a glowering set of hungry eyes – the man with the knife.

"Whatcha thinkin' there, champ?" said the man. He spoke casually with calm, evenly spaced words.

Vincent felt his face redden at the sudden and unexpected confrontation – but he replied at once: "That I might hurl." He clutched his gut and reeled toward the man, puffing his cheeks in a false pre-vomit fashion. The man backed away in revulsion.

And Vincent struck without hesitation; a quiet thrust with his thumb to the man's throat. The man, choked from the crushing impact to his trachea, gasped noiselessly. His defenses down (however temporarily), Vincent plucked the knife from his groping hands with ease. With a quick flip and thrust, he jammed the blade into the man's throat. Blood sprayed and, thinking on the fly now, Vincent unholstered the man's gun, leaned into the spray, and screamed.

The other *hillbilly fucks* (as Vincent now thought of them) whirled at the sound. He knew what it would look like to them, standing at a distance, with their accomplice's back blocking any true view.

One of them said (Vincent thought it may have been the portly fellow), "Oh, what the hell, Richard? You're s'posed to wait for Pete." He continued mumbling, inserting obscenities here and there, as he trudged through the wet grass.

Vincent bided his time, wishing for a pointblank belly shot. But the man – it was, indeed, the portly fellow – noticed something was wrong while still a few paces away. "What the hell...?" his words dragged out as he unslung his rifle from over his shoulder.

BLAM! –he would never speak again as a round from Vincent's newly acquired pistol ripped through the man's throat, hence silencing him once and for all (well, save for the choked gurgles as the portly fellow asphyxiated on his own blood).

The shot caught the others off-guard, but this lapse wouldn't last long. In retrospect, Vincent realized that killing these men, though armed to the teeth with hard calibers, was far easier than taking on a horde of half their numbers; headshots required far more accuracy than center mass. And, with a ghost of this thought subconsciously controlling his aim, Vincent fired three shots in quick succession, all of which landed squarely in the chest of each of these men – one even landed a heart shot, though Vincent had little time to take note of this.

Feeling the urgency of his situation, Vincent pushed through the man whose throat he had slashed (Richard was his name), and took off toward the house. Running faster than he had in years, Vincent traversed the expanse in seconds. He stopped at once when he reached the back porch, and sidled up to the house, his back flat against the siding. The rear slider was within arm's reach then, but he waited.

Cries from inside produced a tight heat in his chest – his breath hitched and caught at the thought of the scene within. Something shattered – it sounded like a lamp – and Vincent thought that for every scratch he found on Ryn, the paunchy fellow would receive one major reprisal. Not to mention what he planned on doing with the blade when all this was through with and only the paunchy fellow remained. (He *prayed* that the paunchy fellow wouldn't die outright in the coming minute or two.) The waiting killed him; moments dragged torturously onward as he listened to the commotion within the house.

The slider opened a moment later, and Vincent could hear Ryn's cries at full volume now; she was just inside that door, no more than a few yards away. His heartbeat galloped, his chest grew tighter – his face was hot with fury.

The man that opened the door was not the paunchy fellow, and for this, Vincent thanked the Universe. Nor was this man suspecting an ambush. Vincent thrust the pistol upward, under the man's chin (he was the near replica of the thin one – a supposed spawn of the paunchy fellow) and – *BLAM!* – painted the underside of the awning with his brains. As this man's body fell to the cement, Vincent stepped over him and into the house.

Directly before him was the paunchy fellow, his back to Vincent, and his drawers at his ankles. Ryn's squirming form was just beyond his, stripped of all her clothes. She was bent forward over an awfully outdated floral couch, her face forcibly buried in one of the pillow-back cushions.

Vincent's eyes tracked movement in one corner; he lifted the pistol and, with a cursory glance at the man in the corner (his pants were also at his ankles, his member stiff and pointing excitedly at the ceiling), and squeezed off another round – *BLAM!* – that penetrated yet another heart.

By now, the paunchy fellow was beginning to turn. Dropping the pistol to the floor, Vincent strode right up to the half-naked, inbred *fuck*, and buried the large knife into his swollen belly. With a hand on the paunchy fellow's shoulder – Pete, this fellow's name was Uncle Pete – Vincent pulled him in close and thrust the blade deeper still into his belly. The embrace looked nearly loving, if the observer (of which there were none, other than Ryn) could discount the blood. The tension on Vincent's face slacked as relief washed over him; his chest loosened, as well. Uncle Pete, however, tensed at once, his face contorting into a shocked grimace.

Vincent was reminded of that day in Vancouver – the day he killed Konrad. The man's belly was softer (Konrad's had been firm and fit), but the action was nearly identical. Granted, the situation was far different, and Konrad had indeed struggled some, whereas the paunchy fellow (Uncle Pete, to some) seemed to merely accept it without a fight.

Vincent was thankful that Pete – this disgusting pig of a man who was irreverently named for a saint – did not immediately succumb to the wound by either death or plain unconsciousness. It was his desire to make the paunchy fellow suffer for his actions.

VI

The paunchy fellow – *Just call me Uncle Petey*, he'd said to her – fell to the floor in a heap at Vincent's feet. The knife remained in Vincent's hand, and dripped blood on the dirty-brown carpet. The scarlet droplets melted away on contact, and were only discernible by a slightly darker spot of apparent wetness. Ryn would be sure to avoid that spot when she stood.

But she was far too aware of her own nakedness to do more than curl into a ball on the couch, covering what she could of herself. Vincent saw this, and he plucked a throw from a nearby recliner and draped it – oh-so-gently – over her nakedness. And then he returned his attention to *Uncle Petey*. She watched as he dropped to one knee and dragged the flat of the blade across *Uncle Petey*'s face.

Ryn ignored this as she wrapped herself and rose from the couch. She snatched up her scattered garments from the floor, cursed and spat at the prone figure of *Uncle Petey*. And then she retired to an adjoining room in order to dress. Not a word had been exchanged, yet, between herself and Vincent. But she saw something in his eyes before retiring to this room – some animalistic hunger. She sensed his dark energy and was grateful for it, thankful that his dark side saved her from violation.

And then the scream; it was bloodcurdling, at first, and ended in a muffled whimper. All subsequent cries were muffled as well, and she wondered just what Vincent had done to her attacker (and purported rapist, had he been allowed to continue in his actions).

She dressed with a touch of haste and curiosity (however morbid it may have been). Once redressed, she wore signs of her struggles: a mildly torn tee and jeans that were now missing the primary button (though her zipper still worked and she still had her belt – *thank the heavens!*). And when she returned to the desecrated family room she found Vincent standing over the shrouded body of *Uncle Petey*. Blood had yet to soak through the shroud (it was a heavy quilt of blues and reds). But he was clearly dead and Vincent was hiding his corpse from her.

"What did you do to him?" Ryn heard herself ask.

"Nothing I should admit to in polite company," Vincent replied. "Let's go. There's nothing left for us here – if there ever was anything to begin with." He thrust an arm around her shoulders, tenderly, and led her out the rear slider, not caring one bit to close it in their wake.

Ryn cast a fugitive glance at the blood-spotted sheet, another at the dead body in the corner, and stepped cautiously over the other dead body that stretched across the threshold. Still guided by Vincent, they emerged into the cloudy, midday suffusion of light.

CRACK! – the sound reached them with surprising volume. John, across the expansive yard, held a smoking rifle over the corpse of the portly fellow. He moved languidly toward the next body – this one writhed in a feeble attempt at backing away, with one hand over his chest (covering the gunshot of Vincent's well-trained marksmanship). *CRACK!* – another round to another head, and this one stopped squirming. He did this a third time – *CRACK!* – and all three were now irrevocably lost to the world.

And we're better off for it, thought Ryn with malice.

Louis was sitting up now, cradling his broken arm against his chest.

Vincent continued on without hesitation toward the truck, gently pulling Ryn with him. After her recent encounter, she had an instinct to draw back from his hold; but she corrected this thought process and leaned into his embrace, instead. Without him, she would have been violated. She couldn't imagine just how he'd managed the rescue, but she was thankful – *to all the heavens!* – that he managed to pull off such a courageous act (or, rather, *series* of actions).

She allowed him to usher her into the back of the truck (after a quick glance within to check for danger). She instantly curled on the couch and awaited his return.

VII

"You okay to drive?" Vincent said to John.

Louis was still woozy, and John was aiding him across the lawn. "Yeah," he replied. "Never been better." The sentiment was overladen with sarcasm. But Vincent knew that it was fairly true – at least that he was capable of driving, anyhow.

And Vincent had no immediate desire to drive.

Together, they assisted Louis in climbing into the passenger seat. Once he was comfortably settled (relatively so), John closed Vincent into the back with Ryn, and climbed in (once again) behind the steering wheel. It took him a moment, but after a quick consultation of roadmaps, he started off down the road.

It was only by a stroke of luck that they found the forest road gates standing wide open, thus allowing them to continue along their backroad route without any fussing or fiddling with the locks themselves. This was fortunate, considering they had no bolt-cutters, none were proficient at picking locks, and, though it was large, their truck was surely inadequate for ramming such a heavy gate – irreparable damage would undoubtedly result of such an attempt.

And from this fortune, they soon found themselves cruising along the tightly packed, bumpy gravel roads that cut through a thick forest in the hills. From the recent rains, the roads were muddy and slick, but John's extensive driving experience – which included many mudding and rally excursions in various vehicles – helped him keep control while maintaining a steady, yet relatively swift pace.

Granted, not a single one of them (save for John, and even then it was in a limited way) paid this fortune any notice. They hardly registered anything; they managed balance only by instincts as their minds where all preoccupied with the terribly recent and most unsavory events.

So it was that when they crested a hill overlooking a clearcut valley with a fair, unrestricted view of Mount Rainier, only John noticed the scenic beauty spread out before them. But again, this was only in a limited fashion, as he was still troubled with thoughts of sadistic hillbillies. Without warning, he pulled the truck to a stop amidst the predictable smattering of shotgun shells, tarnished bullet casings and broken glass one might find at any roadside campsite.

"What's up?" called Vincent from the couch.

"Two things," replied John. "First, I gotta piss. Second, we should probably eat. Maybe figure some shit out, too." He jammed the gearshift into park and climbed outside. After opening the rollup door, he stepped behind a tree, discharged his bladder.

Louis was coming out of his daze some. A cracked version of his voice floated from the cab: "I don't think I can stomach anything right now."

"Me neither," murmured Ryn.

Vincent nodded slowly. He stood and hopped out the back door just as John was returning. "Why don't we give it a minute?" he said. "To eat, I mean. They're kinda beat-up in there."

John's brow furrowed and he looked displeased. But he said, "Yeah. We'll give it a minute."

Vincent climbed back inside and sprawled out on the mattress. John closed him in and returned to the driver's seat.

Ryn was curled into a corner of the couch, gripping her locket tight. Vincent wanted to comfort her, but didn't know how. He figured that it might be best if he just let her be. And so he did.

Fifteen minutes later, John cursed and eased the truck into another litter-strewn pull-off. Once the truck was in park, he started wrestling with the maps. The mad crinkling of paper drew Vincent forward. John was muttering mostly obscenities under his breath.

"What's the matter, boss?" Vincent asked. He tried to sound casual, but thought he came off as patronizing.

"Must have made a wrong turn somewhere," he replied in a huff. He cursed some more, and another folding map fell from the midst of the one he was currently wrestling.

Vincent picked it up and started to unfold it.

"Oh, that's the one!" John dropped the open map and snatched the other one right out of Vincent's hands. He immediately tore into it (not literally, though).

Louis sighed. "I'm gonna water the foliage," he said. He seemed to muster some energy from somewhere deep within before reaching for the handle. While climbing out, he used the open door to steady himself. His lack of balance was certainly a sign of a serious concussion.

Vincent recognized this. And then he wondered what signs he might be displaying. He noticed that John, having taken a much more fierce beating, wasn't displaying any of the classic signs of concussion. But he knew that John wouldn't display any such signs; such was John; quite the embodiment of thick-headedness.

Ryn breezed by Vincent and through the cab without a word.

Staring after her, he said to John, "Wish I could help you." He watched her march off into the forest and marked her path in case he had to fetch her on the fly. "I wasn't exactly paying attention to where we were," he said.

"I'll get it," John grunted.

Vincent slipped through the cab and out the door. His feet crunched on gravel and shotgun shells. After a brief assessment of his inner workings, Vincent decided he'd better urinate as well. He followed Ryn's path for a few paces before veering off behind a cluster of trees.

Through the thicket he watched scant sunspots dance along the valley below. The sky was mostly overcast without any immediate threat of rain, though Vincent could see the haze of scattered showers in various far off locations. A pair of hawks mingled above a clearcut – he smiled when their strident screeches reached his ears. To him, the sight of hawks along one's journey signified good luck. And though their luck had not been very swell as of late, he became suddenly optimistic about the remainder of their travels.

Just thinking about how foul their luck had been wiped the smile from his face. He finished his business, zipped-up, and returned to the clearing by the truck. He found Louis there, propped up against a tree at the far side of the clearing. Vincent thought he was panting until Louis coughed and spit a chunk of something at the ground. And then he noticed the puddle of vomit at Louis' feet.

"You alright there, buddy?" Vincent asked as he patted Louis' back.

Louis spit again. "Yeah," he said. "I'll be fine. Just got a little nauseous is all."

"We should probably get some food in your belly," said Vincent.

"Yeah," breathed Louis. "Probably." He scrunched his face.

"Let's start with water." Vincent started for the truck just as the driver side door popped open. "Yo, John," he said. "Wanna grab me a bottle of water, please?"

John said nothing; he whirled, rummaged around in a plastic sack, and came back out with a large bottle of water. "There ya go," he said, tossing the bottle to Vincent while sliding out the door.

Vincent uncapped the bottle and handed it to Louis. "Don't drink it too fast," he said, knowing full-well that Louis already knew this and would do whatever he damn-well pleased. He turned back to John. "You get it all figured out?" he asked.

"Think so," John replied. "If we follow this around we should be back on track before long. This road intersects with the main one again. It's just a longer route, is all." He looked around at the clearing, the forest, the glimpses of valley beyond it all. "Beautiful," he said.

"Hmmm?" Vincent was caught somewhere between keeping an eye on Louis and worrying over Ryn; she'd been gone a while now.

"Couple summers ago," said John – he wasn't concerned whether anybody was paying attention; he was simply voicing his sorrowful nostalgia. "Came up here with Lucy once. We camped out there some-where." He waved a finger at the valley beyond the clearing, beyond the trees. "Couldn't tell you where, though; we took a random side road, blazed a small trail and posted up in a little clearing by a creek." He paused, smiled – a tear stung his eye. "It was beautiful."

Finally hearing John's words – and recognizing them for what they were – Vincent set a concerned eye on him and placed a comforting hand on his shoulder. Lips pursed, he released an empathetic sigh – but he did not speak, understanding that no words were required of him at that time.

They watched the sunspots dance – the hawks mingle – until Louis retched on the tree again.

"It's okay!" Louis proclaimed at once. "I'm okay. Just drank too fast. Don't worry about me."

Vincent believed him – they both believed him. But Vincent re-gained some immediacy to his previous concerns of Ryn. *How long's it been now?* he thought. "Hey," he said to John. "You watch him. I'm gonna check on Ryn."

John looked around real quick, as though just noticing her absence. "Yeah," he said with a nod.

"Thanks, bud," Vincent said. He slapped the bottle cap into John's hand. "Be right back."

VIII

Ryn hadn't gone off to *water the foliage* (as Louis had so eloquent-ly referred to the act of urinating in the forest). The truck had begun to feel claustrophobic, and she had escaped to the solace of nature. Living in the boonies for all her life, she had developed a tight bond with Mother Nature, and had often run into Her arms in times of distress. Seeing as she had grown up mostly friendless (and motherless), Ryn had found many such occasions throughout her life. At times, she had even chosen the cold embrace of Mother Nature in winter over that of her father, whose hold was a far cry from cold, no matter the season. Even at such a young age, she recognized that the serenity and balanced chaos of the world could bring a person back to center when out of alignment.

—A possibly interesting fact: such early revelations resulted in Ryn frightening the piss out of countless babysitters when she was younger. Her disappearances often followed an argument or disciplinary action in which Ryn was upset enough to run off – into the comforting embrace of Mother Nature. Most of these babysitters cited her reckless abandon as warrantless heartache, and would quit after only a night or two of watching her. This led to her father staying home more often, and thus the reason he'd never remarried (though she wouldn't piece together this logic for many years to come – and without the possibility of corroboration, it would remain pure supposition, regardless of how apt a theory it was).

Just as the snarling image of her father's infected face split the image of his kindly smile, a twig snapped behind her. With her locket still gripped firmly in one hand, she whirled on her haunches, brandishing a tire iron. She wasn't really expecting an attack, but she also wasn't about to let her assumed sense of security undermine her actual safety. She wasn't surprised to find that it was Vincent who had snapped the twig; he was trudging her way through the thick underbrush.

With her assumed security ratified, she returned her distracted attention to the valley below.

"You're okay?" she heard him say.

She shrugged. "Sure," she said, barely loud enough for him to hear.

He hesitated, uncertain of how to proceed; she sensed his discomfort. And from the lack of rustling ferns and twigs, she could tell that he had stopped walking her way, apparently uncertain of whether to approach her or not. After a few beats, he said, "Looks like you're fine." Leaves crinkled as he turned to go. "I'll leave you be."

"No," she said, whirling back around on her haunches. "You can join me. Might be nice to have company." Her lips smiled at him, but her eyes were still frowning.

"Kay," he said, and slowly trudged the rest of the way. He knelt beside her and gazed out at the valley. After a moment's observation, he withdrew a cigarette pack from his breast pocket. He waved the pack at her – she nodded – and he lit two of the smokes. "It really is a bad habit," he reminded her while handing over one of the smokes.

"Yeah," she said. "I know."

The hawks were still circling in the distance. Their shrieks echoed up the walls of the valley. For a time, the only other sound was that of the wind in the trees and underbrush (and the occasional, barely audible sizzling of their cigarettes whenever they would pull another drag). And then, as if on cue, Vincent's mind rambled back through these hellish days, before he'd become a murderer, to a time, not so long ago, in which he was happy. At least, he believed he was happy back then. But if he had been so happy back then, why had he felt the need to rile things up so badly? By his own actions, he was robbed of his life. Hindsight was no help in this respect; if anything, it highlighted his flaws and brought into question his motives. To this very day, he still couldn't identify his exact motives, let alone justify them. The entire debacle of the last year mystified his sensibility.

"Thank you," she said suddenly. "I don't think I told you that yet."

This startled Vincent out of his dolor. And then, "You're welcome." He didn't know what else to say.

"Did John help you?" she asked, still uncertain of how he'd pulled off such a daring rescue.

"No," he replied. "Managed it all on my own." He replayed the scene in his head, marveling at himself as it played out. "Wow," he said. "I *did* do it all on my own." He gazed somberly at her. "I don't think I was thinking straight when I did it," he said. "I don't remember one coherent thought until we were back in the truck."

"Impressive," she said. After a couple beats, she thanked him again.

He nodded in response. "You would have done the same thing for me," he said. "I hope."

She looked him up and down with a shrewd eye. "Maybe," she said at last. "Depends on the situation, I guess."

"Wouldn't want you to strain yourself," he said.

The silence that followed did not, for once, assail Vincent with deprecating thoughts of self-pity or guilt – nor did he think about the phantom aches and pains or his lack of pills. This was the first silent moment in a long time in which he was thinking about something other than his faults; he was thinking about how he had *shined*. Saving Ryn had seemed to save a piece of his soul, if only a small piece.

And then it was he who broke the silence next: "I'll do everything in my power to make sure I never have to do that again." He felt quite resolute in his tone and manner of conveyance of that statement.

Ryn smiled – and this time her eyes smiled, too. "Likewise," she said. She released the locket and hugged Vincent. She planted a wet one on his cheek and stood up. "We should probably get going," she said.

"They'll be worried about us." Before starting away, she dropped the remainder of her cigarette and crushed it into the damp earth.

With a pleasant smile touching his own face, Vincent flicked away the cherry of his cigarette and stamped out the embers. He pocketed the butt, picked up the butt of Ryn's discarded cigarette, and pocketed that one, too. Then he stood and followed her away.

"Thanks again," she said as they walked.

"No sweat," he replied.

She caught the irony and giggled lightly at it.

                                    IX

Back in the clearing, they found John and Louis leaning against the side of the box truck. John was smoking a cigarette and drinking one of the canned espresso drinks. Louis was pallid and still gripping the water bottle. He had drunk over half since Vincent had departed and returned.

"How ya feeling there, champ?" Vincent asked him.

"Oh, you know," Louis began. "Doin' just fine. Got a slight head-ache and my elbow's a bit *throbby*. Other than that, though, I'm doing quite well." He gulped at the water. "But seriously, man: don't call me *champ*. That's just weird. You sound like a pathetic stepfather who so desperately wants to bond with his new son. Want me to start calling you *Vinnie*?"

Vincent chuckled. "Glad to see your sense of humor wasn't lost."

"Everything okay with you two?" John inquired.

"Yeah," Ryn replied. "Just had to clear my head and find a way to put it back on my shoulders." She shot a smile at Vincent. "Wouldn't have a head to speak of without my Knight in Shining Armor, here." She latched onto his arm at that.

Vincent gave her head a curt pat and pulled free of her embrace. "Thanks for that," he said. "But I just did what I had to do. If I hadn't, we'd all be dead by now."

Louis murmured, "Or mutilated and *wishing* we were dead."

"Thank you, Vin," John said. "We all owe you our lives."

"Y'all don't owe me shit," he said, his face now red (Vincent was never very good at receiving praise). "Just don't make me ever do that again."

"Like we wanted any of that to happen," commented Louis.

"That's not what I'm saying," huffed Vincent. "You know what I'm saying…"

"Don't go getting all hot and bothered now, Vinnie," gibed Louis.

Vincent glowered at him momentarily.

But before their banter could persist, a hungry groan floated down from the hillside.

"Damn it," blurted Vincent – and he rolled his eyes and sighed.

"Load up," said John.

After latching the rollup door behind Vincent and Ryn, John reclaimed the helm. And, still being cautious of Louis' condition, John was adamant about him returning to the copilot seat; he was afraid Louis might get too comfortable in the back and doze off, which was an obvious no-no for a concussion victim.

Just as the truck started rolling, something smashed into the side of the box – a shrill shriek was startled out of Ryn at this unexpected *bang*. In the sideview mirror, John watched the lurcher bounce off the side of the truck and grope after it as they trundled away.

For hours, this lone lurcher – a scraggly logger wearing ripped flannel and a yellow hardhat – would continue after the truck that had long since left it in the dust. It would stumble along until the twinkling of a campfire in the trees would draw its attention off the road. Soon after, it would feast on an unfortunate camper. Before this man's final breath – before the lurcher's rotting belly was filled with this man's flesh – the camper's girlfriend, who had been *watering the foliage*, bludgeoned it with a massive rock. The girlfriend would die – and subsequently turn – from kissing her infected boyfriend before he passed.

So it goes.

X

They traveled along a dusty road that twisted them about a valley and the surrounding hills. Overhead, there was a breathtaking canopy of screaming reds, pungent yellows, and palpable greens. When the rain started, the pungency of the conifers became especially palpable. Save for the occasional clearcut (and the rocky road with its various trash-littered pull-offs and campsites), the scenery was very nearly devoid of man's footprint. It was a beautiful, iconic Washington landscape.

But despite the serenity of it all (which was hardly visible to the pair in the back – not that they would have paid it any mind anyhow), Vincent became a little anxious for an end to the bumpy ride. He had been silent for quite some time – all of them had been. And, not wanting to bother Ryn in her fragile state, he had just lain there upon the mattress while his own mind was assailed by torturous thoughts of his shady past as well as a series of *what-ifs* regarding their recent encounter with the blood-thirsty, inbred, would-be rapists.

Unsure of how much time had passed since their last pitstop (it felt to him like a good while), Vincent was ready to be done with the uncomfortable, teeth-chattering ride. But his discomfort paled in comparison to the reels of disquieting thoughts that were streaming through his head at breakneck speeds.

After a cursory, yet concerned, glance at Ryn – still curled up on the couch (and clutching her locket with tears streaming quietly down her cheeks, though all Vincent could see was her back) – he crawled toward the cab and stuck his head through the doorway. His gaze shifted between John and Louis, and he posed the question to either: "Where we at, fellas?"

To which John harrumphed and shook his head. "I think we're lost again. Thought I made the right turn back there, but I'm getting the feeling that we're backtracking now."

"Shit," hissed Vincent.

"You got that right," murmured Louis.

Vincent checked the dashboard clock: 4:19 p.m. He wondered where all the time had gone; the hours had slipped away from him. "We oughtta stop and refuel," he said, referring to their bodies, not the truck.

"Yeah," agreed Louis. "I could eat now."

John sighed. He pulled over at the next roadside campsite. "I'll open the back," he said. "You wanna dig out that camp stove?" He opened the door and hopped out before Vincent could formulate even a simple response. Not that a response was entirely required; John's question was mostly rhetorical.

Vincent rummaged about the grocery sacks until he found the stove and propane. It was a single-burner, collapsible job; a rather remarkable convenience store find. When folded, it looked like a segmented, triangular hunk of metal with a spout and tail. The legs twisted out around the spout, which acted double-duty as the center post. The "tail" was the connecting hose that fastened to the propane bottle. Vincent set it up just as John was running the back door up on its tracks. The truck was flooded at once with daylight.

"You wanna get it going?" Vincent asked. "I'll grab the –"

A pair of grocery sacks was placed in his lap as Ryn took a seat beside him. Her eyes were red and puffy and her lips quaked here and there, now and then. "Soup sounds nice," she said. "Maybe some ham and potato." Her breath hitched as she stifled a sob – and her lips quaked some more.

"Thanks," said Vincent. He stroked her shoulder. "And yes, ham and potato sounds great."

Using the small camp pot they'd also found at the Littlerock convenience store, John heated up two large cans of ham and potato soup. Ryn and Louis split the first batch; John and Vincent split the second. Plain whitebread was also served. Ryn passed on the bread.

During his post-meal cigarette, Vincent cracked a beer. "What be the plan, folks?" he asked. "I feel as though we're hopelessly lost out here. Do we push on? Wait 'til morning light? It's gonna start getting dark in the next couple hours. And it'll be full dark in about three."

"Plenty of time to reach the summit," said John.

"Barring any obstacles, of course," said Louis.

"But that's true for any day now, it seems," countered John.

"Three hours is kind of a tight limit," said Louis.

"I'm up for whatever," said Vincent. "It's guaranteed to be rough going regardless of when we go. But Lou's right: at our current rate of travel, three hours is kind of a tight limit."

Louis nodded. "It'll definitely be rough going. And I'd rather not get caught outdoors after dark. And not just because of the *lurchers*," he said the word with spite and undertones of uncertainty. "After what we went through today, I'm a bit trepidatious of the *people* we'll find out there." Again, he spoke with spite (understandably so).

Ryn visibly cringed at the reference.

"And yes," continued Louis. "I'm aware that we're currently outdoors. But we're not really out here with them. Not like back in town. Or even on the highway. Not too many people out here; none that we've seen so far, anyway."

"We saw that one," John said feebly.

"Yeah," said Louis. "One whole *lurcher*." He flashed a wan scowl at John. "But, like I said, I'm more concerned about *mentally* infected people and being caught in their backyards at night. They'd have the upper hand, for sure; we don't know the lay of the land out here."

Vincent thought about how terrible it would be to be confronted by more militants in their current location – at a bottleneck on an unfamiliar forest road. He decided against voicing this thought for fear of unsettling Ryn – and then he pushed it right out of his head. Instead, he said, "I say we get back on course and see what time it is. Then we reconvene this committee."

John snorted at this. "Committee," he mocked. "Some committee we are."

"Whatever we are," said Louis, "Vincent's got a fine point. Let's unstick ourselves before making any decisions."

John shrugged. "Sure," he said. "Can't really argue with that logic."

XI

With Vincent as the new copilot, John continued feeling his way through the forest. And after a few more wrong turns, they discovered just how far off track they were. A familiar sign for Elbow Lake told them they had just done a large loop. Well, to be more precise, one large loop comprised of a great many smaller loops. But regardless of how many loops they made – or however big or small they were – they found themselves back where they had started. Or near enough (it would seem) to their original point of entry. Realizing this considerable loss of time and energy (and fuel), Vincent cursed their avoidance of highways and standard surface streets.

Together in the cab, the truck idling patiently – and their companions waiting equably in the back (Louis was settled upright at one end of the couch, his good arm sprawled at length across its back; Ryn was seated at the other end, curled into herself with her knees up to her chin and her locket clutched tight in one hand) – he and John quickly triangulated their position. And thus they resumed their journey.

And with some pride at having regained their footing on this taxing leg of their journey, Vincent found he could properly navigate their travels with only minor difficulties. (He began to see how John had lost their way in the first place.) But they weren't very long into these travels again – crawling slowly away from the impending sunset, as it were – when the sky appeared to darken a touch. The dashboard clock read 5:13 p.m. Still around an hour until sunset, and already it was gloomy. Or so it would seem. Vincent aptly attributed some of this gloom not only to the heavy cloud cover, but also to the overshadowing canopy of the sky-scraping foliage.

They rolled along the narrow forest roads; up and around, down and about, crunching over gravel and cutting through mud. Sometimes an angular sunspot would break through the clouds and play upon the forest's natural beauty. A glowing, golden leaf; a shimmer in a puddle; a shifty lattice of shadows that played across the road – and the general wetness of it all highlighted the lovely, colorful chaos of Mother Nature in all Her splendor and glory.

"It'll be dark before we're outta this mess," mumbled Vincent.

John sighed. He could only pilot the truck so fast down these roads. For one, it was wider than most vehicles, which made it tough to maneuver around many corners. And secondly, the rain had turned the dusty gravel road to mush. The mud was so deep in some places that both pilot and copilot were certain they'd get bogged down. But they didn't. And then, with the last shreds of light falling toward the unseen horizon behind them, they rolled up the crest of a hill that overlooked a grand dam. John eased the box truck into a rather convenient pull-off.

The decision was quickly – and unanimously – reached that they would stay put for the night. Nobody had the will or want to press on any farther, and not just because of the darkness or dangers. All had become travel-weary over the course of the day. Add to that the stress of coping with their collective near-death experience, this foursome was utterly kaput. They barely found the energy to fire up the stove. They boiled hotdogs and, having no buns, wrapped them in whitebread. Thankfully, someone (John) had thought to add a bottle of ketchup to their inventory when looting the convenience store back in Littlerock.

"We're gonna have to resupply pretty soon, I imagine," said Louis over dinner. "Probably tomorrow, if possible."

Even with four mouths to feed, they could make their rations last another couple days without having to starve themselves. But, using water for cooking as well as hydration had greatly diminished their supply. Other than that, they were all starting to feel a bit grimy and wanted to grab some basic essentials. (In the throes of haste and fear, not one of them had thought to pack a toothbrush, even.)

With an accord having been reached and silence having reformed, dour faces returned to them all. But John wouldn't have it. He sparked up a cigarette and, in a blatant attempt to keep the past at a distance, he started off on a tangent about modifications to the truck. His ideas ranged from small details – like a mechanism that allowed the rear rollup door to be latched, unlatched, or locked from within – to outlandish additions of a crow's nest that housed a human turret who could fire guns or arrows or fling knives or rocks or Molotov cocktails in any direction.

"Or maybe slits in the walls to shoot or stab through," added Ryn.

John apparently approved. "Yes!" He was very nearly really excited – moreso, actually, by the fact that Ryn seemed to be coming out of her daze. "That's a great idea. And a lot simpler, too."

"Yeah," said Vincent, dragging out the vowels to sound like the boss from *Office Space*. "About that *human turret* thing…not sure it's the most feasible of ideas there, buddy."

"Whatever, Vin," John said dryly. "You know you'd chuck cocktails from a turret."

"Yeah, Vin," said Louis. "Just because it's not feasible doesn't mean it's not a fun idea."

Vincent raised an eyebrow at either of them. He chuckled lightly and a corner of his lips rose in a wan smile. "You got me there," he said. "Speaking of arrows, though…we might try to acquire some."

"You know how to use a bow?" inquired John.

"Not yet," replied Vincent. "So the sooner we grab one, the sooner I become proficient." He punctuated this with a smart smirk.

"We'll get right on that," said John.

"It would be a good skill to have," Ryn interjected.

"Agreed," said John. "But we'd have to settle down somewhere relatively comfortable in order to properly practice."

"Well," said Ryn, "I foresee the four of us settling down somewhere quite comfortable in the near future. We're not too far from Paradise here. Should get there by midday tomorrow." She added a perfunctory nod to this.

"Barring any obstacles, that is," commented Louis.

"Don't jinx us!" Ryn bawled.

"I'm just sayin'," said Louis. "It just seems as though we can't get two feet without something shitty happening to us."

"Don't be so pessimistic," she said.

"It sure does seem to be so," said Vincent. "But I think we'll be fine." He really didn't think they would be fine.

After a little more conversation, they all decided it was time for a restroom break. Once outside, they scattered to the four corners of the map. Being full dark by then, none strayed far from the truck. They reconvened by the cab, where Vincent volunteered to keep watch. Referencing their lack of security on the previous night, he recommended that they begin nightly watches. Nobody argued this. Louis opted to join him. John protested this, but lightly; he was tired. And he acquiesced without having put up much of a fight on the matter. But when Vincent suggested a higher perch (i.e. the roof of the truck), both John and Ryn balked. Again: they were too tired to put up a fight. John eventually helped Vincent boost Louis up top. And then he boosted Vincent.

(Louis promised he could make his way back down just fine.) Then John handed Vincent a grocery sack with a couple bottles of water and a box of granola bars.

"Would you hand me up a snatch of that heavy plastic, as well? And maybe a couple beers?" Vincent asked. "I'ma fashion a couple ponchos – in case it rains." This quelled any befuddlement or querulous looks. Moments later, he had a hefty snatch of the industrial plastic that's been littering the truck. And a pair of beers.

"Be sure to wake me up around midnight or so," said John, once they were settled. "You'll need some sort of sleep tonight."

"I'll try to remember that," Vincent replied. "But I make no promises." He flashed him a wry smile.

"Or don't," said John with a shrug. "But I ain't carrying you when you pass out on the road." He climbed into the cab before Vincent could retort. The truck swayed and jounced with his movements.

With a smile, Ryn wished them a good night and climbed in after John. She pulled the door shut behind her and crawled through the door to the couch. "Thank you for taking me in," she said to John. "I know you probably aren't so hot on the idea of a little girl tagging along with you. But I'm happy you took the chance on me."

"You're welcome," replied John. "I'm happy to help." And then, as a deflection for any further thanks or praise, he said, "But you'd better start pulling your weight if you wanna continue to tag along."

She giggled good-naturedly at his gibe. "Will do." She smiled with a warm heart and fell asleep within minutes – long before John began to doze, despite his weary body and bleary brain.

XII

They sat atop the roof of the truck — atop the box — with their feet dangling over the cab. The dingy white metal was a little slick from rain and it wet their pants at the seat, but none too bad. And, of course, a light sprinkle started falling from the sky shortly after they got settled.

Vincent was cutting plastic with the knife he lifted off the sadistic militants. Louis was aiding him in his limited way; with only one functional arm, he could only do so much. (His busted arm, splinted ramrod straight with ice scrapers and cheap medical tape, throbbed uncomfortably as it rested on one knee.) The finished products weren't exactly the most fashionable, but they were serviceable. After helping Louis into his, Vincent donned his own.

"That was a right fine idea, Vin," Louis hailed. He watched (with admiration) as the rain beaded off the heavy plastic. And then, quite casually, he wondered aloud: "What do you supposed this was used for?"

"From the size, shape, and condition of it," Vincent replied, "I'd guess this was the inner wrapping of a sofa. And I'm guessing the couch and mattress in there are haul-aways from this truck's last job."

"Haul-aways?" said Louis.

"It seems quite obvious that this was a delivery truck," Vincent explained. "And I'm betting that on one or more of their last deliveries, the deliverymen of this truck exchanged the new furniture for the old. And that means the couch and mattress in the back of this truck would be somebody else's trash. The term for such an exchange is a 'haul-away."

"How do you know all this?"

"Remember when I used to work for that furniture store?"

Louis had an obvious moment of consternation. But then a mental light flipped its switch and he nearly exclaimed: "Oh yeah!" And then, a bit more subdued: "Damn…that was a while ago."

"Yeah," said Vincent. "I think I was nineteen or twenty. Wasn't even there a year."

"I remember that," said Louis; his eyes were focused beyond the physical world, searching the past. "I think I recall you calling your boss a *stupid bitch* – if not something worse."

"*Stupid bitch* sounds about right," said Vincent – he also believed his words may have been a bit harsher in the moment. "But it's not just that; she came in and switched everything around in a day, and tried to tell me how to run my warehouse when she had no idea how to properly organize furniture by priority, size, and weight."

"You're getting a little hot on the matter,' said Louis. "You know, after all this time, one might think you'd be over it."

"I'm over it," Vincent said defensively. "Just explaining the circumstances as they were." He popped a cigarette between his lips – any suavity that may have been pronounced on any normal occasion was hampered by the awkward cut of the homemade poncho. He sparked the cigarette with an equal lack of suavity.

They conversed idly for some time, reminiscing about the past. But eventually, as always, the gravitational pull of weighty matters drew them into a darker realm of conversation. Louis wanted more answers to the shady areas of Vincent's recent history. "You left me high and dry, man," he said. "I was prepared to shut down the business – we'd discussed that already. But you bailed all at once and without a word."

Vincent hung his head and shook it dismally. "I was in a bad place. The way he laid it all on me, it felt like a grand adventure. Like maybe I'd be making a difference in the world. I just had to get my hands a little dirty, was all." He thought hard for a moment. "But that doesn't excuse me ditching out on you and our business. Nothing does, really. It just *is*, at this point."

"I guess it is," breathed Louis. "I'm not sure how much it really matters anymore, either. Everything seems to be crumbling around us. But I still have this nagging feeling in the pit of my stomach that wants to know *why*."

"I don't know why," replied Vincent. "It's almost like he put a spell on me or something. I knew it sounded crazy – I should have reported him at once. But something inside said *do it*." He flushed and went momentarily dizzy. *Something inside* did *tell me to do it*...He had started on the pills before Tod had requisitioned his services. In his drug-addled mind, the idea had been almost romantic.

Vincent leveled a wary gaze at his friend – his *brother*. He went right ahead and blurted it out: "I was so high it sounded almost romantic." There: all of his dirty laundry was out to dry in Louis' front yard.

And Louis just nodded. After a few long beats he said, "I had a feeling." He paused a moment longer, eyes locked on Vincent's. "You still using?"

Vincent felt his face grow hot and hoped that Louis couldn't see this in the dark. "No," he said, his voice small.

"But you were," said Louis. "What happened? You run out when the Army snagged our shit?"

"Yeah," sighed Vincent.

Again, Louis just nodded.

"I'll never do them again," Vincent proclaimed.

"Sure, Vin," said Louis.

"You've every reason not to believe me," said Vincent. "I don't exactly have the best track record. But if there's one surefire way to open a man's eyes to the world, it's the fear of imminent death. And we're constantly surrounded by any number of imminent deaths now."

Louis made no move, no reply – he wasn't even nodding.

"I promise you, Lou," he said, clapping Louis on the shoulder. "Never again, as long as we both shall live."

"I'll try to believe you, Vin," said Louis.

"I hope you do," said Vincent.

After a weighty silence in which they smoked and finished up their respective beers, they returned to some semblance of normal conversation. Every subject they touched on was carefully worded so as not to return to any unsavory subject. Eventually, they even began to feel mildly uplifted, despite all the world trying to crash down upon them. And their conversation began to reflect this.

At one point, Louis even announced: "After all that we've done and seen, brother. After all that: this is our lot in life. And if this is where we're supposed to be in this world, then I say we grab hold of our destiny and ride it out, kicking ass all the way and living up to our full potential. After all, we are strong people – all of us are, even that girl (you can see it in her eyes). And, in my humble opinion, not even Armageddon can keep us down."

Vincent chuckled and nodded at this and threw an arm around his brother's shoulders (mindful not to rattle the right one). "You sure got that right, brother."

Purple light forked the eastern sky soon after, and both would wonder where all the time had gone. Still, they did not wake the soundly sleeping pair inside. Neither felt the Sandman's Spell that night.

XIII

Somewhere along their back path, an exhausted young man parked his bicycle in a clearing and climbed a tree. Resting now in the tree's tentative embrace – using a heavy sweater as a pillow – this young man munched on trailmix and sipped water until his heavy eyelids could no longer stay open. The bag of trail mix slipped from his hand during his nap to scatter about the earth below. A squirrel would find some of the nuts and gorge itself until scared away by a wandering ghoul. Sensing the young man's presence, this ghoul would mill about, groaning, at the base of the tree until a rumbling in the distance would draw it away. The young man posted in this tree would not know of this ghoul. But he would curse himself when after finding the trailmix scattered below.

So it goes.

Day Seven

Prophecy of Man

I

The dawn was bright and beautiful. Somewhere in the night the rain had ceased and the clouds had dispersed, leaving scattered remnants of the former overcast. Yellows and pinks and oranges cascaded across the otherwise featureless blue sky. As the blue faded from the darkness of night into a light aqua, the contrasting shadows encasing the far hillside – not yet touched by this day's light – darkened to the deepest green upon which either man had ever laid his eyes.

"Stunning," breathed Louis.

These tendrils of light that painted the sky a multitude of intermingled colors rendered this pair silent for nearly an hour. During this early hour, the colors gradually melted from the sky, the clouds morphed and moved and mingled. Two cigarettes apiece were burned upon this perch throughout this period. And eventually a rustling came from below; the truck shook a bit, shimmied a tad.

John emerged from the driver side, curious, confused. "You two still alive?" Despite the typically lighthearted nature of this phrase, it now bore a worrisome weight. Cautiously, he craned his neck up and around. He spotted them on their perch.

"Yar," said Vincent. "Never got tired." His breath came out in plumes.

"Any sign of trouble in the night?" John stepped to the ground and lightly shut the door.

"Not one bit of trouble," said Louis. "It was cold and rainy, but otherwise uneventful."

"Good," John croaked through a crunchy backward stretch. "Very good," he said, righting himself. "Maybe this is the spot for us," he said sarcastically while casting a dismissive glance about the surrounding woodland.

"Right," replied Vincent, matching the sarcasm. After slipping out of his improvised poncho, he slid off the box onto the slippery roof of the cab. Keeping his footing required a touch of delicacy. "Let's hope and pray that we get through today without too much trouble."

"No shit," said Louis, still seated and unwilling to join Vincent atop the limited surface of the cab for fear of overcrowding the small and slick surface. Once Vincent was safely on the ground, Louis slid carefully down so as not to jar his busted elbow. With some aid from his friends, he made it safely – and relatively painlessly – to the ground.

"First things first," said Vincent. "I need some coffee and grub." He yawned.

Louis then yawned, big and loud.

And before either's yawn subsided, John added his own contribution to this cacophony of inarticulate vocal resonation.

Once the a-melodic chorus was finished, Louis responded to Vincent's earlier statement: "Dude, I'm feelin' ya there. My belly be grumblin'."

After a quick morning munch, they took off down the hill with John at the helm; Ryn sat copilot while the pair of night watchmen sprawled out in the back. Sleep came easily for this tired pair, despite having refueled their bodies and minds with food and caffeine. Before reaching the far side of this quaint dam, they were snoozing soundly in the back.

Pilot and copilot were in awe of the natural beauty growing all around them. Rising on either side of this shimmering reservoir were hillsides of old conifers with a smattering of multicolored foliage. Fluffy clouds – large and small – speckled the cerulean sky and drifted slowly to the south.

They rounded a corner and a glimmer caught their eyes.

Slowing the truck, John locked his door. Ryn followed suit by locking her own.

A short distance down the road was a state utility truck; it had apparently careened into a tree at the bottom of a steep dirt road and was now blocking their path. The fated driver of this truck, having been ejected through the windshield, was motionless on the hood, his skull crushed from impact with the tree.

"Just push through it," Ryn said shakily. "I'd rather not get out here."

Nodding, John did just that: he rolled their bumper up to the rear fender of the wrecked utility truck and eased the accelerator down until both vehicles began to move. As he made room for their passage, a deranged utility worked crashed into the passenger door, its eyes were red and lifeless. It tried the door handle.

Ryn shrieked.

John floored the gas.

Louis and Vincent sat straight up from their very brief rest.

"What the fuck?" cried Louis, having woken up from a particularly disturbing dream of angels and devils and a most frightening vision of his own death (it's amazing how fast one's subconscious can conjure such imagery). He patted himself up and down, reassuring his troubled mind of his continued state of terrestrial life and cognition.

The utility truck slid out and away (the fated driver was flung to the ground) and the deranged worker was left in a cloud of dust. John then slowed a bit and, by careful manipulation of the rear-wheel drive, he expertly slung the box truck around the very corner the utility truck had skirted in its final voyage. Being on the floor, Vincent was flung into the couch in this sudden maneuver.

"I thought you said the night was uneventful!" cried John.

"It was," Vincent replied while pushing himself away from the couch.

"Then when did *that* happen?" he thrust a thumb over his shoulder.

"When did what happen?" he asked.

"That damn wreck!" cried John. "The one we just broke through!"

"I know nothing of any wreck," said Vincent; he looked at Louis. "Do you?"

"Not at all," said Louis. "What the fuck's going on?"

"It's okay," said Ryn, her heart still thundering. "Just another scene. Just another..." she trailed off.

John grumbled unintelligibly to himself – Ryn couldn't even make out his mutterings.

Vincent looked curiously at his agitated friend for a moment before lying back down.

Visibly wearing distress upon his face, Louis remained seated a moment longer. His breaths were quick and ragged, his heartbeat elevated. Topping the startlement of his rude awakening, his mind was still flooded with angels and demons and the troubling image of his own demise. With an effort – after a time – he laid back down, but his troubled mind would not rest.

John drove up the hill along a narrow dirt road that cut through a dense wood. A few minutes later, they were out of the thicket, off the dirt and onto the paved highway that could lead them anywhere they saw fit.

When he spotted the jackknifed semi that blocked their eastward path, he said, "We're not out of the woods yet," not entirely unaware of the irony as they were finally back on a major thoroughfare – back on a state highway.

Louis sat up again; from the couch he caught a view out the windshield. However feeble his view was, he could clearly see their path was blocked.

(Vincent remained half-conscious on the mattress, unable to lift his exhausted body, and was therefore unable to see the jackknifed semi. He pondered John's previous statement, understanding the irony of it as the bumpy gravel road gave way to pavement, but was still curious as to the catalyst for such a statement.)

Swooping, loopy skidmarks sketched the pavement for dozens of yards before the toppled semi. The mangled trailer had leveled the fence of a small utility station. And, using this station's driveway as a detour, John managed to find a safe route around the wreckage. Something told John that this jackknifed semi and the utility truck at the reservoir were connected in some way.

His postulation was absolutely correct.

A ghoul came shambling out of the trees on the south side of the road and continued shambling after the truck as it trundled away.

At a bend in the highway, they passed a rundown, rickety storefront. Someone had painted large red crosses over the peeling façade; the windows had been painted over in the same red paint (John was praying that it was paint and not blood). Smoke was billowing from the old building's rusty chimney.

Inside the storefront – the business office for a salvage yard – were four men, two women and three beheaded corpses. The men were covered in the blood of the fallen (two of these men were unknowingly infected from bloodsplatter); the women were covered in a matching hue of actual paint. All six live bodies were huddled together, kneeling before a wood stove, heads bowed in silent prayer. Sitting between them and the stove were the three infected heads of their fallen colleagues and compatriots, all of which were still seething and snapping, despite having been detached from their bodies – none groaned, however, as they no longer had vocal cords. The remaining members of this group would, by morning, all fall prey to infection.

So it goes.

"Please," said Ryn, "just get us the fuck out of here."

"Workin' on it, love," replied John, matching her fervor.

And then Vincent found the strength to sit back up. "What's goin' on?" he asked.

"Nothing," said Ryn. "This place is creepy as fuck is all."

"Gotcha." He collapsed back onto the mattress. Within minutes, he was sleeping again.

II

A moment of tranquility for the passenger –

Heavy shadows cut with bright interstices striped the road black and orange from early morning sunshine that glimmered off the lake. The trees, mere silhouettes that flitted by, gave the view of this lake a choppy film noir quality; glitters and glints of reflected sunlight strobed between these flitting silhouettes.

The sky above was a beautiful bright azure, speckled with scattered white poufy clouds floating here and there – in the east the horizon was slowly melting from orange to blue. The treetops were stretching upward, swaying in the wind, waving at the passing clouds.

Soon, there were no more trees lining this highway. The view, now unobstructed, offered a languid expanse of water – a crisp cerulean mirror tarnished only by scattered ripples – set before a series of vibrant rolling hills. A stump-speckled isthmus jutted out into this lake.

And then it was all gone as the highway looped them around a park and spit them into farmland – but the lake was still near, its scent remained heavy on the wind.

The sights afforded this young woman planted a smile on her face as all unpleasant thoughts and images drained from her – proof to mankind's willing shortmindedness and selective ignorance in times of great distress. The vessel for this girl's selective ignorance was the everpresent craving for distractions, particularly those offered by Mother Nature's persistent aesthetics. This particular girl also had a weak heart for water and sunrises.

III

"It's nice to see the sun again," commented Ryn, still wearing her peaceful grin.

"It sure is," John responded absently – he remained on high alert; his eyes continually scanned the road for obstacles and potential threats.

After two miles of smooth sailing, they came across a large tract of grassy farmland that stretched across the hillside. It was near the end of this tract that they were forced to stop from a pair of blocking utility vehicles – they were identical to the wrecked one at the reservoir. One stood upright across the westbound lane with its front tire resting against the windshield of the toppled truck that blocked the eastbound lane. Surrounding this wreck was another intricate weave of tire marks.

Both truckbeds were stacked with drawers and racks. Debris from the toppled truck – scattered items that once sat loose and unrestrained in its bed – was scattered about the road; cones and flares and tools and helmets and signs.

"Well then," said John, surveying the mess. "I guess it's time to wake the boys." And with that, he called to the back, through the small doorway, and woke the two men who had thusfar slept so little this morning.

But they were up and they were out, armed and ready (and more than a little groggy).

Ryn was hoisted onto the roof with a rifle and explicit instructions to watch everything.

Armed with his pistol, Louis stood at the nose of the box truck while the other two flanked either side of the wreck – Vincent had to hug tight to the toppled truck to avoid slipping down the steep embankment. (At the bottom of this grassy slope was a quaint country home – baby blue with white trim and subtle decorations – surrounded by thicket.)

Sweeping around the other side, John stopped to inspect an orange reflective vest that was caught on a barb of the farmland's fence. He looked about, but found no sign of the vest's owner. With a shrug, he dropped it and eased himself over the fence, careful not to catch his clothing, his gear – his skin – on the rusty barbs.

Louis tensed when his friends disappeared around the wreck. For a moment, he was frozen in place, listening for any fervor.

A bird whistled.

A crow laughed and took flight.

Boots shuffled along pavement without haste.

Somewhere far off, a dog barked – just once.

Louis stepped toward the wreck, gawping at the bloody handprint that streaked the passenger door of the upright utility truck. His abhorrence quickly abated and he approached the door. Through the murky window he spied a lifeless body that sprawled across the bench seat – he recoiled at the sight. Aware of the possible danger, but feeling no immediate threat, Louis catalogued this body and moved carefully toward the next truck.

The windshield of the twisted truck on its side was spiderwebbed and coated in blood. Careful to avoid the crunching of debris underfoot, Louis stepped closer. Something within the cab was moving. Through the cracked and spattered windshield, he could see bloody jowls chomping down on something large (a dismembered arm, though he could only guess at this).

His stomach emptied at once, painting the windshield a less gory – yet still repulsive – color. The thing inside started at the spattering, then dropped its meal and flung itself into the windshield. The damaged safety glass flexed with each heave, but did not give way.

Vincent appeared over the hood of the upright truck, rifle ready. "What's the matter?"

Still bent – still reeling – Louis waved him off, fighting another urge to retch.

"Ah shit," said Vincent when he noticed the windshield flex.

Ryn watched on with curiosity, white knuckles wrapped dubiously around the rifle.

John hurdled the fence, racing to Louis' side.

Marginally recovered – still bent, but no longer reeling – Louis said, "I got it." He righted himself and raised the pistol – the glass flexed again and two soulless eyes stared sideways through the muck and gore.

*Those eyes...*he thought.

BLAM! – the bullet punched a jagged circle in the windshield and the eyes fell away.

Those eyes were not human...

Dismissing the thought, he nodded to the other truck. "There's another one in there."

John leveled his weapon at the door; Louis holstered his pistol and readied his good hand at the door handle. John nodded once and the door flew open. The body within was still lifeless – still motionless. Trepidatious, they watched it a moment, and still it did not move.

Vincent eased the driver door open with his rifle firmly tucked into his shoulder. After swinging it out to its apex, he quickly slapped his other hand back onto the foregrip.

"Is it dead?" asked Louis.

"I don't know," replied John. He took a step forward.

Vincent reached his rifle in and poked an unresponsive leg. Daring closer inspecting, he jabbed the barrel into an unresponsive belly. And with a second, more forceful jab that rocked the body back, they found that this truly was a corpse; a screwdriver protruded from its ear.

"Well," he said, easing his grip on the rifle. "I think we're fine here."

BLAM! – a lurcher fell to the grass thirty yards away.

"Holy shit!" cried John. "A little more warning next time, maybe?"

"Sorry!" Ryn called back. "Didn't have much warning myself!" She pointed down the highway. "We should probably get going!" she hollered.

They turned and spotted a series of bobbing heads shambling up the embankment near the dead lurcher.

"Oh my lord," breathed John, dragging the syllables. "We done emptied the entire trailer park, boys and girls."

"Move that thing!" cried Ryn. She popped a few more rounds at the growing horde – and then a few more. Each shot landed a target, but her hurried shots – her racing heart and uneven breaths – caused her to miss the most vital organ on more than one occasion.

Shoving the dead legs aside, Vincent turned the key; the engine squawked, the exhaust coughed. He turned it again; more squawking, no coughing. "C'mon," he pleaded through clenched teeth. "C'mon." He feathered the gas, put his foot on the brake, twisted the key –

The truck rumbled to life.

After a dismissive wave to his friends – they quickly backed away – he dropped the truck into gear and floored the gas. He pushed through the toppled truck – breaking through the spiderwebbed windshield – and stopped just barely shy of the embankment.

Ryn continued firing into the horde, but still it moved closer. "C'mon, guys!" she cried. "Get your asses over here and let's get the fuck on!" She popped a few more rounds into the encroaching horde. "Let's go!" she cried, hopping smoothly onto the cab. *"Andiamo!"* She skated down the windshield onto the pavement.

Hopping out of the truck, Vincent's leg was caught and he flopped onto his back – the wind was knocked from him. Dazed, he laid there a moment, unsure of how he wound up on the cement – almost unsure of where he was.

Something groped at his foot and pulled itself closer. He kicked, but it held tight. He stomped, but it held strong. One high-arching blow to the head with his rifle knocked a hand loose; a second high-arching blow knocked the other one loose. He stood up, kicked its face and stomped until he felt the bone give way and the head compress.

His face was mad: lips curled, cheeks flushed, nose flared, brow furrowed – eyes burning. And for a moment in this madness – this *fury* – he could not move to save his life or hear his friends as they pleaded for him to hurry – *c'mon, just run, let's go.* For this moment, he stood there, grinding an infected skull further into an infected and pulverized brain.

A lurcher slammed into the truck; his head snapped in that direction, blind fury still upon his face. Time slowed down; he could see every speck of blood, every bared tooth, both dead eyes. The thing (*this thing is* not *a woman!* cried his mind) was moving toward him. Lightning-quick, he brought the rifle up and –

BLAM! – she fell straight back with a mask of shock and disappointment –

These things don't feel shock! They don't get disappointed!

Smoke curled upward from his rifle; with time being sluggish from the overabundance of adrenaline pumping through his system, he could discern each tendril as it drifted into the air.

And then time and substance coalesced with the real world once more –

With his first step, Vincent almost slipped – the curdled blood and brainmatter that covered his foot was slick. With his second and third steps, he found stability – and he was running back to the truck. John was behind the wheel and Louis was already seated in the back; Ryn was in the cab, staring anxiously out the open door.

Lurchers shambled around the wreck.

"Two seconds," said Vincent – and he whirled, bolting back toward the wreck.

"What are you doing?" cried Ryn, poking her head over the door.

Vincent snatched up a duffel bag and some flares from the scattered debris and darted back toward the truck.

"Move!" he cried, shoving Ryn aside and climbing into the truck. "*Go! Go! Go!*"

A lurcher slammed into the grille, pawed at the windshield.

John hit the gas, mowing this ghoul over – mowing over many more as they passed through the horde that now swarmed the scene.

IV

They raced along until the surviving horde of shambling bodies became little more than specks in the mirrors. John slowed it down to a comfortable, cautious pace – when maneuvering around wreckage, he was careful to avoid any debris. Soon enough, they were driving alongside the glittering lake once more without a hint of carnage in sight. Of course, this respite wouldn't last forever.

"I think we're good," said Vincent, still excited from his narrow escape. "Could you pull over somewhere so I can take a leak?"

Before answering, John's eyes lingered a moment on the sideview mirror. "Sure," he said at last. "But you need to hurry. I don't know how long they'll follow us, but I'd rather not find out."

"No problem," replied Vincent. "I'd like to get to a safe location today."

"My grandparents have a cabin up past Paradise," said Ryn. "But I don't really know how to get there..." she looked down, clearly abashed.

"I'm not worried about where we end up," he said. "I'll take any random place, so long as it has heat and water and no cannibalistic residents." He huffed. "Shit, I'll take less than that so long as there are no cannibalistic residents."

Easing the box truck onto the shoulder by a shady gravel lot, John said, "We'll probably have to bypass Paradise to find such a place." He scanned the road, the lot – checked his mirrors. "Especially one with heat. And we'll definitely need heat if we're up in the damn mountains."

Vincent scanned his own mirror. "Agreed," he said. He looked over at John and nodded – John nodded at him – and they popped open the doors. Without unshouldering his rifle, Vincent vaulted the guardrail and bolted behind a tree to unload his bladder (with great relief and satisfaction). Before finishing his business, Vincent extracted a cigarette from the breast pocket of his heavy military jacket and sparked it. The nicotine in conjunction with relief instantly calmed his edgy nerves.

Without a pressing bladder, John stood guard by the truck, staring west – staring down the way they came. When a shadow flickered or trembled, his eyes would jump. Occasionally he would glance east, inspecting the path they were set to take. Nothing, save for the quivering shadows, was moving in either direction.

Being in no particular hurry, Louis strolled down the drive while grabbing out a smoke of his own. He sparked it and found a relatively remote tree upon which he could comfortably urinate while watching the glittering lake, the vibrant hillside, the scattered puffy clouds that rolled southeast across the sky.

After a moment of indecision, Ryn hurdled the guardrail and blew past Vincent, causing him to flush and turn, attempting to hide himself. But she paid him no mind as she was far more intrigued with the day's beauty – she was staring at the same scene as Louis, captivated by the distorted mirror of this rippling lake. Greens and blues and yellows and whites and grays all comingled and danced along the rippling, shimmering surface.

A smile touched her face and she listened to the music of this place; the whistling of wind and chirping of birds up in the trees, the light sloshing of water on rocks. Even the tinkling of the boys' urine added its own interesting note to the natural tunes.

And then the shriek of an eagle carried across the lake and her smile grew. She gazed up to the sky and watched the noble bird soar in large, sweeping circles above the lake. It shrieked again and dipped toward the water only to flap its broad wings and regain altitude.

Twenty yards away, Louis was gazing at the same eagle; his mind was somehow eased as well from the mere sight of its majesty. But unlike Ryn, he was conscious of this meager delight and it's absurdity in relation to their struggles in subsistence. He watched it for a time still even after his business was done, leaning against a tree, casually smoking.

Even Vincent spotted it before returning to the truck – he smirked at the luck he believed all birds of prey brought to travelers. But his eye didn't linger; he spied it, smirked, and sauntered around the guardrail to join John roadside.

"Nervous?" he said to John, sensing his anxiety. "You know they won't catch us anytime soon."

"You never know, man," replied John; his eyes quavered between the road and Vincent.

"Look around," said Vincent, aware that John was already looking at everything. "You're on an empty road with water to one side and hills to the other." He waved his arms about, displaying the facts he just stated. "Nothing's gonna get us here. Not soon, anyway."

"Still, man," he looked nervously at Vincent. "You never know. If the dead can walk the earth, then anything can happen."

"Okay," said Vincent. "I hear ya. But don't talk crazy, man – you can't call these people the walking dead, because they're not. It's a disease, not a curse." This argument wasn't entirely convincing, even to himself. "And I assure you that this is not the Apocalypse. We're not all gonna die, we just gotta play it smart."

"What other explanation do you have for this?"

"North Korea," replied Vincent, managing a straight face.

John missed the dry sarcasm. "Really?" he nearly bellowed.

"No," said Vincent, shaking his head and waving the thought away. "Not at all. I was just being a smartass. But something like that is possible – it's certainly more plausible than the *walking dead*." After an interval and a drag: "I'm just not quick to jump to theories of the supernatural sort very often."

"No, your theory is more akin to a spy novel."

"It's a bit more plausible than science fiction, at least," Vincent countered – he meant this as a harmless gibe, but knew that it would also stoke the flames of John's argumentative tendencies (especially in regards to religion).

"Nothing about Hell spilling over is science fiction," replied John.

"It's certainly not science fact," said Vincent – he knew he should end this dicey debate but found himself falling prey to his own obstinate nature.

John scowled at him.

"I'm sorry, buddy," said Vincent. "I'm not trying to knock your beliefs. You know that."

Sighing, John said, "I know. You're just a stubborn, argumentative prick."

"Likewise," said Vincent, clapping his friend – his brother – on the shoulder. "But I love ya nonetheless."

"They certainly look like the walking dead to me," called Louis as he ambled their way.

"Yeah," agreed Vincent, nodding, smoking. "I can definitely see the resemblance. I just can't believe in Heaven and Hell and Jesus and God and Satan and his minions – especially not at this moment in time. And I sure as shit don't believe in the walking fucking dead, either. I do, however, believe in science and pestilence and surely this is a depraved concoction of the two."

"And I tend toward that train as well," said Louis – he leaned back until he was half-seated on the guardrail. "But I'm also not one to dismiss such a thing as a possible Apocalypse, whether it be related to God or science or whathaveyou. And these *things*, these *ghouls* – these fucking *lurchers*, if you will – could definitely be the walking dead."

"I won't deny any of it," said Vincent. "I was just debating to debate at John's unfortunate expense." He looked over at his friend. "Sorry – again."

"No worries," said John. With passing glances up and down the road, he relaxed enough to lean against the truck and spark a cigarette.

Vincent nodded and looked across the lot at Ryn with admiration. "She sure is something," he said.

Louis craned his neck around. "Damn right," he said. "Tough as nails with a quick wit. And after all she's been through she can still stop to smell the roses – even during the Apocalypse."

Vincent tittered lightly. "Even during the Apocalypse," he echoed.

V

On the road again, John remained their pilot with Vincent sitting passenger – Ryn sat in the middle while Louis laid out on the couch in back.

"So," said John, "what's with the bag you risked your life for?"

Vincent scooped it up from the floorboards between the seats. "Looks like a survival bag," he said. "Figured we might get use out of some road flares and space blankets and –" he tossed a reflective vest over Ryn's head, into the back. "Probably won't get much use out of that," he said. "But there's also a first aid kit in here and even a couple flashlights." He pulled one of these out – it was long and heavy and met-al. "This thing can do double duty," he said, flicking it forward in mock attack.

"Not bad," said John. "Not sure it was worth the risk, though."

"Potential life-saving tools are always worth the risk," said Vincent.

"Don't be so smug," said John. "You put us all at risk with that."

"I didn't feel any of us were in grave danger back there," countered Vincent. "It was all under control."

"You didn't have to –" began John.

Ryn cut him off: "Quit bickering, children! What does it matter if we're all safe now?"

Louis perked up on the couch – his eyebrows raised and he half lifted his head to look toward the cab – but he remained silent.

Both John and Vincent were stunned into silence.

"Vincent's overzealousness paid off and we have extra supplies," she said, exasperated. "There's no point in berating each other over something that can't be undone. So why don't we move on and focus on the present?"

The following silence was their acquiescence to her mediation.

"That's better," she huffed.

For a moment after this, Vincent watched an eagle – the very same one from before – soar over the lake. The moment was unfavorably short, for he would have liked to gaze upon this good omen for a while longer, and would have, had their circumstances not changed so drastically – so quickly.

"What the fuck…" John began, trailing off.

Over a half mile down the highway were multiple sets of red lights, flashing alternately, signaling a railroad crossing. But the hulk of a train behind these lights sat stolid, silent. Somewhere beyond this train – beyond these warning lights – rose two separate plumes of smoke; one was bluish, the other was straight black.

As they closed in on this dismal scene, their morale began to fade.

"It's blocking the whole fucking road," spouted John. Increasing pressure on the brakes now, the expanse of the goliath confirming his bleak statement, he said, "Yep. It's blocking the whole fucking road. Fan-fucking-tastic." He stopped a few yards from the lifeless train.

"Well, shit," breathed Vincent – he was looking down the tracks, hoping to find a viable path through which their box truck could travel. He wasn't shocked to see no such path existed, and his morale markedly diminished a few more notches.

With further inspection of the train – and retrospection of the previous wrecks along this highway – Vincent said, "I wonder …maybe this…" he reflected further upon the previous scenes – he scanned the length of lifeless train once more. And then he finished his thought: "Maybe this is where those utility trucks were heading."

"The possibility is definitely there," said Ryn, contemplating the supposition.

"That hardly matters," grumbled John. He shrugged and said, "But you're probably right."

Louis moved forward and gazed out the windshield over Ryn's head. "Looks to me like we're fucked," he said. "Might have to hoof it."

"Ah, hell no," blurted John.

"What do you propose?" inquired Vincent. "Flip around and find another way?"

"I don't think so," said Louis. "All other routes are dangerous and distant."

"Who gives a fuck?" replied John. "This is sketchy. Who knows what's beyond that train? What if the town's just overrun with those things?"

"If it were overrun," began Vincent, "they'd be clamorin' for us by now." He stopped and listened, his window cracked, ears perked. After an interval, he said, "And I don't hear shit out there, 'cept for the birds 'n' the bees."

"I'm okay with walking," said Ryn.

"This is the quickest," began Louis. He shook his head. "No," he resumed, "it's the *only* route toward Paradise from here. And if I can walk it with one arm and constant pain, then so can you." It was a dirty, cheap trick, but Louis was adamant about staying the course.

John huffed and looked between the three of them. "Guess I'm out-voted," he said.

"It's okay, big guy," said Vincent. "So long as we have you around to protect us, nothing bad can happen." He smiled cheekily.

"Shut the fuck up," said John, cracking open the driver door. "Grab your shit if you want it," he said, motioning toward the duffel bag. And he slid out of this faithful – useful – comfortable – truck for the last time.

Vincent stuffed the bag full of water and maps, adding to its already plentiful supply of survival gear. He was only a moment behind John in sliding from the cab of this box truck one last time, strapped with a rifle, a pistol, a duffel bag and enough ammunition to combat a small horde and nothing more. But the moment struck him as different and he recognized the finality of this hop, making his peace with the transition seamless and almost comforting.

With an underlying hint of campfire and pine trees, the crisp air was redolent of autumn and childhood and high adventures through the forest. And for the first few moments, this pair stood just outside the truck, allowing these scents to send them down a blissfully nostalgic road. Even the rifles strapped to their chests – even the military fatigues – even the goliath blocking their path – these two men were capable of briefly slipping away.

Once again, the aesthetics of Mother Nature worked their magic.

Ryn threw open the passenger door, startling Vincent out of his revelry. Immediately, her face contorted and her nose flared. "What's that *smell?*" she groaned, cupping her hands over her nose and mouth.

"Something's burning," said Vincent, simply. Then he detected a sour undertone on the breeze and his face contorted similarly. "Something..." he began, searching for the right words. "Something *not right* is burning," he said at last.

Peering distrustfully over his shoulder at the road behind them, John said, "We should get on it."

"Get on what?" asked Ryn. "The train?"

"No, honey," said John, turning to face her. "We should get going. Get moving." He paused for a beat. "We should *get on it*," he said.

She flushed. "Oh," she said.

"Grab some of that food," Vincent said to Ryn, "and put it in here." He slapped the duffel bag hanging at his side.

After two minutes of rummaging and repacking select items, the four of them were out and off and cautiously crawling between boxcars. Their supplies were now minimal – they were down to the food and emergency supplies in the duffel bag strapped to Vincent's back – and their ordnance was thinning – a rifle apiece for all but Louis, who was armed only with a pistol that he found difficult to reload one-handed – with a mere two or three clips remaining for each of their respective weapons. None carried a silent weapon any longer, save for the heavy flashlight in the duffel bag; they lost their stealthy defenses to the military four days prior.

Safely beyond the train, Vincent scanned from trees to train to tracks to town – he could see the smallest corner of a green roof around the bend in the road. He nodded. "I think this'll be just fine," he said. "And if we can keep it quiet, we might actually survive to sing another day."

Louis nodded. "That would be the key."

Taking up the rear of their pack was John. Once the other three were through and securing the area, John laboriously pulled himself up and over the hitch between boxcars. His heel caught a chain that rattled and clinked and smacked him lightly on the back after stumbling from an unstable landing. The chain, jangling and tinkling off the cross-hitch, startled the group – their guns waved this way and that.

The moment passed – John flushed – the others sighed relief and lowered their weapons.

"So much for quiet," breathed Louis.

"Sorry, guys," John said, still red.

"Damn near gave me a heart attack," said Vincent, not entirely exaggerating – his heart, though it wasn't racing, was thudding uncomfortably hard in his chest.

"Sorry, Vince," said John, still red, now at his side.

With an overdramatic scowl, Vincent said, "Don't call me that. It's about as bad as callin' me *Vinnie*." He added to this ersatz melodrama by scrunching his nose at this last, most unfavorable moniker. He held this cheesy expression for a moment, allowing them to grasp his sarcasm.

"Your propriety," piped Louis, interjecting his opinion on the false matter, "is of little or no concern at this point in time. I'd just as soon call you 'ass-river' as our current circumstances do not allow for pleasantries or peeves."

"If they don't allow for pleasantries," began Ryn, "then we should get going already and stop flappin' our yaps."

"Agreed," said Vincent.

And they set their backs to the train.

VI

"According to this map," said Vincent, "we should be able to follow this highway all the way to Paradise." Puffing on a cigarette, he traced the route with his forefinger while Ryn looked on curiously. "We're not to follow it when it shoots straight south, though," he explained. "We'll just stay forward on 706 when the highway splits."

A chilly breeze tousled their hair, whistled in the foliage – the treetops swirled, dancing this way and that.

Peering sideways at the map, John asked, "And how far out would you suppose we are?"

"Oh, I don't know," said Vincent, scrutinizing the map, tracing the lines back and forth, back and forth. "Thirty miles," he said. "Maybe more, maybe less. We could make it tonight if we find a vehicle. By foot, we'd be lucky to make it there by tomorrow."

"Aren't we optimistic," Louis said sardonically.

"It's all about confidence," proclaimed Vincent.

An eagle shrieked above the road – it was circling the town now.

A crow cawed and perched atop the red caboose of a small train – no, this train was actually a cleverly disguised lodge. *The Hobo Inn*, read the sign out front. Each boxcar was a different color. The third car in – the green car – was spattered with blood and brains. Two windows on the fifth car in – the orange car – were shattered from the inside.

No bodies were to be seen.

Pools of dried blood speckled driveways and parking lots – and still, no bodies.

At the edge of town, behind a spotless white picket fence, a small church was ablaze – the steeple was a tall pyre of flames. The thick black plume of smoke they had spotted before entering this town was jetting skyward from this fiery sanctuary.

Mouth agape, eyes wide, John slowly crossed himself.

Ryn gasped. "Holy Hell," she breathed, a hand over her heart.

Despite their agnosticism, such profane irreverence affected Louis and Vincent as well.

John muttered a prayer under his breath with a finger over his lips and sorrow in his eyes.

"Who would do such a thing?" Louis whispered.

Caught up in tumultuous awe, their pace slowed drastically until they stopped entirely. Being so very distracted by the blasphemous pyre and its wicked pillar of smoke floating toward the heavens, none were even conscious of having stopped.

And when they were about to resume their trek, a dark and tall figure emerged from behind the general store. Below the figure's stark-white head – pale skin, a platinum horseshoe of hair – was a long black cassock. From this distance – over fifty yards – they could see the white notch on his collar. And, from this distance, they could see his cassock was spattered with blood that glistened in the sun.

John readied his rifle.

"Hold up," Vincent suggested, pushing the barrel of John's rifle down. "Let's not alert the whole town if we don't have to." He looked fervently around, scanning the road for something. And then he found it – "Here!" he hissed, grabbing up a gnarled walking stick from the side of the road.

"I'm not getting close enough to use that," said John, raising his rifle again.

"I will," said Vincent. "I'd rather that than have the entire town converge on us." He started off, intentionally placing himself between John's gun and the plodding figure. "C'mon," he said. "I'ma need some backup, kids."

Louis was fast on his heel – Ryn paused, apprehensive, and started slowly after them a moment later.

Lowering his weapon and shaking his head, John followed in turn.

The figure – the priest – stopped suddenly and raised his arms to either side – a revolver dangled from one hand. He was babbling something to the ground – and then he whipped his face skyward and began babbling at the heavens.

Vincent stepped back – hand on his sidearm – the moment the priest began babbling.

Scattered in tow, the others took a similar pose, leery of this enigmatic figure.

For nearly a minute, the figure – the priest – stood as such, quietly babbling at the heavens. The quartet held their pose with mounting concern. Holding his exalted stance, the figure began turning slowly –

(for a moment – an incalculable fraction of a second – Vincent was sure the priest was turning to address him directly – for this incalculable moment, he was certain the priest would curse him and strike him down where he stood – and, quicker than this moment lasted, he assured himself that the priest was turning to face a currently unseen threat, though a residue of his previous paranoia lingered and would eventually resonate and fester in his mind, his soul for some time to come)

– without once looking at this weary crew or ceasing his incessant babble. After turning completely around – now facing back the way he came – the priest dropped his arms and his head, mouthing his silent prayers now to the pavement, to his feet (*or maybe communing with the devil*, Vincent thought fleetingly). With a practiced grace, the priest crossed himself, lightly kissed the crucifix hanging from his neck and motioned to the sky, to the earth – his silent prayer was now at an end. He lifted his head, gazing gravely down the road.

A scraggly figure then limped into view after the priest. He was tall, gangly, bald and potbellied and wore tattered overalls. Between broken steps – it was dragging a twisted leg – it reached for the priest, soundlessly gnashing its teeth. Something – or someone – had torn out its throat and it couldn't howl or groan, despite all its best efforts at doing so.

The priest let this lurcher trudge within ten feet before –

CRACK! – he fluidly raised his pistol and plugged a round into its skull – the sound was no louder than a cap gun, though it would certainly alert nearby lurchers.

The sound set this quartet on edge; each of them visibly tensed.

The priest stared down at the infected corpse for just a moment before stooping low over it. Whispering a quick prayer, he gently closed the lids of those infected, inhuman eyes. Once this task was undertaken, his pale face turned unmistakably in their direction (Vincent couldn't help but feel the priest's gaze pierce his soul). Smiling, the priest stood to a staggering height and waved.

They were stunned – and baffled – into further immobility.

Showing them a toothy grin now, he continued waving.

Cocking his head, Vincent looked sideways at this exponentially enigmatic figure – John and Louis exchanged uneasy eyes – Ryn felt compelled to wave back at him, though she wasn't quite sure why she felt so inclined.

When Vincent took off toward the priest (still gripping the gnarled staff), the others instinctively – protectively – started after him.

The priest was tall and wiry with a wily white horseshoe surrounding a lone white thatch that stuck out amidst an otherwise shiny dome. His face was clean-shaven and similarly shiny. His eyes were faded blue, his pupils clouded over (he claimed to see but those ghostly eyes suggested otherwise). Not a speck of red blemished his sclerae.

As they approached, he regarded each one of them with a faint smile and these eerie eyes. In contrast to this smile, his left eye twitched when regarding Vincent – and again when regarding Louis. His focus shifted quickly back toward the others. The smile remained and Vincent passed the twitch off as some possible neurological condition related to his cloudy eyes (though his previous paranoia started to fester some, eating at the free space in his head).

"My children!" bellowed the priest. "Oh, my children, how happy I am to have you join me." He grinned again – his pearly teeth showing through thin lips – before reverting to his former, faint smile. "Please," he said, "come with me. I have been expecting you." His toothy grin reappeared again – just as briefly as before.

He's mad, thought Vincent.

The priest's eye twitched – he glanced at Vincent.

"Excuse me?" said John. "You've been *expecting* us?"

"Well, of course," said the priest. "I've been cleaning up for you." He waved his arms around, motioning to the town. "Can't you tell?" Madness shone through those thin lips of his once again – sincerity shone deep within his cloudy eyes.

Standing there, listening to this mad priest gibber, Vincent noticed the burning church again. This structure was still standing tall behind the perfect picket fence – its cross and steeple were still burning impiously.

"I wish I'd had more time to prepare," continued the priest. "I regret that the fire is still burning, but it took me so long to lure them all in there." He gazed solemnly at the lurcher by his feet. "I doubly regret at not having lured this one in there as well," he said, "but, as you see, its vocal cords did not work and it was locked away from my prying eyes." He looked at them with wide, expounding – nearly humorous – eyes. "Took me by surprise, he did!"

"Who'd you lure?" inquired Louis, already knowing – and dreading – the answer.

"The Damned," replied the priest. "Come," he said. "Let's get some real food in those bellies of yours." He started off with gusto through the yard in which the potbellied dead lurcher now rested. "Come!" he called. "I've got food and clothing and room and board!" He stopped halfway across the yard to wave them along. "Come!" he cajoled.

They hesitated...

VII

Despite a crucifix in every room, it was clear to each of them that this man – this strange priest – did not live at the house to which he brought them. Details of the home's interior were skewed ever-so-slightly: a tapestry leaned to one side; a lamp was shattered in the corner; mirrors were busted; picture frames were empty. Every window was blacked out with heavy blankets – towels for the smaller ones.

Laid out on the couch, the chairs, the coffee table were an assortment of clothes – double-kneed jeans, thick cotton shirts, heavy flannels and wool jackets. Upon the coffee table were two pairs of boots and about a dozen pairs of various socks (large, small – cotton, wool). The quartet was stunned at this array of clean clothing – and still baffled at the priest's uncanny foresight.

Ryn was shown into the master bedroom where an array of girl's clothing awaited, spread out across a massive four-post bed. She told him that her bag contained plenty of clothing, but he insisted that her supply was insufficient. After pointing her toward the bathroom for an overdue shower, the priest let her be.

With ridiculous haste and zero modesty, the other three had already changed into fresh clothing, leaving their soiled garb (formerly stark-white, now dingy and speckled with blood and dirt and muck) in a heap below the curtained front window. Their camouflage jackets were laid over a wingback chair.

All three wore blue jeans over longjohns with white cotton under-shirts. Vincent found a black button-down shirt and a plain black baseball cap to match – he was eyeing the jackets while pulling on a pair of wool socks. John simply wore a brown and green flannel over his un-dershirt and found a clean black Stetson with a braided leather band to wear. Louis was carefully pulling a black thermal over his jury-rigged splint when the priest walked back into the front room.

"I have provided bags as well," said the priest. "They're in the kitchen. I've included some supplies you may or may not still have, as well as a couple I'm sure you're lacking." His eyes flicked to Vincent (it twitched again!), then to Louis and finally rested upon John.

"Thank you, Father," said John, removing the Stetson to fiddle with it some. "But I must ask, how did you know we were coming?"

"It came to me," said the priest, brimming with pride. "It came to me on the night – on the first night. It came to me in a dream – a vision! I was told to go east in search of two grand souls. Two grand souls that would either damn us – or save us."

Vincent recalled his dream of a week prior – the king, the faceless woman, the headless servants, the omnipotent eyes – imagery of this dream assailed him without notice.

"But there are four of us," commented Louis, pulling on a blue and gray checkered skullcap. "How did you know to prepare for all of us?"

"I was told that for these grand souls," he said somberly, "there would be two fated servants of power."

Vincent's eyes fell to the floor – his lips pursed.

"What do you mean by that?" asked John.

Louis said, "He means that two of us are going to die." He gazed into the seemingly soulless eyes of the priest. "Isn't that what you mean?"

With a faint smirk – an expression that never truly faded from his face – the priest nodded.

"Are you serious?" barked John.

The priest regarded him with silent assurance.

"In this vision," said the priest, his murky eyes lighting up, "I saw the crimson angel of light and beauty beside a glowing figure of iridescent darkness – such a paradoxical entity could only be the tangled identity of the prophet of death." In his fervor, the priest's voice was escalating. "Serving this quizzical pair's every whim – every desire and every need – were two dissipating clouds. Such has been –"

"Listen, Father," began John.

"My child," replied the priest, cutting him off. "There's no need to be formal. Just call me Salem." He grinned.

"Fine," said John. "Try to keep the volume down, Salem."

The priest did not respond. Instead, he stared expectantly at John for a moment. And, without warning, he said, "Who's hungry?"

"Sir," began Vincent. "Salem – that's really kind of you, but we should really get a move on. There are only so many hours in the day and we would really like to get to the summit by tonight."

"If you leave now," said the priest, "all will be lost."

They stared with curious, uncomprehending eyes.

"I know you," he said to Vincent. "You are the prodigy of evil – the prophet of death. But don't you fear, my chi –" he cut this axiom of priesthood short. "Don't you worry, son, for even though this is a frightening evil – a bone-chilling, soul-shaking evil – it is also a necessary evil." His murky eyes bore a tremendous gravity. His smirk faltered for a moment.

Vincent was nearly speechless – he was able to squawk out one question: "Excuse me?" His face was red and hot with anger and insult.

"Though you are a prodigy of evil," began Salem, "you are not necessarily evil yourself – thus the paradox inherent in the prophet of death. You can still manifest your own future and you are not obligated to fulfill any of his grim requisitions. But –"

"Listen, old man," Vincent interrupted, his eyes now burning, flinging fiery daggers at this mad priest. "I don't know what you're babbling about here, but this is obscene and unnecessary and I take high offense to your words."

Salem stared, his face a blank canvas (save for that everpresent smirk).

Cooling some, Vincent said, "I don't believe in your vision."

"The vision!" cried Salem.

"Yes," said Vincent, rolling his eyes. "The vision. I don't believe in it. I don't believe in your God. I don't believe in Satan. Nor do I believe in Heaven or Hell or the Four Horsemen of the Apocalypse. And I sure

as shit don't believe in crimson angels or prophets of death – or prodigies of evil, for that matter.

"I do, however," he continued, "believe in life and death and the
consequences of inaction. And I believe that if we don't make tracks
soon, our collective survival –" he motioned to his friends "– just might
be compromised."

"Ah, but you are wrong, Vincent," countered Salem.

"How did you learn my name?" He tried feebly to remember if his
companions had used his name since encountering the priest.

"The vision!" he cried. "If you leave now, all will be lost."

"You've said that already, Padre. But I've told you that I do not believe in your vision."

"Then you are to be one of the fated and another will rise in your
place – for there is another of you who is equal to your prodigal level."

"Are you fucking kidding me right now?" exclaimed Louis. "This is
madness! Visions and prodigies and angels and devils – nonsense! You
speak nonsense!"

"Believe me if you wish," said the priest, "or don't believe – it
makes no difference to me – my fate is sealed. But it will make a difference to you," he regarded each of them in turn, "it will make a difference
to all of you – all four of you."

Ryn emerged from the bedroom just then – the air that wafted out
after her was fragrant, pleasant. She was pulling a plaid button-down on
over a white cotton tee-shirt. Her short red hair was dark and tangly and
wet from the shower. "What'll make a difference to us?" she asked.

Salem went on as though he hadn't heard her: "Leaving now would
be the most detrimental act you could subject your party to. 'Twould be
even more detrimental than disregarding my premonitions regarding the

angel and the prophet."

"Your words are nonsense," Louis reiterated in a huff.

"Be they nonsense or divination, I beg the lot of you to stay. For a short time, at least. Leaving now would be a terrible mistake."

"I'll stay at least for a quick shower," said Vincent. "And maybe a proper meal. But, if you don't mind, Padre, please stow your babblings of visions and whatnot." He stepped past the priest. "There's only so much of that psycho-religious bullshit that I can handle in one day." He breezed past Ryn with a nod.

Salem's eyebrows rose and he nodded to himself. "Well then," he said. "I'll get cookin'."

VIII

Warm water washed over his head – filthy with muck and grime and blood – and down his clammy, odorous body. Pooling at his feet was a steady stream of dirty water – sometimes this water was predominately red, other times it was a brackish, rusty brown color. For minutes, he let this water run over his head, down his face and over his body, the temperature soothing his strained muscles and achy joints. Absently, he watched the grime stream off his feet to form the mucky pool and how this pool slowly, steadily flowed down the drain.

Scrubbing away, his thoughts turned to Isabella. He did not fret over her this time – did not pine. Absently working suds into his armpit, Vincent closed his eyes – a loud, vivid picture of her filled his head and, silently, he prayed for her safety. Briefly, he thought of this prayer being broadcast over a loudspeaker that spoke directly to the hearts and minds of the collective human subconscious.

With a sigh, he continued scrubbing. He wished for something to assuage his pains.

Some hundred miles to the northeast, in a cabin in the mountains, an older man with long white hair, a matching beard and thick spectacles that covered half his face watched a charred and beaten ambulance roll up under the awning of a nearby lodge. The occupants were all uninfected, but the militant guards outside the lodge detained the driver and passenger before opening fire on the bloodied woman who was cuffed to a stretcher in the back.

This old man, watching from a third-floor balcony – with a coffee in one hand and a cherrywood pipe in the other – grinned at the blind obedience of his ignorant soldier-boys. The detainees would remain in the basement of this lodge for many days with very little food or water until it was proven to all who were concerned that they were not infected.

Once the scene was through, the old man went back inside to augment his memoirs – the current addendum regaled the days of his youth when a silver-streaked old man offered him the choice of life or death (he chose death, but not for himself).

A shudder ran up Vincent's spine as he was toweling off.

IX

"Did you save any water for me?" John teased when Vincent walked out (so fresh and so clean and so very well-dressed!) into the front room. "You were in there for-fucking-ever, dude." He strode quickly by Vincent, into the master bedroom. "If this water isn't warm," he said, turning back to face him, "you're gonna get it." He scowled facetiously and shut the door.

Vincent shrugged and plopped down on the couch.

"Feel better?" Ryn inquired – she was curled up on a wingback with a book in her lap.

Opposite her sat Louis, the warm fireplace between them. He was snoozing on an overstuffed recliner with an open book on his knee and an untouched snifter on the end table. The awful ice scraper splint of his had been replaced with three small pieces of oak on the sides and back of his elbow and one thin, narrow piece of padded steel along the front – all of which was taped to his arm and covered with a flesh-toned, breathable elastic wrap.

"Oh yeah," Vincent replied in a long, heavy breath. "Much better." He eyed the new wrap on Louis' arm. Lazily, he pointed at it with his chin. "'Bout time he got a good splint," he commented.

"Yeah," said Ryn. "John coulda been a doctor with such skills. Lou hardly made a face through the whole thing."

"Probably hurt like hell, though," breathed Vincent. He stretched out on the couch, brought the bill of his cap down over his face. "I'ma take a cue from him and nod off for a bit." Savory scents drifted in from the kitchen, making his stomach rumble. "Wake me when it's time to eat," he said.

"Will do," replied Ryn, diving back into her book.

Within minutes, the room was filled with battling snores (Vincent's were far louder).

And soon after the snoring began, John stepped out of the master bedroom in his new undershirt and jeans with his flannel draped over his arm and Stetson in hand. His blonde hair was wet and messy – his beard, now thick and full, was gleaming. With his free hand, John scratched one cheek followed by the other. "I was thinking," he began.

"*Shh!*" insisted Ryn. "They're *sleeping*," she hissed.

"My bad," whispered John. He continued in the same low voice: "So, I was thinking that we could really use some sidearms." He set the hat on the coffee table and slipped into his flannel. Buttoning it up, he said, "Preferably ones that don't go *bang*."

They began scouring the house at once.

In the upstairs bedroom, Ryn found an assortment of possible weapons and laid them out across the bed while scavenging for more. Once she was certain there was nothing more to find in the room, she looked upon the pitiful array – among the most pitiful were two softballs, an empty wine bottle, a short, heavy piece of wood with a sculpture of Buddha's bust at the top and a blowdart gun. She grabbed the most promising – an aluminum baseball bat, a hatchet and a wristrocket, sans marbles – and headed back downstairs.

She found John in the front room with a wooden baseball bat resting on his shoulder. Shaking his head, he whispered, "Not much down here. I found more rifles, but they can't replace our military hardware. And I found no ammunition, so that's a bust…"

"Well, I got these," she said, displaying her weapons.

Nodding, John snatched the wristrocket, turned it over in his hands, tested the band and shook his head. "Cheap crap," he said, setting it on the coffee table. He grabbed the hatchet. "Not bad." He set it beside the wristrocket. "Always a handy tool. But not the greatest sidearm. We'd still need something else."

From the kitchen, Salem said, "Try the shed. All sorts of tools and gadgets, I'm sure. And it should be safe – I have cleansed this town of The Damned."

Heeding his advice – yet still wary of *The Damned* – they took off out the back door. Their travels were safe, indeed – no howls or moans, not distant or nearby – not even a critter scuttled through the bushes or trees.

The shed was well organized and dirty. Cobwebs hung in every corner, racks were dusty, the floor was dingy with pine needles, grass and sawdust – but every tool was in its place. Everything was separated by type and size with rakes and spades and shovels and hoes hanging in a row along one wall and various power tools and handsaws arranged on shelves. A workbench stood opposite the rakes and spades with a small assortment of manual tools hanging from pins along the paperboard back.

Beneath the bench was a gas-powered chainsaw – John went straight for this with a devious grin upon his face.

"That's highly impractical," said Ryn while eyeing some axes that stood in one corner. "It's loud and heavy and inefficient. Besides, you'd need to keep a gas can, too."

Grumbling something about his shattered dreams, John replaced the chainsaw. He glanced at the tools hanging from the paperboard, briefly considered them – the hammer might work, or maybe the mallet. But he turned soon after to face the wall of rakes and spades. Some were short, some were long – some of the rakes were flimsy, others were solid and sharp. The shovels were all too beefy, the hoes were too awkward. He took a fair spade off the wall – not short, not long, not heavy with a decent balance. But after testing the business end of it, he found the blade was wobbly and would likely fall off after two or three swipes.

He replaced the spade.

"How about this?" said Ryn – she held an axe out with both hands.

"That's not bad," he said, taking it from her. The head was blunt on one side and dull on the other and the rusted metal was covered in dust, but it held strong to John's tests and attempted manipulation. The wooden handle was worn and smooth and comfortably weighted. After flicking it a few times through the air, he said, "None the worse for wear. I'll take it."

"Do we need anything else?" she asked. "What about Lou?"

"Well," he began. And, after a pause, he said, "I hate to say it, but Louis won't be much use in a melee with only one working arm." His eyes flicked toward the workbench. "But maybe..." He grabbed the hammer. "Maybe he could use this."

"You're horrible," she said with a mock scowl.

"I'm serious," he said. "It's either this or one of the bats inside. Or something else that he can use with his non-dominant arm."

While they bickered over weapons – and then supplies – the priest put a hold on the afternoon meal to stroll into the front room from the adjoining kitchen. He looked between the two men asleep at either end of the room. His shrewd eyes lingered on one in particular.

Both were satisfactorily asleep – both were lightly snoring – and he decided a surprise would be in order for the man he called the *prophet of death*. From an unsuspecting seam in his cassock, the priest withdrew a thin, black scabbard that had been tied by ribbon to his belt. The scabbard was old leather, worn and faded around the edges. From it stuck the long black-red diamond-wrap handle of a katana.

With a few long strides, he crossed the room to where Vincent slept. Smiling, he brought the scabbard up – one hand on the handle, the other on the leather –

Cha-click! – the distinctive double-click of a pistol being cocked behind him.

"Set it down," commanded Louis, his voice deep and authoritative. "Do it easy, do it now, or I will splatter your unholy brains across the walls."

Without protest, Salem bent – slowly – and placed the katana at his feet. He kept his back to Louis. "You can put the gun away, son," he said, his voice calm – no hint of pleading or concern. "I will not harm this man," he said. "I will not harm you. I was simply giving him a gift." No lies.

"Sure not what it looked like to me, Padre. You say he's pure evil and then go at him with a sword? I don't think so, buddy." He stepped around an ottoman, into the open. "Turn around," he commanded.

The priest turned graciously – his hands remained upraised – his smile remained faint.

"Move away from him. Move away from the sword."

The priest stepped right; Louis stepped right, keeping his distance.

"Keep moving," said Louis, stern.

The two moved in step, one strafing toward Vincent, the other strafing away. And when their positions were officially reversed – Louis standing over the sword and Salem behind the ottoman, by the chair – Louis instructed the priest to take a seat by the fire.

Salem sat at once. "The food will burn," he said. "Nobody likes burnt casserole."

"And nobody likes a wormy priest," countered Louis. "What was the plan, huh? Kill him, take me next? What then? Kill Ryn and John and dance around our flaming corpses?"

"I would never kill any living human being," Salem said. "It would not befit my beliefs to do such a thing."

The back door opened. It shut moments later.

In walked Ryn and John – she held a crowbar while he proudly wielded his axe.

All pride or sense of accomplishment vanished when they saw Louis' gun.

"What the fuck's going on in here?" cried Ryn.

Vincent stirred.

"I caught this worm trying to kill Vinnie," Louis alleged.

"Don't call me that," mumbled Vincent. He peeked at them through a squinty eye. When the scene finally registered, he leapt to his feet. "What the fuck's going on in here?" he cried, completely unaware of his mimicry.

"This guy was gonna kill you, Vin," Louis alleged again. "He was gonna slice you up with this sword." He kicked at the scabbard by his feet.

"What?" cried Vincent – he had heard and understood all of what Louis said, but did not instantly comprehend the weight behind the words. "Salem tried to kill me?" Eyes wild, he looked at the priest. "You tried to kill me?"

"I did not try to kill you," replied Salem, his hands still upraised in surrender.

Louis badgered him: "Then what were you doing with that sword? I saw you pull it out of your robe! You were sneaking up to him while we slept! I saw you!" The general volume in the room began to rise with every passing word.

"Simmer down, Lou," said Vincent. "Screaming won't solve anything."

"I'm sorry," he said, gruff and sincere. "But I saw him coming at you, Vin. I saw him coming at you with a sword." He stared accusingly at Salem.

"I can assure you, young man," said Salem. "I was not going to kill him – I was not going to kill anybody. I told you already: it would not befit my beliefs to do so. I was simply –"

"Why would you want to kill me?" Vincent interrupted.

But Louis answered – rather sardonically – before the priest could: "Because you're the *prodigy of evil*."

"I do believe," began the priest, "that we were all born of sin – born of evil. Each one of us in this room was born of sin. And we were cleansed of this sin. And then we dabbled in the sin. And then we bathed in it. And now we are submerged in the sin. But this sin we live within will be our path to life – our path to *righteousness*!" Though excited, he monitored his volume quite well – his murky eyes were alight – his toothy grin reappeared.

"That doesn't answer my question," said Vincent.

"I don't want to kill you," replied Salem. "I was giving you a gift."

"What gift?"

"The Crimson Katana." His eyes flicked to the scabbard at Louis' feet.

Vincent stooped, snatched up the scabbard.

Just then, an enormous clatter erupted outside, setting these four on pins with a shudder. The priest sat calm, as though he expected this to happen at this very moment. The sound they heard was that of the church steeple toppling over and crashing through the roof, thus crushing the toasty remains of all the infectious corpses that had been lured inside by a crafty old visionary.

X

"I don't trust you," said Louis, pistol now dangling at his side. "I don't trust your lies."

Salem replied, "That may be, but could you at least trust my food? I'm sure it's about ruined by now. But for you four, I can always make more." His faint smile broadened a touch, but his perfect, pearly teeth did not show this time.

"I don't trust you," Louis said again. "And I think we should get a move on." He looked about the room for affirmations from his friends, but saw only thoughtful or contradictory faces gazing back at him or staring purposefully at some spot on the floor.

"I don't know," said Vincent at last – he looked back toward the gangly priest whose arms were still upraised. "As much as I want to get a move on, I think we could spare some time for someone who's given us so much already. And since we clearly have the upper hand here…" using the scabbard as a pointer, he motioned from Lou's pistol to the submissive priest, "…then I see no reason to worry."

Salem's nostrils flared – the casserole was clearly starting to char.

"Get back to it, Padre," Vincent told the priest. "I'ma lay back down."

"You've got to be kidding me, Vin," said Louis. "This guy just tried to kill you, and you *still* want him to cook you lunch? You want to trust him not to kill the rest of us as well?" He was becoming a bit irate.

Salem remained seated, watching them with his murky eyes and persistent smile.

Seating himself on the couch, placing the scabbard on the coffee table, Vincent said, "I'm beginning to think his premonition is eating at you, Lou." He nodded at the priest. "You can get back to it, Salem. Don't let this guy bother you." He stretched out. "And, Lou," he began, "if you're so damn worried about it, then why don't you keep an eye on him?"

Without hesitation, Salem stood and breezed into the kitchen, lowering his arms only when he was clear of Lou's scowling eyes. With impressive grace – though none of his guests were watching him – the priest pulled open the oven with one hand while sliding the casserole out with the other (using, of course, an oven mitt).

"Put your gun away," Vincent told Louis. "Pop a squat. Or go watch the priest. I don't care which, just ease up already."

After releasing the hammer and engaging the safety – leaving a round in the chamber, as always – Louis slipped the pistol back into its holster. He bent and gingerly picked the scabbard off the coffee table. Respecting Vincent's wishes, Louis shut his mouth on the subject of suspicion and sat down to inspect the katana – *The Crimson Katana*, the priest called it.

From his seat, Louis could watch the priest. And at first, his eyes would flick between the scabbard and Salem, but soon his interest in the priest flagged as the katana began to intrigue him more and more. He unsheathed it, astounded by the red sheen along its edge and intricate filigree that stretched the majority of the blade. Within the filigree were swooping characters – foreign characters. It took him a moment, but once he could isolate the symbols from the filigree, Louis recognized them as Arabic.

An Arabic Samurai sword? he thought in bewilderment.

"What's that look for?" inquired John, having noticed Louis' clearly befuddled face.

"Check this out," he said, displaying the katana. "Look at this inscription."

Attempting to read the foreign characters, John was equally baffled. "Is that Arabic?"

"I believe so," replied Louis. "But doesn't that strike you as odd?"

"Just a bit," said John. "And why is the blade red?"

Seated on a pillow between them, Ryn said, "Since when do Arabs use Japanese katanas?"

"That's what I was wondering!" husked Louis, attempting to keep his voice down.

"It is a one of a kind Meitou katana," called Salem from the kitchen. "It was forged by a soldier of Saladin's army in the late twelfth century. They say the blade is tinged red from spilling the blood of the wicked and the righteous alike."

"I don't think I understood anything you just said," commented John.

"He's talking about the Crusades," explained Ryn. "Saladin was an Islamic hero."

John scoffed at this – Ryn glared disapprovingly.

Turning the blade over in his hands, Louis said, "I've never heard of any sword that's been stained by blood."

"It is not stained with blood," replied Salem. "It is stained with their souls."

"Umm, okay," said Louis – he dragged the syllables while absorbing Salem's mystical explanation. Letting these dubious words sink into the past, Louis said, "Next question: how did a Muslim soldier forge a near perfect replica of a katana? Was he some sort of *Arabic Samurai*?" This last was not devoid of sarcasm.

"That is a fine question," said the priest, now standing in the door-way – his appearance at the doorway was startling and sudden; nobody saw him move from the stove. "The sword was forged by an exiled dip-lomat from Kyoto and it helped win battles for both sides."

"If that's the case," murmured John, "this should be in a museum."

"Why are you passing it off?" asked Louis.

Before he could answer, Ryn said: "I have a better question: Why does an Evangelical priest have an Arabic sword – pardon, an Arabic *katana* – that was forged by a Japanese outcast who somehow found himself in the largest holy war in the history of the planet?"

"I am merely passing it down the chain," replied Salem. "And none too soon, either – my time is growing short." His eyes flicked to Ryn, hovered on Louis and settled on John. "But I did not fret, for I knew I had time enough to pass it on – such has been inscribed in the book of fate since the dawn of time."

"I'm sorry, Father," said John, "but I must ask where your faith does truly lie."

"Isn't it apparent?" replied Salem. "I am faithful to the Holy Trini-ty."

"It's not as apparent as you might think," said Louis. "Christians aren't usually open to the beliefs of others."

Salem turned slowly toward him – his persistent smile sent a chill down Louis' spine. "Angels and demons battle for purchase while divi-sions of man flail with false understanding." He shook his head. "Some mysteries of life are often better left undisturbed. Pry not at these fruit-less mysteries."

After a lengthy silence in which Louis and John – and Vincent, for he was not yet napping, despite his best efforts – mulled over his words,

Ryn said to him, "What did you mean when you said you were just 'passing it down the chain'? Is Vincent some sort of divine being or something? Because, after what you've said, I doubt he's a part of your chain."

"Divine?" mocked the priest. "Nobody born of sin can be divine."

"Then how is it you're a priest?" said Louis.

"I'm not divine." His persistent smile confounded the statement. "Divinity has no play in priesthood – it has no play outside of the Holy Trinity. I just bear the Word of God to all who may listen." His toothy grin appeared – his murky eyes fixed on John's broad face. "Is there anybody here who would listen?"

"So how is it Vincent is next in this chain of yours?" persisted Ryn.

Slowly, his head turned toward her – unlike Louis, Salem's faint smile did not send a chill down her spine. "His soul is intertwined with mine, just as your soul is intertwined with his – just as all your souls are knotted to the divine aiúa. And the purpose of the divine aiúa is to bear the word of peace."

"Peace?" she asked. "What of the Word of God?"

"I do not concern myself with personal beliefs," replied Salem. "Nor does the divine aiúa. All one needs is faith in life and progress and peace. Man's petty fumbling of religion is how we arrived at this dreadful predicament in the first place."

"False understandings…" Ryn murmured.

Salem nodded.

"Do you realize how farfetched this sounds?" Louis asked.

"What of The Damned – the *walking dead* – the *lurchers*?" countered Salem. "Were these unholy beings not farfetched just one week ago?"

"Well, yeah, I guess," she said. "They're weird *and* far-fetched – as is God or Allah or the *divine aiúa*, whatever that is. But you're talking about Vincent," she motioned at the man feigning sleep across the room. "You're talking about him being some successor in an extremely far-fetched chain of peacekeepers or whathaveyou. Not to mention this mysterious katana that you're so obsessed with for some reason." She huffed. "I'd say all that is just a bit weirder than *zombies*." She exaggerated the word, accentuating it with jazzy fingers.

"Beliefs are rooted in tall tales," replied Salem.

"Now I'm not sure if you've covered this or not," said Vincent, giving up on feigning sleep. "But what's the deal with the sword?"

"I thought you were asleep," said Ryn, genuinely surprised.

"Not quite, dear," he replied, strenuously rising to a sitting position – his weary muscles protested this shift – his joints sang their displeasure. He suddenly felt older than his years. Grimacing, he said, "It's kinda hard to sleep with such a lively conversation raging around me."

"Since you're awake," began Salem, "might we move to the kitchen now? Our food, though lightly burnt, is getting cold. And nobody likes burnt *and* cold casserole." He looked from one to the next, to the next, to the next – that persistent smile chilling all but Ryn.

"Sure," said Vincent. "Let's eat."

XI

Their meal was held around a green Formica table with all five transitory occupants of this house present. The priest served them a classic home-style tatertot casserole and bold coffee – with farm-fresh creamer and sugarcubes for those who desired to cut the bitter dark roast beans. When the meal was served, conversation was light as these four travelers shoveled bite after bite of the casserole into their mouths.

Between bites, Ryn praised the meal: "This is *amazing*, Salem. And I'm not just saying that out of malnutrition; I really truly mean it. I don't think I've ever had anything so awesome." She scarfed down another savory bite and groaned with pleasure.

"Thank you, my child," Salem replied. He ate slowly, with a refined sophistication.

With his stomach filling up now, Vincent found his voice: "So, Padre – Salem," he began. Before continuing, he washed down his last bite with a gulp of water. "What exactly is the deal with the sword?"

"This blade," replied Salem, "was forged by a Japanese outcast during the Crusades – this, I already told you. Legend has it that while fighting against the Christians in Syria, Saladin himself took interest in the blade, thus requisitioning the warrior to forge other swords (though, none were of the classic Meitou design any longer). And while he forged these new weapons, Saladin wielded the katana.

"When his job was complete," he went on, "this warrior reclaimed his blade, only to lose it in battle when taken prisoner by Crusaders. The sword then made its way from his captors to King Richard. Though it is not known whether or not King Richard used this weapon himself, legend says the katana was found in the aftermath of a battlefield near Damascus by a Muslim soldier.

"When the bloodstains wouldn't wash off the blade, this soldier handed the blade off to his superiors. Frightened by this seemingly devilish blade, they did not bother passing it before Saladin. Instead, they dispatched of the blade in a nearby river." Salem sipped his coffee, allowing for comment.

"What ever happened to the Japanese dude?" Ryn asked.

"Nobody is entirely certain how," said Salem, "but as the legend goes, before the year's end, he returned to Syria from his prison on Cyprus and, guided by a vision, he found the katana in a river just outside of Damascus. Before his death in the early thirteenth century, he passed the Crimson Katana down to a Christian girl in a village just outside Acre."

"That's one helluva tale," said Vincent – his plate was clean, his mug nearly empty. "But a tall tale it is, indeed. And as intriguing as this story is, it does not prove the existence of your chain of peacekeepers."

"Sure would make for an interesting flick," commented Louis.

With his forefingers steepled before pursed lips, John broke his long silence: "I believe in God," he said. "I believe in Jesus Christ and the Holy Bible. I believe in bits of your story – heck, I'll even agree that it's possible King Richard handled this weapon, though highly unlikely." He leaned back in his seat, clasped his hands in his lap. "But I find it hard to believe in your prophecy regarding this katana's power and importance. Peace is to be found in the actions of the individual; it doesn't rest in some pious chain of peacekeepers that supposedly balance out the world and all its wickedness."

"Then do not believe," replied Salem. "But I implore you to accept this gift if for no other reason than to utilize its blade to aid in your collective survival." He turned to Vincent and – with some effort – was able to hold his gaze for more than just a moment. "If you do not accept this gift," he said with a sigh, "then my life's work will have been for nothing." His persistent smile began to falter. "That would be too challenging to my own beliefs."

Returning the somber gaze, Vincent slowly nodded. "I see no harm in accepting an efficient weapon for the hard road ahead," he said.

"Thank you, Vincent," replied Salem, his smile returning. "May it serve you well."

With genuine concern, Ryn asked, "But what about you, Salem? Won't you need protection of some sort?"

"God will watch after me."

XII

After the meal – while Louis showered – Salem let Vincent and John pick from a trio of compact hiking bags. Salem had already packed each bag with a few tools and supplies; pocket knives, canteens, flashlights, water- and wind-proof matches, stick lighters, maps of the region (each bag had a different map). In the front pocket of each bag was a small leather-bound Bible – a simple edition with no other marking than a golden cross set into the black face.

Though she kept her own bag, Salem gave Ryn the same supplies to add to her own.

After Vincent divvied up the supplies from the duffel bag amongst their new packs, they stuffed extra clothing into the remaining space. Having grown fond of the boots, both Vincent and John opted not to take the ones offered by Salem – John even kept the camouflage jacket while Vincent changed up for a heavy wool jacket two shades lighter than his shirt and hat.

Once Louis was showered and dressed and packed – and feeling quite refreshed – each of them offered their most sincere gratitude to Salem for his hospitality (Ryn even asked if he wouldn't join them, but Salem graciously refused). They inquired about a possible vehicle to aid in their journey, but the priest informed them that the last car drove out of town two days prior – just as he had arrived to *cleanse* the town of its evil.

Feeling abashed for his accusations of attempted murder, Louis apologized and begged forgiveness for his belligerence. To which – naturally – the priest had told him, "Don't you worry, son. I take no offense to such allegations. Nor does the Lord. Your behavior was not at all belligerent. In fact, I view your behavior as noble and brave. You honor your friend by ensuring his safety."

"Thank you, Father," replied Louis, awkwardly shaking Salem's right hand with his left.

There was no struggle in Salem's eyes when approaching Vincent any longer. Nor was there any when he gently took Vincent's right hand in both of his. "Thank you," he said. "This blade will give you the protection of God. And one day, when your time is nigh, you will know to whom this blade must be entrusted."

Vincent nodded, clapped his other hand over Salem's. "You're a good man, Father."

The priest grinned. "Safe travels," he said, releasing Vincent's hand.

He watched them out of view before balefully regarding the smoldering remains of the old church.

XIII

Upon their departure – new clothes, new bags, new tools, new supplies, new weapons – the sun had passed its zenith and was on its downward arc toward the western horizon. Each of them gazed somberly at the flaming pile of rubble that was once a landmark of this small town. The smoke that drifted skyward looked like demons escaping Hell.

"Well, that was a trip," said Ryn after a mere minute of travel.

"Yep," agreed Louis. "I'm not quite sure what just happened there."

The highway split off to their right – to the south – over a canti-levered bridge. Faint babbling of an unseen river rose up from below the bridge, beyond the guardrail. A light breeze whistled through the trees, tussled their hair – Ryn's flew forward, whipping her eyes, but she paid this no mind.

"This is heavy," said John.

"Agreed," said Louis.

"So…" began Ryn, searching for words. "What do we do now?" is all she conjured.

"Hoof it," replied Vincent. "We got aways to go, but I know we can do it."

"That's encouraging," she murmured, sarcastic.

Spread out across both lanes, they continued at a fresh pace; brisk, yet conservative – the bridge was now fifty yards at their backs. Soon enough, the road became claustrophobic – the limbs of trees stretched overhead from either side of the road; they nearly touched across this expanse. Shadows over the road were dense, dark – cold.

With a quick stop – and quicker debate – they veered off the main highway at a nearby railroad crossing. Quickly, their path was crowded by trees whose only trimmings came from passing trains. Minute after minute passed under a tall, dark canopy – until eventually, the highway at their backs was lost in a growing haze that separated them from it.

Uneventful hours ticked by, tracked only by the nerve-wracking passage of interspersed driveways that crossed the tracks. Occasional gaps in the surrounding trees would give way to scenic farmland on the northern hills or southern flats – the highway ran mostly parallel to the tracks and was visible to the south, beyond the fields.

Near sunset came the first disturbance on this afternoon journey; rapid gunfire in the distance. At first, the gunfire came in bursts. And as it grew closer to their position, it became steadier – louder. Before long, they could hear the underlying roar of a pickup truck.

To the right of the tracks – to the south – was a clearing. A scattered horde that was previously lurching north – lurching right at this quartet – whirled at the sound of oncoming gunfire.

"Get down," said Vincent, stooping behind a fallen tree.

They all ducked down beside him.

Moments later, a green pickup zoomed by with a .50-caliber mini-gun mounted in the bed. The gunner unleashed a spray that cut through the horde and peppered the log behind which this quartet was hiding, showering them with splinters.

Ryn shrieked; all four dropped, covering their heads.

Vincent could swear he heard some maniacal laughter between bursts, but that could not have been possible.

All remaining lurchers in the clearing (of which there were few) began stumbling after the raucous truck. The roaring engine faded quickly – the gunfire faded slowly. After a few minutes, the reckless truck was somewhere to the west and still blindly blasting away at everything in its path, wasting round after round of grossly misappropriated ammunition.

Before starting back down the tracks, Ryn worried over Salem's fate should these maniacs cross his path.

A mile down the road, a crow cawed twice, catching their anxious attention.

Defenses heightened – heart hammering – the katana handle felt hot under Vincent's white knuckles.

A moment later, a lurcher crashed through the foliage and into Ryn. It knocked her back a few feet – she stumbled cleanly over the tracks and tripped on a vine, thus tumbling into the bushes. She screamed until the breath was knocked out of her from the impact.

Without hesitation, John slammed his axe into its back. And, while it lay across the tracks, squirming under the embedded axe, Vincent sliced clean through its neck with one swipe of the katana. The inhuman eyes of the decapitated head stared up at him while its teeth continued gnashing.

"Oh my god!" breathed Ryn, pushing herself up. "That's awful! Kill it! Kill it!"

Vincent placed the tip of the katana on its eyeball and pushed – he swirled the blade until the head stopped gnashing.

Covering her eyes, holding her stomach, Ryn turned away.

"Let's go," said Vincent. "We should find a place to crash soon." He started down the tracks, holding the katana at his side – it dripped bits of curdled blood and chunks of rotten graymatter.

XIV

Just as the sun was setting and the color was draining from the sky, they found a spot to camp in the foliage about thirty yards off the tracks. Their camp was maybe twenty square feet of rough, knotty ground in a sea of ferns and evergreens. Without daring to light a fire that might attract unwanted attention, they ate cold hotdogs in silence.

All of them were exhausted and achy and mentally strained, wandering the labyrinths of their delirious minds while absently ingesting minimal sustenance. At first, the cold, slimy surface of the uncooked hotdog was difficult for them to chew, but after a few bites, none of them noticed.

Despite the uninviting, lumpy, cold forest floor, Vincent was quick to sleep – Louis was a few minutes behind him. The day had been long for them after having foolishly stayed awake throughout the previous night; their naps this day had barely amounted to an hour apiece.

John and Ryn stayed awake for some time, though they rarely spoke. When John began nodding off, Ryn told him to sleep – she was wide awake and would rouse him after a few hours. He protested lightly before laying back with a massive yawn. He was asleep within a minute.

Ryn grasped the dainty gold chain with heart-shaped locket that hung from her neck. She opened the locket and, being sightless in the gloom of night, rubbed her thumb over the picture it held. A tear rolled down her cheek as she thought of her father.

XV

On the highway, silent and cautious, a boy pedaled a sturdy mountain bike past a horde of ghouls. He unsheathed a three-foot bamboo staff from his back and readied himself. Something groaned to his left and he swung high, striking one straight in the dome – he swerved, but leveled his course within a moment.

Another groan – closer – came from his right. It was too late – he was not quick enough to fend it off; the ghoul lunged at him. It grabbed the back wheel, its hand caught in the spokes, and the rider tumbled to the pavement, scraping his exposed skin in places and burning through his jeans, his shirt in others.

The boy fought by starlight and sound – his ears uncannily keen – swinging his staff at every step and snarl. His wild swinging landed multiple hits that kept a handful of his attackers at bay. When afforded the space and time, he would calculate a strike against the nearest aggressor in his limited view.

When the onslaught abated, he hurried back to his bike – verified the lunging ghoul wasn't still attached to his back wheel – and took off again.

A group of latecomers hobbled after the bicyclist. They would continue down the road long after the boy was gone. Eventually, they would follow a mewling cat through an empty tract of farmland toward the northern hills.

Day Eight
Life & Death

I

It was pleasant enough to begin with – they were walking serenely down a wooded trail, hand in hand, with smiling eyes and fluttering hearts. They were happy, as they had always been. Each satisfied thoroughly in every facet of their lives, both individual and combined.

Sunspots speckled the forest floor, these aimless wanderers; shadows danced about in the sunlight, playing on bushes, on trees, on dirt and on lovers. Birds chirped near and far while rodents rustled in the shrubbery.

One bird in particular caught her eye. It was yellow and black and fat and cute, singing a special song just for this couple. She broke his tender hold and, with grace uncommon, she bound upon a mossy and green nurse log with many small sprouts that shot skyward. So calm was she that this young finch did leap onto her outstretched finger and sing a song for her – a solo serenade.

And he was happy to see her smile as she beamed her ecstasy at this friendly finch.

This is the way it should always be, thought he of her. *This is the way it* will *always be*. And his woes did melt away – his body, his soul

were now at ease, sublime. He glowed while she whistled in collusion –
a duet! – with this strangely friendly finch.

A breeze combed this forest, taking with it this goldfinch – this
friend of Isabella.

Upon this breeze came a wall of leaves, a chill – her face became
obscured by this wall and her flowing hair. She watched her friend flap
away; he watched the floating wall move as one along the path. He
watched it out of sight and turned to find his beautiful Isabella's flowing
hair (*red?*) settle into place revealing a gorgeous, youthful face (*Ryn?*) –
his mind raged for answers to this strangely sudden change.

And from the forest came a handsome young man – his face was a
blend of every soldier he had met – from Lee to Cooper to Sanchez to
Johnson. This menagerie of a man emerged from behind the moss-laden
tree with a goldfinch upon an outstretched finger. As he raised this bird
up to this lovely lady, his young face paled, drooped and sprouted a
snowy, stringy canvas and the bird grew large and fat and black.

The young lady (*Ryn!*) shrieked – Vincent froze.

In a deep, dark, remote corner of the forest, a crow cawed and a
beautiful person was taken into the abyss. He watched those last strands
of her luxuriant (*red!*) hair chase her into the shadows – into the darkness. A ghost of her twisted face was stamped into his subconscious.

II

Vincent sat bolt upright, breathing heavy. White lights flashed
about the foliage. He could vaguely make out the image of something
trundling through ferns. When the light flashed elsewhere, he could see
another trundling figure. With dancing lights cutting randomly across his

blurred vision, he relied on his other senses (namely his hearing) to relay the situation to his brain.

Groans and moans and the rustling of bushes hit his ear –

Large hands hoisted him to his feet. "Grab your shit!" hollered John.

Out of sorts and off-balance, Vincent snatched up his bag and un-sheathed his katana.

"C'mon!" called John – he took off, plowing through the under-brush, the beam of his flashlight jumping this way and that, illuminating his path – the dancing shadows were heavy and deceptive.

With his light still tucked away, Vincent started after John's sil-houette. Half blind and bounding through ferns and over logs, he fum-bled with the backpack, his arm bent back and up, reaching for the bag's side pocket. He thumbed the flashlight and smacked into a sapling – he was spun around and nearly tumbled.

He had almost regained his balance when something caught his an-kle and dropped him to the soggy earth. A brief yelp was cut short when the air in his lungs was forced out on impact. He managed to hold the sword safely to one side in the fall. Gasping for air, he was blinded as John's flashlight beamed directly into his eyes.

"Look out!" cried John.

Something groaned, groped at his ankle.

The world remained a white explosion to Vincent – the light had flashed out his vision entirely, leaving only a black ghost that shrouded the world. He flipped onto his back, carelessly swinging and scuttling away from his attacker. One wild swing found the lurcher's skull and stuck. With an effort, he was able to yank it free again.

And finally his vision cleared enough to see the skeletal ghoul at his feet.

Once again, John's large hands hoisted him up. Radiant light cast a twirling myriad of deviant shadows across John's animated face. He yanked Vincent's flashlight free of its snug home and slapped it into his hand. "Let's go!" he commanded, his teeth barred (the sight of which bolstered his malevolent appearance).

Twenty yards ahead of them, twin beams danced amidst inconsistent shadows. These lights marked the brazen exodus of Louis and Ryn from this midnight terror. John tugged at Vincent's arm and started after them; Vincent chased his heel.

Ryn shrieked, Louis bellowed – an audible *TING!* rang out through the forest followed by a hushed exchange. They were blinded to the incident by distance and darkness; all they could see was the wild fusion of intersticed light and shadow in this dense wood. Driven harder by these alarming sounds, Vincent bounded nimbly through the foliage, bypassing John, who had also increased his pace (despite his long, powerful legs, John's size notably diminished his mobility when high-stepping ferns and hopping logs).

Dipping and dodging – and just about losing his footing with every other step – Vincent raced toward the frantic lights. With fear and adrenaline pumping through his veins, time slowed – mere moments of underbrush negotiation seemed to stretch into minutes.

The katana was hot under his white knuckles.

His light landed on a lurcher – it was lunging at something ten yards out. He rounded a tree and watched Louis brain it – *TING!* – with the aluminum bat; it fell with just one blow. Another one lunged and Louis caught it on the backswing. He whirled, stopped, crooked his arm; Ryn's hands shot up from the underbrush and he lifted her to her feet.

Vincent rushed past them, meeting an oncoming horde head-on. His boisterous attack – the raucous trampling of ferns and twigs – the bright and wild beam of his light – attracted the horde. Their numbers were spread and their fervor made them trip and fall. Scattered as they were, Vincent carved a path with ease.

The others followed close behind.

Together, the four of them sliced straight through the horde. They were clear of the mass – still running hard with hammering hearts – when Louis was tripped by a crawler. Instinctively, his hands went out to break his fall and two of the wooden splints on his right arm snapped – the metal splint dug painfully into his skin. His elbow bent audibly backwards and cracked in two more places.

And he bawled, the sound shrill and bloodcurdling.

The crawler pulled itself toward Louis as he writhed in the underbrush.

As it groped at his leg, Vincent raced back; as it chomped on his boot, Vincent buried his blade in its skull. Another moment or two and it would have found flesh on which it could feast. "C'mon, buddy," he said, offering a hand. "We gotta go. Now." He shined his light on their back path to find glowing eyes and bobbing heads.

Louis relinquished the grip on his busted elbow and slapped his hand into Vincent's.

They were off again, fetching a sizeable rift between them and the devastated horde of disjointed (and, in some cases, dismembered) lurchers, of which very few now remained. Occasional groans and snarls would catch their ear from ten or twenty yards out, but none were close enough to attack.

Before long, they found the edge of this wood.

III

None of them saw the fenceline – all of them crashed into it.

Due to his height, John folded over the taut cable of this chest-high fence while his friends bounced straight off. Each had been running at a full sprint and, from their velocity, the impact knocked each windless. Louis, still dizzy with pain, stumbled back and fell into a fern, bumped his elbow again – he did not bellow this time, only seethed and grimaced and groped at the pain.

Still holding her chest tight from impact with the wire fenceline – still gasping for air – Ryn started off toward the railway, silently cursing the fence and the field beyond. In reality, she was cursing the false hope this vast field gave her when bounding out of the forest only to be so painfully rejected.

In similar fashion – gripping their bellies, their chests, cursing the field, the fence – the others followed with John hunched at the rear, still half bent from folding over the cable. He quit cursing when he thought of how much worse it could have been had the fence been barbed instead of straight cables.

A large swatch of the bejeweled night sky – a touch of color was now beginning to creep into the darkness – stretched overhead, over the misty field. And, somewhere beyond the treeline and rolling hills, the sun was gradually working its way toward the horizon.

With the pain in his abdomen receding some, Vincent gazed out at the shifty fog, the field and its carefully interspersed trees. He stared at the stars – marveled at the lack of clouds – picked out the few constellations he knew. He spotted the new moon – a dark circle amidst a sea of shimmering stars.

Leaning against the cornerpost before the tracks, Ryn held her head with one hand and her belly with the other. "That's one helluva way to wake up," she said. Her pout turned to a facetious sneer and she dropped her hands.

"Not too banged-up, I trust," Vincent said in passing – he stepped onto the tracks, admiring the natural beauty surrounding him.

"I think I'll survive," she said, stepping up beside him.

"That's the goal," commented Louis. He stopped short of the tracks, turning to check that they were still four; John was plodding along, though his gait was not so hunched or staggered and he no longer clenched his belly.

Ryn was staring down the tracks. "What do you suppose is down there?" she asked.

Vincent followed her gaze; a flickering light – small and almost unnoticeable – shone through a distant attic window. "Looks like a house to me," he said. "Probably another whacko priest."

"Oh, God, I hope not!" she sighed.

"Please no," John panted.

"You okay there, big guy?" Vincent asked.

"Never been better," John replied, feigning a smile through his grimace. "Now let's go." He started off down the tracks first to show them just how fine he was, though pain still blazed across his midsection. A colorful bruise would soon bloom, stretching from side to side.

Genuine curiosity coursed Vincent's veins regarding the occupants of the house ahead. Typically a pessimist of humanity, he was wary, but somewhere in his soul he discovered a strange hope. Something inside told him there was nothing to worry about – they would be treated with muffins and milk instead of hostility and gunplay.

Running his hand over the katana, Vincent slipped into a cascade of ephemeral thoughts.

BLAM! – pellets sprayed the trees, the tracks and the four travelers.

John rolled down one embankment, into a tree while Vincent rolled over the embankment, into the fence. Somebody was shouting obscenities from a distance – from the attic of the house – something about demons and slugs.

Before another shot could be fired, Ryn pushed the words she thought she heard together to form a cohesive sentence and started pulling at Louis' sleeve – he was still writhing, delirious from the fresh birdshot implanted in his shin and his busted arm that took yet another pounding.

He rolled out of her grasp, daft to the matter.

She pulled at him again, snatched his jacket and yanked him backward; they tumbled down the embankment together, sliding into the shrubbery just a few feet from John. *"Keep your head down!"* she hissed.

BLAM! – the upper half of the fencepost nearest Vincent exploded.

A crow cawed nearby – a flock of birds sang their fears – groans rose on the wind.

"Go back to Hell!" croaked the weathered old man in the attic.

Vincent crawled over the raised tracks to join his friends behind the other embankment.

"Wait!" cried Ryn – she stood up, waving her arms. "We're not infected!" she screamed. "We're not infected! Please!"

"Leave me be, hellspawn!" he cried, shucking another round into the chamber.

John yanked her back down –

BLAM! – a massive hole was punched into a nearby tree.

"Fuck this!" growled John, rolling onto his belly. He drew the rifle up to his chin and sighted the attic window. When the old man's head popped into view –

CRACK! – the bullet splintered the windowsill; the old man dropped back out of sight.

"Let's go!" barked John.

They bolted single-file through the underbrush at the edge of the embankment, each keeping a keen eye on the attic window. And when the old man reappeared – *CRACK!* – John splintered the windowsill again. As they ran further along – too far along to worry about being shot, but not far enough to stop running – the old man poked his head out again and openly fired three wild shots near the spot he last saw them.

"*Demons be gone!*" he cried, firing more slugs at the tracks and trees before ducking back into the darkness.

Later this morning, attracted by the continuous thunder of his shotgun, "real" *demons* and *hellspawn* would overrun his house. Swarmed by ghouls, the old man would eat one of his own fiery lead slugs. The undead masticators would chomp until his body was little more than a dismembered skeleton that was missing the top half of its skull.

While munching on the old man's heart, one of the lurchers – a one-eyed haggard farmer with a flayed cheek – would stumble straight out the attic window, blindly chasing distant gunfire. It sustained many broken bones in the fall – including a snapped femur – but somehow managed to stand and even stumble onward.

When the gnarled farmer started down the tracks, the old man's heart was still clenched firmly in its hand.

IV

Throwing his weight onto a tree at a crossroad and speaking in a breathy husk, John said, "Stop. Please." He ran a hand down his leg and winced, feeling the scattered birdshot embedded there. "Sonofabitch got me!"

"Yeah," said Ryn, dropping to one knee. "Me too." A few beads speckled her ankle and foot, but not so many as to hobble her.

Nauseated by the thundering pain in his arm, Louis did not notice the beads scattered up and down his leg. He seethed and paced and groped at his elbow (which did nothing at all to ease the pain).

Heart hammering, ripe with adrenaline, Vincent hunched over in the middle of the crossroad, stroking the birdshot in his hip; one of the beads had found an old wound in which it could bury. Exacerbating this pain were the various aches in his joints that were spurred on by a physical desire for drugs to which he no longer had access.

"We gotta find someplace to take these out," said John.

"Let's get back to the highway," suggested Ryn. "We'll probably find transport there."

"I like it," said John, pushing off the tree.

Something groaned from down the tracks. Another groan followed, further along the tracks. And then a waterfall of groans cascaded into the distance and swelled again as nearby lurchers groaned some more.

"Yeah," breathed Vincent, still hunched. Craning his neck, Vincent searched the shadows for movement – maybe he saw a head bobbing here, an arm flailing there – or maybe he saw the trees and shrubs shuffling in the breeze. Or maybe – just maybe – his bleary eyes and sleep deprived brain were playing tricks on him.

Uncertain of the answer to this fundamentally futile question (and indifferent, as well, since the groans alone were enough to spark alarm), he started down the road. With a noticeable limp in his stride, he fell in step with Louis, who was still cradling his elbow. "How you doin' there, buddy?" he asked.

Before answering, Louis gazed balefully at his friend. "Not so hot," he said at last.

"How's your leg?" he asked.

"Can't feel it – yet," he replied, adding emphasis to the last.

"Damn," breathed Vincent.

"How 'bout you?" inquired Louis.

"Could be better," he replied, rubbing a light hand over the beads and wincing. "Got my bad hip."

"That sucks," said Louis – a stock response (he only half-heard Vincent due to his own painful preoccupations). Pain shot up his arm, radiating from his elbow – he grimaced and groaned and threw his head back without losing a step.

Another cascade of groans drifted after them from the tracks.

Distant shouting and gunfire sounded – the old man in the attic again. The groans then grew thick and unrelenting – they became a deathly chorus of moans that chilled Vincent to his very core. Fortunately, this chorus appeared to be moving toward the gunfire rather than after this group (though Vincent thought of how unfortunate the old man would be when this horde of "actual" *demons* and *hellspawn* closed in on him – not even the birdshot in his hip could ease the grief he felt for this frightened man).

A vast field stretched out to their right on the western side of the road – acres of treeless land between the tracks and the highway. Above

this featureless field, a cloudless sky glimmered with innumerable stars –
Ursa Major was tilted toward the trees, spilling her sparkling contents
carelessly about. The starlight, as beautiful and bright as it shined, offered little visibility with the moon darkened by Earth's shadow.

Plagued by injuries, this cadre's progress was surprisingly exped-
itious. But despite their relatively decent clip, this leg of their trek – this
short, narrow, dark and eerie backroad – could never end soon enough.
Every whistle of wind and flitter of leaves did set these travelers' nerves
on edge. Groans like waves rose and fell at their backs, further grating at
their wits.

Something skittered across the road, halting their march, and Vincent almost drew his sword. The thing squeaked and skittered faster.
They heard it scamper through the field, squeaking once more before it
was beyond earshot. After a brief pause to ponder this animal (both its
fate and its role in the world), they continued down the road.

And five mentally taxing minutes later, they were heading east
along the highway.

Without pursuers, each of them felt at ease enough to walk at a lei-
surely pace. They doused two of the lights to save power; only John and
Vincent kept theirs burning at the flanks. John wrestled a canteen from
his pack and handed it down the line until everyone had their fill.

After a half mile of travel, Vincent dug through his bag until he
found the map Salem had stowed there. Illuminating it with radiant light
(he kept the main beam of his flashlight upon the road), he narrowed
down their position and estimated the distance to the next town along the
highway – Ashford – at roughly two miles. Too much can happen in that
timeframe. And he could only imagine what – if anything – awaited
them there.

He didn't voice his trepidations, but was sure to pass along the pertinent information of estimated distance and time.

Ashford was, in fact, a rather sleepy town. The residents – more than a few of which were already infected – had mostly fled to the east, though some lucky few had thought better of this and fled to the south, by way of Elbe. A small faction of stubborn mountaineers – and a couple tourists – stayed behind to protect the town and wait for rescue from this unprecedented scourge.

V

Stirrings in his gut had Vincent's mind in a knot.

The road was too dark now – overhead, the trees formed a nearly unbroken canopy. Beyond this shroud was the star-speckled sky – a touch more color had crept into it, but Vincent felt the darkness was deeper than at any other point throughout the night. The brightness of his flashlight did nothing to ease this sensation.

He continually scanned the southern treeline while John kept watch to the north. Walking between them, Louis and Ryn also kept their eyes trained on the twin beams as they swept back and forth. Occasionally, someone would swing around to check their back path.

Marching down the highway – even in this nearly unnatural darkness – Vincent felt they were too exposed. He envisioned ghouls popping out of every bush, from behind every tree – up and over the guardrails and racing after him. He thought of high-caliber trucks barreling down the road and mowing him down one way or another. He thought of unnatural and extremely farfetched predicaments, unduly frightening himself beyond reason.

And something else nipped at the back of his mind, but he couldn't associate a name or a cause with this muted alarm.

Fifteen minutes passed before Louis said, "Hold up, guys," and veered off to the shoulder. "I gotta rest a minute." He dropped his pack and sat on the guardrail.

Without a word, John followed suit.

"You doing alright there, buddy?" Vincent asked.

"I'm fine," replied Louis. "Just sore and hurtin'. You know: the usual."

"I gotcha." He popped a cigarette in his mouth and took a seat next to Louis.

Ryn dropped her pack at Vincent's feet. "Well, I'm gonna pee," she said. "Keep an eye out." She hopped the guardrail and stepped behind a tree. They could hear the light tinkling of urine on leaves.

Something rumbled in the west; the trio on the guardrail turned as one.

The rumble flared a few times; rubber chirped on wet pavement.

"Someone's coming," said Vincent.

"What should we do?" asked Louis.

"Let's hitch a ride," suggested John.

A faint glow danced about a bend in the road.

"Good idea," said Vincent. "But let's play it safe. I'll flag 'em down with the three of you covering me."

"Sounds dangerous," said Louis.

"Everything's dangerous now," said John. "Sure you don't want me flagging 'em down, Vin?"

"I'm sure," replied Vincent. "You're a bit too intimidating sometimes. And I'd rather have your deadeye covering me – just in case."

The glow at the bend grew steadily brighter.

"Then let's do it," said John. "I'll take the other side of the road." He grabbed his pack, shouldered his rifle and started across the highway.

Holding the cigarette between his teeth, Vincent rummaged through his bag until he found a road flare. "You and Ryn stay together," he told Louis. "Be ready in case this gets violent." He slipped on the pack and, after a second thought, handed his rifle over to Louis. "Take this. I don't want them getting all paranoid."

"What about your sword?"

"No time. But I'll try to keep it out of sight."

"Gotcha."

Vincent stepped into the middle of the road.

"What's going on?" said Ryn, emerging from behind a tree.

"A car's coming," Louis explained. "Vincent's gonna flag 'em down."

Just then, the flare in Vincent's hand erupted, bathing the road in brilliant red light.

"And what are we doing?" she asked. "Just watching him risk his life?"

A pair of high-beams roared around the bend; Vincent started waving the flare and his flashlight.

"No," said Louis. "We're covering him. Nothing's gonna happen."

"Damn straight nothing's gonna happen." She hopped the guardrail and raced to Vincent's side.

"*Shit!*" hissed Louis. He ducked down and scuttled into a fair cover position, cursing the girl's recklessness.

"What're you doing?" barked Vincent.

She froze, staring at the lights bearing down on them.

"Fuck it!" he husked, still waving the flare and flashlight.

The vehicle slowed – Vincent could barely make out the shape of a minivan – its breaks squalled as it came to a stop ten feet away.

Vincent smiled, still waving the dueling lights, careful to keep his eyes dead ahead.

The driver revved the engine.

Vincent dropped his arms and started toward the driver's door; Ryn was on his heel.

"Hold it, buddy," said the driver – his voice was familiar.

They stopped – Vincent's trepidations roiled.

"Where are your friends?" the driver asked.

"Excuse me?" said Vincent.

"Where's that *fuckhead*, Webb?" asked the driver.

Vincent flushed – the driver no doubt saw this as he started chuckling.

The passenger door opened. And then a silhouette lunged through the lights, tackled Vincent. "What now, motherfucker?" cried Sanchez as he slammed a fist into Vincent's face. "Y'all left us for dead out there in B-F-E!" He socked him again. "Goan give you a good ass whoopin' now, bitch!" He bloodied Vincent's nose.

Ryn smashed her rifle stock into the side of his head before Sanchez could land another blow; he fell to one side, holding his face, dazed.

The driver opened his door – "Whoa there, little lady," he said with a titter – and leveled a very large pistol at her. "Don't go getting all crazy on us now. Put that thing down."

Sanchez writhed and moaned. After a moment, he pushed up onto wobbly feet.

"Where are your friends?" Cooper asked.

"Right here," said Louis from inside the old minivan – he pressed the muzzle of his pistol into Cooper's abdomen.

"Here too," said John as he sighted Cooper's head with his rifle.

Never having a chance to drop her rifle as Cooper had instructed, Ryn sighted Sanchez.

"Told you they had backup," said Cooper. "Where's Webb?"

"Drop it," insisted Louis.

Cooper let the pistol dangle from his finger by the trigger guard. "Dead, huh?" He snorted. "Figures."

Wiping blood from under his nose, Vincent rose to his feet. He regarded Sanchez with a malicious eye, but stood fast, biding his time. He rapped his fingers along the katana's handle. "I do believe," he began slow, enunciating every syllable. "The last time I saw you...I told you...I think I told you...I wouldn't be so kind...as to leave you with weapons...and good health...and *not* tie you up." He paused, cocked his head, gripped the katana. "And here you are," he said, "in the middle of nowhere – once again." He drew the blade. "How fucking poetic."

A moment of silence followed – blood dribbled from Vincent's nose, over his lips; scarlet droplets clung to his chin until they grew too heavy. Direct light from the minivan's high-beams accentuated this trickle and turned his malicious eye sinister.

"Disarm them," he said at last.

John stepped toward Cooper, intent on taking the pistol dangling from his finger.

But when he neared, Cooper flipped the gun back up and slammed it into John's cheek, sending him whirling and dazed –

BLAM! – a bullet from Louis' pistol punctured Cooper's abdomen, pierced his liver, shattered three vertebrae and punched a sizeable hole in his backside.

As Cooper fell, Sanchez charged – *CRACK!* – but a bullet from Ryn's rifle lodged itself in his shoulder and knocked him to the ground. The defected soldiers hit the pavement simultaneously. Sanchez writhed and groaned, groping his injured shoulder.

Vincent knelt beside him. "You can live on knowing one thing," he said, slipping his hand around Sanchez' neck. "At least I won't tie you up for the *stenches*." He applied pressure to the carotid, the jugular – Sanchez stopped groping at his shoulder and started wrenching at Vincent's arm. "Don't worry," said Vincent. "You're just going to sleep for a little while."

Ryn stood aside in awe.

VI

"You probably should have just killed him," said Louis from the passenger seat.

Vincent was driving the rundown minivan. He said, "I'm done with cold-blooded murder." He didn't mean for that to slip; he flushed, his breath hitched. He checked the mirror, but neither John nor Ryn had fathomed the depth of his statement. He noticed a sideways glance from Louis. "At least he has a chance," he blurted so his last statement wouldn't linger.

Glancing in the mirror again, Vincent noticed that Ryn was still in shock. He sighed and said nothing, pining for the right words to say. But he couldn't think of any to assuage the turmoil rolling around inside her. Really, all he wanted to do was thank her; if she hadn't reacted so quickly, his katana would have ended Sanchez – if Sanchez hadn't somehow foiled his defenses and ended his life instead, that is.

"Cooper's probably gonna die," murmured John.

"Yeah," breathed Louis. "Nothing we can do about it now."

"I'm not upset about it," said John. "He was about to kill me. Probably shouldn't have tried that."

"No," said Louis, sighing. "Probably shouldn't have."

And as Vincent maneuvered the minivan into the outskirts of Ashford, a young man in the hospitable confines of a makeshift lodge was gathering his gear and sneaking out – his total transitory residence there amounted to no more than nine hours. Armed with a bamboo staff, he mounted his bicycle and started east. His stealthy flight wasn't even noticed by the night watchman as he was preoccupied with headlights approaching from the west.

VII

Frantic lights bounded into the street, illuminated the minivan, shone through the windshield. Startled and cautious, Vincent slowed and angled the van toward the oncoming lights. The men holding these lights abruptly shaded their eyes and planted their heels. Vincent brought the minivan to a stop a few yards away.

"What do you suppose this is about?" inquired Louis.

"I have no idea," replied Vincent. "But they don't appear hostile."

"No, I suppose they don't." Louis rolled down his window. "Yo!" he called – the men shifted, still shading their eyes. "What can I do for you?"

The men looked quizzical, disappointed. "You're not military," called one (he was shaggy with gray hair and red flannel).

Louis thought this sounded like a question; "No," he replied. "We're not." He thought of the soldiers – of shooting Cooper and leaving Sanchez for dead (once again) – and shuddered. "Do you have medical supplies?" he asked.

The men exchanged a distressed gaze. The shaggy one turned back. "What're your injuries?" he asked.

"Buckshot," Vincent called through his window. "And a busted arm."

"Any infected?" asked the shaggy man.

"No," Vincent called back. "Any infected in there?"

"No." The men exchanged another look – the shaggy one seemed to be pleading with the younger one. And then the younger one flopped his arms in apparent exasperation. He waved them over and stepped back onto the deck of the lodge.

The shaggy one started to the driver's door. "Park around the side," he said, studying the minivan's occupants. "We'll see what we can't do for you."

"Thanks," said Vincent, his face still bloodied – bruises were blooming under his eyes.

"No problem."

VIII

Instructed not to use any lights and stay tight, they were led through the dim lodge by the pair that flagged them down outside. But even without the aid of light, Vincent was able to sense the disarray surrounding him – something was toppled in a corner, the register was missing. Glass crunched underfoot and he could only imagine where it came from.

Something stared at him from behind a merchandise rack –

He gripped the katana (it was cold to the touch) and eyed the silent observer. The person didn't seem to be tracking his movement, but Vincent was poised and ready. He scanned the rest of the place – was someone else watching him in the other corner, too?

A door opened; light spilled out and revealed the silent observers to be nothing more than mannequins; extremely nonthreatening inanimate objects. Inwardly, he felt foolish. Breathing again (though he couldn't recall when he stopped) Vincent released his white-knuckle grip on the katana.

They were hurried through the open door and into the back office, whereupon the door was swiftly shut at their backs. The room was lit by two electric lanterns – one hung from the ceiling, the other rested on a desk beside a dark computer monitor. More thin light filtered in from a back room.

"What's the damage here?" asked the younger of the pair – his eyes immediately focused on Vincent's colorful face. "Whoa there," he said. "Are you sure you're not infected? That looks pretty nasty."

"I'm sure," said Vincent. "Lurchers don't punch."

"He don't look infected to me," said the scruffy one. "Looks like he had his bell rung nice 'n' good, but he don't look infected."

"You could say that, yes," said Vincent.

"Which one o' y'all got shot?" asked the scruffy one.

"All of us," replied John, showing off his speckled thigh – his pants were soaked with blood from the multitude of wounds.

The scruffy one gawked, his eyes wide under furry eyebrows. "Holy cow!"

The younger of the pair (he was barely younger than Vincent or Louis) stood silently in mild shock. He briefly assessed each of the others – and then his eyes landed on Louis. "Alright," he began, "I'm going to fix up your arm before anything else – I think I have some painkillers around here somewhere, if you need them. And Bucky here," he thrust a thumb over his shoulder at the scruffy old man, "will get to work on the big guy's thigh." He turned to face Bucky. "Lay him up on the cot in back. Shouldn't need too much –"

"I got it," said Bucky. "Tweezers, alcohol – yada-yada-yada."

"Don't forget the –"

"Yada-yada-yada." Bucky stood up. "Come with me," he said to John, snatching the lantern off the desk.

Louis was splinted and relieved of his birdshot (and medicated) before Bucky finished with John's leg. Vincent declined any attention until Ryn was helped – the few beads embedded in her foot took just a few minutes to extract. For his wounds, Vincent was given ibuprofen – how he longed for the drugs Louis was given, but he resisted the urge to ask for any.

(He did take note of where the drugs were stored, though…just in case.)

Fuzzy morning sunlight filtered in around the curtains when all were patched up.

"Thank you so much," gushed Ryn. "I can't tell you how much this means to us."

"You're very welcome, young lady," replied Bucky.

"What the hell happened to you guys out there?" asked his younger counterpart.

"It's a long story," replied Vincent, plucking a cigarette from his pack.

"Hey now," said the young one, "you can't smoke in here."

Vincent chuckled and sparked it anyway.

"I'm serious!" squawked the young one. "There's no ventilation!"

Vincent raised his eyebrows and drew deep of his smoke. "I got more pressing concerns than *ventilation* right now."

"If you want to smoke," he said, "then go up onto the roof. I'm not trying to breathe your secondhand for the next three days."

"Three days, huh?" mused Vincent, taking another puff. "You think you'll last that long?"

"I don't imagine it'll take them that long to save us," he said, confident.

"You think you're getting saved?" Vincent barked a quick guffaw. "World's going to hell in an express handbasket and you *still* think you're getting saved!"

"Ease up, Vin," said Louis, his voice low.

"Sorry," said Vincent, obviously not apologetic in the least. "My bad. Just trying to inform the good doctor here of some current affairs. Which, by the way, aren't so pretty."

"How bad is it?" Bucky asked. "Radio don't say shit 'bout nothin' no more. Last we heard, all the cities were being evacuated."

"Don't know where they're evacuating to," grumbled John.

"It's bad," said Louis.

"National Guard can't even do shit about it," said Vincent. "We're on our own now." He puffed and gazed stolidly at the younger one. "So I'm not too concerned with *ventilation* at the moment." He blew the smoke out slowly, relishing the flavor. "But," he continued with dramatic pause. "In the future, I'll be sure to hit up the roof."

"I do apologize," said Louis. "It's been a rough week for all of us – I can't even begin to tell you how rough." He looked a moment at his busted arm. "I guess we're all wearing proof of it, though."

"No," replied the young man. "I understand." He plopped with a huff onto one of the cots. "It hasn't been easy for us either. I'm sure you figured that. We were just trying to hold onto some sort of hope, I guess."

"You get so used to the system," said Bucky, "that you never expect it to fail."

"Smartest thing I've heard all day," said Louis, wearing a grim smirk.

A silence followed in which they all ruminated on Bucky's statement.

And then Ryn asked, "How many of you are there here? It can't just be the two of you."

"We got four, total," replied Bucky. "Some drifter was here overnight, but he disappeared at some point before you showed up. Heck," he snorted a quick guffaw at himself, "can't even remember the kid's name." He shrugged. "Anyhow, two of us are on watch right now – we always double-up on the watch after a disturbance, such as your arrival – or that boy's arrival last night. Rhea and Jothan are up there. Sweet little couple from –"

"Did you say *Rhea?*" Vincent asked. He exchanged an uneasy gaze with Louis.

"Yup," said Bucky. "Rhea and Jothan. *YO*-than – spelled with a *J*. Guess it's German or something."

Jothan, thought Vincent, searching for a connection that wasn't there – he had never met anybody with that name. And he doubted it was the same Rhea he knew. But still, he couldn't escape the discomfort he felt at the name.

"Jothan's been on minor expeditions with us," said the young one. "Apt young lad," he added, ignoring his own youth. "Never met his girl before, though. Nice enough. A little crass at times. But still nice."

"I knew a girl once with that name," said Louis. "Didn't like her much."

"If y'all're gonna be hangin' around for a while," said Bucky, "we'll need you to help with the watch, too."

"We'll probably get a move on before long," said Vincent.

"Places to go and people to see?" Bucky said.

"Something like that," Vincent replied, snuffing his cigarette on his bootheel. He thought of the priest and his presumed psycho-babble about angels and demons and tall tales regarding the Crusades. He glanced at the katana, curious of its true origins. "You mind if we rest here for a few hours?" he asked. "We'll be out of your hair by midday, I'm sure. And we won't use up your supplies."

"Don't mind at all," said Bucky. "And take what you need. We ain't selfish."

"Thank you again," said Ryn. "You're kind people."

"No problem, girlie," replied Bucky.

"There are blankets and pads for beds," said his younger counterpart. "Take the cots if you like, too. Nobody's going back to bed anytime soon, I imagine." He stood to leave. "I'll leave this lantern. If you need anything, we'll be in the next room."

"Where are the stairs?" John asked. "In case I need a smoke."

"Through the office, around the corner." He pointed in the general direction.

"Thanks." He went to shake his hand. "John."

"Greg," he said, taking John's massive hand.

"Nice to meet you," said John. "And you too," he said to Bucky with a nod.

Pleasantries and introductions followed for a minute before they were left to crash out. Vincent was surprised to find he could fall asleep after the morning's raucous events. Sleep didn't immediately fall upon him; John was snoring well before he drifted away. At one point, he was vaguely aware of Ryn snuggling up to his side and whispering in his ear. She nuzzled into the crook of his arm as he passed into slumberland.

IX

She was opening her mouth, trying to speak – but he could not hear her words.

They were standing under a spotlight on a dark and deserted highway through the forest – the only spotlight on this eerie highway. The light was bright and white – and he couldn't find its source; it disappeared when he looked for it, but he could always feel its shining heat.

Louis stepped up behind her. His eyes were empty and his mouth was stitched shut; one of his arms was a blackened stump. He held a broadsword in his only hand; the blade was green and reflected no light.

She was frantic now, silently jabbering at him, frightened. She pointed down the road.

He turned. A spotlight shone on a wicked priest wielding a red katana. He raised the blade over his head and a painful light flooded the highway – Vincent turned away, shielding his eyes.

The girl was gone; Louis was gone.

When he turned back, the priest was gone – where once there was blinding light there was now only darkness. But the spotlight above remained – the spotlight always remained, always kept him shrouded in white hot light.

So when he started down the highway, the spotlight followed.

He felt a presence behind him, but was unable to turn.

And then he was flying down the road, aware of a vast army of evil nipping at his heels. He ran – he flew – he floated away, always wrapped in light and fear. And then he stopped, twisted and turned and otherwise wriggled in air and was deposited onto a railway, immobilized and on his back.

When the screams reached his ears, he knew it was over. The ground shook as a steamer whistled and shrieked along the tracks, rapidly bearing down on him. He was terrified of the wailing payload that was about to run him down, yet found that he was strangely comforted by the fact that it would all come to a merciful end soon enough.

                              X

It was too bright when Vincent opened his eyes.

And everybody was in a frenzy.

"What the –?" he rubbed his eyes and looked around – second time in one day he found himself waking to madness. "What's happening?" he asked. And then it was the second time in one day that he was hoisted to his feet by John so soon after waking.

"Lady was pounding on the door," he said.

"What lady? What?"

A shrill voice started yammering in the next room.

"What happened?"

"I don't know," replied John. "I heard gunshots. And then I heard her pounding away on the side door. And from the sounds of it now, she might be infected."

Greg's voice rose over the woman's nonsensical yammering: "How many were there?" he boomed – and she was silent. In an even tone that barely floated through the open door, he asked her again: "How many were there?"

She stammered and sputtered. "Can't say," she said at last. "There was Kyle, in the car. And there was a boy in the yard. And a mailman in the driveway. And a soldier. And a cook. And a whole lot more on the highway. And –"

"Which way were they heading?" he asked.

"They were…" she began. "I don't know. They were after me."

"And you came straight here?"

"Yes. I ran – I left him there!"

"How far did you run?"

"I left him there!" she repeated, her breath hitching as she began to sob. "I left him to be eaten by the *dead*!" she cried.

"For God's sake, woman, *lower your voice*," snarled Greg. "And please, for just a few minutes, stop your blubbering long enough to help me here. Now," he paused, cooling himself. He continued in a much calmer voice: "About how far back were you when you wrecked?"

Her sobs faltered as she recaptured something reminiscent of composure. "Maybe a half mile," she replied. "Maybe more, though…maybe less. I don't know."

"She sure don't know much," John grumbled under his breath.

"That doesn't give us much time," remarked a woman – a different woman – from the other room. Vincent recognized her voice – so did Louis.

"No," replied Greg. "It sure doesn't. We need to get this place locked up tight – and quickly. You and Jothan keep an eye out while we corral our guests. We'll be up there shortly." After a moment's hesitation, he added, "And take her with you."

A door opened – feet shuffled – and then it closed.

A moment later, Greg stepped into the back room. He addressed the room as a whole: "Alright, guys. Look sharp. We have a potential threat heading our way. Lady says she encountered *bobs* less than a mile away – a whole ton of 'em. Grab your stuff – grab your guns. We'll do a perimeter check and head to the roof." He waved his arm, motioning them along. "Come with me. And bring a lantern."

John started immediately after him with Ryn a step behind.

Vincent grabbed the lantern; he and Louis followed dazedly, attempting haste.

Bucky was reinforcing the blockade at the front door.

"You two," Greg pointed at John and Ryn, "stay with me. And you two," he pointed at Vincent and Louis, "stay with Bucky."

Faint popping and muffled shouts hit their ears – gunshots from the roof.

"*Shit!*" seethed Bucky. "Help me with this!" Vincent pinned another board over the existing window barricade while Bucky tacked it in with a pneumatic nail gun. "This one too," he said, handing another board to Vincent.

Glass shattered in another part of the lodge. Someone hollered and cried out.

Ryn shrieked and Vincent's heart stopped. Rage filled him; he dropped the board, drew the katana and ran toward her fear. Having never been in this place before, he was frighteningly uncanny in his navigation of fallen racks and blind corners. The darkness of the lodge gave way to light and he saw her cowering on tiptoes against one wall. Greg was across from her, crawling along in a pool of blood, holding one arm against his chest, his face twisted in agony and terror.

At the window – ripping through the curtains – was a ravenous boy.

John smashed the boy's head with the side of his axe, sending him into convulsions on the hardwood floor. With one fluid sweep, he brought the axe over his head and dropped the blade, chopping through the boy's skull, terminating his infected existence.

Through the open window came a cascade of gunshots and groans.

"Help me!" gasped Greg. He coughed and sputtered and sat up against the wall.

Bucky and Louis rounded the corner, momentarily stunned by the scene.

Bucky knelt beside him. "Let me see it," he said, reaching for Greg's wounded arm.

"Was it glass or the boy?" asked Louis.

Greg seethed and moaned as Bucky took his arm. One deep gash was slit down his wrist and his hand was lined with ragged gouges. All the wounds were clotting. "Looks like both," said Bucky.

Vincent stepped over to Ryn and put his arm around her shoulder. "You okay?"

"Fine," she breathed, sinking into his embrace.

Through clenched teeth, Greg said, "I'm a goner, aren't I?"

"More than likely," replied Louis. "Why don't we get you upstairs?"

"No!" snapped Greg. "Gimme a gun. I'll kill these fuckers and then myself."

"There might be a way…" began Louis, unsure of how to finish his thought – discomfited at the futility in trying to save this man.

"No," said Greg, wincing. "There's no saving me now. All I need is a gun." He directed a stern gaze at Vincent. "And maybe a cigarette," he added. "No reason to worry about cancer or ventilation now."

A lurcher groaned and tumbled through the busted window at John's feet. He jumped back and brought the axe down on its head before it could claw or swipe.

"Now!" growled Greg.

Louis slapped his pistol into Greg's good hand; Vincent lit a cigarette and placed it between his lips.

"It doesn't have to be this way," said John.

"I want it this way," replied Greg, drawing hard off his smoke. "I'm not turning into one of them."

"I don't blame you," said Bucky. "I just wish it wasn't so."

John stepped over to him. "Godspeed," he said, patting him on the shoulder.

Another lurcher tumbled through the window –

BLAM! – rotted brainmatter splattered the walls.

"Get out of here," said Greg – a wisp of smoke drifted from the barrel of his gun.

People hollered on the roof and bullets rained down outside the window.

"Just go," said Greg. "They could use your guns upstairs."

Reluctant to go, Bucky stayed by his side as the guys started slowly, solemnly out of the room. Vincent lingered behind his friends – his brothers – as Ryn crossed over to Greg. She bent low, laid a kiss on his forehead and whispered her thanks; she managed to restrain her loaded tear ducts while facing him. She whirled and stepped briskly past Vincent, out of the room. She didn't want Greg to see the rogue tear that rolled down her face.

They all started away a moment later.

"Hey, Vin," said Louis, falling in step with him. He lowered his voice: "I don't know how I'm gonna get up to the roof." He raised his busted arm until it screamed and lowered it. It throbbed when he let it dangle, so he tried to keep it cocked and resting on his gut or held in his lap.

"I know, Lou," replied Vincent. "But we'll figure it out."

The gunfire from above was persistent and Vincent wondered over their reserves of ammunition. From the sound of it, this little group was stocked to the gills. And though he was no expert on gauging a weapon's caliber by sound alone, he was certain their weapons were more than your standard civilian models. He also recalled the two large, army-green metal boxes of .223 ammunition that were stacked under the desk of the office. He imagined Rhea wielding an Army issue M16 and suddenly had no desire to climb up to the roof.

Just as this foreboding paranoia began creeping into Vincent's brain, something slammed into the front door. Vincent jumped – they all jumped – at the sound. And then another slammed into one of the bay windows. Right on the heels of this was another. And then another. And soon, there were so many pounding at the windows and door that Vincent was sure they'd break through any moment. He wanted to get out of there, but had no desire to jump out into the swarm.

"The stairs are back this way," said Bucky. He started away with haste.

But nobody was hot to follow. They just stood in the shadows of the darkened store.

"We should dip," suggested Louis. "This shit's all bonkers."

Another shot rang out from around the corner as Greg blasted another *bob* that was trying to climb inside. Soon there would be an unstoppable flood of them pouring in.

"I ain't goin' out there," Ryn said with a quake to her voice.

"Are ye comin' or not?" Bucky growled at them.

Glass shattered and the room was instantly filled with the hungry groans of countless *bobs*. That was enough to motivate them. Without a word, the foursome darted after Bucky. The slapping of their shoes and boots on the hardwood floors rang loudly off the walls. When they caught up with Bucky, their pace slowed, thereby diminishing the noise that served as a beacon for all those hungry *bobs*.

Through the deepening shadows he led them to a stairwell at the rear of the store. "Up we go," he said, ushering them ahead of him. He shot a wary eye at their backpath, but caught no movement through the darkness. Though they had smashed through the bay windows, he assumed they must be stymied by the barricade.

BLAM! – another shot from Greg's gun. *BLAM-BLAM!* Bucky was frightened by this rapid succession of gunshots. Greg would surely run out of ammo before too long.

He sighed and started up the stairs.

He was chased by the painful echoes of two more shots and Greg's wild, delirious voice as he taunted his attackers. The next shot he heard bore a chilling finality, and Bucky knew – without actually knowing for sure – that the kid was dead. He wondered briefly how long they would feast on him before seeking out a fresh meal – he pushed the thought from his head.

The others were already waiting at the top.

"Right around here," Bucky said, motioning for them to round the corner. Further instructions were not necessary once they were in the hallway; the stepstool beneath the open window was instruction enough for anybody with half a brain.

John eyed the opening with apprehension. He wasn't sure it was large enough for his girth.

"Let's go, big boy," Bucky said, slapping John's shoulder. "You ain't much bigger than Jothan, and he fits through just fine." He flashed him a wan smirk and climbed out the window with ease.

Vincent followed a moment later. The drop was higher than he'd approximated and he nearly lost his footing on the damp grade of the roof. Bucky stabilized him. Together, they helped Ryn down from the window. Louis was a trickier ordeal; John had to help him settle onto the sill and lower him to the waiting arms of Bucky and Vincent – both of whom eased him the rest of the way out.

Already halfway out the window in his efforts to assist Louis, John tried with all his might to retain his balance and not go tumbling after him. Once he was free of the burden – after Louis was safely on the roof below – John kicked out and twisted in an attempt to right himself and grab his axe at the same time; he intended on handing it down before climbing out. But the rifle – it was slung across his back, over his shoulders – snagged, and he couldn't move. He was stuck uncomfortably sideways with one arm bent painfully between his body and the windowframe. In his current position, he wasn't even able to twist his legs enough to locate the stepstool and ground himself, if only minimally.

And, of course, that's when he heard the howl of a nearby *bob*. His face went slack and drained of color.

"Wha-what's that?" Louis stammered. (He knew what it was, he just didn't want to believe it – the timing couldn't be worse.)

"*Shit*," John hissed.

The ghoul latched onto his leg and he kicked violently to shake it loose – which worked, but only temporarily. He knew it would be back in just a moment. So he tried twisting back around again, but for all his efforts, he still couldn't move. The rifle was now jammed from one corner of the window to the complete opposite corner, and was digging in further with his every frantic shift.

There was a rope ladder hanging from the upper roof and Bucky was up it in a hurry. Looping one arm through the rungs of this ladder, he stretched out, grasped the edge of the window and pulled with all his might. John's massive frame nearly filled the window's entire cavity. And he had to reach up and around John's squirming shoulder to reach the barrel of the snagged rifle. What made this task all the more difficult was his strenuous – and tentative – finger-hold on the window's frame. He felt his fingers slipping when Vincent and Ryn got underneath him to help hold him in place. (Louis felt useless and full of dread watching the entire ordeal unfold; he was standing aside, silently cursing his broken arm – and wishing that it was him, instead of John.)

Although he was still squirming and kicking, awaiting the ghoul's imminent return, John helped as best he could by taking hold of Bucky's grip hand with his one free arm. And sure enough, just as he took hold of Bucky's wrist, he felt the ghoul's fierce grip on his boot. He yelped and kicked, but this time it held firm. Any moment now, he would feel its teeth or nails sink into his leg.

More hungry howls and moans filled the hallway.

John was bucking violently and squalling through gritted teeth. The ghoul was strong, clamped to his leg now with a vice-like grip and he could feel the pinch of infected nails trying to claw through his jeans. The feel of it was so intense that he wasn't entirely certain that it hadn't already pierced his skin.

All this squirming and kicking, as vital as it was to John's survival, made Bucky's efforts at freeing the rifle seem nigh impossible. There was a point, though, when he found a decent hold on the barrel – a little too near the business end for comfort, but a hold nonetheless – and gave it a good yank. The barrel kicked out and the stock slapped John's ass – hard. He was jolted forward, lost his hold on Bucky's hand – and the gun went off when the trigger was somehow depressed. The bullet missed Bucky's head by inches. And his hand was burned from being so near the business end. He released it immediately and simultaneously lost his grip on the windowframe.

Ryn shrieked, and Bucky's leg – the one she'd been supporting as he freed the snagged rifle – slipped out of her grasp.

Vincent's feet slid out from under him after the sudden shift in weight distribution. The rope ladder swung back out from the window. With an arm still wrapped around Bucky's leg, he snatched the taut, silky rope ladder – firmly, with white knuckles popping on either hand – as it continued its outward arc. His timing could not have been better; just after snatching a hold of the ladder his feet left the relative safety of the damp roof. (He nearly yanked Bucky right down from the added weight around his leg.) A number of *bobs* were converging on the space below. Vincent could envision plummeting into their midst, breaking a leg, and being ripped apart, piece by piece. He could only hope to break his neck if his grip should slip, and be done with it before it ever started – before becoming an appetizer for these bloodthirsty, *ravenous* cannibals – or whathaveyou. (He wasn't sure, any longer, if they could be considered human enough for such a title as *cannibal*; the appeared to be a different breed altogether.)

They swung back to safety without incident. And though his feet skidded on their return swing, he managed to plant them firmly enough to forestall another flight above *no-man's land*.

He was panting; reeling with fear and anxiety.

CRACK! – the sound of a high-powered rifle from inside.

Apparently, while dangling and swaying above a certain broken leg or neck (and subsequent infection, if not worse), John had slipped back inside. Vincent stepped back to try and see through the meager view afforded by the tiny window. He hollered, "John?" hoping that his voice would travel to his friend's – his *brother's* – ear.

CRACK! – was John's only reply. (He hadn't actually heard Vincent call to him; the timing of this "reply" was purely coincidental.)

Vincent tried again, louder: "*John!*"

Instead of more shots – or an actual response of any other sort – he just heard grunts and groans and thuds and the unmistakable *thunk!* of heavy metal chopping into hardwood and drywall (presumably John's axe destroying infected brains). From the window – from inside – also came John's vociferous taunts and curses as he pummeled and chopped and stomped a number of his aggressors to death.

But this courageous, if not heroic, racket did nothing to assuage their fears. Still, Vincent was frozen – they *all* were frozen. All, except for Bucky. Already on the ladder, he pulled himself back over to the window and crawled back inside with surprising ease for a man of his age. *Truly a mountaineer*, Vincent thought. *Through and through.* Still standing helpless – a "deer in the headlights," as the saying went – he hoped (and prayed) for John's safety and Bucky's security.

And just as he was sending his mental prayers upstairs, a flaming bottle arced down from the upper roof. Vincent's wide eyes followed its arc all the way. It fell to the ground below and exploded in the midst of the growing horde with a light *crack-whoosh*. It doused the surrounding *bobs* with fiery liquid; the flames quickly spread amongst their ranks.

Vincent followed the cocktail's backpath, wondering who would be so foolish as to risk burning the place down while taking refuge upon the rooftop. What he found up there was a hulky man with disheveled blonde hair. He stood away from the flat platform beyond, upon the roof's apex, and was firing a tricked-out AR15 at the now-flaming horde. Vincent assumed – correctly – that this was Jothan. But he could not see Rhea or the other woman – *what's her name again?* Vincent briefly pondered. A row of unlit Molotov cocktails were lined up behind Jothan, along the building's squared façade, which extended only a few feet above the makeshift platform, which was currently not in use (for whatever reason). More were on the makeshift scaffolding that ran the length of this façade. This scaffolding provided a flat, strafing surface for the rooftop watchmen. A surface that, as far as Vincent could tell, was not in use by any of these rooftop defenders.

Hollering from inside brought him back to his previous – and, in his opinion, more pressing – concerns for John's safety.

As it turned out, Bucky's security was not required for John's safety on this occasion. Just as he touched down on the stepstool, John was racing back down the hall. "*Go-go-go!*" John bellowed frantically.

Bucky was a bit too wide-eyed and startled to react at once (almost like Vincent; a *deer in the headlights*, and John was the steaming freight train that was about to run him down). The room was a virtual bloodbath – if the curdled substance that was once blood in a *bob*'s previously un-infected body could still be considered as such. The meager light spilling in through the hall windows hardly illuminated a thing, but Bucky could still clearly see the chunky spray-pattern of infected blood along the walls, the floorboards, and everything else (shelving, boxes, crates, et cetera) up and down the hall. On his initial observation, Bucky counted seven bodies. But he assumed there to be more on down toward the stairwell. Had he checked, he would have found his assumption to be quite accurate. However accurate his assumption was, his estimate on the number of bodies was still low…

"Let's get the fuck outta here!" John wailed, still bearing down on him like a freight train. He was closing the distance with astonishing speed.

The sight of John's massive frame racing directly at him at such a clip made him want to cower. But he was no fool. Bucky snapped out of his fearful trance and slipped back out the window. He dropped down and landed on shaky knees.

John thrust his axe out the window at Vincent – handle first – who took it without hesitation. John tucked his rifle, so as to prevent a repeat of his last bout with the window, and wriggled his way through the tight opening. "Get up that fucking ladder!" he bellowed to nobody in particu-lar. "They'll be here any damn second now!" He was able to shoot Ryn a look that told her to get a move on.

And she took the hint.

John joined them on the lower roof just as Bucky was starting up the ladder; Ryn was nearly to the top already.

Vincent dropped a heavy hand on John's shoulder. "Holy shit," he said, breathless and relieved.

"You're tellin' me," said John. He was still panting from battle (and from having run so hard and fast). "Get on up there," he said. "I'll push, you'll pull." He was referring to helping Louis up to the next level; the upper roof. Vincent wasn't sure whether he meant to help Louis up the ladder, or – and he thought this more likely – by just boosting him all the way up, with minimal, if not *nonexistent*, aid of the rope ladder. John was tall enough and Vincent and Bucky could more than handle Louis' smallish frame.

Vincent knew that death was coming at him from inside – he knew they'd be pouring out that window any moment now. Hell, their moans were growing louder by the second. And, with the rising numbers on the ground below, he knew the only remaining option was *up*. But he was still a tad trepidatious about what he might find up there. Was it really *Rhea*? *The* Rhea? The one that he and Louis had busted and processed on multiple occasions – *that* Rhea? If it was *that* Rhea, and she was strapped with a supposed AR15 – or M16, or pistol, or any damn weapon, for that matter – and murder in her eyes, he feared that death might find him no matter what he did or where he went.

But he figured – wisely – that he'd rather risk a quick and relatively painless death from a gunshot to that of the gnashing, ravenous jowls of the undead ghouls that were rapidly forcing his hand. Without much of an option – or the space and time to think of an alternative option, of which he was certain there were none – he flashed his friend a wan smile and started up the ladder after Bucky. His hesitation to move was curt enough that John paid the lag no mind at all.

XI

Another cocktail arced overhead as Vincent, with Bucky's aid, pulled Louis up. He tried to avoid bumping Louis' busted arm, but he ended up doing so all the same. John heaved from below until Louis was beyond his grasp, and the rest was on the pair up top. They managed to not bang him up too terribly, but Louis was seething and groping his arm at the end, nonetheless.

Ryn, the little diehard, was already at the strafing platform, assessing the situation below. Jothan paid her little mind as he fired another flaming cocktail at the encroaching horde. She saw the woman that Vincent feared at once; she was hunkered down at the base of the platform, firing a subcompact rifle around the corner. The other woman – the intruder who had brought this horde upon them – was huddled at the edge of the platform, hugging her rifle, eyes squeezed tight, with her back to the façade. Ryn scoffed aloud at the woman's pitiful survival instincts.

Short as she was, Ryn found it difficult to shoot over the facade. Instead, she moved to the other end of the platform, away from the cowering woman. She added her own rifle fire to the cacophony, sighting and killing three *bobs* in her first four shots. The lack of blood made her feel as though it were some crude, *teen*-rated video game. (Though, her other senses reminded her that this was definitely a real scenario, and not virtual reality.) Bloodlust overtook her, and she barely heard Vincent unleash a verbal lashing on the man who was throwing the flaming bottles.

"Are you trying to kill us all with those?" Vincent cried at Jothan. "The place is gonna burn with us up here!"

As if to spite him, Jothan lit another wick and chucked the bottle. He said nothing.

Vincent fought the urge to tackle him. The survivalist within wouldn't allow him to tumble to his death when alternative solutions were still at hand.

Before he could holler some more, John's large paw landed on his shoulder. "Let me take care of this," John said. His face was calm, but his eyes were burning with excitement and anger. The man he was approaching was a decent build, nearly his own size. But John wouldn't care if he was eight feet tall and built like the Hulk; he felt no fear of any man, no matter their size.

Jothan was lighting another wick when John approached him. He caught Jothan's arm before it could unleash another flaming bottle. He was vaguely aware of Ryn in his peripherals. "I'd rather face a thousand of those *things* than burn to death from your ignorance," he said. His voice was surprisingly serene. "Now I recommend that you stop before you get yourself hurt."

Jothan yanked his arm free. The wick was nearly burnt all the way down. "Don't you tell me how to defend this place," he growled. He cranked his arm back again –

And John caught him with a right hook that knocked him backward. As he tumbled down the steep grade of the damp roof, the cocktail exploded. His cries were horrific, and he nearly bowled Rhea right off the roof. But he didn't fall at once. Even engulfed in flames and screaming his big head right off, Jothan managed – somehow – to grasp the gutter and hang on for just a few moments. Rhea stared down at him with very little emotion in her eyes. Mostly, she was stunned – but even that emotion did not show. When the flames started licking up around the shingles, she risked her boot to kick his hand free. The flames charred a corner of her pants, and nothing more.

She turned to find three newcomers standing at the roof's apex – right in the spot that Jothan had previously been. Two of the faces were stunned, mouths agape. And it was these two faces that she recognized. And so it was her turn to be stunned. She had no idea how to handle the arrival of this pair in such a time and place as here and now.

It's her! cried Vincent's flabbergasted brain. *It really is* her*!*

Louis' thoughts were similar, though he hadn't put much previous thought into this possible predicament. After initially hearing her name, he had paid her possible presence little mind. Unlike Vincent, who was now silently screaming in his own mind, Louis was just shocked.

None of them heard Ryn's anxious cries until she was at their side, screaming in their faces. "*The place is on* fire*!*" she bellowed, her voice cracking at her highly elevated pitch and volume.

John whirled to find thick smoke billowing up over the roof's edge.

She went on: "They're climbing on top of one another, like a ramp, and the fire is spreading quickly. We gotta go! We gotta *go*! They'll be up here in minutes, if the fire doesn't reach us first. Let's *go*! *Andiamo*!"

Vincent heard this last, but his eyes were still locked with Rhea's. He was waiting for her to make a move – to raise her rifle or some other threatening motion. But she didn't. Instead, she spoke just loud enough for them to hear her: "I knew he'd kill himself with those damn things." She turned, almost casually, back to the horde below and resumed firing (she killed with every shot).

"*There!*" cried Ryn, thrusting a finger at an awning below. It was roughly the same distance as the roof from which they had just come. But it was a smaller surface. The van was just below that, parked at an angle between two other vehicles; a lifted pickup and an old station wag-on. "We can get down there!"

Louis found himself wondering why they ventured up here in the first place. He also wondered how much more damage would be inflicted upon his arm on the descent.

Vincent allowed his gaze to shift long enough to gauge the drop.

"What happened?" inquired Bucky. He was in a frenzy – and late to the game, it would appear. The effort of pulling Louis up had winded him, and he finally made his way to the apex. He hadn't seen John punch Jothan, but was able to surmise a great deal from the aftermath.

"We're getting the fuck gone," said John. "This was a bad idea." Before he could answer, John said, "We need a distraction." The van was just below Rhea, which told him that the entire building was being swarmed. "She's only drawing more to this side." He pointed his chin at Rhea. "Let's get them all around the other side."

"The fire's spreading fast," said Bucky.

Ryn was nodding her assent to this statement – vehemently.

He went on: "And she's right; they're ramping up. They're almost up to the lower level already. And then their numbers will grow with the ones that are crawling out the second level." He had seen plenty while catching his breath at the ledge.

"There are too many over the other side to safely descend," said Louis. "They're probably ramping up as well. We'll be swarmed in no time if we go now."

Rhea's gunfire ceased and she started up the roof, but not toward this indecisive group. "I gotcha," she said. She tossed a scowl at Louis and shot daggers at Vincent – but not bullets, and he was thankful for this. "Y'all getcher pasty asses down there when it's all clear." She stepped up onto the strafing platform and snatched up a Molotov cocktail. "I'll be right on yer tails." Lightning-quick with her Zippo, she lit the wick. She rolled it to catch better flame before tossing it. And then she unleashed on full-auto at the horde.

"Come get some!" she hollered. And then she howled before letting loose another long burst of fully automatic rifle fire.

"Go," John insisted. "Keep low. I'm gonna help her draw their attention." He traversed the roof's apex with skill – and very few steps. Together, he and Rhea strafed along the platform, howling and hollering while blindly firing at the horde below.

Vincent regarded Bucky with stern eyes. "I'm entrusting you with their lives," he said, meaning Louis and Ryn. "Get them down safely. I'll be right behind you." He started toward the platform; each of his steps was deliberate and cautious.

Ryn's eyes were wild, but she couldn't find any words.

"Just wait," Louis told her. "They haven't drawn enough of them away yet anyhow." He suddenly felt naked. After Vincent's statement ("I'm entrusting you with their lives"), he felt the heavy absence of his pistol. Despite the emotional weight of Greg's very recent death, he sourly wished that he hadn't relinquished his pistol.

Louis turned his attention to Bucky. "You got any more firepower?"

"Just got this," he said, displaying his rifle.

Louis nodded. "Guess this'll have to do." He grabbed at the handle of the bat that stuck at an angle from his backpack. But he did not draw it; he would need his hand free on the upcoming descent.

"I got your back," Ryn said with a wink.

While Louis was worrying over his weaponry, Vincent was slinking along the platform toward the cowering, cowardly woman. She yelped when he snatched at her rifle – it wasn't nearly as sophisticated as the military hardware the others carried, just a semi-automatic .22 with a ten-round clip. In her fear, she squeezed the trigger – *Pop!* – but the bullet went astray by the imposed angle of Vincent's action.

With a finger over his lips, he shushed her. "No more of that," he said, his voice low."

Her eyes were wide and crazed, without comprehension. She didn't say a word or utter another yelp.

"We gotta get going now," he said. "The building's on fire. It's not safe here anymore."

She blinked a couple times.

"Let me have this," he said, pulling the rifle away. It slipped surprisingly easily out of her deathgrip. He peeked over her shoulder, checking on the horde below. They were slowly making their way around the front of the building. "C'mon," he said. Keeping low, he shuffled back down the platform and out onto the roof. The woman remained where he left her, but she stared after him. He held little hope that she would snap out of her paralytic shock.

After a glance at John and Rhea – she was firing over the façade while he was directing all of his efforts at the ramp of flaming *bobs* – he addressed the others as a whole. "It's working," he said. "They're moving away from the van – toward the commotion." After a moment's thought he said, "Just another couple minutes and we should be able to head down."

Rhea breezed by them just then, with her subcompact slung over her shoulder. Lithe, with graceful silence and surefooted confidence, she crossed the slick surface and eased herself down to the awning, hence dropping out of sight.

"Well alright then," murmured Bucky.

XII

John was still firing at the ramping *bobs*, hollering and howling to attract evermore; the cowardly woman was still cowering against the building's façade; Vincent, Louis, Ryn, and Bucky were staring after Rhea's departure, moving not an inch and speaking not a word; and Rhea, now out of sight to these three, was crouched beneath the cover of the awning's peak. On the walkway below, Jothan was no longer burning; he was now just a lifeless, smoldering hulk that even the *bobs* ignored.

With the horde still distracted, Rhea slid down the short surface on her belly. She found little purchase on the ledge and dropped with a clatter on the gravel below. The drop was not so far as to disorient her completely, and she quickly rolled behind a small, decorative boulder for cover. (Two of these were set only a few yards from the side entrance – perhaps to prevent people from plowing through the doors.) She then scuttled behind the nearest vehicle; a dingy blue minivan. If she had cared to think on the matter a bit, she would have realized that this was the very vehicle in which Vincent and Louis – and whoever else – had arrived only a few hours prior. But, circumstances as they were, Rhea had little care for such trivialities.

In the few moments she was positioned here, waiting for the horde to dissipate, she started to wonder on the two people missing from this showdown. Greg was the one she especially pondered over – what had happened to him? And secondary to this, she wondered about the wiry and young, hippie-chic and hairy boy who'd rode in on a bicycle at some point in the night. Though she hadn't met the boy, as she was on watch at that hour, she distinctly recalled radioing down when he rode in. Jothan relayed his story when he joined her on watch.

But enough of that – she hadn't the time for such futile tangents of the mind.

She peered around the van's front fender; only a handful of stragglers remained. She noticed that these ones were especially deformed, having lost limbs or ears or eyes to whichever bob – or bobs – infected them in the first place. She ducked away again, counted slowly to five, and made her way around the backside of the van, careful to keep low – and always silent.

While rounding the next vehicle – a lifted white pickup truck that was stained red and brown with blood and mud – the gunfire and commotion ceased upon the roof. This sudden ceasefire rendered her immobile and breathless, fearful of drawing the horde's attention. After a few beats, she dared a peek around the truck's tall tire. From her low vantage, Rhea spied the staggering legs of some straggling bobs. None were in her immediate vicinity. And instead of pausing to gauge their surroundings, the bobs marched on after the phantoms of gunfire and racket.

Wielding a machete, Rhea emerged from behind the truck. Still crouched, she scuttled after the last straggler – it was once a middle-aged white male, but was now bloody and mottled with only one arm and gray skin. Before Rhea could rise and strike this bob, the raucous descent of Vincent (*and his numbskull crew*, she thought with scorn) shifted its attention. It groaned – it *howled* – thus alerting its mindless brethren, and stopped dead in its tracks. Not expecting this, Rhea barreled right into its legs, and together they went down in a tangle. She was thankful that the finely honed edge of her machete buried not in her own body, but in that of the one-armed bob that was now flailing overtop of her.

They struggled together – her and the ghoul – and all the while the blade was burying deeper into its back. She was hardly afforded any angle to wrench the weapon free as the damn thing kept thrashing around, trying constantly to get at her. And of course, during all of this, the horde, no longer distracted, was closing in on her. Feeling the rise of urgency in this instant, she kicked hard and twisted the blade. She felt something pop and the bob's thrashing all but stopped – she had managed to sever its spine, thus paralyzing its legs. And so, in one fluid motion, she rolled out from under it, hopped to her feet, and brought the machete down in a heavy arc to slice clean through its head.

The encroaching horde was nearly upon her then, but still she dared to glare up at Vincent (and his numbskull crew) before they arrived. The assault came a moment later…she kicked the first one, chopped into the next one's head, kicked another, dislodged her blade, and sliced into one more brain (she was vaguely aware of all the gunfire that was aiding in her defenses) – and then she was tackled. Her machete went clanging away, across the pavement.

XIII

"They don't even know she's down there," Ryn hissed.

Vincent could feel her anxiety at their inaction – all this damn *waiting* was driver her crazy. He looked about the others, sensing the same anxiety from each in turn. "Alright," he said with a curt nod. "Let's do this thing."

His first step was quite the opposite of graceful; John had to steady him lest he trip over himself and tumble to his death, if not severe – and painful – incapacitation.

"You alright there, buddy?" John asked him.

"Yeah," replied Vincent. "I got this." He started away with haste, unmindful of the audible clomping of his heavy boots. The others followed, similarly unmindful of their raucous clomping.

Vincent glanced at Rhea as she wrestled with a *bob* on the pavement. He scoffed at her lack of tact in this encounter, completely unaware that it was his raucous descent that was the catalyst for this impromptu bout of hers. It was over quickly, and just before he dropped down to the awning below, Vincent caught the glare that Rhea shot his way. He failed to catch the very moment she was tackled as he was preoccupied with lowering himself from the awning. She was already on the ground when he landed a moment later.

Seeing her there, trapped by a ravenous ghoul, he had the notion to let the thing eat her. She was defenseless and only inches from its gnashing jowls – it would be so easy to just let it have her. And then the world would be rid of one more foul example of humanity. He smirked at the idea. But he knew he couldn't let this happen –

BLAM! – from the rooftop; the ghoul atop Rhea dropped dead.

Wisps of smoke were visible, rising from John's rifle. And when he gazed up to see who had fired this shot, Vincent was met by a nasty sneer from John. But John's expression changed in a heartbeat; his face grew long and frightened and he started to motion at something. But before Vincent could even begin to whirl, something hard crashed into the side of his head and sent him sprawling.

He was too dazed to figure out what was happening. But the moment he went sprawling, a crazed – and rather tenacious – Latino man was on top of him, pummeling his face and body with a flurry of fists. Through the haze, Vincent could hardly mount any sort of defense. This man – who Vincent would have recognized as Corporal Diego Sanchez, had he been coherent enough to focus – was spouting obscenities in two languages, cursing Vincent for not having killed him.

But Vincent heard none of this over the pounding of his skull. And for all he knew at the time, this pounding lasted an eternity. When in reality, it lasted only a few seconds before Ryn intervened with a full baseball swing of her crowbar to the back of Sanchez' head. He fell away at once, his body stiff and lightly convulsing.

Vincent's memory of this entire episode would be wiped clean. But the others would remember it for as long as they lived.

"Get him into the van," Bucky instructed once they were all on the pavement.

John picked up the bloodied, mostly limp and helpless body of Vincent and set him on the middle bench of the minivan. As he did this, Louis and Bucky were fending off the swarming horde. Most of which – *Thank the Heavens!* thought John – were tromping after Rhea and the blatting of her subcompact. She was backpedaling toward the highway in a serpentine fashion, drawing the majority of this surprisingly massive horde. *Where'd they all come from?* John absently thought.

Ryn was still standing over the convulsing body of Sanchez, the crowbar still clutched tight in her white-knuckled hands. John gingerly grasped both her shoulders in his massive paws and looked deep into her terrified eyes. He blinked once and nodded toward the minivan. "Vincent could use your help in there, if you would," he said to her.

She shot a glance back at Sanchez – still rigid, but not convulsing quite so much – and then gazed with woe at Vincent. Livid bruises were already sprouting, visible where the blood wasn't. Not that he was such a bloodied mess that she couldn't see his face, but he was split open in two places around his right eye, his nose was dripping, as well as a puffy, cracked lower lip. His head was tilted back on the headrest, and she could see that he wouldn't even notice if a ghoul climbed in beside him to set upon his face or neck with ragged teeth. So she climbed in beside him and set upon him with a cloth to clean up the blood.

"Can you drive, Bucky?" John hollered over the din.

"All day long!" he heard him reply.

"Then let's get the fuck outta here!"

"Copy!"

Bucky and Louis made one final push and peeled back. John climbed into the very back of the van, sliding the door shut behind him with power. He tapped Ryn on the shoulder. "Keys should be in his front pocket," John told her, gesturing to Vincent's jacket. Louis was in the passenger seat a moment later, and Bucky climbed in behind the wheel just after. Ryn handed him the keys and he fired up the old beater.

The van rocked with the force of Sanchez slamming into the slider. His eyes were wide and distant, and he pounded a fist against the window. At that moment, he closely resembled the *bobs* that would crash into the van if they lingered for much longer.

Bucky threw the gearshift into reverse and hit the gas. "What about Rhea?" he said while shifting into drive.

They all looked for a moment at the horde. It was turning their way and Rhea was starting to serpentine her way back toward the lodge. But then she was swarmed. Gunshots continued to ring out – they heard no screams or cries – but she was gone from sight and presumed overwhelmed. Not that Vincent or Louis would wish for a ride with that woman anyhow.

"Forget her," Louis said, trying to hide the malice he felt.

"But what if she...?" Bucky didn't know how to finish the question.

"Forget her," Louis reiterated. "She's gone." *Farewell*, he thought with scorn. *Crazy fucking bitch...*

Bucky threw the vehicle into gear and ripped across the driveway, the courtyard. They swayed to and fro, slipping and sliding across damp grass – and then they caught traction on the highway. Louis watched the horde diminish in the sideview mirror. *Crazy fucking bitch*, he thought once more. And just then, from amidst the horde, he saw the muzzle flash of his death.

Glass sprayed John from behind – something nicked his Stetson.

Blood spattered the windshield. Mostly on the passenger side.

XIV

Ryn shrieked and blubbered.

Vincent couldn't breathe.

Bucky swerved and shouted – he corrected and stomped on the gas.

Beside him, in the passenger seat, Louis' head was tilted forward, dripping blood and brainmatter onto his lap.

John was unable as of yet to fathom what had just transpired.

Moments of bewildered shrieks and shouts filled the van before understanding gradually crept into his detached brain. And when it finally settled in, he remained silent. His lips moved slowly – his jaw worked mechanically – as he attempted to vocalize disconnected thoughts; his mouth opened and closed – opened and closed – opened and closed...

His eyes welled up and tears began to roll.

Vincent threw himself forward, onto his knees – he shook Louis' shoulder – he called his name. Louis' head lolled and fresh blood spilled onto his lap – some splattered Vincent's hand. He stared at the specks in disbelief.

Ryn bawled, holding her locket and her face.

John's head swam, his face went slack – and he fell sideways across the back seat.

XV

His first thought was: *They're both dead!*

Through the rear window – falling farther behind them – he could make out the dark figure standing alone amidst a field of corpses. He may not have had the greatest vision, but he knew it was Rhea and knew that she was firing at their escape.

TCHINK! – a bullet struck the rear quarter-panel.

Just before losing sight of her, he watched someone – or some*thing* – tackle Rhea. He was hopeful that karma's justice was swift in repaying her for Louis' death, figuring that becoming a *bob* might just equal her atrocities. Nothing of what he saw detracted from this hope and in the coming days he would frequently recall her supposed demise over time. Occasionally, whisperings of doubt from his subconscious would nip at him, but he learned to hush them and instead imagine her shambling, bloody body that would effectively wreck her beauty and epitomize her evil.

These deep-seated whisperings were – curiously enough – accurate; what he saw was not a *bob* – a *lurcher* – a *ghoul* – tackling her. Rather, it was Sanchez and he was saving her from a crawler. Together, they would run east until locating a deserted cabin on the edge of town in which they would remain safe for three days. Hardly straying from the cabin's second floor, they survived on canned goods and bread and bottled water. After a short time, Rhea would grow fond of Sanchez – she admired his will to live and ruthless nature.

They formed a strong bond that would endure.

But Vincent believed they were both dead or dying.

And he also believed his brothers were now dead.

He flew over the middle seat and started shaking John – Ryn continued wailing. He shouted John's name, slapped his face and shook him harder. He felt for a pulse, but with trembling hands and a rocking vehicle he couldn't definitively locate one.

"Pull over!" he called to Bucky.

"No can do!" Bucky called back – he swerved around a lurcher; Vincent was thrown into Ryn, abruptly halting her braying. He cursed, offered her a curt apology and shook his friend's shoulder some more.

Bucky swerved again (Vincent managed to avoid slamming into Ryn this time). "Where did all these people come from?" Bucky shouted to nobody. He clipped a gnarled teenager and lost a mirror to its groping hands.

John groaned, pawed at his furrowed brow.

"John!" cried Vincent, gripping his shoulder. "You're okay!"

Groaning more, John sat up, rubbed his head. "I guess so." His voice was gravelly.

"I thought she got you, too," said Vincent, relieved that she had not.

"No," John croaked. "I just…passed out." He looked up at Louis' lifeless body as it flopped around from Bucky's evasive maneuvers.

Stalled, wrecked and otherwise derelict vehicles now speckled the road, adding a less carnivorous (or mobile) threat to the already swarming number of lurching obstacles. "Is he really...?" he couldn't finish the sentence.

"Yes."

"How?"

"Rhea." Vincent gazed at Louis, mortified, furious. "She shot at us."

John took a moment to process this information. And then he said, "Go back. She needs to pay."

"She's dead," Vincent alleged. "I watched a lurcher take her down right after she shot Lou."

"Then I want to kill her infected body and piss in her eye."

"Ain't no turnin' back now," said Bucky. He met John's glower in the mirror. "We're in the thick of it now. Too many *bobs* up here and as many still back there. Won't turn around now for Hell or high water."

John glowered a moment longer, but did not argue.

Unfazed, Bucky continued piloting through the mass of groping hands and hungry eyes. He tried to avoid their reach whenever possible, but clipped them whenever the alternative was another vehicle or larger horde. The further they traveled, the denser the horde grew. At one point, the numbers outside were so intense that gnarled, bloody hands were constantly slamming into the windows and door panels. A good few he mowed over, each time thanking the heavens their beat-up minivan didn't catch or flip due to a perfectly placed arm or leg in the axle or struts.

But eventually their numbers thinned and the massed vehicles were less chaotic (though still quite numerous on their own). Vincent noted that every vehicle now pointed east (more or less; some were sideways or angled between lanes). Apparently everybody in the area figured the mountains – or the plains and farmlands beyond the mountains – were their best bet. And apparently they didn't get very far.

Trepidations mounted in Vincent.

And soon they found the epicenter of this horde.

Beyond the arch leading to the park gates sat an astounding mess of derelict vehicles. And beyond all this they could see the white tops of canvas tents surrounded by razor wire. Chills ran concurrently down the spines of Vincent and John.

"Can you find a way through?" Ryn asked.

"I can only try," Bucky replied.

Having been lured from this spot by the morning battle in Ashford, fewer *bobs* were now lurking amidst the wreckage. This was definitely advantageous for Bucky as he attempted to squeeze through gaps, but not quite as advantageous as any of them would have hoped. In the end, a sprawling mess still stood between them and the checkpoint's impressive perimeter.

"We gotta make a run for it," said Bucky. "And I don't think we have much time."

"We can't just leave Louis like this," said John. "It just don't feel right."

"You don't have a choice right now," said Bucky. "Not if you wanna live, anyhow."

"I can't leave him to be eaten by *zombies*!" bawled John.

"Get it together!" Vincent demanded. "Lou's dead and we gotta live. So let's get the fuck going already!" He snatched up his pack and rifle. "It's what he would want."

John seriously wondered what a life like that could be, making such grim bargains.

Vincent slapped him – hard. "Louis would rather be eaten than see you die today!"

Though he was hot from being hit (John was never able to strike Vincent in all the time they knew one another, though he contemplated it on more than one occasion), he slung his rifle over his shoulder and grabbed his pack. As an afterthought, he plucked the Stetson off the seat (he absently noticed the hole at the front of the brim) and popped it onto his greasy head. "Let's do it then," he said with affected conviction.

Vincent threw open the sliding door and they spilled out into the world. With one last look at Louis – roiling thoughts of sorrow at his loss and leaving his body behind welled in each of them – they were off around the van.

Bucky led their winding path through narrow running lanes. More than twice they were forced to climb over the hood of a car. All were on point in the matter of sweeping for danger, but – as history has proven many times over – man is fallible. So despite their best efforts, the crawler that tripped Ryn went unseen until the moment she fell hard – the impact dislocated her shoulder.

Vincent very nearly tumbled and crushed her; he skidded to a halt at her side. He kicked the crawler's hand away and bludgeoned its head with his rifle until the skull cracked and popped and rotted brains squirted out one side. He hoisted Ryn to her feet and they ran after the others. Her injury slowed her pace; the pain disrupted her equilibrium. Vincent remained patient and assisted her when she listed this way or that.

Surprisingly, neither Bucky nor John heard the incident.

The perimeter of this particular checkpoint – another National

Guard outpost meant to curb the spread of infection – ran the length of the park gates. It was comprised of coiled razor wire and jersey barriers set before double chainlinks that were topped with more razor wire. In the middle of this impressive barrier was a gap where Vincent was hoping to find a path.

"This way," he said, leading them along the perimeter's edge. "Just like before," he murmured, thinking of the razor wire mazes he had to navigate at the start of all this madness. And he was thankful when he found the mazes were indeed the same (he managed to overlook the mangled corpses strewn about the razor coils and focus on the opportunity afforded them by this handy pathway). "We should be a bit safer inside," he said. "Doesn't look like there are very many –"

Bucky screamed as a lurcher tackled him into the razor wire. He hollered and struggled, accumulating countless gashes and gouges. The lurcher – the *bob* – felt no pain as chunks of skin were torn away from it in droves. Within a moment – before anybody could react – curdled, infected blood gushed out and onto Bucky, mixing with his once healthy blood.

Still hoping for the best, John pulled the *bob* off of him. He tossed it aside and shot it in the head as it tumbled into the grille of a truck. He whirled to find Vincent and Ryn freeing Bucky from the coils. "Are you alright?" he asked. "Did it get you?"

"No," panted Bucky. "I don't think it did. But…" he looked down at his bloodied body, wincing at his various wounds. "It bled on me," he said. "Its blood got *inside* of me."

"Are you sure?" John asked.

"Dead sure," replied Bucky, ignorant to this statement's inherent irony. "I can feel it – it's like death in my veins."

"Well let's get inside the perimeter and check you out," suggested Vincent.

"No," said Bucky. "I know I'm done for. I have maybe an hour, if I'm lucky. I've seen people change sooner with just a scratch. And this is worse than a scratch."

Nearby groans interrupted them.

"I will take one of your cigarettes, though," said Bucky, racking his pistol. "Greg and I kicked the habit a couple years ago to go pro at climbing." He took the lit cigarette offered him by Vincent. "Thanks," he said, drawing deep. "I hope to see him soon in whatever afterworld I can find." He started toward the nearest groans. "Go," he said. "There's still time for you three."

And for just a moment they watched him march away, trailing smoke – every step he took was marked with a red bootprint. They watched him shoot at something behind a car – *BLAM!* – and continue marching without a hitch.

"C'mon," breathed Vincent – he started down the razor wire maze.

XVI

They could hear his gunshots for minutes after making their way beyond the perimeter. Sometimes he would shout or bellow at his assailants. Sometimes he would howl or cry out in pain. After nearly ten minutes of his ultimate procession, they heard one more gunshot – and never did they hear him cry out again.

Before the final gunshot – as the three of them were clearing the courtyard of the few remaining lurchers – Bucky climbed behind the wheel of the faded blue minivan. He looked at Louis' limp corpse – a man he hardly knew – and decided he looked rather undignified slouched against the seatbelt. After reclining the passenger seat so Louis could spread out, he reclined his own. He recited the Lord's Prayer and then one of his own, begging forgiveness for his sins and mercy on his soul for the act of taking his own life. He spoke individual prayers for Vincent and Ryn and John and crossed himself (*the Father, the Son and the Holy Spirit – amen*).

He looked at Louis once again. "Let us find sanctuary in oblivion," he said.

And then he slipped the gun into his mouth and pulled the trigger.

So it goes.

XVII

As they rested at an abandoned guard's post, the horde filtered through the web of derelict vehicles. Unmindful of flesh wounds, the lurchers thrashed at the razor wire barriers. A few overly ambitious specimens managed to work through the coils and thrash at the fences, but to no avail as their numbers were too low. And not a single lurcher in the horde could fathom navigating the simplistic maze; they all stumbled straight into it and tangled themselves in the coils.

Vincent studied their behavior with abject curiosity.

"I think it's broken," said Ryn, grimacing and holding her shoulder. "It hurts real bad."

"How'd that happen?" inquired John.

"I fell," Ryn answered.

"Let me see it," said Vincent. Working gingerly with his fingers, he felt along her collarbone and scapula. When he touched her shoulder, she yelped. "Sorry," he said, releasing the pressure. "I gotta feel some more, though. Probably gonna hurt a bit worse, too."

"It's okay," said Ryn. "Go for it."

"Here," said John, offering his hand. "Squeeze when it hurts."

She took it; her tiny hand was swallowed up by his massive paw.

When Vincent replaced the pressure on her shoulder, she choked out a whimpering yelp. And when his fingers worked deeper, she sucked in air through bared teeth and seethed. Her eyes were shut tight and she dug her nails into John's hand; he returned her grip with lighter, pulsing squeezes to let her know he felt her pain.

"Well," said Vincent, releasing her shoulder, "it ain't broken. That's the good news." With the course of events as of late, simply uttering the phrase "good news" fundamentally upset him; after losing his best friend – his *brother* – nothing about this day could even be considered relatively *good*. Had he known the phrase would upset him before saying it, he probably would have chosen a different aphorism.

"What's the prognosis, doc?" John asked, not without a touch of sarcasm.

"My *diagnosis*," replied Vincent, "is a dislocated shoulder. And my *prognosis* would be to pop it back into place." He caught Ryn's trepidatious gaze. "It'll hurt. It'll hurt worse than *real bad*. But it's gotta happen."

"Just make it quick," she said, bracing herself – her grip on John's hand tightened.

Nervous from a lack of experience (Vincent had never actually popped any joint back into place and was certain he would mess it up), he hooked himself under her arm and placed one hand on either side of her shoulder – already she was groaning from the torque and added pressure. He took a deep breath, summoned all the power he could muster and channeled that power into one supreme heave –

POP! – Ryn bellowed, fell into John's chest; her arm went limp and Vincent thought for a moment that he must have broken it.

"Are you okay?" he asked instinctively, aware of her tremendous pain.

Whimpering – her face still buried – she nodded and took her arm back from Vincent. She moved it cautiously, testing her boundaries. She pulled away from John, released her firm grip on his hand (four little crescents were carved into his palm from her nails). Her tears dried (though her face was still wet) and she caught her breath. She continued testing her arm and watched with wonder as it passed back and forth through her vision.

John flexed his hand, rubbed his palm.

"Should we see what sort of supplies they got in there?" Ryn asked, referring to the tents.

"No," replied Vincent without hesitation. "There's nothing of use in there."

"Might be weapons," she suggested.

"I plucked enough extra cartridges off the bodies out here," he said.

"We could stay here for a while," she said. "Seems secure enough. Probably got beds in there, too."

"No beds," said John. "Just cots." He looked over at the fenceline. "And I don't trust this place's security too well if it's been abandoned like this." He remembered their flight from the checkpoint in Olympia. "So long as we're right here, where they can *sense* us, they'll keep trying to get at us."

"Didn't even leave us a vehicle," muttered Vincent – he was surveying the grounds. He shifted his focus to the eastern perimeter (tall fences and razor wire – go figure). His interest in this fenceline was piqued when he noticed the lurcher differential: a hundred or more and counting to the west and zero in the east. "Why don't we check out that gate," he motioned toward the eastern perimeter. "Maybe there'll be a car or something."

"Where else are we gonna go?" she asked.

"Paradise," Vincent replied. "Just like we planned."

"Is any other place gonna be as secure as this?" she asked.

"You see it as secure," said John, "but I see it as a cage – a trap. We could get boxed-in and have nowhere to go."

"If we find a car," said Vincent, "we could be up there and locate a defensible property in no more than an hour."

"Vincent's right," commented John. "I know I'd feel safer elsewhere."

"Oh, c'mon guys," said Ryn, apparently exasperated with them. "This place can't possibly be as bad as the other one." She was well aware of their previous encounter with the Army National Guard. "For one thing, there's no more people here. And for another, there's no *zombies* here, either."

Vincent was sure that Louis – despite their circumstances – would have commented on her poor grammar. Instead – being as he was not a stickler for such benign issues – Vincent decided to respond logically; "This has less to do with our failed military than it does with *them*." He pointed his chin at the growing mass at the western gate – their mounting groans were starting to wear at his psyche.

"Seriously, Ryn," said John. "We should skedaddle. Besides being wary of this place, one could go insane listening to that racket."

And he was right; in the coming months – the coming *years* – many cases of insanity would result from extended exposure to the incessant moans of infected hordes. Most incidents would go undocumented as witnesses of such phenomena would often die or be driven insane as well (quite expectedly, of course). But in time, these occurrences would become apparent to the remaining scientific and psychiatric community. As disintegrated and disconnected as this community would become, experts in the field would still coin useless phrases on the disorder (such as "zombie overexposure" or "auditory psychosis syndrome"). No matter the terminology used, those who suffered from this disorder were plagued with never-ending audio-hallucinations that drove them to suicide or murder. In extreme cases, the victims would believe they were infected and begin acting as such (until, of course, they were shot or eaten by survivors or lurchers).

"Got a lot of day ahead of us, anyhow," said Vincent. "And I'd rather not see how long it takes them to topple those fences."

"You really think it'll be safer up there, eh," she said.

Interpreting this as a question, Vincent replied, "I sure do. Especially since I don't see a single lurcher on the other side of that fenceline."

Their attention finally shifted to the east.

"Don't see any cars over there, either," said John.

"Yeah," breathed Vincent. "We might just have to hoof it. We'll probably find one up the road aways."

"We'd be lucky to find one with keys in it," commented Ryn.

"I don't see much of an option," said Vincent.

"Well," said Ryn and she motioned to the tents.

"No way," replied John.

"Then I guess you're right, Vin," she said. "Don't really have an option." She rolled her eyes. "But can we maybe rest for a little while longer?" she pleaded. "Maybe have a smoke and let me stretch out on the bench for a minute?"

"I guess we're not in any immediate hurry," replied Vincent – he handed a smoke to her. "But let's not try to set up shop; damn moans are startin' to irritate me already."

"Deal." She sparked her cigarette and laid out across the metal bench. She clutched her locket and bore both the fond and the frightening memories of her father as they careened through her weary mind.

XVIII

Nobody went more than ten yards from the guard shack – and rarely did they even have a reason to leave it. Vincent pissed around the corner once and John mostly paced or stared at the growing horde along the western perimeter. Relatively cozy upon the cold, hard bench, Ryn rarely puffed on her cigarette and very nearly passed out.

Fifteen sluggish minutes dragged on as growls and groans swelled at the fenceline, grating at Vincent's fragile sensibilities. His patience gradually faltered over this mere quarter hour and he marched back into the guard shack. He tapped Ryn's boot with one of his own. "Ready?" he said when she opened her eyes.

She nodded and stretched, incidentally crushing what was left of her cigarette.

Beyond the eastern perimeter was a barren road and quiet forest.

"I'm not excited about this," mumbled Ryn.

"I know," replied Vincent.

"Do you even know how far it is to the top?" she asked.

"If you have to ask," he said, "then you don't wanna know."

Unwilling to check the maps, she sighed, accepting the journey ahead as indefinite.

They started through the razor coil maze.

XIX

Almost immediately, they were gaining altitude. After about an hour, rain began to fall; the cool droplets soothed their aching bodies and aided (if only slightly) in staving off fatigue. Their pace slowed considerably from the grade; after two hours, they made it just over two miles and had to break out of the rain.

Unmindful of the damp earth, Vincent flopped onto his back, panting and absently rubbing his hip. He grimaced at the various pains shooting across his body.

"How the hell did we come to be here?" murmured John – he stood at the edge of the forest, staring at the increasing rain, his arms crossed over his chest. Without pausing to receive responses, he started rattling off all the queries that plagued his troubled mind: "The greatest nation with the greatest technology and military force in the world and we still couldn't quell such a threat on our own land. And where the hell did these things come from? Is it truly *the end*? Has Hell come to Earth? Or is this just one big nightmare from which we'll all soon awake?" He huffed and fell against a tree, rubbing his temples with one hand. "How far will it go before we return to normality?"

"I don't know," Vincent wisped. A tear stung the corner of his eye as reruns of Louis' exploding head played over in his mind – how the blood and brains (his unusually intelligent brains, at that) spattered the windshield. "I don't know," he wisped again, loosing a tear.

Holding her ankle, Ryn sat against a tree near Vincent, watching them both. She could see the stress eating at their sanity – their composure. Being the youngest (and arguably the most frightened), she was startled to find her own composure holding strong. She was tempted to respond to some of John's rhetoric, but decided her words might cause more damage; she would wait to pose these observations.

Instead, curious thoughts of this area's complete lack of lurchers intrigued her until they started off into the deluge twenty minutes later. The rain sang as it pounded the pavement and drew rivers across the road.

XX

Their pace was incredibly slow and in the next hour they barely hiked a mile.

"I can't go any farther," panted Vincent. "We need to find a place to crash. Preferably off the highway aways." He was delirious from mounting pains, but managed to exude some semblance of equanimity.

"How 'bout up there?" suggested Ryn, pointing up a stream that ran under the highway.

"Sure," breathed Vincent. "Fine. Whatever. We can crash wherever I fall over. Which won't take long. Let's go." He veered off the road with John and Ryn on his heel.

Chilled from a brisk autumn wind and the deep shadows of the thick forest canopy, they tromped through the underbrush, careful to keep the babbling stream in earshot at all times. And just when Vincent's hip started to lock up, they stumbled upon a suitable clearing.

Vincent flopped on the forest floor, unmindful of the cold earth.

Similarly, his companions plopped down against nearby trees.

From his bag, Vincent withdrew a bottle of water and started guzzling. He quickly found his thirst was insatiable; he downed over half before realizing he should save some for later. He capped the bottle and dropped it at his side.

Nobody moved or spoke for ten minutes.

But Ryn couldn't contain herself any longer; feeling strangely spry for the day they had, she hopped to her feet and marched into the forest.

"Don't go too far!" John called after her.

"Two seconds," she replied.

Thirty seconds later, she returned with an armload of heavy sticks.

"No fire tonight," said Vincent. "Too risky."

"Check," she said – and she marched back into the forest. A minute later, she returned with another armload of heavy sticks along with a grip of ferns.

"What're you doing?" asked John.

"Shelter," she replied. "Don't wanna get rained on all night." And she marched away.

"Well shit," said John – he looked at Vincent, eyebrows arched. "Might as well help her." He laboriously stood, stretched his back and looked at Vincent with purpose. He smiled as Vincent sighed and stood.

They erected their shelter against the trunk of a fallen tree, using ferns and moss to patch holes in the woodwork and leaves to line the floor for bedding. Exhausted and sore, they crawled inside when their work was done. Huddled together for heat – with Ryn sandwiched between the boys – they were asleep in minutes.

Nobody sat watch that night.

Day Nine
Threshold

I

Something escaped him – something vague and disjointed – when Vincent awoke. His first thought was, *Save yourself!* – and he gasped. Ghosts of terror lingered; his head was foggy and far away. His hip flared and he winced at the pain.

"It's okay," whispered Ryn. "You were just having a nightmare." She hugged him and sat up. She stretched her arms out and yawned. "Not surprising, I guess," she said. "Pretty scary shit lately." Touching the locket around her neck, she looked back at him, her eyes large and sorrowful. "Who's Isabella?" she asked.

The question was startling. "Did I talk in my sleep?" he asked.

"Just that name," she said. "*Isabella.*" She tasted the name, sensing a sort of romance in it. "Pretty name," she said.

"Pretty name for a pretty girl," he said. "But that's a long story," he said, trying to skirt the subject. He sat up and stretched his long arms. "Probably best for another day. For now," he started to crawl out of the shelter, "I gotta throw a wizz."

"Did you lose her?"

He stopped midway through the little door. "You could say that," he said. He crawled out and wandered behind a cluster of trees to unload his bladder. A snapshot of Isabella being chased by a gnarled version of Konrad flashed before his eyes and he shuddered. He made a dim link between this vision and his forgotten dream.

When he returned to the clearing, John was trying to start a fire with wet wood and paper. Ryn was seated on the damp earth with her knees pulled up to her chin, hugging them close for warmth.

"Where'd you get the paper?" Vincent asked.

"Blank pages at the back of the Bible Salem gave me," John replied.

Raising an eyebrow, Vincent said, "Burning the Bible now, John? That's unlike you."

"Har-har," said John. "I don't see any other purpose for those pages right now." He blew on the smoldering paper, trying to catch a flame. But the embers burnt quick and died in a puff of smoke. "Damn," he breathed. "Shit burns too fast."

Vincent recalled the tricks of his youth when rolling papers were nowhere to be found; he chuckled, knowing why the Bible paper burnt so fast. He was certain that John knew this trick as well. "Just a second," he said. "You keep trying that – I'll be right back." He rifled around in his bag for a moment and twice dropped items back before snatching a sizeable knife. He marched away from the creek, into the trees. He scanned the trunks until he found one that was bleeding and started chopping away at the bark.

He did this a few times on different trees until his palm was full. He topped the pile of bark and sap with moss (still wet, unfortunately – but that was hardly a bother to him) and returned to the camp. John was still huffing and puffing away at smoldering bits of Bible paper when Vincent tossed his natural fire starters into the mix. He drew a box of wind-proof matches from his pocket and waved John away.

"I got this," he said, striking a match.

The sap did not catch very quickly – it mostly sizzled and popped and died. But after a few matches and more breathless efforts, a small flame licked across a chunk of bark. He caught a few more pieces with that one flame and surrounded the lot with wet moss. And when the moss started to catch, he built a small teepee around it all and shoved a few more crumpled pieces of Bible paper into the middle. Within a few minutes, the sticks were burning hot and he added a ring of heavier wood chunks to dry.

All three of them started snapping fallen limbs and added them as the fire grew. After an hour, they had enough flame and coal to relax on the chore of hunting for wood. Ryn popped a large can of beans that would be their breakfast and set it to heat in the flames. While it cooked, John took leave to piss and clear his head.

"Don't go too far," Ryn reminded him. Despite the lack of danger on this stretch of highway, she still felt such a reminder to be prudent. And it was, of course; danger seemed to have a way of sneaking up at the most inconvenient of times.

"I'll be within earshot," he assured her. He found the nearby creek and sat beside it, his head awhirl with memories of Louis.

"Well," said Ryn suddenly (to which Vincent raised an eyebrow at her). "I'ma romp around a little more. I shouldn't be long, but would you watch the beans for me?" she asked him.

Vincent shrugged (and dropped his eyebrow). "Sure. Just don't go too far." He smirked with a wink.

"I'll be sure to stay within earshot," she replied with a return wink.

II

Alone and cross-legged beside the fire, Vincent withdrew the katana. He held its reddish blade straight up before his face and traced the blood-caked filigree with his eyes, wondering over the foreign inscription. Though he couldn't read it, he was overcome by a deep chill, and flashes of Louis and Konrad and Tod erupted in his head. His eyes grew wide as he stared at the gleaming inscription; for a brief moment, he thought he was staring at the very blade that ended Konrad's life. He felt the very fear and adrenaline of that incident pumping through his veins, soaking into his porous brain. And then he saw the priest on the darkened highway, an image from a dream of which he had absolutely no recollection. The priest wielded this very blade – this tarnished and cursed blade – at him with malice in his eyes. And again, despite its red tinge and mysterious inscription, he had a flash of the blade that ended Konrad's life. Already, he wanted to break down.

But the images weren't done. He saw the blade slicing clean through Rhea, though her image in his head was amoebic and shifted hazily between her and Louis and Ryn and Cooper and Konrad and Sanchez and Isabella – and others – until it sliced clean through his own body, as well.

This last image shook him from this trance.

He lowered the blade until the tip rested gently on the dirt floor. The handle felt cold, despite him having been gripping it so tightly just moments ago.

Ignoring this peculiar sensation, he straightened his back, breathed deeply of the fresh mountain air, drew his knees in tight, and spread his arms out with the katana poised across his upturned fingertips. With closed eyes, he exhaled slowly before drawing, once again, long and deep of the fresh mountain air. He breathed as such – posed as such – until his mind was clear of all such negative and disturbing thoughts. He called up happier thoughts and images; a warm, bright day at the lake with Isabella in one of her light sundresses – the yellow one specked with subtle daisies.

He always liked the way she wore that one; it hugged her perky breasts with sexy sophistication and flourished just above her knees in a gentle breeze. She always accented this with a bright orange belt that ringed her petite midriff; her flats and headband matched the belt. And, as always, she wore the citrine pendant he'd bought her for her birthday some years back (the pendant won him his first date with her); it was set into pure silver and hung right between her flawless breasts on a dainty silver chain. She wore a matching ring on the third finger of her right hand (she wished it was the third finger on her left hand, but had yet to press him on such a matter).

Her smiling beauty on that lovely summer day was a stark contrast from his lazeabout, paint-stained khaki cargo shorts, faded old tee-shirt (it was once black with a crisp Atari logo on the front, but that was long ago), ratty and ripped Guinness baseball cap, and brown plaid flipflops. Being the semi-geeky, smalltime bounty hunter that he was, it always amazed him that he'd landed such a gem of a woman. Her heritage was half-Colombian/half-European (a good portion of which was heavily Sicilian); she was a wonderfully amalgamated American mutt with a slight olive complexion (and the softest skin he'd ever felt). Vincent was solely of European descent, making him the typical white American mutt. Together, they would have created some of the brightest (if not most beautiful or handsome) children.

Vincent cringed at the thought; they had just begun talks of having children right before he blew town on his fool's errand. She wanted a family more than anything in the world, and he still felt too young – probably always would. He was starting to entertain the idea, as she was becoming restless in their relationship. She felt as though they were stagnant water in a rut – and he could see why she felt that way. Work, make dinner, watch the tube (literally; they owned an old forty-inch tube television), make love (sometimes), and go to sleep. And sometimes, he'd work late to apprehend someone at a specific time or location, in which case she'd be left to her own devices until God-knew-when. Maybe they'd go out on a Friday night for dinner followed by drinks and some pool or darts or bowling. Or barbecue on a Sunday. There was no "spice" in their relationship anymore, as she had so eloquently complained one night. So he tried taking her out more often – on a random Tuesday or something, just to change things up. And he tried different moves in bed, but nothing so different or exciting as to "spice" up his lovemaking.

He couldn't figure out what else to do to spice things up, save for giving her the only thing she really wanted: a baby. What he couldn't understand was that all of his efforts had failed because he never actually knew what she wanted – or *needed* – in order to give new life to their relationship. And she certainly didn't want more of the same speckled here and there at weird and random times (i.e. more trips to the same bar or the same bowling alley or the same damn restaurant). What she really needed to spice things up was spontaneity. A weekend trip to somewhere she'd never been before; a road trip through the countryside or forest or even the hills that were just outside of town; fishing at the lake in the summer or sledding down the street in winter; or baseball games or football games or basketball games (and she didn't even care for the sport!) or maybe even hockey or roller derby – anything besides more of the same. But, more than any of those things, she wanted to visit her parents more than once or twice a year. They had a ranch just over the mountains – not even four hours away – and still they rarely found the time to make the journey. They loved Vincent, so she never understood why he didn't take her there more often; something just always seemed to come up.

Unfortunately for Vincent, he was too blind and timid – and unimaginative – to figure out any of this. A baby – a *family* – may have been her dream for them, but she needed a *life* as well. Vincent just couldn't figure out what that really meant. It's a wonder they lasted as long as they did; it's a wonder why he left her, and not the other way around. Which made the event all the more shocking to anyone who knew them.

Despite thoughts of failing her in some unfathomable way – and all the thoughts related to leaving her on such a ludicrous whim – he filled his mind's eye with images of her soft, smiling face on that lakeshore; her fingers intertwined with his; the light feel of her yellow sundress; her supple lips pressed gently against his. She was small, but not short; beautiful without makeup; classy and smart and everything he wanted – or *needed* – in the world. The weight of her absence pressed hard on his shoulders, his chest – his heart and his soul. But thinking of her and her beauty (in character and presence) was all he could do to remind himself of all that made life worth living. Even in this wild new world, there was something that would make it all worthwhile. He prayed – in his agnostic way – that he would find his love again and all would be forgiven. And if all couldn't be forgiven, he prayed that she was at least alive. Without her beauty gracing the world, he wasn't sure he would want to be in it any longer.

He would make it his life's goal to find out her fate – and find her, if at all possible.

Crackling leaves and twigs roused him from this mediocre meditation, though not unpleasantly so. He opened his eyes just as Ryn stepped from the foliage into the clearing with an armload of sticks and short, spindly branches. He could tell by her dour face and stiff mannerisms that something was disturbing her, if only slightly. He noted that her pants were darker in spots, perhaps from hastily cleaning off something or another – mud, perhaps – or blood. *Yes*, he thought, scrutinizing the discoloration as she got closer. *Fresh blood*. The darker flecks were apparent now, standing out like nasty cherry stains.

"What happened to you?" he asked, motioning to her pants.

She flushed and clutched her armload of soggy sticks and limbs to her chest. "Nothing," she said. "Just a little mud." She was lying – her reaction to his seemingly benign question betrayed her. Ryn wasn't used to lying – even minimally – and she was bad at it.

But Vincent detected nothing malevolent about her fib. He guessed that he truly didn't want to know what had happened, that perhaps it wasn't something a man wouldn't want to discuss. Had he pressed her further, he would have discovered that such was indeed the truth. But even without this certainty, he was trig enough not to press her on the matter. He figured she wouldn't hide a wound if she had been bitten. He also figured that he would have heard at least some commotion if she'd encountered a lurcher. If not a scream or a yelp, he surely would have heard its hungry snarls or her grunts of violence – or a gunshot. But there had been no recent commotion – this he was sure of.

"Alright," he said, dismissing the subject. He gazed back at the katana's tainted blade. Brownish blood of the many infected he killed caked the grooves of the filigree. Vincent couldn't help but think about the priest's story regarding the blade's reddish tinge. *If they thought it was tarnished by the blood of infidels and the righteous back then*, he thought, *then I can't imagine what they'd think of it now; surely, the infected are* worse *than infidels, if not a direct relation to the devil himself.* Though, he was certain they would have deemed its use on these infected *demons* quite righteous, indeed – no matter who was wielding it.

Ryn tumbled the bundle of sticks at the fire's edge. The redness in her face diminished slowly as she noticed Vincent had dropped the subject and returned his attention to that of the katana. Carefully, using the sleeve of her jacket as an oven mitt, she pulled the black and steaming can of beans from the fire. "Forget something?" she asked with a sarcastic smirk. She displayed the blackened can, waggling it with snarky admonition.

"No," he lied. "You returned just as I was getting to that."

"Uh-huh," she said, setting the can aside to cool. "Looked like you were nodding off to me." She made a face at him, stopping just short of sticking out her tongue.

"My nose would have told me if they were done," he countered.

"Or if they were burnt," she replied – but this time she couldn't help herself; she scrunched her nose and stuck out her tongue.

"Nah," he said with a wink, still playing her game. "I had it all under control."

"Sure," she said, dismissing the subject.

She took a seat across the fire from him on a nurse log, the surface of which was mossy and damp. She no longer cared if she dirtied her pants and paid the blooming wetness of her rump little mind.

From his pack, Vincent withdrew a rag and began cleaning the blade; the dried and caked blood flaked away with ease.

"So, Mister Bounty Hunter," Ryn said to him. She was reluctant to shatter their previous banter, but she had to know. "What happened to Isabella?"

Vincent's face simultaneously slacked and flushed. "Like I said earlier," he began, his voice trembling just a touch, "that's a long story."

"All we got is time," she said.

Before he could toss out another dismissive response, John interjected his opinion: "He dumped her for money." John stepped into the clearing; he had been at the creek's edge doing a little meditation of his own. "The way it went down, it felt like he dumped us all." He spoke to Ryn without so much as a sideways glance at Vincent.

And Vincent's complexion flushed a brighter shade of red. His cleaning of the katana had since ceased; the rag was draped motionlessly over the blade.

"What happened?" she asked John.

"One day he was gone," John replied, taking a seat beside her on the nurse log. "He never even said goodbye. Just broke her heart and left." His eyes now bored into the top of Vincent's downturned head. "Soon after, she moved back to her parents' ranch. I contacted her via Facebook, but she was rather vague on the circumstances."

Both of them were gazing expectantly at Vincent.

After a few beats, Vincent addressed their questions and comments without lifting his head; "That's just about it." His voice was low and weak. "Thanks for explaining it so succinctly, brother."

John slitted his eyes in a searching glare.

"But there's gotta be more to it than that," Ryn said. "Why?"

"Yes, Vincent," John said. "*Why?*"

His cheeks were still warm, but Vincent felt the redness draining from his face and turned to meet their gazes. "I thought I needed a change. And our relationship was becoming rocky."

"Relationships require maintenance and compromise," John said. "You can't just throw in the towel when things get tough."

"Yeah," Vincent breathed. "I know." He dropped his gaze and resumed his cleaning of the blade. "It was a bad move on my part. As was leaving without a word to you or Lou."

"Or your parents or your brother or anybody at all," John scorned. "So tell me now, and tell me honestly: where did you go?" He waited patiently, giving Vincent the time to collect his thoughts.

Without a brain clouded by drugs – and the sour effects of his detox now in the past – Vincent managed to collect these thoughts with some ease. His response was only delayed by a lack of courage to actually *speak* the words aloud. And so, when he did speak, he did not raise his eyes out of shame. "I was contracted to kill a very bad man," he said at last with a quaky voice and fluttering heart – his head swam with fear and plenty more shame.

John was stunned, his mouth agape; Ryn was just confused.

Save for the crackling of the fire and a few chirrups in the trees, silence filled the air. After over half a minute, Vincent raised his head to find their awed expressions.

"His name was Jackson Friedrich," Vincent said, using Konrad's pseudonym. Telling them he'd killed someone was bad enough; he wasn't about to tell John he'd killed someone they knew. He would have to hold that information until a later date – if not forever. (Thinking back on it now, he wasn't sure how he had been so candid with Louis.) "He was a domestic terrorist." He almost explained the connection to Rhea, but feared John would snap and blame him for Louis' death. "It was the only contract I took. And it's been killing me ever since. So much so, that I was doped-up and drunk for months – right up until we reached that military outpost just outside of Oly." He swallowed hard and watched as they digested this flood of information.

"I don't really care who it was," John growled. "You *murdered* someone. And not like we have been lately; you actually fucking *murdered* a *living* human being!" Knocking the Stetson off his head, he ran a rough hand through his hair, launched himself up and off the nurse log and started pacing angrily around the fire.

Vincent thought that he was due for a beating, and he would have let it happen. He set the katana aside and closed his eyes, awaiting the blow from John's powerful fist that surely would follow.

Even Ryn shrank back, expecting the worst. She remained silent and fearful – and felt more than a little betrayed.

But John just paced and pulled at his hair. "How could you?" he bawled. "How could you throw us all away for *murder*? And then just come crawling back when the shit hit the fan?"

Vincent couldn't reply; he remained silently seated, his head swimming worse than ever and heart pounding so hard he felt it might burst through his chest. He thought he might keel over while awaiting the beating he was certain would follow.

John stopped pacing, both hands in his hair. He wasn't about to beat Vincent, despite his burning desire to do so. After a silent prayer to calm his nerves, he lowered his voice and said, "At least Louis died before learning of this. It may have killed him to know such a thing."

Vincent's cheeks burned. And without a word, his reaction to this statement told John that Louis did, in fact, know of such a thing.

John knelt before Vincent and gently grasped his shoulders. "He *did* know," he breathed, his voice barely above a whisper. The betrayal he felt trebled at this knowledge. His eyes were wide and crazed, searching Vincent's silence for an answer. His jaw worked mechanically, but he had trouble vocalizing the jumbled thoughts that bounced violently about his head.

Vincent met his gaze with sorrow. "Yes," he wisped. "Louis knew. I asked him not to tell you. I was scared. I didn't want to hurt you." *And I thought you might hurt me*, he thought, *or worse…* but he let that thought hang in his head, not wanting to finish it, even silently. His eyes flicked toward Ryn. "And now I've hurt you both." He dropped his head and squeezed his watery eyes.

John slumped and touched his forehead to Vincent's.

Once she realized John wasn't going to pummel him, Ryn's fear began to subside. She still felt the pain of Vincent's admission, but she couldn't forget all that he had done for her…

"I forgive you," she said.

And the floodgates opened up; tears fell from his downturned face as his body shuddered with quiet sniffles and sobs. With the weight of this secret off his chest, he felt relief, but he didn't believe that he deserved any forgiveness. Her kindness was too much. As was John's; brothers in arms, there was an unwritten rule of forgiveness, no matter the transgression, and he knew John would abide this rule. They had been through far too much together – especially as of late – for John to dismiss him at this point. But still, he deserved no forgiveness on the matter; just acceptance of the transgression as something that could not be undone. He knew his image would be forever tainted now.

And in a way, it was. But neither John nor Ryn would let this tainted image affect their love for him. Though, he would always assume that it would; there was nothing they would ever do or say to make him think otherwise. Such was the guilt and shame he felt. But eventually, Vincent would manage to harness these emotions for the best.

A lone tear eked its way out of John's right eye. With their foreheads still touching, John grasped the hair just beneath Vincent's hat and pulled him in closer, increasing the pressure on their foreheads and shifting the gesture of gentle commiseration to that of gruff, brotherly love. "I forgive you, too," he husked.

Before they broke this hold, Ryn rounded the fire and hugged them both. Though she forgave him already, she was still apprehensive on the matter. She wasn't sure how to face a murderer. Worse: she wasn't sure how to act around a murderer that she already loved and respected and who had saved her from certain death – and later, from certain sexual abuse. (She could only imagine the sheer magnitude of abuse that would have been inflicted by all those men...) All she could do was try to stand behind her forgiveness and love him the best she could. If John could, so could she.

III

There was little conversation for some time after they broke this rather emotional embrace. Vincent absently wiped down the remainder of the katana's blood-caked filigree while Ryn ate her share of breakfast from their communal plate. He was done cleaning it by the time she handed the plate over to John. It was around this time that their minds started to work their way back toward the larger issues concerning their lives and the collective fate of the world in which they did reside.

"You think they might actually have this thing contained?" inquired Ryn, with genuine curiosity (though, not even she truly believed it could have been remotely true).

"Not in the least," said John. "What makes you think they do?"

"Well, I don't really," she replied. "But we haven't seen a single lurcher since we crossed through that checkpoint."

"We also haven't seen a single *person* since then," countered John. "And the last person we saw was Bucky and he's dead or infected by now."

"Maybe they have it contained to this state," she said. "Maybe life is still normal beyond our borders."

"Maybe the Columbia's a natural barrier for all this," Vincent wondered aloud – really, he was thinking of finding Isabella alive and safe at her family's ranch…

John pondered Vincent's optimistic postulation. And even though he had an inkling of this epidemic's true scope (thanks to the radio), he said, "That's actually plausible." He thought a moment longer, wondering on Vincent's own notions regarding the state of the world in these dark times. "Only one way to find out for sure," he said. "I guess we'll need to make it over the mountains."

Vincent sighed. "We better find transportation. 'Cause I am not walking that far."

"Me neither," said Ryn.

IV

Loaded with their gear – bags and guns slung over shoulders with silent weapons in hand, on the ready – they smoked and stood around the dying fire.

After a sizeable rift in the conversation, John turned to Vincent. "Why did that woman try to kill us?" he asked, fighting to keep an even tone. "Why is Louis dead right now?" His voice quavered at the last.

The sudden questions startled him – he was worried about where this conversation might lead. But Vincent answered just a moment later: "We have a history," he said. "Louis and I processed her more than once. And she used to run with a group of radicals that were against big business – as well as big brother." Vincent worried that one of them would connect the dots between "Jackson Friedrich" and Rhea.

"And she had it out for you?"

"I guess so," he replied. "Pent-up aggression and an unsavory history. And maybe she was pissed that we left her behind." Vincent snorted with disdain. "Knowing her, she probably blames *us* her boyfriend's death." He was pleased to see that neither had connected the dots yet. Perhaps they wouldn't at all.

"She was a little unruly," muttered Ryn. "Looked like she was gonna kill you right then and there. Looking back on it, I'm happy she's not with us."

"So Louis is dead over petty bullshit?" John growled. Anger boiled under his skin, but he managed to keep his tone softer than his mood (if only by a fraction).

"Yes," Vincent replied. He wondered if Rhea knew of Konrad's death. Or worse: if she knew of his killer. If she even had any reason to suspect Vincent, she'd find a way to kill him – or have him killed. "Louis is dead because of some *stupid* bullshit." As these words escaped him, logical revelations of her behavior patterns streaked his thoughts. Vincent suddenly grew confident that she had no idea it was he who had committed the murder; if she had, she wouldn't have hesitated to shoot him back in Ashford. Even if such an action resulted in her own demise – which John would undoubtedly have felt obliged to dispense...if Ryn hadn't beaten him to the punch, that is.

Still, this did little to assuage his troubled mind.

John crushed his cigarette butt under his bootheel and walked back to the creek – again, to clear his head. Though he could see how a criminal like her would despise both Louis and Vincent for having arrested her (on multiple occasions, evidently), John still had a hard time wrapping his head around Louis' death. Deadly vengeance was beyond him. When it came to administering punishment or reprisals, he was of the face-rearranging variety. Such was his line of thought after departing the campfire...

Once he had left, Ryn gazed cautiously at Vincent. "What did this Jackson Friedrich dude *do*, exactly, to warrant a *contract* on his life?" She spoke with feinted affectation over words that, to her, felt surreal and implausible – in the real world, at least. Such things were fantastical notions found only in books or onscreen; there was no-way, no-how, that such things were possible in *the real world*...or so she wished...She sighed in consternation before he could reply.

"I'm not sure what he did, *exactly*," Vincent replied. "All I know is he pissed off the wrong person. Probably a very wealthy, very powerful CEO or corrupt senator or something. Or a deadly mix of both bunches of unsavory, money-hungry, capitalist pigs." Wary of telling her the *exact* truth – the way he had explained it to Louis – Vincent chose his words carefully, omitting anything that might give Ryn probable cause to link "Jackson Friedrich" and Rhea to one another.

"You said he was a terrorist," she said – Vincent could nearly *smell* the gears turning in her head. "I wonder what he did…" If she'd figured it out, she kept her own vigil on the matter. He wondered if she could know his reasons for such omissions.

After a few beats, Vincent said, "Well. We should probably get going. We got a long, hard walk ahead of us. We can discuss this matter further when we get *someplace* cozy." This was a fantasy he clung to tightly; if they pushed themselves, they could reach Paradise by nightfall. And if they reached Paradise, they could find *someplace* suitable – at least for the night. Perhaps they could find Ryn's family cabin. If not, they could always search tomorrow. If they managed to make it, that is, and if they didn't succumb to the perils of the mountain or – *Heaven Forbid!* – fall prey to the lurchers and become bloodthirsty drones in their own right. But Vincent figured likeliest calamity to befall them would be keeling over from sheer exhaustion. And, given their current physical condition and the upward struggle of the mountain's slope still before them, this was quite the apt postulation.

Yet he still remained confident in their success; he had a strange sensation deep in his gut that told him the Universe wasn't finished with this lot just yet. And he believed this gut feeling with every fiber of his being. Such blind confidence would often yield one with a favorable outcome; this was how a person could manifest their own destiny. Such philosophies as these were etched so deeply into Vincent's heart that he had no choice but to believe in their success. They *would* survive – he could *feel* it in his soul.

"Yeah," said Ryn, looking up at him and away from her own mind, which was churning as much as his. "Daylight's a-wastin'."

They started off through the ferns and foliage toward the creek.

"Isn't it beautiful?" John asked when they arrived. "This is nature at its finest."

They were indeed in the heart of nature, standing astride this babbling creek in a mountainside forest. Birds chirped their morning songs in the windswept trees that lined the banks, stretching toward the gray sky. Leaves were falling to the flowing water in heaps, turning the water into a flowing bed of browns and reds and greens and yellows, leaving hardly an inch of visible water. The scent of crisp mountain water was accentuated by the warm musk of autumn – the combination of which was deliciously palpable.

"It almost makes you forget that the world is so ugly right now," said John. "Louis would have loved it."

"He sure would have," said Vincent – a tear touched his eye. Louis was the biggest nature lover of them all. If they weren't working, it was a fair assumption that he and August were hiking or camping – or both – no matter the season. They were quite the survivalists. Yet somehow, the universe had decided to subdue them both. Such a realization brought on a flurry of pessimism regarding the fate of the world. Vincent had to shake the thought away. *I hope you made it out, August,* he thought. *I hope you're surviving, just like you're meant to do...*

Vincent reached into his pocket and thumbed a round from one of his spare clips. He squeezed it tight and brought it up to his lips. With a silent prayer for the lost souls wandering this world and those that were recently departed, he kissed the bullet and held it out. "For Louis!" he announced. "A great friend, a beloved brother and a true warrior through all his life. His absence in this world will be noticed. He will be missed. And he will always be loved."

"Amen," said John.

"Amen," Ryn echoed. Gingerly, she touched her locket; her heart wailed for her father and for Louis and all the others lost to this wicked epidemic. Squeezing her eyes tight, she issued a silent prayer for all those she knew and those she didn't. And she prayed for her new friends and protectors – her new *brothers in arms*…her new family. She opened her eyes again, but left a finger on the locket and kept an image of her father in her mind's eye.

Vincent dropped to one knee beside the creek. He set the bullet on a misplaced stump and stood up again. Ryn popped a round out of her rifle and placed it next to his; John pulled one from his breast pocket and placed it next to hers. They gazed at the bullets – each a different shape and caliber – and at the leaf-laden river for a time before motivating away from this transitory – and depressing – encampment.

And so, with nine days gone, countless lives lost, and a pandemic on the brink, this trio of courageous (if not *stubborn*) souls emerged from the forest with grim understanding of the new world order. They would march on creaky bones; their muscles would protest with every step. But when the day was still young, this travel-weary crew would stumble upon a veritable haven set into the majestic mountainside.

V

The sign read:

Longmire ➔
National Park Inn

The symbols below suggested local accommodations of camping and food and lodging. Two of the three appealed to these weary travelers – camping was the obvious black sheep of the local accommodations.

After spending a couple nights out of doors on the cold, hard ground with naught but shared body heat for warmth, this trio—

(the thought of three travelers instead of four shivered whatever strength was left inside Vincent; a life without Louis was unimaginable to either him or John)

—they longed for the comfort and warmth of blankets and beds. And a shower wouldn't hurt, either; it has been, and always will be, nigh impossible to remain clean of hand and hair after two nights in the forest. A simple rinse in the (ice-cold) stream did little to wash their hands of all the muck and mud of foraging about in the forest.

After passing the sign (which presumed to place them in or near the town of Longmire), the lodge presented itself without delay. With every step of their jellied legs, the storybook edifice of this lodge slowly emerged from beyond the treeline. Even through the morning haze, its tan façade, capped with the sheen of frosty shingles, shone brightly as a beacon in the night. Add to that the picturesque stone chimney, the cobble-lined paths that cut through the tree-specked courtyard, and the surrounding wood, this locale's storybook image was complete.

(In his near-delirious state, Vincent thought the place may very well have been ripped straight from a fairy tale – which made him wonder whether he was still dreaming or not. He shed this thought right quick; such ideas were nothing more than whims of the imagination, and could lead only toward darkness of mind. And he could not afford any darkness of mind at this time. Not when others depended on his proper cognition – and he on theirs. Despite all this, he still felt as though this well-manicured property was too good to truly be. But it was.)

And so, before actually approaching or entering this place, Vincent had the sense that it truly was a veritable haven. And there was absolutely no question about it: the mountainside was, is, and always shall be (until the end of times, barring any of a million calamities), majestic. Given enough time, Vincent was certain he could discover all sorts of natural treasures sprinkled about the surrounding areas. Unfortunately for him, he seriously doubted he'd have the time for such adventures.

Alas: so it goes.

While gazing blandly at the hanging wooden sign (which read **National Park Inn** and was streaked in blood and shot to all hell), something caught Vincent's eye. His focus shifted at once to the upstairs window in which he had (could swear he had, at least) seen movement. His right hand instinctively fell to the heft of his sheathed katana; the other fell to the handle.

Whether they spied this same movement or not, his companions readied themselves as well; rifles were clutched in tighter to their bodies and their eyes drew to studious, shrewd points. The corner of Vincent's mouth twitched momentarily upward with admiration for his friends.

"What do you think?" John asked in a hushed husk.

Ryn's lips quivered, and she could not respond.

"I say we try it," Vincent replied with equable hush to his words.

"What if it's filled with *lurchers*?" posed Ryn.

Vincent surveyed what he could of the state of things: save for the one in which he'd seen movement, the windows were all blacked out with shades or paint or, presumably, both; the doors, though under cover of shadows cast by the expansive awning, also appeared to be blacked out. Vincent wondered if they were chained or barricaded on the inside. But not a single window was busted out. Blood stained the courtyard in places, mostly along the concrete paths, where stains were less likely to fade. But there were no bodies to be found. This suggested murder (or self-defense) and cleanup. Lurchers weren't likely to clean up after themselves since they couldn't even conceptualize any act other than feasting, and even that was a rudimentary conceptualization. Actually, "instinctual" would describe their actions more aptly than "rudimentary," and he highly doubted their ability to conceptualize a damn thing.

His mind had wandered and he corrected its path.

As they neared the lodge – carefully planned steps brought them slowly, cautiously closer – Vincent noticed even more about the state of things: namely, the faint flicker of light behind in the upstairs window (which could really have been nothing more than a trick of daylight glinting off the window); but he also noticed what appeared to be boot-prints in the frost of the awning, just outside the one clear window. He couldn't tell their shapes for sure since most were streaked; whoever had been upon the awning had apparently not held their footing so well on the slick shingles. Vincent wondered if this person had made it back inside without falling; it wasn't a long drop, but it was long enough to break a bone or crack a skull. Fall wrong from there, land in the wrong spot or at the wrong angle, and someone could even die.

But again, there was no sign of any such casualty to be seen on the ground below.

Vincent's attention was just beginning to shift toward the doors, the porch, and the steps leading up to the aforementioned – and then he saw it clear as day in the window above: a head poking up and dipping back down like a Whac-A-Mole in the eleventeenth level. Despite being so ephemeral in its permanence, Vincent could discern that this head belonged to a bald black man. But it was ephemeral enough that he could not discern the man's approximate age or the expression he wore.

He smirked and his grip on the katana lessened. "I think we're in the clear," he said, not bothering to lower his voice.

"What makes you say that?" said John, still near a whisper.

Vincent nodded toward the window. "Might be that I just saw an uninfected tenant of this here establishment."

John saw nothing when he looked up to the window. "Where?"

"He's in there," said Vincent.

A light jingling came from just inside the front doors and Vincent felt, rather than saw, the eyes that peered out at them. He let go of the katana and held his hands up by his head. "It's okay," he called. "We ask aid and succor and nothing more. We'll be on our way, if you deny us."

The man upstairs stood up at this and regarded them with due caution. He made no move for the window. Vincent saw that he wore fatigues and carried a carbine rifle – one quite like those they acquired from Cooper and Sanchez and Webb. The stern set of his face gave no argument to him being a soldier.

After a few long beats, the soldier upstairs finally opened the window. "Lay down your weapons," he said to them. "Or you can leave and forget you ever found this place."

Vincent exchanged a wary gaze with his companions. And then they all resigned to this instruction with a nod; they laid down their arms and took two backsteps away from them.

More jangling came from the front doors. A moment later, another soldier emerged onto the front porch, followed closely by a portly ginger with a red goatee and small, wire-framed spectacles. Both were armed, and each brandished his respective weapon with a boldness that was tainted by jittery nerves.

At the sight of their shaky aim, Vincent pulled Ryn back and stepped forward, thereby positioning himself between their unpredictable trigger fingers and her. *Who put these jokers in charge of answering the door?* he wondered. His eyes darted back up to the man in the window and silently accused him of this breach of healthy decorum.

"Whoa, guys," he said to them. "Steady those weapons, please."

"We're unarmed," blurted Ryn.

"What about that blade?" said the soldier – he was young and white and scrawny and still plagued by pimples, and his voice quavered at the every syllable.

"We mean you no harm," said Vincent. Slowly, he reached for his hip, to undo the katana's strap.

"Leave it!" cried the young soldier.

The portly ginger jumped at this sudden outcry. He was slow in re-composing himself. Vincent feared a hair-trigger might be tapped in the man's fright. He was thankful when nothing of the sort came to pass.

His katana fell to his feet with a clatter and he kicked it forward. He winced as the scabbard scraped and skidded across the cement path. It came to a crashing halt when it struck Ryn's rifle. "There," he said, holding his hands back up by his head. "We're unarmed. And, like I said before, we mean you no harm."

Just then, a middle-aged, apple-bottomed woman came stomping out the front door. She was vaguely pretty with olive skin and long, dark hair. "Put them things away!" she hollered at the men on the porch. "Can't you tell these people are hurtin' and hungry?" Hidden beneath her careful allocution, Vincent thought he detected a hint of Southern twang – or maybe French Creole – in her voice.

But he wasn't certain. And it hardly mattered.

The woman pushed each of their guns toward the ground and scowled. "They've obviously been through a lot. Why don't you give 'em a break, boys?" She whirled to regard the newcomers.

"Sorry 'bout all that, folks," she said to them. "We're a bit sketchy on visitors these days. But, from the looks o' ya, I think ya understand just what I'm talkin' about."

They nodded in silent affirmation.

And the woman nodded solemnly in return. "Well, then," she breathed. "Let's have a look at ya. Hold up yer shirts so I can see your skin." She nodded and twirled her finger, signaling for them to twirl as well; they did, and she nodded some more. "Now the pant legs," she said. "Up with 'em." They did; she twirled her finger again, and they twirled their bodies; she nodded once more. "Lastly," she said, "collars and cufflinks." After another superficial inspection (this time of their arms and necks), she nodded one last time (though, not nearly the last of her life – not in the least) and bade them entrance – wait, the stupefied young soldier was shoved from their path first...Okay then. After shoving this young soldier further down the front porch, she bade them entrance to the lodge.

VI

Their induction was swift; lest they were infected in some ways unidentifiable to the naked eye, these three were swept away to their new digs, which were located on the third (and highest) floor. Upon entering, all the promises and prayers that Vincent had sensed regarding the rest and respite and warmth and comfort within the walls of this storybook lodge appeared to be true. Beds, blankets, a bathroom, and heat; this place had it all!

But it wasn't long that Vincent realized he knew little of this place, and the people residing within its walls. What he did know he'd siphoned off the nurses who cared for them.

An old lodge, this haven was now occupied by locals who transformed the place into a fortified sanctuary. This trio did not meet very many of the occupants (of which there were few) on their first day. Escorted by the woman and both men who'd "welcomed" them, they were rushed upstairs to a large suite that was set up as a convalescence room with a row of beds lined up along the outer wall. These three were the only patients in the suite.

Once officially declared free of infection (after a more thorough inspection of their bodies and eyes – special attention was paid to their eyes), they were treated to fresh food and water, hot showers, clean clothes and soft mattresses. (After surviving so long without a real bed, each of them melted into the pleasure of cool sheets and fluffed pillows.) Their wounds were treated and patched – and Vincent found himself riding a familiar river of opiates soon after they were done with him.

Each was attended to by a pair of experienced nurses. The woman – the vaguely pretty one with sharp Mediterranean features and Rubenesque physique who'd finally bade them entrance to the lodge – paid special attention to Ryn. She worried over the circumstances behind the bruises on Ryn's face. Vincent was unable to tell if she was convinced by Ryn's tale of their heroism. But, at that moment, he didn't think it mattered much.

The male nurse – the stout ginger with short-cropped red hair and matching goatee who'd greeted this trio alongside the shaky, young soldier – seemed to believe her tale. He dealt mainly with Vincent and John and moved languidly between the two. He was particularly curious about the fresh pocks that peppered their legs.

After some more light questioning, the nurses left them to rest.

They drifted in and out of sleep, occasionally aware of people returning in shifts to monitor their condition. When they were thirsty, the nurses brought them water; when they were hungry, food. And when they were restless and in pain, they brought drugs.

Nobody berated them with questions of the outside world – nor did they divulge any new information about it. Mostly, they were left alone to recover from their struggles. When the sun went down and candles were lit (the power was out up here, as well), Ryn crept out of bed and crawled in beside Vincent.

"I know we're safe here," she whispered, "but I still feel safer with you." She nuzzled her head into the crook of his shoulder and draped an arm over his chest. She was asleep within a minute.

Wrapped in the warmth of opiates and bundled between soft sheets on a real bed with a protective hold of this fragile young woman, Vincent started to drift away. Though plagued with recent terrors and hardships, his last thought before drifting away was of the familiar drug coursing through his system – *Hello, my old friend*, he thought with a smile.

His dreams that night were not so pleasant.

So it goes.

tributations

Tribulations

Of Honor & Malice

I

Her first thought was: *They left me!* Fury immediately washed over her.

Ignoring the bobs swarming from every direction, she watched the rickety minivan tear through the courtyard. She stood in disbelief, her rifle cradled lazily in her hands. The hot and heavy thumping of her heart in her ears drowned the groans at her back and even the garbled cries of her fallen lover at her side.

Just seeing him had set her emotions on edge; their history and this coincidental encounter under such circumstances baffled and irritated her. And when he dismissed her entirely, she found herself seething. She would have shot him as he ran, but he was tackled before she could pull the trigger. But she smirked at the scene that followed; watching the crazed Latino man pummel his face had evoked from her a wicked pleasure.

Unfortunately, this good cheer ended all too abruptly when Jothan was swarmed. She tried to free him from the mass, but the giant at her side kept dragging her away. But still she fired and fired and fired until her rifle was empty of bullets. The bodies piled atop Jothan were mostly dead now – a fair portion of her shots landed true – but from his gurgling, pathetic pleas, she could see her efforts had indeed failed. She switched out her empty clip –

And then the engine roared to life and the van pulled away.

Her heart turned to stone and her vision blurred around the edges. A darkness glowing black and red filled her and she pulled the rifle into her shoulder. Her deafening bloodflow muted the subsequent gunfire. If asked after the incident of what she had been doing, Rhea would have been baffled and unable to answer; everything before and during her blind firing was a diluted haze. She could recall emotions and nothing more until the moment she was tackled.

II

There was no pain when he was hit and none when he fell. The only pain he felt was at the uncontrollable seizure that overtook his body. In his mind, he was fighting a brick wall of centurions and losing horribly. But when he came to, he lunged at the beastly automobile that purportedly brought him to this position. Multiple occupants jumped at his attack – but they quickly were gone and he met the pavement once more. (The centurions returned to whoop him up and down again and again.)

His delusional vision clarified some, illuminating the angelic enigma with her explosive rifle. Her skin was soft, yet rough; her fierce eyes exuded integrity and compassion; her rugged clothes and resolute demeanor suggested intensity in life and love alike. When he realized this woman was a stranger to him, he also realized he had no recollection of his own entity. Something was definitely wrong with this.

And though he did not recognize the thing now crawling at this woman, he did recognize it as a potential threat. Bursting into action, he leapt from the pavement where twice now he met the sentries of his subconscious. Oblivious to anything but her target, this angelic enigma fired repeatedly without once noticing the aggressor or the unknown savior.

He hit her blind side just as the crawler groped at her ankle. And when they slammed back into the pavement, his brain sloshed uncomfortably within his skull. Dazed, he hardly noticed her tiny fists wracking his head. Between inarticulate groans (groans sounding quite like the masses that slowly encroached from every direction) he managed to croak out something intelligible: *"Please!"*

And she stopped.

III

No way, she thought. *You're hearing things.* An overwhelming fear of her own humanity – her own *weakness* – flooded her body and mind; the thing attacking her would most certainly eat her now. She started flailing, kicking and backing out from under it. The thing was covered in blood and muck and stared with empty eyes. *No*, she thought. *There's pain in there.*

Something like hot steel gripped her arm; she felt her skin tear. If not for the heavy jacket she wore, the crawler would have poisoned her blood. She ripped her arm free and plunged the barrel of her rifle into its eye.

The thing that tackled her was pushing onto its feet. In one deft move, she pulled her rifle from the crawler's face (with it came a mushy,

tattered eye and chunky brainmatter) and swung it at the man now standing over her –

He smacked the barrel and dropped his weight on her midsection.
But he did not move to bite or claw. Instead, he spoke: "I'm not one of
them," he said, his voice a little crackly and hoarse. Blood dribbled from
his temple, his nose, the corner of his mouth. "I'm still alive," he said. At
last she recognized him as the crazed Latino man that was previously
pummeling Vincent.

She blinked, her mouth agape, her confidence wavering.

"Quickly," he said, pushing off of her. "We gotta clear outta here."
He extended a hand.

Regaining focus and form, she detected danger in her periphery and
instinctively swung the rifle at the crawler groping for his ankle. *BLAM!*
– its head exploded, its body went limp; the man above her hardly
flinched. She shot three more dead in their tracks. The fourth failed to
fall as the firing pin of her rifle struck an empty chamber. The urgency of
their situation rose a few notches at the *click* and she grabbed his extended hand at last.

Any strength displayed in assisting her dissipated once he lifted her
to her feet. He reeled and blinked, gazing through all substance and matter before his eyes. "You okay?" she asked, bracing his shoulders to
steady his sway, careful not to touch the wound on his left shoulder. But
he couldn't hear her over the buzzing of his injuries. She glanced around
and decided she wasn't going to wait for him to recover. "C'mon," she
said, pulling his arm around her neck, shouldering his burden. "We're
going now."

Their gait was hobbled and slow. Fortunately for them, it was no
worse than a lurcher. For the first half mile, they were closely pursued

and Rhea was becoming fatigued. Her burden was capable of nothing more than staggered steps that constantly tested her balance. Though he was hardly taller than she was, his wiry figure was muscular and heavy. Incapable of checking their back path, she was aware of their pursuers by sound alone.

Gradually, though, his head began to clear some and he started taking charge of his muscles once more. And as this happened, their collective pace increased some. The snarls and groans at their backs slowly receded. But their path was taking them directly toward another horde, though this one was preoccupied with something further along the road.

"*This way*," she hissed, steering him off the highway. "We gotta throw 'em off our tracks a little." She huffed, panted and spit to one side. "Just try to keep up."

Still entwined, they blazed around a cottage, into the forest. Their gait was immediately hobbled from the underbrush, but she refused to let him go. *And besides*, she thought, reasoning the situation out in her mind, *damn bobs will get stuck worse 'n us in this mess anyhow*. Careful to keep civilization somewhat close, they weaved through the edge of the forest, hardly dipping too deep into the thicket. The few bobs that managed to hold a relative pace with them quickly fell back as some tripped on vines or entangled themselves bushes. Others just were too slow to navigate the foliage, even if they didn't fall.

His breathing became heavy and he started tapping her back. "*Hold*," he husked between breaths. "*Hold. Please.*" He reached his other hand out to brace himself on a fat tree (his shoulder flared at the stretching of his injured muscles) and pulled his good arm free of her aid. "Please," he panted, his face sketched with a terrible grimace.

She gazed back and saw distant heads bobbing this way and that.

"Fifteen seconds," she said. "That's all you get." Having remained so close to civilization, she wasn't too surprised to spy a two-story cabin just beyond the edge of the wood. "In fact," she said. "You have no time. Let's get inside there. Then you'll get to rest."

He shook his head and started hacking.

"Yes," she commanded, grabbing at his arm.

He pulled free of her grasp and shook his head again. "No," he groaned, lurching forward and reeling on his heel. "Not yet," he said, the words slightly choked. He hacked some more, cutting off any reply she might have given. And then he hurled all over the tree against which he was leaning. The spray was specked with blood, but his eyes were too clenched to take note of such things.

The bobbing heads were gaining ground.

"Are you all through?" she asked, quite impatient with his retching.

He spat the bile that coated his mouth onto the tree. "Two seconds," he said. "*Por favor.*"

Rhea grumbled incomprehensibly and stared down their pursuers.

He spat twice more and pushed off the tree – a fleeting thought of his situation passed across his consciousness. But it quickly escaped him and he said, "All better. Now where are we going?"

"Right there," said Rhea, pointing at the cabin with her rifle.

"You know them or something?" he asked.

"Know who?" she said, her face twisted with perplexion. "I don't know anybody around here. I just know we need to get inside – get away from them damn *bobs*." She said this last with a snarl.

"Bobs?" he said. "What the fuck are *bobs*?"

"The infected," she said. "The goddamn *zombies* that are chasing us!" She directed his attention to the bobs that were now too close for comfort. "Now," she said, clutching his arm. "Let's get going." She ushered him to the fenceline at the edge of the wood.

The word *infected* resonated deep in his well of memories and another fleeting thought crossed his mind. Again, it was too elusive for him to catch. "What's wrong with them?" he asked. "What are they infected with?"

"I don't know," she said, pushing him along the fenceline. "The jury's still out on the *what* of the situation. But if we're to stay alive out here, we need to ditch the bobs. And we gotta do it before they call for reinforcements." She stopped him short of the corner and stepped into the lead. "Just do what I do and we'll talk later," she whispered.

A dingy old motor home was parked along the side of the cabin. It both obstructed their view and offered more coverage to stealthily slink around the property. The bobs in pursuit were still stumbling through the foliage, out of view once they rounded the corner. And thusfar, the property itself was devoid of any lingerers. The highway beyond was another story entirely; droves of bobs lurched eastward.

"C'mon," she breathed. "Keep low and don't make a sound." Still crouched, she started around the motor home. She was glad to find that her tagalong was indeed following her instructions. And when they rounded the motor home, she was even happier to find a gate to the back yard. A handy little cable dangled over the door handle; Rhea yanked it down and pushed slowly through the gate. Despite her care in the matter of silently opening the gate, its rusty hinges uttered a curt squawk. She grimaced and bounded over the threshold.

"They heard!" he hissed, scrambling after her.

She shut the door with haste, but was sure not to slam it and alert more bobs than necessary (as if any were necessary, really). "Back away," she husked. "Over here," she said, tiptoeing over to a sliding glass door. And he was right there at her side without hesitation.

Groans sounded from the side yard.

And more from the forest as their pursuers stumbled closer to the property.

"We gotta get inside," he said.

"We will," she replied, her voice low, her composure surprisingly strong. "Just give it a minute. Let them forget we're here."

"What?" His voice almost squeaked with anxiety.

She held a finger to her lips. "Shhh. They'll forget soon enough. Just stay quiet. Please." Her voice remained low and composed throughout.

Something slammed into the gate, rattling its hinges and latch. That same something snarled and pushed. And then some more somethings were snarling and pushing and smashing into the gate. But it held firm on the one small latch. For the time being.

"That thing can't hold," he said, his breath quickening.

"It'll hold," she replied, her voice soft and soothing. She slipped a machete from a sheath on her leg. Its blade was tarnished with blood and rust, but the edge was keen and glistened in the light.

The gate flexed with the surging horde.

"It's gonna buckle," he panted – he was nearly hyperventilating.

"Look at me," she husked. And when his frightened eyes met hers, she said, "If you don't calm down, you won't need to worry about them breaking through. Just hush up and catch your breath. You're stronger than this – I know you are. You're a soldier, for fuck's sake. Now act like one." Despite whispering this diatribe, her words bore enough weight to strike a chord in him. "Get your shit together, man."

He took a few deep breaths, leaned his head against the glass door and tuned out the creaking wood and snarling ghouls. After a moment of this, he opened his eyes and gazed out at the yard before him. Really, it was one large garden. Half the crops in the garden had been harvested; the other half was covered in tall rows of corn that were practically popping out of their husks. And he noticed a string of lightly electrified wires lining the inner walls of the fence. And then he refocused his attention on Rhea. "Thank you," he said at last. "That concussion must have really messed me up." He looked at her weapons. "Got anything for me?"

"I was hoping you would ask," she said. Extending her rifle, she said, "Take this. I prefer my pistol and blade anyhow." Before he could drop the clip, she said, "It's loaded and ready to blow. Just keep quiet until they go away or get through…don't go poppin' off too early."

He dropped the clip anyway; the sound of which incensed the horde.

"*Fuck!*" she growled. "I told you to *keep quiet*." She drew her pistol.

The gate flexed, the hinges protested, the latch reached its apex of integrity.

A distant gunshot in the east halted their barrage.

"That's right," breathed Rhea. "Chase them guns down."

One of the bobs pressed against the gate; the wood, the hinges creaked.

Another gunshot in the east distracted them again. One of the bobs at the back of the horde, having never heard or seen the prey it now chased, started off toward the highway once more. Another followed. And another.

But the ones at the gate weren't so convinced and pressed against the gate again.

A rapid succession of gunshots erupted, clearing all but a few stragglers from the cabin's property. One more flurry of gunshots was all it took to clear the rest; within minutes, the gate was free from its assault.

"That's better," he breathed when he was certain they were gone.

"We'll give it another minute, though," she whispered. "Think some are still stumbling through the woods." She motioned toward the back fenceline; through the gaps in the boards they could spot movement. "They're usually quieter when they don't see food."

"What are they?" he asked – and yet another fleeting thought flashed through him.

"Shhh," she said. "Not yet. Once we're safely inside."

Ten minutes later, when she saw no unusual movement through the fence, Rhea checked the door; as she had figured, it was locked and a heavy bar blocked the tracks – just for good measure, of course. Fiddling with that would undoubtedly cause a commotion. Before trying the windows, she instructed her tagalong to help her with the wooden picnic table. Together, they lifted it from the cement patio and set it snug against the gate. It was light enough that he didn't have to use his injured arm to move it.

"There," she said, her voice still low. "That should strengthen the gate."

"So..." he said. "How do we get in?"

"That's the tricky part," she replied. "Gotta be very careful entering a residence these days. There could be people in there – scared people – that might just blast us away because we're intruding and possibly infected. Or the place could be filled with bobs."

"I didn't hear any," he said.

"Neither did I," she replied. "But that don't mean they're not in there. Could be behind any door, in any crevice. Could be they didn't hear us and are right behind that door there." She gestured with her rifle. "Or that window there."

"Only one way to find out," he said and marched to the sliding door. He knocked – softly, though Rhea was still unnerved by the sudden action. He repeated the rhythmic knock a few more times.

"Stop it!" she hissed, pushing his arm away from the glass. "Jesus Christ, man! You'll alert the neighborhood with shit like that!"

"Oh, c'mon," he said. "I was quiet. And hey: I don't think they're home right now. So we may just be in the clear here." He paused a moment. And then: "Now what?"

"After my heart attack," she said, holding her chest, "we'll try the windows. Break one if we have to."

"'Cause that's quiet," he muttered, trudging to the nearest window. It was high, but not too high to test; locked. He nodded and moved on to the next one; it was at the same level as the last one and was also locked. He nodded some more and went to the next one; this was near the gate and small and way too high to reach on his own. "Hey, uh…" He searched for her name in his memory banks, but came up empty. "Whatever your name is," he said, "would you help me here?"

"Sure," she said. "And it's Rhea." She spelled it for him. "What do you need?"

"Think you could slip through that window?" he asked, motioning up the wall.

With a shrewd eye on the small window, she marched toward him. "Maybe," she said.

"Let me boost you up there, then. Can't hurt to try."

"You hope it can't hurt," she said. "Just don't drop me." She slipped the machete back into its sheath and snapped it into place.

By lacing his hands together, he formed a step for her and crouched beside the wall. She placed her right foot into his hands and steadied herself on his shoulder. "Ready?" he asked. And when she nodded, he hoisted her upward (bending at the knees, of course; mindful of injury to his back). But his shoulder flared and his arms dropped out – she stepped easily back to the patio.

"You gonna be okay?" she asked.

"Yeah," he said. "Just give me a moment." He huffed and mentally readied himself for the task at hand. And then he said, "Let's go," and laced his fingers together once more. This time, he managed to hold her weight – though it hurt like hell to do so.

Cautiously, she snaked her hands up the wall, constantly steadying herself, until she reached the glass. With an effort (moreso a test of her balance than actual strength), she pushed the little window up.

"Got it," she breathed. "Can you go higher?"

"Hold on," he replied; veins bulged over his strained muscles. He strained some more; he huffed and grunted, but made no headway. "Not like this," he said. "If you grab the ledge real quick, I can adjust and get more leverage."

"Ugh," she growled. "Fine." *I've done worse*, she thought. She spread her hands out and gripped the windowsill. "Got it," she said. And she looked down just as he let her feet go; the drop would be maybe five feet, but from this vantage it might as well have been three floors. The sheer face of the cabin's outer wall and the strain of her weight resting solely on her fingers nearly instilled a sense of vertigo.

But then he thrust a hand under either foot and pushed until his elbows were locked. "How's that?" he asked, holding back the howl his shoulder wished to elicit.

"Perfect," she replied. She could see through the window now; it was poised above a toilet in a cramped restroom. Before climbing through, she poked her head in to check for danger. When none presented itself, she reached inside and grabbed hold of the sink with one hand and the toilet tank with the other.

And even when her weight was lifted, he stood below the window, arms upraised (the pattern of her boots imprinted on his palms). He watched her wriggle through the tight window, her legs kicking comically whenever she lost balance. All at once, though, she disappeared into the house with a clatter. He winced and brought the rifle around front.

Seething through a grimace, Rhea rolled from shoulder to shoulder on the linoleum, bumping the wall on her left and the toilet on her right. One hand held her forehead while the other caressed her raked stomach. "Shit," she breathed. "That was stupid." She bared her teeth, cursing herself for being so clumsy.

From the hall came an eager groan. The bob inside had wandered in through the open front door after their earlier racket and was further incensed when her tagalong had rapped on the back door. And, having not found its way back out of the house, it was lurching now toward this closet of a restroom.

"Oh, great," she husked, rolling her eyes. She unsnapped and withdrew her machete. But before she could make a move to stand, its hand gripped the door jamb. Instinctively, she kicked the door, breaking its brittle fingers. It slammed the door back at her feet and squeezed its head through the opening. She kicked again and caught the satisfying *crunch* of breaking bones once more.

But it wasn't enough; the bob heaved against her protesting legs. Red froth dribbled from its nasty, unhinged jowls and it bellowed a hellish, keening snarl. With its broken hand still on the jamb and the other on the door, it heaved again, testing its weight against her strength.

Bracing herself against the pedestal sink, she kicked with all her might; her healthy muscles were unmatched by this thing's infected deterioration. But one kick wasn't enough; the second kick caught its head between the door and jamb (more *crunching* as bones in its hand and wrist and arm and face broke). She kicked and kicked until its arms were completely busted and useless (though it was still quite spry in its attempts at lunging through the door). And then she kicked some more, crushing it until curdled chunks of brainmatter and blood squirted out its fractured skull to paint the walls, her legs – and even her torso in places.

(Outside, her tagalong was left to listen to this commotion with mounting anxiety.)

"*Gross*," she said, pushing away from the door. The compressed bob fell in a heap at the threshold. She was on her feet and moving just a moment later – *no time to waste*, she thought, mindful of another possible attack.

Hoping to keep it silent (though the noise generated in her recent struggle was not audible on the road), she drew her pistol and disengaged the safety. Entering the hallway (stepping over the former bob on her way), she led with the machete; the pistol, though gripped tight in her left hand, was at her side.

The house was dark and silent. The only light she could see spilled in through slits in the blinds. She stepped lightly through the hall, listening and looking for anything and everything. And when she approached the arched doorway to the dining room, the darkness faded some. She paused to peer around the corner.

The dining room was lit mostly from the front of the house; light radiated through another arched doorway and was reflected off a mirror on the far wall. The table – a heavy antique made of mahogany – was set for a meal that only partially happened. Glasses were tipped or smashed, plates were abandoned with cooled veggies and potatoes; a platter, set beside a multi-tiered candelabrum, was in the middle with its silver lid just slightly askew. The room smelled musty and rotten.

She slunk into the room. Keeping to the perimeter, she sidled along the wall until she reached the next doorway – the backlit doorway. She stole a glance around the corner; front door wide-open, view of highway...view of the shuffling horde. Crouching and using the shadows for cover, she crept across the hall into the tiled foyer. Hiding behind an entry table, she timed her movement according to the horde's density; when it thinned in the middle, she stepped around and behind the front door in one deft move. Then she eased the door shut, wincing at the squeal that never sounded. She winced more at the click of the door handle in the jamb then threw the bolt (it squawked lightly) and hurried back through the house.

Afterword
Thanks & Adieu

†

To all the authors that have inspired me throughout the years, I must give a heartfelt thanks. Stephen King was probably the man who first sculpted my style and way of thinking about the English language. From the time I was just a boy until the present, his literary expertise and voice has bled through into my own style. I must give him a grand round of applause for all he's done for my work; *The Dark Tower* series has been the foremost inspiration to everything I've done since childhood. Secondly, I must thank Kurt Vonnegut for his satire (nuggets of his wisdom can be found throughout this novel). From *Cat's Cradle* to *Timequake* to *Breakfast of Champions*, his straightforward satire and social commentary have inspired the very core of my themes and theories and views of the mysteries of life and death (so it goes...). And then there's Douglas Adams with his ever-popular *Hitchhiker's Guide* series. His tangents inspired many of my side stories, and his skeptical view of the world helped form my own way of thinking. The natural byproduct of this helped form the undercurrents of my style, plot, and themes (sorry for the inconvenience...).

But I must not forget all the others, either: Isaac Asimov (namely the *Robot* series); Orson Scott Card (*Ender's Game* and *Ender's Shadow* and the subsequent series' for each); Max Brooks (*The Zombie Survival Guide* and *World War Z* – both helped enormously in the creation of this novel); Thomas Harris (*Red Dragon, The Silence of the Lambs* and *Hannibal*); and, more recently, Ernest Cline with his super-amazing novel *Ready Player One* (this is a must read for any sci-fi fan or big-time gamer)...this might actually be my all-time favorite novel. For the time being, at least...

But I mustn't forget all the local authors I've met so recently. If you don't know them, you should look into Michelle Kilmer (*When The Dead...* and *The Spread*), her twin-sister Becky Hansen (co-author, *The Spread*), Matt Dinniman (*The Shivered Sky* and *The Grinding*), Charlie Jack Joseph Kruger (*Spoken Tombstones* and *Setting Son: A Haunting*)... Each is splendid in their own right.

And then the poets...a proper thanks wouldn't be prudent without mentioning Edgar Allan Poe, Emily Dickenson, Allen Ginsberg, Charles Bukowski and – of course – the Bard himself, William Shakespeare.

To all the authors I left off this list, I apologize; it's late and I'm running on empty. But there are many, many more authors, both modern and classic, that have shaped the way I write today.

And before I move on, I must thank every writing teacher I've had, no matter how much I frustrated you with my failure to turn in homework. I meant well, but *creative* writing has always been a hindrance to the rest of my life. Elana Freeland, you will always hold a place in my heart for pushing me to write my best. (I also think you're the only English teacher to ever grant me a passing grade...) And Mr. Underland, I do apologize for showing you promise only to dash your hopes of my success to the dirt. Maybe now, if you see this, you'll smile and realize that I do have a little drive...I just had to grow up to find it.

So now, with such pressing matters as thanking all the authors and teachers out of the way, I must now thank my artist, Todd Liggett, for all the harassment he received – and still receives – in regards to past, present, and future cover art, as well as other random artistic needs inherent in being an eccentric, needy writer...I thank you, from the depths of my bloody heart, for not telling me to fuck off. I appreciate all your fantastic artwork. And someday (hopefully someday), all your hard work will pay off. (Now get to work on book two!)

I also, of course, must send a special thanks to everybody I have encountered throughout my lifetime. Everybody I've ever met (from those I've loved, to those I've lost – from those I've hardly known, to those I've known but no longer know); each one of you has inspired every word I've ever written. Don't stop being yourself. Not for one moment. After all, it's all of our differences that make our dysfunctional society what it is – for better or worse...

I am so very happy to finally share my mind with the world at large. I'm even happier to be part of this world for as long as I may be. And I'm much more positive (really, I swear it's true!) than this story might make you believe. I sure hope this is not what we are to become. But more than that, I hope that the flaws I highlight here (and in the future) will be reconciled before we overstep our communal bounds.

And so I bid you a fond farewell with this little haiku:

> Before we implode
> We must unravel the stars
> For they hold the key

~Kurtis Bissell

About the Author

Prosed self-abstraction

†

Kurtis Bissell is plagued by a variety of stories and scenarios which are bubbling beneath the vaguely humanoid head of his. Each of these cacophonic tales is itching to burst forth from the fleshy prison in which they've been captive for so many years. But instead of collecting dust, these stories are fermenting. And one day, when the time is right, these intoxicating tales will spill forth for any and all to imbibe.

Trials: Death and the Undead is his first completed novel. He is currently working on the second installment (entitled *Tribulations: Of Honor & Malice*) in his breakout series (tentatively entitled *Manifest Destiny*). *Tribulations* is slated for self-publication, to be released by late 2015 or early 2016...whichever comes first (har-dee-harrr).

Kurtis fell in love with the written word at a rather young age. He wrote many poems and short stories before graduating himself to more in-depth, entangled, and lengthy storylines. And for somebody who flunked nearly every high school English course, he turned out to be one talented wordsmith.

Kurtis Bissell was born and bred in Washington State.

He still lives there to this day.